ACCESS TO CAPITAL

A NOVEL BY

GARY HOBBS

For

Mom, Dad, & Josie

That Virtue owns a mortal eternal foe

Than Force or Fraud; old Custom, legal Crime,

And bloody Faith, the foulest birth of Time

- Percy Bysshe Shelley

ACCESS

TO

CAPITAL

A Novel
GARY HOBBS

CHAPTER ONE

Luke Boyd leaned back in the plump, gray, first-class window seat. He dropped the *New York Times* into his lap and adjusted the headphones plugged into his black plastic portable cassette player. He felt edgy and tense, but the billowing layers of clouds soothed him. His flight had been delayed, and he had lost another hour to the time change. It was after ten thirty in the morning, and he still needed to land. Grabbing a taxi, reaching the hotel, dropping his bags, and getting to the appointment would take another hour, if there were no more delays. The lunch would take an hour or so, and then he'd need more time to get the wire approved and sent, if they would do it. It was Friday, and he needed $6 million transferred to his company's Tulsa bank account by three o'clock Eastern time.

Within the moment Luke recognized he was more tired than anxious. Last night he had caught the last flight from Tulsa to Chicago, taxied to his downtown hotel, and then hailed another cab to meet his bond broker, John Elliott. They ate at the Bakery, a tasty restaurant on Chicago's near north side. The meeting was a preliminary to the lunch in New York. The deal was simply undoable, he had been told. Luke's company needed money to fund mortgage loans that were scheduled to close in the next few days.

Failing to close the loans on time would destroy the last ten years Luke had spent building his reputation and the last three he had spent building his company. It was the early 1980s, and the average home value was $75,000; the average mortgage loan was around $60,000. Luke knew a hundred sets of buyers and sellers were waiting. They were all links in the chain.

The buyers had fretted for weeks over their purchases—planning the wallpaper, the fixtures, the landscaping, and tossing between remorse and exhilaration. Their possessions were packed and boxed, and their daily routines were destroyed and uncomfortable. Family and friends had been told, pictures had been exchanged, and boasts had been made. They had walked through the homes describing their dreams, etching their plans, and investing more of themselves than time or money. Pickup trucks and movers had been scheduled.

The sellers had also packed their possessions and scheduled their movers. They lingered, remembering their children's births, their holidays, and their most perfect evenings. They now lived out of boxes in spaces stripped of memories of who they were. They were usually moving to larger houses—the dream—the home with the pool, the second story, and the larger lawn. All they needed was to sign the papers, get that check, and drive to the next closing, where another seller waited.

The closings were flanked and buoyed by agents and brokers with nametags adorning their chests. Many were living commission check to commission check. Each closing helped the broker pay the office rent and buy more ads; each gave the nervous agent the money for the house payment, the car payment, or the credit card payment he or she had sweated. They understood their plight more than the process; delays and bad news were countered with tempers and threats. It was all they knew to do.

Luke had built his reputation understanding the chain. If Luke said it would close, it closed. If he and the staff had to stay late to make it happen, they stayed late. Luke understood the humanity in the chain; he knew the emotional roller coaster would force those trapped in the process to say things they never intended and never meant. He knew what drove them. He also knew it took years to build the reputation and only a day to destroy it. Hopes and dreams without a check made for venom, rumors, and hatred.

He knew all of this without thinking about it. It was simply a fact, an ordinary part of his life, as certain as the puffed clouds now swirling like cotton candy around the plane's window. It was what he did to make money. He still did not know that some people do not do things to make money; they make money when they break things.

Luke's bank was increasing his company's line of credit from $20 million to $35 million, but Luke had been told the increase would not be available for at least another week. Luke's company, FRM, had sold mortgage-backed bonds to the investment firm Stiller Stevens. The bonds would be delivered in the next five days, but they had not been delivered yet. Luke's proposal was simple. Luke wanted Stiller Stevens to give Luke's company the money now, before it received the bonds. That would let him fund the loans on schedule without the credit line increase.

"No way," John Elliott had told him. "They agreed to meet with you, but only as a courtesy. I don't see them funding before they get the bonds. Frank Ryan is your best hope. Stay with navy, gray, and red. No browns. He's going to be pleased you don't wear cowboy boots. I think he just wants to see what someone from Oklahoma looks like." John finished with a shrug.

"I don't own cowboy boots," Luke had answered. He didn't. His suits were custom tailored, the shirts crisp, and the colors bold and traditional. Everything said conservative, young businessman, except the hair. "And I can conjugate verbs."

"I know," John allowed. "Listen, I want all of your business. When we first talked, I didn't think you would produce large numbers. But in three years, you've grown to the top fifty nationwide and you're the biggest in your state. You issue more bonds than the other three top companies in Oklahoma combined, and they've been there for years. Frank is smart and fair, but I really don't think he can do it."

"I have to ask in person," Luke had concluded. "Thanks for setting it up."

Luke's eyes drifted back around the plane's cabin, and he noted the conservative commentator and publisher in his blue blazer, crumpled and dabbled with dandruff, seated in the aisle seat ahead of him. The man was still devouring his cadre of newspapers and was now buried in the *Washington Post*. Luke had noted his poring over the *New York Times* and the *Wall Street Journal* as Luke had read his own copies. Fifteen years earlier, Luke had watched the PBS commentator's unceasing praise for the escalation of the Vietnam War. Luke's left hand absently flipped his hair over his collar, which was too long for business but much shorter than it had been years ago.

The commentator had never bagged groceries for the poor in a country market, mopped floors after midnight, or worked on highway construction crews with men who could neither read nor write, so he could pay tuition. Luke smiled, pleased with himself, aware of his disdain for benefits inherited and not earned.

Seeing the commentator reminded Luke he had started the company to prove new talent could surpass the old money that owned the industry. Luke had worked as a loan officer making mortgage loans. His job had been to find the loans, make the loans, and supply them to his employer, who had the credit line.

Luke would not have needed a credit line to open his own mortgage brokerage. He could have made and sold loans to mortgage bankers. Some big companies would have bought loans, but they would have decided what kinds of loans were made and when, and they would have demanded the servicing rights and the steady monthly flow of fee income the servicing provided. Mortgage brokerage was essentially what Luke had done as an employee, and Luke had no desire to be a mortgage broker and be bound by the dictates of the big companies.

Having a credit line enabled Luke to form a mortgage banking company, to pool the loans as collateral for bonds, to sell the bonds in the capital markets, and to keep the servicing rights, and the fees for collecting the monthly payments. The servicing income gave the company value and stability. Creating a new mortgage banking company was the challenge that drove him, and having a credit line was the key. He had been a sharecropper with his employer, and now he wanted the tenants to own the land.

In those days Luke defined the world by what he knew and what he believed, but most of the world is made up of things we do not know. The only part we know is what we experience and can comprehend, and what we believe can keep us from knowing. He had learned that new money got the attention of old money, but he did not know they played by different rules.

The plane knifed below the clouds, and the light drew Luke's eyes to the window, where he could see the southern tip of

Manhattan, the Statue of Liberty, and the Twin Towers. The blur of last night's dinner, the abbreviated sleep in the Whitehall Hotel's pressed white sheets, and the quick rattling taxi back to O'Hare eased away. The Psychedelic Furs sounded good as "President Gas" tingled in his ears.

CHAPTER TWO

Luke quickly checked his bags with the bellman but did not check into his room. There wasn't time for a taxi. Stiller Stevens was only seven blocks away. He grabbed the cheapest black umbrella from a news store rack, slid a ten on the counter, picked up his change, and emerged from the Park Lane Hotel on Central Park's south side. The carriage horses seemed not to notice the smattering of drizzle as the drivers huddled under their jacket hoods. Luke rapidly covered the blocks, turning left at the sign labeled "Avenue of the Americas"—Sixth Avenue to him. The rain held back until he was safely in the lobby of the tower, and he headed straight to the elevators.

Luke smiled at the receptionist and patiently stood until an assistant led him to the corner office. Frank Ryan was tall, athletic, and forty-six. His hair was full but beginning to thin with tinges of gray at the temple. His blue eyes were sharp and his features chiseled. His suit was navy; his shirt was bold stripes of blue and white, and his tie was bright red. The two shook hands firmly, their eyes at the same level. Luke liked Frank Ryan immediately.

"Please, have a seat," Frank opened. "I've asked some of our people to join us."

As if on cue, two men entered the office. Luke stood and greeted Louis Freeman, from accounting, and Dave Greenfield, a trader in the mortgage-backed securities department. Luke shook hands with both and noted Louis's brown suit.

"Our company president, Alex Stewart, will meet us there. He's the president of Stiller Stevens. I'm just the president of Stiller Stevens Securities," Frank said.

"Just the president," Dave chided as Louis eyed Luke.

"OK." Frank grinned boyishly.

The locals grabbed their umbrellas, a must in the city, they said. The few blocks to Ben Benson's, a steakhouse, were dry. The overcast skies lay in abeyance, but the air was cool as Louis and Dennis gently peppered Luke with questions. Where had he gone to school? How long had he been in the business? Had he really started his own firm? How old was he? Bachelor in business from a state university and a few hours shy of political science and history degrees. Worked for a mortgage banking company while going to grad school at night. Quit grad school to go to law school. Passed the bar but didn't practice. Ten years in the business. Started his own company using the net worth he had built from real estate investments. Thirty-three. He answered as quickly as they fired.

They each felt the chill abate as they entered the restaurant and were led to a round table. Within moments, Alex Stewart arrived at the door. Several patrons at other tables stood and shook his hand and chatted as he slowly made his way through the dining room. "See," Frank nodded to Luke, as the group watched Alex inch toward them, "there's the real president."

Alex Stewart was in his sixties, his midriff softening but his gaze stiff and sure. His strong pose was detached, and the New England accent gave him a learned air. "How is the agriculture business in Oklahoma?" he started as he seated himself.

"I really haven't a clue," Luke responded. "I think high interest rates have to be hurting. For rural lenders the declining value of farmland has to be a concern. But honestly, I don't know much about farming."

"You must come from the oil business then," Alex offered.

"I fill the tank once a week and change the oil every twenty-five hundred miles. No, sir. Sorry, I don't know the oil business, either."

"You weren't involved in all of the oil speculation…the boom and bust of the last few years?" Alex asked, referring to the rapid rise of oil prices in the late 1970s, after the Arab oil embargo and the shortage at the gas pumps had fueled runaway gas prices. After a couple of years, the Saudis had unleashed their reserves, driving down prices and creating huge losses for oil lenders and speculators.

"No, sir, I stick to real estate and mortgage loans. Obviously, the boom-and-bust cycle of the oil industry affects our business. Many over speculated in real estate as energy prices peaked inflation. I guess I was more conservative than some."

"Oh, that's right. You're the young mortgage fellow Frank was telling me about," Alex said and turned as the waiter approached. "I thought everyone in Oklahoma wore boots and a hat, and was either in farming or oil." A Cheshire smile seemed poised to appear on Alex's face.

"You're much too traveled to think that," Luke bantered. "You know full well there are six of us who have neither boots nor hats."

Frank laughed. Dave smiled, and Louis studied the menu.

Hearty orders followed: steak au poivre, veal chop, liver and on-ions, and shrimp. Luke ordered veal piccata and settled into the room.

Alex turned to the firm's top accountant. "Louis, I understand Mr. Boyd wants us to give him six million dollars with his promise to deliver six million dollars in mortgage-backed bonds in five days. Doesn't seem like good business to me. Tell me, Luke, what's the problem?"

"Growth. Profitable growth. Business is good. Our primary bank, Malson, has agreed to increase our credit line to thirty-five million dollars, but the documents won't be available for another week. In the interim, we have a shortfall. We have about six million dollars to fund in the next few days, before the end of the month. We have six million dollars of mortgage-backed bonds that will be delivered to you on the first of the month. Those certificates have been approved, and the bonds will be issued directly to you. We would like for you to buy the bonds five days early. The money would repay a portion of the credit line with the bank and give us additional capacity until they can implement the increase. The bonds will be delivered to you on the first and repay the advance we receive from you. A few days later, we'll have our increase from Malson, and our short-term credit crunch will be solved."

"Don't you have other bank relationships?" Alex asked.

"A couple of small ones. We have lines of credit with three other banks, but they each have one-million-dollar legal lending limits. That's all they can lend to one borrower. Oklahoma doesn't have branch banking, so most banks are small and have low lending lim-its. We're at capacity with them now. They're holding loans pledged for bonds you have agreed to purchase later in the month."

"Isn't your father-in-law a banker?" Alex asked.

"Yes." Luke paused. That was a sore spot. "It's a small bank. His is one of those with the low lending limit. Honestly, his rate is too high. We hate to use it."

"No family deal?" Frank interjected.

"Oh…there's a family deal, all right. But not a good one." Luke forced a grin. His face was younger than his years, but he wrinkled his forehead at the mention of his father-in-law.

"How do we buy bonds that don't exist?" Louis interjected. "The bonds don't exist until they're issued. We can't buy something that doesn't exist."

"I don't know all of the rules," Luke admitted. "But you have all the paperwork. You have the certificates showing the custodian has the mortgage documents, and you have the certificate numbers showing the bonds are approved. I have already signed the PD 1832s transferring the bonds to Stiller Stevens, so the bonds will be issued directly to you. I can't get the bonds back unless you transfer them to me."

"Honestly, Luke, the solution seems to be to delay closing new loans, get your credit increase, and resume normal operations. Every business has a crunch from time to time," Alex answered.

"Yes. But banks have the Fed Funds window where they can borrow overnight, sometimes for weeks or months to shore up their liquidity. You can do similar things with repurchase agreements between brokers. But a mortgage banker doesn't have that last resource. To disrupt our loan closings, even for a day or two, sends a bad message to our customers. It's similar to a bank run. We can't afford to delay any loan closings without creating rumors and running the risk of destroying our business. Oklahoma is a sensitive market. There has been an oil bust, and a medium-sized bank was closed last year. We need to be seen as stable and dependable."

"You have one primary bank. Why's that?" Alex asked.

"There are only four large banks in the state. Two have mortgage companies, and I worked for one of them. They didn't want me to resign. One bank doesn't do mortgage banking lines. So, we deal with Malson. Ultimately, we will have to go out of state, but we're not there yet. Frankly, many lenders are avoiding the region due to the oil bust. Colorado, Oklahoma, Louisiana, and Texas have been nicknamed the 'COLT states' and have been blacklisted."

"How have you managed your delinquencies? Yours are below the national average, and Oklahoma's delinquencies are double the national average," Alex said.

"We have done two things. First we have avoided adjustable rate mortgages; in my opinion, they are a time bomb. Common sense tells me borrowers are getting loans only because they qualify at a starting rate below the market. Those loans have escalation clauses adjusting the borrowers' interest rates to the market after a year or two. Interest rates have to go down significantly for their payments to stay the same. If the market stays the same or goes up, the borrowers' payments will increase. How are they going to keep the home when the payment increases? People are betting on good news that will only let them break even. If things stay the same or get worse, they lose. I think that was one of the lessons we were supposed to have learned from the Great Depression and the reason the government started sponsoring fixed rate loans.

"Secondly, rates have been volatile. When rates drop significantly, one of two things happens, and they're both bad for us. If the borrower is credit worthy, he will refinance, and we lose the monthly servicing fees we get for managing the loan. If he is no longer credit worthy, he can't refinance, and the loan will most likely go to foreclosure. Either way, we lose. So, as interest rates move, we sell the servicing on all loans that are one and a half percent higher than market rate."

"Savings and loans are the buyers?" Alex asked.

"Yes. They want the escrow deposits, and they pay a good price, usually around two and a half percent or more of the loan balance."

"So, you make money on the origination fees and the servicing, either collecting the monthly payments or selling the rights for an upfront fee?" Louis asked.

"Yes, sir," Luke quickly replied.

"How do we buy bonds that don't exist?" Louis repeated.

Dave quickly chimed in. "Luke, I know our trading desk is risky. I occasionally enjoy it." He gave Alex a smile. "But, you guys are out there. Making loans, banking the loans, running to pledge them for bonds, selling the bonds, getting paid, paying off the bank, and starting all over. You won't live any longer than bond traders." All laughed.

The entrées arrived, and the conversation settled into generalities of weather, markets, and sports. Over desserts the business conversation became more pointed.

"Luke, we like your business, and we would like a long-term relationship. Please understand your request puts us in a difficult position. It's just not possible for us to purchase bonds before they are issued. You are asking us to loan you six million dollars with no collateral."

"Alex, I fully expect to be charged interest. You can charge the regular repurchase agreement—that's about the same rate we are paying Malson. And that's higher than the Fed Funds rate, so you would still make a small spread for a few days. Please remember, we are at risk every time we sell our bonds to you. These bonds are going to be delivered directly to you, and I have already put them in your name. If anything were to happen to Stiller Stevens, where would I be? I am not suggesting that is even a possibility, but long-term relationships are built on trust." He paused a moment and added, "And long-term relationships are the only ones worth having."

Alex's eyes remained fixed on his coffee. "Will you stay in town for the weekend?" he asked.

"I'm not sure. I may try to find a theatre ticket for this evening. Otherwise, I will wait for the next trip."

When Dave had paid the bill, they all stood. Luke thanked them for lunch. At the curb Alex excused himself, saying he had another meeting. Luke, Dave, and Louis crossed Fifty-Second Street, as Frank lingered with Alex.

"Do you like New York?" Louis asked.

"I love New York." Luke smiled and inhaled the swirling scents; the city's growl echoed between the towers and whisked above the concrete and asphalt.

"Well, come back and visit us. Please understand, Alex is doing the right thing. We can't advance the money until we have the bonds." Louis's voice was sincere.

"Do you have time to see the trading floor?" Dave asked. "You know you can call me if you can't reach John in Chicago. I can do your trades, and he'll still get credit. You know he's calling me to get the price quotes when you call."

"Yes, I can hear your voice in the background. You have some great one-liners," Luke said.

"What do you mean?" Dave deadpanned. He knew he had an arsenal of zingers and wondered which ones Luke had overheard.

"I loved the one, when I told John he was trying to buy my bonds too cheap—an eighth of a percent under the last trade—and I could hear you on the squawk box saying, 'Tell him they're for my mother.'"

"That was probably Artie's voice." Dave bit back a smile.

"It was yours," Luke laughed.

"You know, my mother is a heck of a trader," Dave quipped.

Frank caught up to the group as they entered the building lobby. He winked at Luke, leaned toward him, and whispered. "You know, I learned something today. I used to think all of the hustlers came from Brooklyn." Frank turned to Dave and said in a normal voice, "Are you going to show him the trading floor?"

"Sure," Dave offered.

"Great," Frank said. He turned to Luke. "I'm going to leave you with Dave. He can show you around. I need to get to a meeting. I'm sure we have the wire instructions for your account. Louis will be sending the six million dollars within the next hour. We do have the PD 1832s, don't we?" Frank asked Louis as he draped a hand on his shoulder.

"Yes, we just don't have the bonds," Louis replied, his face in disbelief.

"Well, they should be here in five days. Let's be sure we get Luke's wire sent right away. We'll just charge the Fed Funds rate." Frank nodded, took back his arm, and turned to Luke. "That will be four-point-five percent, instead of six percent. And of course, we won't charge any fees for early funding."

Dave patted Louis on the back, and the two headed toward the elevator.

"Thank you for your help," Luke said as he and Frank shook hands firmly. "I'm not a hustler," he added softly.

"Oh, you're a hustler. And that's a good thing. I'm from Brooklyn." Frank nodded. "Thanks for coming to see us. Catch up with Dave, and I'll see the wire is taken care of."

Frank and Luke rejoined Louis and Dave at the elevators. Everyone exchanged pleasantries, and then separated in the congestion of the building. Dave and Luke made their way to the trading floor. Luke shook hands with more than thirty traders, reaching over and around terminals as they swiveled to smile with headsets in place, shirt sleeves rolled up, and ties dangling from open collars. Luke nodded greetings to more assistants, wedged between stacks of trading sheets, with pens and pencils cocked behind their ears. Within a few minutes, he said his good-byes and headed for the elevator and the tower exit. Thin beams of sunlight sliced through the overcast skies, and he sensed the threat of rain was over. He slid the umbrella onto the security guard's desk counter without a word and quickly spun onto the street, heading toward the Park Lane Hotel.

CHAPTER THREE

uke briskly stepped through the hotel lobby and grabbed the first black receiver from the row of coin telephones. He glanced at his watch. There was a late flight to Dallas with a connection that would arrive in Tulsa before midnight. He wistfully recalled the views of Central Park and uptown from the windows of the Park Lane rooms. He wanted to stay, to sit on the windowsill, to take refuge in the city, and to breathe in anonymity. "Maybe another time," he thought. Chuck Rail answered on the second ring.

"Chuck, it's Luke. I wanted you to know they're wiring the money. It should be there within an hour."

"So, it went well."

"Yes, very well."

"What did it cost you, Big Boy…one- or two-percent fee plus some interest?"

Luke hated when Chuck called him "Big Boy," but he ignored it. "No points. No fees. We have to pay the Fed Funds rate. Met some nice people, and I think they understood the situation."

"Whoa." Chuck leaned back in his chair. "You must have made some pitch."

"I don't know that I was so convincing. I think the audience was sympathetic. Anyway, the money should be there in an hour."

"Don't worry. We received it a few minutes ago."

"Great," Luke said.

"Are you staying for the weekend?" Chuck asked.

"I want to, but I may be able to get back tonight. I'll probably try that."

"Going to the lake?" Chuck asked.

"Probably." Luke flinched, realizing he had given Chuck an opening.

"By yourself?" Chuck asked.

"Yeah." Luke waited.

"Great. How about I come up tomorrow and introduce you to Fluffy?"

"Fluffy?" Luke sighed. Chuck always seemed to be chasing a new, young girlfriend. "Where did you meet this one?"

"Twenty-seven, tight little package, blond hair, daddy's money, and works in the Trust Department. Pretty blue eyes."

Luke smirked to himself. Chuck had been a college acquaintance but the two had drifted apart and Luke preferred that. Chuck had recently been promoted to head Malson's real estate department, and suddenly Chuck was back in Luke's life. Luke knew the two would have to do business together and Luke would have to entertain his banker. "You want to play some tennis?"

"You and I can play tennis. Fluffy may want a few sets of her own. We can leave tomorrow night or"—he paused—"Sunday morning."

"OK." Luke hid the resignation from his voice. "I'm planning on leaving Saturday. You can stay if you want. Give me a call before you head up."

"See you tomorrow morning before noon. Good job in New York. The guys on the nineteenth floor will be impressed."

Luke punched the numbers to call home. One of the babysitters answered.

"This is Luke. Is Beth there?"

"No, she and her sister are shopping. I'm picking up the kids from school. Beth should be back later."

"Tell her I'm staying in New York tonight, but I'll be back tomorrow," he lied. "I'll call her tomorrow."

"OK."

"Thanks."

Luke tapped the receiver and dialed his office. "May I speak to Harold?"

"May I say whose calling?" The receptionist sounded friendly.

"Sure, go ahead."

There was a pause and then she laughed. "Luke, is that you?"

"Yes. How are you? How's everything?"

"Good. Busy. One moment."

Harold Rhoden started, "Hope you're having fun while the rest of us work."

"Is it busy?"

"Lots of phone calls. Lots of closings next week, so buyers, sellers, and realtors are calling to confirm times and change everything at the last minute," Harold huffed.

"Anything I need to know?"

"There's nothing that can't wait," Harold replied. Luke knew there would be a large stack of issues on his desk. Harold hated making decisions, preferring to delay and hoping someone else would solve the problem. "Uh…uh," Harold stammered. "Luke, do we have any money?"

"Yeah, Stiller Stevens gave us the money early, and Malson has the wire."

"So you did some work."

"Got lucky, I guess. Hey, I'm going to check the flight schedule. The markets look steady. Leave quotes for new applications the same for the weekend. Let the branch managers know."

"OK. Phyllis and the others have been asking what we would do on rates. I have been putting them off."

"It's nice to have the same rates for two straight weeks. Feels like the old days."

"Yeah."

"If no one needs me, I'll see you Monday morning," Luke said.

"See you Monday morning." Harold hung up.

Luke turned and reclaimed his luggage with the claim check and a tip, strode through the lobby, scaled down the steps, and stepped onto Fifty-Ninth to hail a cab.

CHAPTER FOUR

The spring afternoon sun shot shards of light ricocheting off the forty-seven floors of white marble and glass called "Malson Tower" and back across the Arkansas River. Still leaning back in his chair, Chuck Rail's eyes flared out the windows of his new eighteenth-floor office and conjured the promise of his future. From his view, he could not catch a glimpse of the river. He could not see the sun or the reflections of Malson Tower shining in Malson Tower II, its thirty-four-story sibling. His office offered the poorer section of the city and the shadows cast from the tall tower. Chuck gazed down at decrepit brick buildings, abandoned and languishing. He lifted his gaze and found rows of low-income housing, weathered gray roofs, and industrial tracts until he finally found the horizon. He still sat on the wrong side of the tower.

Chuck smiled, content with his recent promotion, though he thought it was long overdue. He saw himself as the workhorse of the Real Estate Department. He had left his position with a small law firm, joined the bank, and staked his future by taking the most challenging deals. He had grabbed the daunting task of leading the bank's financing of a risky urban project: Malson Tower II, owned by the real estate affiliate of the bank. Banks could not operate as developers, so an umbrella corporation, a holding company owning the bank and a subsidiary, presented the legal fiction that the bank's owners did not own the buildings. Each day the bank's executives and key directors watched the construction from their office windows. Each executive's lunch on the forty-seventh floor had been served on fine china and in full view of the new rising structure, built of the same white marble with narrow, blue, tinted bands of windows circling the almost oval building, shaped the same as the larger tower. Majestically, the two buildings stood at the river's bend with fountains and waterfalls. Malson Bank served as the lead lender, but its $35 million was only a token of the more than $900 million put up by New York banks for the second tower. The lenders had been paid in full and on schedule when construction was completed, and AMNE National, the nation's largest supplier of electricity, provided long-term financing through its financial subsidiary. Malson's credit card operations, expanding from the acquisition of small bank portfolios, had taken twelve floors of the new building. The remainder had been leased to national firms and local professionals. Already occupancy for the new tower was above 80 percent, and Chuck Rail had been named senior vice president in charge of the Real Estate Department.

The promotion had not fully satisfied Chuck. He was still locked on the wrong side of the building and one floor from where he wanted to be. Sid Fullmer, the former head of the Real Estate Department, had received most of the recognition. He had been named executive vice president, moved to the nineteenth floor, and could see flashes of sunlight on the river. Sid's office gave a hint of Tulsa's south side: the city's rolling hills, the fashionable shopping centers, the huge oak trees shading million-dollar homes and exclusive country clubs.

Sid Fullmer's new role was to develop a network of banks under Malson's ownership. New state legislation allowing banks to open branches was winding its way through approval and would soon be law. Malson was gearing up to purchase smaller banks and to open new locations. "That's where the action is and where I belong," Chuck thought. His success was dulled by Sid's promotion. Chuck thought Sid was too weak to pull off big deals and had ridden on Chuck's toughness and smarts. Chuck resolved again to show the nineteenth floor he belonged and turned to see his secretary approaching.

"Mr. Bivins is waiting for you in his office." She smiled.

"Thanks." Chuck winked and started toward the bank of elevators. Across the lobby he could see the huge spiral stairway to the nineteenth floor. The enormous marble steps were cloaked in thick, cream-colored carpet, exposed only on the ends, and bordered with highly polished brass rails. The stairway was off limits to him when alone. It was to be used only by the executives of the nineteenth floor or those escorting bank customers and guests to and from the executive offices. Chuck turned past the elevators and felt his lapel to ensure his gold-plated bank logo pin was in place. He hurried along the corridor, opened the heavy black door, and climbed the fire escape stairway to the nineteenth floor and the offices of Bill Bivins, president and chief executive officer.

Chuck emerged and crossed to greet Bivins's secretary. She noted his muscular frame and tapered waist, belying his forty-one years, and offered coffee or soda, which Chuck politely declined. One never had a beverage in Bivins's office unless accompanying a bank customer—this was the rule. Never be caught without the logo lapel pin—this was another. She motioned Chuck inside and mimed Bivins was on a call.

Bill Bivins had been recruited by the bank's board to make Malson a premier regional bank. National bank consolidation was on the horizon. The barriers to interstate banking were falling as the Reagan administration argued that small banks were inefficient, siphoned deposits from larger institutions, and left American banks unable to compete internationally. The promise was that consolidation would form larger, stronger, safer, more efficient banks and would drive down costs and benefit bank customers.

Chuck glanced around Bivins's office, almost as large as Chuck's entire department. Leather sofas and hard-edged tables adorned custom rugs. A huge conference table was framed by large, tan, leather chairs. A separate area of more leather sofas and leather winged-back chairs awaited more informal meetings. All reflected the sculpted, edged, and strong persona Bivins had adopted. Chuck sat across from Bivins's oversized desk and enjoyed the view offered by the bank of windows and then turned as Bivins finished the call. The lower chair and Chuck's short height forced him to look up as Bivins started talking before he had put down the receiver.

"So, what did it cost him?"

"No fees. Just the Fed Funds rate. I thought they would have charged him a fee of one percent or more, that would have been at least sixty thousand dollars. But they didn't. He actually saved a little on the interest." Chuck shrugged.

Bivins's eyes were fixed on Chuck. "No fee. Incredible. He borrowed at the same rate we do." Bivins paused for a second without facial expression. He was a no-nonsense manager, interested only in results. "Tell me about this guy, Luke Boyd. How does he go from a five-million- to a thirty-five-million-dollar line of credit in three years? How does he become the second-largest depositor in the bank? Does he know that?"

"I met him when I was in law school and he was an undergraduate. Friend-of-a-friend type of thing. He was younger. She was too." Chuck tried to induce humor, but Bivins's eyes remained fixed. "Ran into him in Tulsa. He was working for CPT Bank's mortgage company and going to law school at night. CPT Bank had no presence in Tulsa before he arrived, and within four years they were the city's largest mortgage lender. He had made some money investing in real estate on the side—buying and selling property. He talked about starting his own company, and I introduced him to Sid. He finished law school, took the bar, passed but never practiced. He's an open book, easy to read. He's a straight shooter; you can see him coming for miles."

"You introduced him to Sid?" Bivins interrupted.

"Yes. And Sid handled his account."

"Sid handled it," Bivins repeated. "Have you handled it before?"

"No, just Sid. I was doing the Malson Tower II loan—that sort of thing."

"But you know him well. Go on."

"His father-in-law is president of Sand Springs Fidelity Bank. He invested one hundred fifty thousand dollars in FRM, about fifteen percent, but Boyd bought him out. Might be his ex-father-in-law soon. Boyd is probably going to get a divorce."

"Really?"

"I think so. It's a matter of time."

"Keep me posted. Go ahead," Bivins ordered.

"Boyd raised another three hundred thousand dollars from two other investors and put up five hundred fifty thousand dollars himself. He's bought all of them out, and he owns it all now."

"Do we have the banker's stock loan…what's his name?"

"George Winney. Yes, he was banking with Second Bank. Tom Cook in the Correspondent Bank Department got him to move his accounts here two years ago. We have his stock loan. He owns less than twenty percent of the bank. It's small but solid. His part of the bank is worth about two million dollars, but he owes us about two and a half million dollars. So, he's technically in default with us. We could call the loan. He invested in oil deals and lost heavily. I think we have added the interest for the past three quarters into the loan because he can't pay it."

"But Winney's not involved with FRM now?" Bivins asked as he made a note to ask Sid Fullmer whether Winney's bank was on the list of potential acquisitions.

"Not now. Winney has financial problems, so after the first year, Boyd bought Winney's share for three hundred thousand dollars. That gave Winney cash to repay some of his debt, but I think Winney still owes more than one million dollars to other banks on top of what he owes us. Might be more. Cook would know. I know he's heavily leveraged. Boyd bought out the other two guys a little later. One of them had some large real estate losses, and Boyd helped him out. The other guy was in good shape."

"Nice profit on FRM, huh. Winney doubled his money in a year."

"Yeah, Boyd was trying to help him out. Winney used the profit to pay some of the debt on his oil investments. Rumor is there are still lots of oil loans but no oil. He's just barely hanging on. I think the bank's OK, though."

"How's Boyd do it?"

"The guy works. He's always calling on realtors, buying lunch, and trying to get their business. He has about eighty employees: five guys and the rest women. Harold Rhoden is the operations guy. One guy manages one of the branches in Oklahoma City. The other guys are gofers. I think one may be a loan officer, but most of his loan officers and branch managers are all women. Boyd always has this spiel about how women are underpaid and never given opportunity. But he makes more mortgage loans than anyone in the state and watches his delinquency rates. He's heavier on business development and marketing than on operations."

"What's the servicing worth?"

"Probably two and a half percent. He has around four hundred million dollars in servicing, so it's worth ten million dollars. That's where he gets the interest-free deposits. The borrowers have to escrow money for insurance and tax, and that money goes into the accounts with us. Sid negotiated for the rate to be adjusted for his interest-free balances, so it's around six percent. That's half of the mortgage rates, so he makes a nice spread on the loans while he's holding them for resale. I don't think he knows he's our second-largest depositor. I'm sure he doesn't have a clue."

"In three years the guy's net worth goes up by at least ten million dollars, he pockets more than one million dollars a year as income, and his deposits in this bank average over sixteen million dollars per day—all interest free. He's making over four million dollars per year. We deal with two other mortgage bankers, right?"

"Yes."

"How do they look?"

"They're OK, but they're nothing like his deal. Both have been around for years. Much smaller market share. They have smaller, older portfolios with smaller average loan sizes and higher delinquencies. They probably couldn't get the same price for their servicing. Probably could get one and a half percent, maybe less. And their operations are stagnant. They make three or four loans a week. Boyd makes twenty to thirty loans or more on some days."

Bivins turned, pulled a stack of documents from the top of his credenza, signed his name, and slid them toward Chuck.

"Here—these are the loan documents for FRM. Don't let Boyd sign them until next Friday. Then they can go to loan operations, and he can draw on the increase the same day." Bivins paused. "Let's set lunch with Boyd within a couple of weeks of that. Tell him I want to meet him and ask him to help me with the United Way drive. My secretary will call to confirm the date." Bivins reached for the phone, which let Chuck know the meeting was over.

Chuck picked up the loan documents and slid toward the door, saying, "Will do."

CHAPTER FIVE

Luke easily caught the flight from LaGuardia. The headphones in place, he spoke to no one, ate the dinner setup—shrimp cocktail and a salad and a glass of white wine—skipped the entrée, and went over the loan production and marketing reports he always carried. The weight of a portfolio aligned to settle with bond brokers and the loan applications processing toward closing left more than $75 million in mortgage commitments exposed to market changes. The volatility of the 1980s had brought huge daily fluctuations in interest rates, with long-term rates jumping suddenly, changing the value of loans Luke's company held. The value of FRM's portfolio could change by more than $2 million in one day. A piece of Luke was always aware of the bond market, and the potential loss hovered over his head.

If interest rates rose, causing bond prices to fall, the bond delivery commitments Luke had sold in the futures market would grow in value enough to offset the loss he would suffer when he sold the loans. If interest rates fell, causing bond prices to rise, Luke would take an immediate loss in the futures market and would have to make the margin calls, paying the loss upfront. FRM would then recoup its money by making a profit when the loans were sold.

The looming prospect of making margin calls required another piece of Luke to always be devoted to FRM's cash position. A sharp drop in interest rates would require significant cash to make a margin call and keep coverage in place. Luke combed through the reports, touched the keys of the HP-12C calculator, and verified coverage and cash reserves available to make margin calls.

The connection in Dallas went smoothly, and he landed in Tulsa before midnight. He retrieved his car from the parking garage and ensured the car telephone was turned off before the slate-gray four-door 500 SEL Mercedes started for Grand Lake and continued cruising steadily five miles over the speed limit. Light traffic followed for the first half hour of divided highway that cut through small hills and trees buried in the dark. Luke's car was alone once it exited onto another half hour's driving on black, rural, two-lane roads, passing through small towns already asleep. The spring air rushed through the windows and swooshed over the open sunroof. Luke veered from the state highway, down the narrow curved asphalt path, through the trees, and into Cliff Point—forty units of multistory condos, lining the peninsula, each with its own view and decks facing onto the lake. Luke saw only one other car as he arrived. It was early spring; the air was cool and the lake water, cold. There was no moon, and the absence of city lights and clouds allowed the stars to burst overhead.

Luke pulled his bag from the trunk, admired the stars, and cautiously found his way down the low-lit steps and to the front door of the blackened condo. Without turning on the lights, he entered, felt his way, and pulled back the wall-length curtains, revealing the upper-level deck and the lake. The water danced slowly, a plate of glass, mirroring soft light, occasionally shimmering from a ripple.

Luke breathed the view, pulled off his coat and tie, draped his suit pants over the loveseat, and leaned into the sofa, his eyes embedded in the lake. The last twenty hours covered his eyes, and he slept.

Luke woke as the sun's rays angled through the trees and splattered across the deck. He stared as the lake's water rolled in the daylight, and the first boat of the day was visible in the distance. He followed the stairs to the lower-level master bedroom, found a robe, stepped onto the lower-level deck, and gazed down to the shoreline twenty-five feet below. His neighbors were not there. Most showed up only in the late spring and summer, and Luke preferred the quieter seasons. It would be a pretty day.

Chuck Rail never called but arrived midmorning and rang the bell. "OK, I brought some Tecate and limes. I know you never have any beer. Oh yeah, this young lady is Fluffy. Some call her 'Melissa Marin.' But you can call her 'Fluffy,'" Chuck announced as he slapped Luke on the back and strutted toward the living room.

Melissa rolled her eyes and gave Chuck a slight glare. "Thanks, Chuck."

She turned to Luke and flashed a genuine smile. "Hi," she said. She was pretty. Her thick, blond curls touched her shoulders. Her bright, blue eyes sparkled, and her porcelain-white skin was creamy smooth as she gracefully glided through the foyer. She was shapely and poised. Her full, pink lips smiled knowingly. She wore an unbuttoned, pale-blue knit pullover, with the collar popped; her breasts were full but not oversized, and white shorts highlighted her narrow waist and trim legs.

Luke immediately saw her beauty. "Hi, Melissa. Nice to meet you." He smiled, and they both paused. "Please, come in," he said. "You know I have beer, wine, and all that," Luke said, turning to Chuck.

"You have the same beer you had a year ago. You never drink beer, and it just sits there and goes flat." Chuck laughed, took a glimpse of the lake, and announced, "Let's play some tennis."

Within minutes they had reached the courts. New nets had been installed, and the bright white top of the net shone against the green and red of the court. Snippets of the lake could be glimpsed in the distance, through the dark green windscreen and the trees that shielded the court. Luke had shown Melissa the pool, but she said she preferred to sun and to watch.

The match was a contrast of styles. Chuck was shorter, five feet seven, with a muscular build. He was untiring, chasing each ball, staying at the baseline, endlessly placing an array of spins without pace, in an attempt to outlast his opponent. Luke was eight inches taller and angular and would press the net with big serves looking for an ace or a winner or a volley off a weak return to take the points quickly.

Luke had regularly beaten Chuck since they had first played. His serve was strong, and he breezed to an early 4–1 lead. Melissa stretched on a chaise lounge and read, occasionally stopping to watch the two. Luke felt confident and played a loose service game to make it competitive. Chuck won that game, held serve, and looked energized. Luke concentrated, and the first set was quickly over. The second set was longer as Luke experimented at times but focused on the big points.

Chuck would tease Luke on the end changes. "She distracting you?" he would pose.

"She's pretty." Luke would smile.

"Pretty—hell, look at that body." Chuck would counter on the next end change.

Luke hit a big serve, and Chuck's return found the net, ending the match. "Sorry if we bored you," Luke offered to Melissa as he walked off the court.

"Bored? She loved it. Two white-clad stallions, lathering in competition for her charms," Chuck countered.

"He's so funny," she said and smiled at Luke. "You played well."

"Thanks. Let's find some lunch," Luke suggested, grabbing his car keys. Soon they had traversed through the budding oak trees around the lake's shore to the North Bay Club. The crowd was sparse and they sat in sunlight on a wooden deck edging over the lake. The conversation was light. Melissa was quick, obviously intelligent, yet trying to be demur. Her eyes glistened smartly though her air was delicate. She knew she was pretty, and she knew Luke thought so also. When she excused herself, Chuck quickly changed to business as Luke watched her walk away.

"How did you get the money? And with no fees?"

"I just told them the deal, and they said, 'OK.'"

"They made you sign a personal note or something?"

"No. They just put it on our account. The bonds will be there Wednesday. So there won't be a problem."

"You never cease to amaze me," Chuck said. He paused and drew a wry smile. "So, how about Fluffy?"

"Melissa? Oh, she's pretty. How long have you been seeing her?"

"I'm just the tour guide. I can't afford this one."

"Hey, if you guys want to stay tonight, feel free. I'm going back this afternoon. I need to go by the office, and I want to see my kids."

"No, I'm going back this afternoon. I told you, I'm just the tour guide. I brought her to meet you."

"Sure, right. Where did you meet her?"

"She's in the bank's management training program. She's working in the Trust Department, but she's really looking for a husband. I don't have the net worth for this one. She's old money."

"Well, she must have an MBA."

"Sure. She graduated from an all-girls school back East and then took a year off to travel with her mom in Europe. Took a couple of years to finish her MBA; then took more time to travel with her mom. Dad finally made her get a job; I think he called the bank. I bet she will pull your financial statement from the Credit Department next week."

"Just what I need." Luke shook his head.

"Oh, she's just what you need," Chuck insisted. "Smart, pretty, classy, and what a body."

"And checking out my balance sheet. I'm still owned goods."

"How's that going?" Chuck asked, referring to the divorce.

Luke's eyes dropped, and he stared at the endless waves rushing the shore. He paused and saw Melissa returning. "The same," he said as they both stood as she arrived.

"We can talk…later," Chuck said, faking a whisper.

"Am I interrupting?" Melissa asked.

"No, Melissa," Chuck countered quickly, "Luke here has been trying to resolve his domestic arrangement. It seems they can't reach an agreement on his buy-out price."

"Oh," she breathed.

"Oklahoma is still a little tough on divorces. A divorce isn't granted until a property settlement is finalized. And that can take years," Chuck stated.

"Oh, I know," Melissa answered. "One of my dad's friends filed six years ago. The last appeal was just finalized, and his divorce granted this year." She barely paused before asking, "Is it what you want?"

"The divorce—yes. The mess—no. I have two children, and I don't want to hurt them." Luke's voice was muffled. He hated to talk about his personal life.

"Well, can't you work it out?" she asked with coy eyes.

"No, it's far too late for that." Luke's eyes dropped and glanced over at the waves.

"Then give her the money. You're young, obviously gifted, and you can make more," she stated simply.

"Thanks for the confidence, but it's more complicated than that," Luke responded. "So…" Luke said, breaking the conversation.

Melissa smiled and never let her eyes leave Luke.

"So," Chuck jumped in, "I have to get back to Tulsa." He looked to Luke. "Are you spending the night up here?"

"No," Luke answered, "I need to get back before this evening, but we can have a beer on the deck or take the boat out if you want."

"No, we'll just grab my car and head back. I know my beer will still be there next time," Chuck laughed.

Luke was relieved his offer had been declined.

CHAPTER SIX

Luke called home from the car. Another of the babysitters answered and said Beth was running errands, and the children were at a neighborhood party. He left a message for Beth to call him at the office. Music blared until he parked in the rear. The brick FRM office building was nestled among oak trees on a major midtown street. Luke had designed the space with offices on the perimeter, each with glass walls looking into the larger center section, where quietly papered, low-walled workstations allowed easy viewing for an informal intercom of hand signals, waves, and shouts while cupped hands smothered telephone receivers. He was surprised but relieved no one was there. He saw the mound of mail, notes, and files stacked on the left-hand corner of the dark walnut desk. The Telerate machine beckoned with market rates and news from the matching credenza stretched behind his desk.

He scanned the pages of the Telerate screens of green symbols and numbers on black background, reviewing the news and final Friday closing prices. He searched the yield charts and world news stories that might affect Monday's opening prices and the value of FRM's loan production portfolio. Then he turned his attention to the phone messages, mail, and notes from the loan officers. He loved reading the ones from Phyllis, the Tulsa branch manager. Everything was urgently scrawled and demanded immediate attention. The size of the loops in her writing painted the direness of the need. He was relieved the stack contained no surprises. He called home again, and the line was busy. He finished the stack and then drove through the southern suburbs of hills and trees.

He found Beth, one of her sisters, and a babysitter in the living room. The children were in the upstairs den, but they heard him enter and came running downstairs. He gave them hugs and promised to join them. He asked Beth to go to dinner. The sitter needed to leave, but Beth knew another was available, so Luke headed to the kitchen telephone to make reservations. There was no dial tone, and a recording repeated a line was off the hook. A tour downstairs found a receiver lying on the master bedroom floor, while the phone cradle sat on the nightstand, partially covered by a magazine and surrounded by four partially filled glasses of soda and milk, accumulated over the past few days. He called the Summit Club, reserved a corner table, and climbed the stairs to watch the children as they watched a video cassette.

The Summit Club sat atop a tall downtown building. The club was packed during the week, but the weekend crowd was smaller. Only about half of the tables were occupied, and Luke thought the place offered a good chance to talk, and he knew the food was good. He let Beth catch him up on the last few days and some tidbits of gossip to which he feigned attention. Luke waited until the Caesar salad had been tossed tableside. He thought he appeared calm; Beth could sense his nervousness.

"Beth," he said and paused. "We've tried, but I really think it's time to come to some agreement. You know I love the children, and I'll always do whatever I can. You know I care about you…" He paused again. The lights on the horizon danced in the dark and made for a romantic view of the evening and the Arkansas River. Her dark brown hair gleamed in the candlelight. She was pretty and looked as she had when they had met in college. Her soft eyes looked to the side momentarily as he continued, "But I think it's best we come to some agreement."

Her eyes returned, and the softness was gone. "Divorce?" she asked defiantly, staring straight at him.

"Yes," he said haltingly.

"Who is she?"

"There's no one. This isn't about someone else. It's about us."

"No," she said. The determination rose in her voice. "You are not going to do this to me and the children."

Luke noticed the grammar, the placing of oneself before another, noted its importance, but said nothing.

"We've gone over this enough," Beth continued. "This is not going to happen." When he said nothing, she challenged him, "Is it Nick?"

"No," he answered.

"You've never gotten over Nick. That's what it has to be."

"No," he said again, meeting her challenge. He wanted to ask how she could have been seeing someone else when they were engaged, how she could have continued the relationship after they were married, and how she could have introduced Nick to him as a friend in front of her sisters, who knew the whole story. Only after the births of their children had his suspicions grown into an unconfirmed conviction he could no longer ignore, and he had finally pressed her until she admitted the affair and said it had been over for a few years. "No, this has nothing to do with Nick," he said again.

"Look, I've put up with who knows how many girlfriends since then. I know you. There's someone. Who is she?"

"There's no one."

"Then it's Nick. Look…We are both adults. We've made some mistakes. But we have two children. I don't deserve this, and they don't deserve this."

"You don't understand," he started and then told her how he hated there was always a babysitter or cleaning person or sister or some combination of the three in the house. He told her he hated the house being in disarray even though a bevy of sitters and cleaners were always there. He told her he hated that a telephone was unplugged, unhooked, or missing in action most of the time. He told her he hated knowing at least four items in the refrigerator did not have tops on them. He told her he was tired of fighting over how much money she spent. He told her he hated the half-filled glasses lying around the house. But he never told her he hated her for having had Nick, for having lied to him, and for having had no respect for him. He did not tell her he hated himself for not having known earlier and for not leaving her the moment he found out. He did not tell her he hated he had never been honest with himself about how he felt. He had never told anyone, even in confidence. He did not tell her he hated himself for having affairs. He did not tell her he hated her—most of all—for using the children as pawns and for fostering an illusion. "Look," he finished, "I have a ton of guilt about the impact on the children. We can control that. Our relationship is not your fault, and it's not my fault. It's our fault. We don't work well together. Sometimes good people aren't good together. I don't want to live a lie." He paused again. "I think it's time I moved out."

"Again," she dismissed him. He had tried this before, but he had been lured back by the children. "Who is she?"

"There's no one. I have a condo that's vacant. The tenant moved, and it's not leased. I'll just be a couple of miles from the house. I'm going to move a few things over there this week."

"You will take nothing out of the house. You will not take the children there. The children are not going to be around another woman. This is not going to happen." By the time she had made her proclamations, they had finished their entrées and never once been overly demonstrative. To anyone watching through flashing flickers of low candlelight, they portrayed a young couple enjoying an evening away from the children.

After a silent drive home, they found the sitter reading in the living room. Luke climbed the stairs. His son slept peacefully, a book on his chest and three others on the bed. The toys littering the floor painted a picture of the frantic pace that had receded into reading and finally sleep. The tiger barbs, striped bright orange, black, and silver, swam under the low aquarium light and above the bright blue gravel. All the colors danced in the ripples from the water filter's flow. Luke smiled, stepped carefully to avoid a toy, and turned off the aquarium light, the video game controller, and the reading lamp, and then turned toward his daughter's room.

Nothing littered her floor. Each item had been put away, and the room appeared pristine. She slept as a princess, her blond hair draped on the pink pillowcase. The pink sheets and white bedspread were turned out perfectly as though awaiting a photo. The blue-and-gold, bright striped angelfish fluttered gracefully above the pink rocks. All the lights were already turned off. Again he smiled.

Luke drifted into the upstairs den, stepped to the door opening onto the balcony, but did not go out. He searched the sky for stars but found too few. Even in the suburban hills, the city's lights threw their glow across the sky. He pulled a blanket from the hallway closet, stripped off his suit coat and tie, folded the pants and shirt onto a chair, and draped his coat across them. In a moment he had cocooned himself on the sofa, his feet and head pinning down the blanket, with only a sliver of space for breathing, and he slept.

Beth visited with the babysitter for another hour before going to bed in the master bedroom downstairs and slept with the light on and the television playing.

CHAPTER SEVEN

Sunday was calm. Beth and the children joined her family for lunch, while Luke drove to the office and worked until he piled a huge stack on his assistant's desk and wrote his list of issues to resolve on Monday. Two hours before dusk, Luke picked up the children and started to Tulsa Country Club. Most of the day's golfers had finished their rounds, and the skyline of the city rose in the background. Luke played the first hole alone as the children rode along in the cart. Seeing the course abandoned, Luke paused at the second tee and pulled out the short clubs that he had tailored for the children. They took turns playing and driving the cart under his constant gaze. He laughed as they hit the ball and ran to the next shot. "Walk, walk," he said to no avail. It was almost totally dark when he made them stop. After they returned home, Luke slept on the upstairs sofa again.

Monday morning Luke trailed the children down the steps to the arc driveway in front of their home. He found them precious in their school uniforms and backpacks. His son bounced, vigorous and robust in his white shirt and blue pants, one book already in his hand, his hair combed down but with a wayward few rising in defiance.

His daughter strolled with a royal gait, smooth and silky, in a white blouse and scotch plaid skirt, never jostling the pink backpack.

Already Luke had called John Elliot to check the opening of the bond markets. The fluctuations were small, and no major announcements were expected. The car telephone sat cradled as he and the children joked during the short drive. On arrival, the children raced gleefully with shrieks to greet their friends and blended into the frenzy of high-pitched voices in the school's entrance. Once out of sight, Luke checked the markets again as the car retraced its path.

He pulled into the arc drive and looked up at the two-story house. He liked the architecture, but nothing in the two stories was home. Once inside, he looked through the dining room at the cherry table and buffet stacked with sacks and then past the open door, where he caught a glimpse of Beth and one of the cleaning people having coffee in the breakfast nook. He knew the sinks and counters were filled and littered with dishes. He turned past the living room, where newspapers, plates, glasses, clothes, and magazines dotted the furniture and floor. He said nothing and angled past the standing vacuum and snaking cord blocking the hall and into the master bedroom, where he found the bed cluttered with hangers, papers, books, magazines, towels, and bags. More filled the chairs and covered the floor. Plates and saucers were scattered on the nightstands. The television played to no one. He turned toward his bathroom and went into his closet; he took two suitcases and a hanging bag and packed. Beth and he had agreed to wait a day or two before talking to the children, although she still insisted there would be no divorce. She would tell them he was on a business trip. He hoped after a day or two she could be persuaded to sit down with the children. He was wrong.

Luke arrived at the office and heard the clattering of typewriters and constant ringing of telephones. The dot matrix printers, the first sign of the computer age in the office, screeched from the Loan Servicing Department. There were over fifty people in the Tulsa office, but only four males.

In his first years out of college, Luke had seen a recurring theme. Every office was staffed with underpaid females, without college degrees but with experience and expertise that kept the business running. Many had the potential and desire to advance, but they received no opportunity and stewed in deference. Going against the grain, Luke had hired the first female branch manager in the state when he worked for CPT Mortgage. He had caught plenty of grief for that. In building FRM, Luke had repeatedly hired and promoted women as the company had grown from five employees to more than eighty in five locations. Some were married, working first to supplement the family income but coming to learn that there were more possibilities. Others were single mothers with the burden of a full workday of performance and pressure followed by an exhausted evening of nurturing children. Luke would quickly admit his hiring pattern was based equally on social philosophy and qualifications. He felt responsible for them, as if he had to match their work with both compensation and commitment.

He grabbed a cup of coffee, smiled hello to his assistant, Andrea, and entered his office with his eyes fixed on the Telerate machine. He had made and taken several calls when Andrea told him George Winney was calling.

"This is Luke," Luke answered with his customary greeting.

"Luke?" George Winney paused.

"Yes," Luke replied as he leaned into his chair, peered out the window, and laughed to himself at the repetition that began each call from his father-in-law.

"This is George Winney." He pronounced the name "Win-knee," with emphasis, still aware of the old grade-school taunts, "Whiney Horse! Whiney Horse!"

"Good morning," Luke said, still smiling.

"Luke…" Winney paused. "Beth needs a little money in her account."

"How much?" Luke answered, sitting up. He had been through this routine as well. At each quarterly meeting, the bank's board of directors reviewed the list of overdrawn accounts and past due loans. Beth would write checks beyond her bank balance. Winney, as president of the bank, would approve the checks and let the account be overdrawn. The day before the board meeting, Winney would call and ask Luke to cover the overdrafts, so Beth's name would not be reported. The first time the overdraft had been four hundred dollars. The amounts had steadily increased to over one thousand dollars. Finally tiring of the quarterly tax, Luke had covered one last overdraft and then told Winney to close the account. After several years of giving Beth cash every Monday morning, she had convinced Luke she had changed her ways, and he had agreed to her opening an account again just two months ago.

"Well, the board of directors meets tomorrow, and of course the list of overdrawn accounts is reviewed. I don't really want Beth's name on the list."

"How much is she overdrawn?"

"She needs a little more than four thousand dollars," Winney said without inflection.

"What!"

"Just a little over four thousand," he repeated almost with a chuckle.

"How much, exactly," Luke said slowly. There was no question in his voice.

When Winney reported an exact figure of $4,725.89, Luke said, "I'll be there in thirty minutes. I want the account closed."

"You can make a deposit with the tellers."

"I'll be there in thirty minutes. I want the account closed." Luke hung up.

He glanced again at the Telerate, grabbed his checkbook, told Andrea he would be back in an hour, and started the twenty-minute drive to Sand Springs. On the drive, he again checked the markets and made several calls. He exited the expressway and turned into the old downtown area. The curved, narrow streets were bound by curbside parking and housed two- and three-story red brick buildings with weathered mortar from the oil boom era of the 1910s. Names and the years of construction adorned the facades, but the buildings now housed thrift stores and law offices. The retail stores, as in many other small towns, had moved to outlying strip centers close to the new Walmart. Sand Springs Fidelity Bank sat on a block of its own.

Luke parked, took a deep breath, and replayed some history. Years before, as a wedding gift, Winney had paid the seven-hundred-dollar air travel for the honeymoon. Beth had taught school then and was due her three summer pay checks. Upon their return, Winney broke the bad news; Beth's two thousand dollars of summer pay had arrived and had been applied to overdrafts on her account. She still owed another two hundred dollars, which Luke covered. His mental ledger had marked his wedding gift as a loss of more than fifteen hundred dollars.

Luke gathered himself and started inside. He turned sharply left and headed up the fire escape to the second floor and the bank's Proof Department. There was no natural light as he crossed under the fluorescent glare to the counter. "May I get a printout of Beth Boyd's account?" he asked.

The young man turned quizzically, and an older lady crossed to the counter. He didn't know her, but he began as she approached. "Hi, I'm Luke Boyd, and I need to take care of Beth's account," he said sheepishly. "May I get a printout of her balance?"

"Do you need just the balance, or do you want the activity?" Her smile told Luke she knew the account was overdrawn.

"The activity?" He liked the idea. "May I have something that summarizes the last few weeks?" His voice was polite and tailed at the end.

"Of course. Just a moment." She disappeared behind a solid wall. She returned with her grin and a green-and-white striped computer print of the activity since the account's opening. Luke glanced over the summary; the account had been overdrawn within the first week. Beth's check writing steadily outdistanced the deposits and the overdraft had grown. Luke's automatic deposit, two thousand dollars every Monday morning, had already posted. She had been $6,725.89 overdrawn at the day's beginning. Some of the checks were written for as little as three dollars, but each check incurred a fifteen-dollar service fee.

"Does the bank mail her a notice of the check and service charge each time?"

"Of course," she responded. "We have to send her a notice for each check."

"Looks like she keeps someone busy around here," Luke muttered and took a deep breath. "Thank you." He forced a smile.

Luke stepped back to the first floor, crossed the lobby, and took a seat on the sofa outside George Winney's office. Luke could see Winney talking on the telephone. His father-in-law took one call and made a succession of others, refusing to glance at Luke. Finally as Winney began a new call, Luke huffed and walked into the office and stood at his desk. Winney quickly ended the call and turned to Luke. "I guess she just needs a little more money." Winney kept his seat, pushed his large belly into the desk, and offered his hand, which reached less than halfway.

Luke leaned, shook his hand, and began talking as he seated himself. "I don't think she needs more money. She doesn't pay any bills; she doesn't pay the utilities or the house payment. I pay for her clothes, the children's clothes, and their tuition. I pay the housekeepers and babysitters. And it looks like I pay for a lot of fifteen-dollar bank charges. And two thousand dollars a week for mad money isn't enough. You need to close the account. If you reopen the account, it's your own fault. I won't cover it again."

Winney tried to sell it softly. He allowed he might not have "placed the proper importance on financial matters" and "may have been too lenient," but he quickly agreed he never let the amount grow so large when his daughters were younger and unmarried. He made it worse when he added, "But you're doing so well. You can afford it."

Luke bit his tongue, paused, and decided to let it pass. "I think two thousand dollars a week is plenty. She doesn't pay any household expenses. She can't handle a checking account, and I want the account closed. I'm serious. I won't ever cover her account again." Luke stared straight into Winney's eyes. "And the service fees…" He paused. "You knew what you were doing." He stopped, knowing the fees would not be waived. Winney could not show favoritism before the board, and in Oklahoma a husband was legally liable for his wife's debts.

Winney watched as Luke pulled his checkbook from his coat pocket, wrote a check to close the account, and laid it on his desk. "What if there are more checks outstanding?" Winney asked.

"You and Beth better work that out," Luke said. They exchanged shrugs, and Luke started toward the teller's line. He cashed a check from his account for Beth's weekly spending money and left the bank.

Winney's "you can afford it" comment played again. He stewed. Yes, he was making money, but he dealt in large numbers, and there was great risk. Not having proper commitments in place could sink the business in a day. The company needed to keep earnings to grow and to reduce risk on market moves. The loan servicing was valuable, but that was only if he sold it; then income would fall, and he would have to lay off people. It seemed the more he made, the more Beth spent; and the dishonesty stung him.

"Where does the money go?" he said into the hollowness of the car. Her allowance was six times more than the average annual income. He simmered and knew one of her sisters was struggling and often wore Beth's outfits. Was the money going to help support her, her husband, and their children? A telephone call broke the thought, and the subject of mortgage banking eclipsed Beth's bank account in Luke's mind as the car scurried back to the office.

CHAPTER EIGHT

The next four days were a blur. Luke dropped off the cash for Beth on Monday, and her father called to say he had closed the account. Monday night Luke walked into a furniture store five minutes before closing and purchased a cheap, dark brown bedroom set with bed, mattress, night table, and a dresser without a mirror and arranged delivery. He slept each night in the cocoon of a blanket he had taken from the lake condo, the first night on the floor and the following nights on the bed without pillows or sheets. He met with a divorce attorney Chuck had recommended, who warned a divorce could not be granted until the property settlement was concluded; he informed Luke bluntly that the process would be expensive. Luke dined each night an hour or so before midnight on the remnants of an extra-large pepperoni pizza he had picked up Monday night, finally finishing the pizza Thursday and watching the quarter moon slice through the evening's clouds as he tossed the box into the trash bin in the parking lot. The lowest point had been Thursday night when he and Beth had agreed to talk with the children. He arrived to find a babysitter, a sister-in-law, and two of her children all sitting down with

Luke's children to a late meal from a fast-food chain. He spent a few moments with his children, who thought he had returned from a trip, told them he had to go to the office, and glared at Beth as he exited.

The four days also had good news. Business was good, and decreasing interest rates had sparked activity. FRM loan production was growing: approaching 20 percent in the Tulsa market and exceeding 10 percent in Oklahoma City. The bustle of new business and the endless series of telephone calls, applications, and closings kept everyone busy and in high spirits. The office was aggressive; only a few were older than Luke, and the high-energy atmosphere was contagious. Employees only started winding down and drifting toward the doors around six o'clock each evening. Others worked later. Luke was rarely the first there in the morning, but he was almost always the last to leave. Even when he left early on a given day, notes were confidently placed on his desk, knowing he would most likely return that evening.

Luke met with Chuck Rail on Friday morning to sign the increase of the credit line. "We rushed to have these ready by today," Chuck said, turning to retrieve the papers Bivins had given him the previous week.

"Thanks." Luke began scrawling his name on page after page of the stack.

"So, how's the love life?"

"Next subject."

"Did you meet with Stan the Divorce Man?" Chuck asked.

"Yeah." Luke shrugged. "He's smart and knows his stuff. It was a horror film without the popcorn."

"And he told you it takes a while. It's a tough state for a divorce."

"In so many words. Fact is she controls the situation. If she won't settle, I have to get appraisals for everything: the office buildings, the condos, the apartments, and the company. I offer her half of the value, which means I would have to sell enough things to pay her off and pay the tax on the profit from the sales. After her half, taxes, and fees, I may net twenty-five percent or so. If she rejects the offer, then we both get appraisers, whom I have to pay. We go to court, and the judge can accept her or my valuations but most likely appoints a third party to do a new set. The problem is the extensions and delays. She can get them. And then the valuations become outdated, and we have to start the whole process again; I support a legion of appraisers and get holiday cards in return."

"So, you live separate lives together," Chuck said, moving Luke along.

"He was talking about how many of his clients did that. He cautioned that the cash drain can lead to financial problems. Don't worry. I won't let that happen. I won't let this threaten the company or the people. No matter how hard it is."

"Tough break, Big Boy," Chuck laughed, feigning sympathy. "You're doing well; there are plenty of young ladies willing to provide solace."

"I don't think I need any involvements right now," Luke said.

"Well, Fluffy wanted to know if you had asked about her."

"You mean, Melissa? I haven't."

"You should."

"She's more your style. Aren't you dating her?"

"No, I told you. I brought her to meet you. She had nothing to do during the day, so I suggested she drive up with me."

"She's your style."

"No. She's perfect for you, Big Boy." Chuck's smile was devilish. "She'll be calling you soon. She'll start in our new Executive Banking Center next week."

"I thought you said she worked in the Trust Department?"

"Oh, she did. She was in the management training program. They move through several departments before being assigned to one permanently. She wanted the Executive Banking Center. It's designed to provide personal services and investments to young doctors, lawyers, and executives. Your name will be up there. She'll be calling you after she's reviewed your financial statements."

Luke shook his head. "I have only one small personal account. Everything else is a business account. I don't think I'm on the screen."

"Oh, you're on her radar. She'll be calling..." He paused. "And she will be offering"—he broke a big smile and paused again—"executive services."

"Yeah, right. You should chase her. She's pretty."

"Sorry, I have already met the next Ms. Chuck, and by the way she's going to be your new loan officer."

"Pardon."

"I'm going to assign your account to one of the new real estate officers. Cindy Cleugh will be taking over your account."

"Who's that?" Luke searched but did not recall the name.

"That's the new Ms. Chuck and my new loan officer out of the management training program."

"Chuck..." Luke shook his head. "I don't need to educate a new person straight out of training. I understand everyone has to start somewhere. I did. But let the young lady start with real estate loans; they're much simpler than mortgage banking."

"Don't worry. She's smart, and besides she's forty-eight, so she's not that young."

"Forty-eight and in the management training program? Wow. Must have come up through the ranks." Luke started feeling better.

"Oh no, she just started. Get this: she's old money. Born with money, married money, and divorced about five years ago. Never had kids, so she decided to go to work."

"What did she do before?"

"Nothing. Nothing since college. No degree. Never worked. Hasn't worked since the divorce. She does charity work—that sort of thing. She's great friends with some of the wives of the directors. She wanted to go to work. They got her in the management program; I picked her for the Real Estate Department, and she's going to be your loan officer."

Luke's mouth was open. "You're kidding me. You're making up all of this."

"Nope. Great legs, single, money—lots of money—and bored. Really great legs. Just my style. Bored and looking to meet Mr. Chuck. She's got a great house near Utica Square. Two-story, grand landscaping, and servant's quarters. Big house stuffed with fine furnishings, but it needs a man."

"Chuck, I don't want to judge anyone too quickly, but I'm not hearing anything that makes me think she understands our business."

"What's so hard? It's real estate lending. You secure the collateral and you can't go wrong."

"Chuck, mortgage banking is not that simple. It's not real estate construction lending. Every day we have credit line advances to fund our new loans. We have payments coming in from loans we have sold to pay off your advances. The markets fluctuate and so does the value of the collateral. The markets move, and we have margin calls on commitments. I'm always managing our cash position to ensure we have liquidity and capacity under the line."

"Don't worry. I'll be spending a lot of time with her. She's classy and smart. And besides she will be working for me and hopefully under me." He smiled.

"Chuck, you haven't handled our account. Sid always handled everything, so there may be a few things that are new for you."

"Oh, Big Boy, c'mon—it's just the two of us. Lending is lending, and your business isn't that tough to manage. Sid's not that bright. I made him who he is, and he got the promotion because of me. The department manager should never be handling accounts. Sid shouldn't have handled them, and I'm not going to. It'll be fine."

"Where is she?"

"Oh, she's off today—a fundraiser for the symphony. You'll meet her next week. I'll bring her out. She's very attractive."

"I'm sure she is, Chuck." Luke took a breath. "I don't have time to train someone. That's why Sid handled the account. Sid handled all the mortgage banking relationships. Let someone else handle us."

"Sid handled you and two old sleepy companies, Osage Mortgage and Tremble Mortgage. We should get rid of them anyway; you do more business in a day than those two do in a month. They are both ready to sell out, retire, or just fade away. There's nothing to handling them. So, all Sid really did was handle your account. And I can oversee that. It won't be a problem." Chuck leaned forward. "Look, the bank is on a growth program—big growth program. The growth of branch banks is the future and that's where we're putting our resources, and that's why Sid moved upstairs. Weldon came from Chicago to grow this bank, but he wasn't getting it done. The board wants faster growth. They've brought in Bill Bivins from Houston as president, and he intends to grow quickly. He wants Weldon's position. That's the future. Cindy can handle this account. She's new, but I can work with her." He smirked. "It'll be fine."

"OK," Luke allowed. "Like I said, I don't want to judge someone before I meet them, but I don't want to train someone right now."

"Don't worry." Chuck nodded. "I want to do some training on this one."

Luke shook his head as both acknowledged the double entendre. "I need to go." Luke looked at his watch. "The increase will go into effect today, right?"

"Sure. I'll get the papers over to operations right now. Oh…" Chuck paused. "Mr. Bivins wants you to join him for lunch upstairs sometime in the next week or so. I think he wants you to help with the United Way fundraising drive. It'll be good politics."

Luke had only met Bivins once before, as they rode in a crowded elevator. "Let me know when," Luke said. "What do I need to do?"

"Oh, I think he wants you to help raise money—that sort of thing. There'll be some United Way people at the lunch."

"Sure, I'll do it."

"Great. I'll let you know when it is."

"Thanks," Luke stood, shook hands, and headed toward the elevators.

Late Friday afternoon brought the empty gloom he felt each week. The staff left earlier on Fridays, and by five thirty, almost everyone had said gleeful good-byes and headed toward long-awaited weekend plans. The last stragglers were gone in another half hour.

Luke looked at his office—the stuffed sofa sitting eight feet away and the two oversized matching stuffed chairs at either side, cornered with inlaid marble tables. He looked through the floor-to-ceiling glass panes, staring at the large abandoned interior office below the high, textured ceilings. He saw the glass panels of the other offices, the desks, and the calm that now waited for another week, just as he did. Luke had no plans for the weekend and realized he had no plans beyond work. The nonstop Monday-through-Friday schedule, the endless stream of telephone calls, the constant checking on the bond market, the impromptu meetings, the lunches with customers, the trade-organizations dinners, and the late nights at the office—everything was over until next week. He called the children, but the telephone was busy. "It's off the hook," he thought.

He stopped at a bookstore and picked up a tome on the French Revolution. By Sunday night, he had finished the book, played a match in the tennis league at a local club, gone to the office both Saturday and Sunday, and finally reached Beth. She said she and the children had plans, so he couldn't take them to the golf course, but he could visit so long as there was no talk of divorce. He told her he had seen an attorney and was going to file the following week. She told him there would be no divorce and hung up.

CHAPTER NINE

uke was eager for Monday morning. The office buzzed, and the five Tulsa loan officers and their loan processors went at full pace. The underwriters pored over loan files verifying qualifications. The four loan closers and their assistants typed the closing statements and the stacks of documents the buyers and sellers would sign. The accounting and shipping departments were at full tilt packaging executed loan-closing documents for delivery to Malson's Trust Department in exchange for certificates pledged as collateral for bonds that would be sold to Stiller Stevens and other brokerage houses and then sold to insurance companies, retirement programs, mutual funds, pensions, and investors. Luke knew the other branches were bustling by the steady stream of calls through the lines connecting the offices. He also recognized an increased rustle of activity and whispering that began just before Andrea walked into his office.

"Chuck from Malson is here with some lady," she said, rolling her eyes.

Luke nodded and finished the call. He noted raised eyebrows and heads listing oddly as he made his way to the lobby. The reception area held large sofas, modern art, a hand-woven rug, and two stand-ing guests.

Chuck spoke first. "Luke, this is Cindy Cleugh." He motioned to a lady an inch or two taller than himself.

Cindy Cleugh quickly extended a firm handshake—too firm. She was medium build, thin, and without definition except for the lines of her expensive designer suit.

"Luke, so delighted," she said, lingering on the *so.*

"Nice to meet you," Luke responded. "Please come back." He led them through the lobby, past the row of loan officers, and to the side where his office awaited. Luke made small talk and noted the bold stride, expensive briefcase, high heels, brilliant scarf, and abundance of jewelry. "Overdone," he thought. The discreet looks from Phyllis and the others told him the accoutrements were expensive.

Cindy and Chuck settled on the sofa in Luke's office, and Luke took his customary spot in the side chair, facing the glass panels look-ing into the heart of the office. The small talk continued. Cindy was confident. She had shoulder-length, bright red hair, meticulously styled but dyed dark enough to highlight the slight, deepening lines of her forehead, the creases around her eyes, and the narrow lips that made her appear older than she was. She was not pretty but well kept, even if overdressed. Luke watched her eyes and listened care-fully. The banter seemed sophomoric. Her eyes gave off a superior air but were shallow. The briefcase and scarf struck Luke as oversized dice hanging from the rearview mirror of a thirty-year-old Chevrolet with two hubcaps missing and a rusty tailpipe blowing gray smoke.

Luke's position allowed him to sneak glimpses of the increased traffic outside his office as staff scurried back and forth to catch a glimpse of Cindy Cleugh. Some tried to be discreet but failed, and others boldly mugged and made faces at Luke with glee. Luke continued the conversation convincingly but found Cindy's act was more suited to a country club charity luncheon to raise funds from those who wrote checks on other people's accounts, only a small portion of which would go to benefit people with whom they never wanted to be seen. Neither Chuck nor Cindy had any inkling of the parade behind them.

Cindy's conversation was peppered names; almost every phrase included "Of course, you know…," followed by another name. Luke's few questions drew dreadful responses, and he was sure she knew little of mortgages or banking and nothing of mortgage banking. He knew none of the people she mentioned, and she knew nothing of what he did. When Cindy mentioned she and Chuck had attended some function over the weekend, Luke for the first time considered Chuck might be seriously interested in her.

Luke almost flinched when Cindy's only substantive comments were that she wanted "to get the FRM relationship organized" and to help the bank "to get a handle on things." Luke was unaware of any problems and dismissed the comments as excessive zeal. He shot a couple of glances of disbelief to Chuck but found him intent on Cindy and watching her dotingly.

Cindy posed only one business question. "What do you like best about having your own business?" she asked.

Luke doubted the sincerity, so he first fed her his standard joke. "I get along very well with management, but I can't quit. I don't know where to deliver my resignation letter." He paused as they laughed politely. He continued earnestly, "There is a major difference. I used to worry about one house payment, one family, and one holiday season. Now I worry about eighty house payments, eighty families, and eighty holiday seasons. I rely heavily on these people, and I know they are relying on me."

Within the next few exchanges, Chuck and Cindy said they had a luncheon downtown, and Cindy promised to call the next morning. Luke was glad they were leaving and avoided thinking of the call.

After leading his guests back to the lobby, Luke hustled to his office. He had just turned to sit in his chair when he saw Phyllis scurry through the door. She toted a huge stack of loan files. One hand propped the files against her tight waist and curvaceous frame. With a coffee cup in the other hand and a pen behind her ear, she sported a broad grin.

Harold Rhoden was supposed to supervise the branch managers, splitting office time between Tulsa and Oklahoma City. However, Harold's hesitancy on decisions led Phyllis and others to circumvent him. She was aggressive and preferred to tackle problems immediately. Despite the title, Harold had been mostly relegated to the Shipping Department, ensuring loans were packaged and delivered to investors and managing the funding and repayment of loans with the banks. Phyllis only went to Harold if Luke was out of town, and then she would often track Luke down by telephone to get an answer. She was barely thirty, had only a high-school education, and had been told innumerable times she would only be a "secretary." Luke took satisfaction knowing she now earned as much as Harold and more than her husband with his college degree.

Phyllis dropped the files onto the table with a thud, leaned back into the sofa, let out a breath, and smiled over her round, rimmed glasses. "Well, who was that?"

"That was Chuck from Malson." Luke kept a straight face.

"And…"

"And what?"

"Who was carrying all of the Chanel?" Phyllis demanded.

"Chanel?"

"As in Coco," she said, rolling her eyes. "Oh, you're so oblivious. Didn't you notice the briefcase, the shoes, the suit, the scarf? That was an expensive ensemble."

"Oh, I saw them. A bit overdone. Probably would play better on Park Avenue."

"And pricey—very pricey."

"Well, that's our new loan officer at Malson."

"Oh, I thought she must be Chuck's new girlfriend."

"Oh…" Luke raised his eyebrows. "I'm afraid she may be both."

"She must have some money."

"I can't see him going for her."

"Oh, I can. I've told you. I don't like him. He leers."

"He's never leered at me," Luke said wistfully, and they laughed. "Well, guess what. Chuck is the new department head, and Cindy Cleugh's our new loan officer."

"Which bank did she come from?"

"I think she's from the Junior League." Luke frowned.

"Oh. No wonder Chuck's all over her."

"She's not his type. Chuck always seems to go for the young shallow type."

"Oh, she's there to pick up the tab, and he'll be all over her. OK," she concluded.

She grabbed the first file and started the routine. She began by telling Luke which realtor had brought in the file and then giving a synopsis of the problem and what she wanted to do. Luke listened carefully, stole glances at the Telerate machine, and usually agreed with Phyllis's recommendations. The meetings were generally short-lived and rarely resulted in a major disagreement. Confrontations were marked by Phyllis's standing, placing one hand on her hip, and pointing. Luke loved her passion, but her displays rarely changed his position. The meeting this day went smoothly, and in less than three minutes, Phyllis had repositioned the stack, grabbed her coffee cup, and headed to update the realtors, shouting instructions across the office to closers and processors on her way.

Cindy Cleugh called early Tuesday morning. She called again before lunch and twice in the afternoon. By her second call on Wednesday morning, Luke was timing the conversations and had already mentally penned the nickname, "Cindy No-Clue," although he had yet to share it. Luke painstakingly walked her through reports FRM submitted. He explained several times the process from loan application to loan approval to loan closing and how FRM submitted the loan files to Malson. Luke walked her through the pooling and sale of loans and the payments coming to Malson to pay back the advance for those loans.

Cindy was overwhelmed. "Well, all of this changes every day. You borrow money every day, and you pay off advances every day. We need to control this. What I think is that you should just close loans once a week and just sell loans once a week."

Luke cringed and took a deep breath. "We can't do that. That's not the way the industry does things. Our competitors would have a field day, and our customers would be memories. More importantly, there's too much work. If we could do it one day a week, we would work one day." He almost fell out of his chair at her response.

"Well, I think it's something we need to look at."

By Thursday the situation had not improved. Luke reached Chuck and asked how he was. After letting Chuck tell him about Cindy's graces, Luke broached the subject. "Chuck, I'm having a bit of a problem. First of all, Cindy calls me four and five times a day. I used to talk to Sid once every other week—maybe. I don't mind trying to help her get up to speed, but she doesn't have the basics. Maybe she can relax a little bit and spend some time with her other customers."

"You're her only account."

"Oh," Luke thought, "then you need to give her some other accounts." He paused, and Chuck filled the gap.

"She's going to be my mortgage banking specialist. You know, we have visited, and she has some great ideas."

Luke winced. "Chuck, she doesn't have a clue," he blurted, forgetting the homophone. A silence followed. Chuck had never handled the account. Suddenly, Luke was concerned about Chuck's understanding of the business. "I'm sorry, Chuck, but she really doesn't understand."

"Relax, Big Boy. Give her some time. Good things will come of this. By the way, next Thursday, lunch upstairs with Bivins. Can you do that?"

Luke looked at his schedule. "Sure. Is this the United Way thing?"

"Yeah," Chuck said, "and a good chance for you to meet Bivins. You need to get to know him. Meet me in my office fifteen minutes early, and we'll go up together."

"All right," Luke said. "Now—" he started, but Chuck cut him off.

"Relax. I'll keep Cindy busy. I think I know how to reduce her tension."

"I'm serious," Luke interjected.

"So am I. She has a nice, big, lonely house. I'll be parking my car there soon," he said, pausing for effect, and adding, "overnight."

"Sid's old secretary knows how to handle things, and have Cindy call Harold instead of me."

"Yeah, I'll have her call Harold. That's a good idea. Sid's secretary will be moving. She's stuck on doing things Sid's way, so I am trading her to another department. But I'll have Cindy call Harold—that's a good idea."

Luke didn't like the idea of Sid's secretary leaving the department, but he felt relived Cindy would be calling less.

"Are you two an item?" Luke asked.

"Hush. That sort of thing is frowned upon around here. Now, have you called Fluffy?" Chuck asked.

"You mean, Melissa? No, I haven't."

"You should. But she will call you anyway. Do you need anything?"

"I need a sofa. I can't get used to sleeping in a bed again. And fewer calls from Cindy."

"I don't have a sofa, but I will slow Cindy down."

"I'll get the sofa, and thanks for the help."

"Tennis? Saturday?" Chuck asked.

"Sure," Luke said and hid the resignation from his voice.

"Oh no, I can't play Saturday."

"Let's see…You and Cindy are going antiquing?" Luke joked.

"No, actually we are going to the Philbrook."

"Save me," Luke said. He was sure there was a fundraiser at the museum that hosted a wide array of social functions.

"Let's play early," Chuck said.

Cindy did not call again that week. Luke worked late Thursday and arrived at the furniture store shortly before closing. He purchased a cheap, extra-long, fabric sofa and arranged for delivery on Friday. When the store called, he hustled to meet the truck and watched the movers exchange glances as they surveyed the vacant apartment. He dashed back to the office and by six o'clock Friday, the uneasy, lost feeling had returned as the office emptied to weekend plans. In the bustle, Luke had forgotten to call the divorce attorney, and the failure added to his angst. He stopped at the bookstore and picked up an autobiography by Mickey Mantle and a nonfiction about Queen Elizabeth I. Then he drove the few miles south to Winding Creek Condominiums and parked in the dusk. Later he curled up in the blanket on the sofa and slept.

CHAPTER TEN

Saturday was a beautiful day. Spring bloomed with a hint of a breeze, blue skies, young dancing green leaves, and temperatures that faintly flicked the skin. By midmorning Luke and Chuck had chased and flailed at the yellow tennis balls, toweled, and gone their separate directions. Luke returned to the condo, showered, stopped for a bagel and coffee, and headed to the office. He entered the alcove at the building's rear, turned right, and unlocked the door to Boyd Investments. The décor was more modest. There was a reception area and desk for his real estate assistant and a small office for his leasing agent, Alison, which sat dark. She had been so excited about a weekend trip to Dallas, and Luke knew he would be alone. Luke had his own office where he kept his personal and real estate investment records.

Luke slipped into his chair and positioned the pale green ledger sheets detailing the previous month's real estate income and expenses under his gaze. His cash flow was good; rents covered expenses and debt payments and left a comfortable margin. He left the profits in the bank for improvements, future investments, and extra payments to pay off the mortgages more quickly. Luke pored over the schedules, fingered the HP-12C, and penned numbers and notes on the reports. Suddenly his eyes were drawn to one of the windows. He had not raised the blinds, as was his habit, but through the narrow slit between the blinds and window frame, he could see the white fender of the BMW coming to a halt on the other side of the waist-high hedges.

Instinctively, he stood, started toward the reception area, and heard the car door shut outside. He unlocked the Boyd Investments door, took three steps, and then unlocked the building's exterior glass doors, so she could enter. She said nothing, smiled with eyes up at an angle, and walked straight to his office. Luke locked both sets of doors and followed; his eyes tracked the slight curve of her back in the pink pullover sweater and the moving pockets of her pressed tight jeans. He was almost sheepish when she turned and found his eyes.

"Hi, Ginny," he said.

"No hug?" she asked.

She noted his stiff embrace and knew she had caught him off guard.

Luke promptly offered her a seat and returned to the safety of the chair behind his desk. His eyes shot up as he realized she had ignored the offered chair, followed, and posed herself on the credenza behind his desk with her chest at eye level.

"Hi," she said.

"Hi," he answered.

"So…what's new?"

"Just some work," he said, glancing at the desk. "Going over a few things."

"Anything else?"

"The usual."

"I've heard there's a dark gray Mercedes parked at Winding Creek Condos."

"Really."

"Yes. Rumor is some guy moved in to one of the upstairs units. Pretty nice car for that neighborhood. Modest two bedroom and one bath. Probably rents for about five hundred dollars a month. He seems to arrive late and leave early. No visitors…" She paused. "Apparently, no visitors…" She paused again. "No reported visitors…" She paused a third time. "Is my information correct?"

He leaned back. "So far, so good."

"Let me guess," she cooed. "A bed without sheets. A dresser. Piles of clothes in the corners."

"And?" he questioned.

"Oh, there's more!"

"A sofa and a nightstand."

"Oh, my! You are serious this time," she laughed. When he said nothing, she wiggled until she was more comfortable on her perch, her eyes dropping for a second and then rising, and asked directly, "Do you need anything?"

"You," he thought, but instead he said, "so far, so good." He thought his response was poised, but she knew he was nervous.

"And you didn't call me," she said, lifting herself off the credenza. She kicked off her flats and stood on her toes, showing the curve of her hips, and turned slowly. "How do I look?"

"Pretty good."

"Well, then…" She retreated to one of the guest chairs on the other side of his desk, sat sideways, and draped her legs across the other chair. "Are you over me?"

He looked at the shiny black hair, the brilliant, sparkling green eyes, and her lingering eyelashes. Her mouth was full and luscious.

Hers was a beauty that had won contests. He knew the beauty that lay beneath the pink pullover and the tight jeans and the firm soft, sweet-smelling skin. "I would have called."

"That sounds better." She let silence fill the room.

"So, how are you?" he finally asked.

"Call me, take me to lunch, show me the piles of clothes you've thrown in the corners of the bedroom, and find out." She stood suddenly and started toward her shoes.

He popped up in response. "Where are you going?"

"I have to go." She was suddenly distant. "I just came by to check out a rumor."

"Ginny," he said and fell back in his chair.

"Luke," she said mockingly. They stared silently, both recounting how they had met years before. Luke had been separated for the first time. She was married and bored. The attraction was there at the beginning. The affair had quickly flamed and then grounded itself in the reality that neither was available. The affair ended abruptly when Luke had gone home.

"So, how's your life?" Luke asked.

"We can talk later. Nothing's changed. He's a jerk, and I'm married to him."

Some of the mist cleared, and Luke was lucid. "You're gorgeous. You know you're gorgeous. You came by to see if I still think of you, and I do." It was what she wanted to hear, and it was true. "You're beautiful—very beautiful. You're married, and I'm going to be divorced."

"Not soon," she said. "I prefer you married but separated. I don't think you'll be divorced soon, if at all. And if you get divorced, then..." She paused. "You can see other women, just don't marry them. Remember, you don't have to fall in love with everyone you sleep with. But you have to love me. You're mine," she laughed. "Now I have to go. Walk me to the door." She stepped back into her shoes.

He grabbed the keys from the desk and followed her toward the doorway. She stopped abruptly, turned, and waited, looking up at him. The temptation was too much, and his hands found her waist as his lips found hers. She pulled him closer, and suddenly he felt the passion of vanishing into her warmth. His hands clutched her closer, and then she pulled back and stared up. "I have to go," she breathed.

"Why?" he asked.

"I have to go."

She had gotten what she wanted, he thought. He had given her affirmation that he still wanted her. That was enough for today. "OK," he said. They kissed lightly again and stared at each other. Then she retreated and waited as he unlocked the two sets of doors. She turned and kissed him lightly again and left without saying anything else. He watched every move as she walked away and struggled to regain his focus.

CHAPTER ELEVEN

onday morning brought the customary early calls to the bond markets. Beth had kept him away from the children for another weekend and refused to discuss divorce. By early morning Luke had called the lawyer and asked for the suit to be filed. He agreed to deliver the $10,000 retainer, knowing it would be spent quickly and legal bills would be arriving soon.

Within an hour Melissa Marin called to tell Luke of her new position in the Executive Banking Center. Luke pleaded he was a poor prospect, but she insisted she had a quota of contacts to make. Luke agreed to meet for lunch on Friday. Phyllis walked in at the end of the conversation, making hand signals for him to wrap up the call. She plopped on the sofa and stared at him impatiently as he talked. As soon as Luke hung up, she rolled her eyes, said sarcastically, "Let's do lunch," and started reviewing files while he laughed. He was back in the flow.

Chuck called on Thursday morning to confirm Luke's lunch appointment with Bill Bivins. Luke was relaxed as he spun through the doors of Malson Tower. The divorce had been filed, and his thoughts drifted to visions of life after the settlement, although he knew it lay far ahead. Luke rode to the eighteenth floor, headed toward Chuck's office, and saw Sid's former secretary packing some items.

She was in her fifties, stocky with flat brown hair. Her face was full and crinkled. She gestured brusquely as her stubby fingers grabbed and stacked with purpose. "Where are you moving?" Luke asked.

"Commercial lending," she said and shrugged.

"They are going to miss you. I'm going to miss you."

"Oh, you'll be fine." She tore a frame from her desk and placed it into the box.

"I thought maybe you were going with Sid."

"No, there wasn't an opening." She started to look over her shoulder to be discreet but dismissed the idea. "I needed a change of scenery," she said in full voice and nodded toward Chuck's office. "So I'm heading to the Commercial Department."

"Can I visit?" Luke smiled.

"Only if I invite you," she snarled and then threw Luke a big smile. "Two floors down. Any time."

"You got it."

Luke found Chuck pulling his suit coat from the closet. They rode to the forty-seventh floor. Chuck felt his lapel twice to make sure his logo pin was in place. Luke asked about Sid's secretary and was told Chuck wanted his own staff. They exited the elevator into a lavish lobby of grand vases, marble, mirrors, luscious plants, and the greetings of five lovely hostesses.

Two grand, dark, closed doors guarded the executive dining room reserved for executives of Malthers & Nelson Petroleum, whose offices occupied many floors immediately below. The Tulsa offices were modest compared with the international offices based in their Houston towers. Malthers & Nelson Petroleum's two largest shareholders owned the controlling interest in Malson Bank and dominated the bank's board of directors.

The other side offered similar doors into Malson Bank's dining section. Luke had never seen the Malthers & Nelson section, but he had been invited to Malson's executive dining room several times. He knew by memory the panorama that waited, offering unobstructed views of the expanses of Oklahoma landscape.

Luke and Chuck had been graciously greeted by the hostesses upon their arrival, but their greeting seemed almost disdainful compared to the reception for Bill Bivins as he stepped boldly from the elevator and surveyed the room with a slight tilt of his head. He nodded in response to the hostesses' effusive welcome and acknowledged others waiting in the lobby. He approached Luke, extended his hand palm down, and looked Luke directly in the eye. "Luke, Bill Bivins," he said confidently as they exchanged firm handshakes. Chuck excused himself, to Luke's surprise, and announced he was meeting other guests.

Within seconds Luke was escorted into Bivins's private dining room and greeted by three others standing and visiting by the windows. Luke was surprised to find all were from Malson. Luke first shook hands with Matthew Frost, whom he particularly liked. Mr. Frost had been with the bank for almost forty years, had served as chairman until Todd Weldon's arrival, and was known for his class and genteel manner. Luke knew Mr. Frost was nearing the end of an agreement that paid his compensation and had given him a ceremonial title.

Luke turned and was introduced to Tom Cook, of the Correspondent Banking Department. After shaking hands, Luke was introduced to Ray Ellis. "Mr. Ellis is the president of our new Oklahoma City branch," Bivins declared. "We finalized the deal this morning when we acquired TNB." Luke knew the midsize Oklahoma City bank located a few miles from the downtown area. "Mr. Ellis was president of their bank, and now he has joined our team," Bivins continued.

"Wow," Luke said, "I read in the papers this week the legislature had passed the branch banking bill. You move fast."

"It's been in the works," Bivins answered. "We have regulatory approval subject to final review. In the meantime we have an operating agreement."

"Well, congratulations." Luke nodded.

"Yes, I put this deal together myself. Sid Fullmer has moved upstairs to help us consider other acquisitions."

Luke noted Ellis did not have a lapel pin of the bank logo. Bivins noticed also and quickly pulled one from his suit pocket, handed Ellis the pin, and said, "Welcome aboard." All exchanged pleasantries while Bivins ensconced himself at the head of the table; the others filtered to the side, and Cook helped Ellis put on the pin.

The United Way segment of the lunch was over before the first course arrived as Bivins explained he wanted someone to help raise funds, and Luke quickly accepted. Bivins promised his secretary would forward the materials. The balance of the lunch appeared to Luke to be an unexpected low-key interview. Luke presumed Bivins wanted to become more comfortable with the recent credit line increase.

"Tell me," Bivins said, "why is it you make more loans than anyone else?"

"People," Luke said without hesitation. "We have a group of young people committed to giving better service than our competitors. It's a people business," he said, starting his mantra. "People are going to buy four or five homes in their lifetime. They are going to rely on a realtor or homebuilder to recommend a lender. The realtor or homebuilder is going to choose someone with competitive rates and quality service. Neither the realtor nor the homebuilder gets paid until the loan is closed. They want a lender who knows what he or she is doing, who can tell them quickly whether the buyer qualifies, and who can handle the communication and document challenges that come during the four or five weeks between signing a contract and closing. The buyer wants guidance and understanding, and the sooner the deal closes, the sooner everyone gets what they want, and the less time there is for something to go wrong."

"But banks and savings and loans can do that," Bivins interjected.

"It requires a different kind of personnel," Luke responded. "It takes a different compensation program. It takes the drive to go find the business personally, rather than waiting for a billboard or commercial to bring a deal to your door."

Bivins led the conversation toward changing banking laws, the expansion Malson had started, and its goal to be statewide within the next year. Cook chimed in supporting the bank's ability to consume other banks. Luke noticed that Mr. Frost said little and Mr. Ellis seemed to be feeling his way into the group.

"How involved are you in Sand Springs Fidelity Bank?" Tom Cook asked. "I know we have a correspondent relationship with them, but I'm not up to speed," he lied.

"I'm not involved at all," Luke said. "My father-in-law is president and a stockholder, but I have nothing to do with the bank."

"Oh, I thought you were partners or something," Cook said.

"No, I have never been involved in the bank. Mr. Winney was one of the original stockholders of FRM, but only for a year. I bought out his interest."

"I see," Cook said softy.

"And your goals?" Bivins asked Luke.

"To do what I'm doing," Luke said. "That means FRM has to be profitable. We may want to expand into other states, but now is not the time. We've had some good growth, but I think we need to digest that growth over the next year or two," he said without thinking. It was the standard answer, and it was true, but it was incomplete. Luke's goal was to turn the key personnel into owners in a few years, and then vanish into the background. He knew that vision would raise eyebrows, and he was still trying to put the team together.

"But what about access to capital?" Bivins asked. "How will you deal with that?"

The question seemed odd to Luke. Capital markets to him meant debt-and-equity markets for stocks, bonds, debentures, and specifically the bonds used to market mortgage loans. "Mortgage bankers have the same access to the bond and mortgage markets as banks and savings and loans. We have to meet the margin calls because we cover our loan production in the futures market. Previously, mortgage bankers could sell directly into the cash market, but the volatility of 1979 and the early 1980s caused many defaults as interest rates doubled. There's been less liquidity in the cash market—fewer brokers willing to buy commitments from mortgage bankers prior to the bonds being certified. So, like most, we sell in the futures market to cover the loan production pipeline and then buy back the futures hedge and sell the bonds in the cash market as the bond is put together. There have been some changes, but frankly, I don't see why those capital markets wouldn't be open to us."

"We anticipate that capital markets may be chan-ging"— Bivins paused, looked to Tom Cook, and then glanced back to

Luke—"including access to capital for companies like your own." Bivins's eyes dropped to his plate. "What is your greatest risk?"

"The mortgage markets. Rates are constantly changing. We must have commitments in place to cover the loans waiting to close and the ones already closed. We need the cash to meet the margin calls as the markets move. The interest volatility of the past few years has been incredible. I am almost always in view of a Telerate machine to watch the markets or near a telephone to get an update."

"I'm glad to hear you mention controlling your growth," Bivins said, referring to an earlier comment. "We expedited your credit increase as quickly as we could."

"Thanks for moving so quickly," Luke replied.

"There are so many changes on the horizon," Bivins said. "Mr. Frost has seen many over the years, and many more are just now coming into our view." Bivins looked at the other members of the table.

Luke was ready to share the spotlight and listened as Cook and Ellis eagerly echoed the opportunity to take advantage of the changes. Malson clearly intended to be the dominant bank in Oklahoma.

"And beyond," Bivins said. "Nationwide banking is on the horizon. We intend to become a significant regional bank and then explore merger opportunities with a nationwide institution. I think we will see nationwide banking within the next three years. But there are still growth opportunities in our own domain. Take the new Executive Banking Center. It's a tremendous opportunity to provide additional services to our preferred customers: investment services, retirement programs, and estate planning services." Bivins paused. "Luke, have you visited the Executive Banking Center?"

"No, I haven't. But I have already received a call."

"Good, good," Bivins said. "You should let them take a look at what they can do for you. Have you talked to our Bond Department? They could help you sell your mortgage-backed bonds."

"With all due respect, we both sell to the same brokerage houses. Obviously, your people would have to mark up the price by an eighth of a percent to cover their costs, so selling through your Bond Department would cost us more than a thousand dollars on each bond. It's certainly more profitable for us to continue to go direct to New York."

"Oh, yes," Bivins said without energy. "That's the equal access to capital you mentioned."

"Yes. Our bond houses have been very good to us."

"That's wonderful." There was no sincerity in Bivins voice.

The lunch wound down, and Luke sensed Bivins had concluded his interview and was ready to move on to the remainder of his day. Luke was eager to conclude the meeting also. He knew he did not like Bill Bivins. The group exchanged their good-byes in the elevator as Bivins and the others exited on the nineteenth floor.

Luke called the bond market from the car. By that time, Bivins had already called Chuck Rail.

CHAPTER TWELVE

Friday started with a bang, but everything was resolved easily and early. By midmorning, Luke found himself admiring the cirrus clouds streaking across the sky as he talked on the phone. Luke's attorney and Beth's attorney had talked. Luke had been dropping off Beth's cash each Monday, but now the payments would go through the lawyers. He knew Beth would soon file for a separate maintenance hearing and request an unreasonable allowance. Luke's attorney promised regular visitation with the children would be arranged in a few weeks.

Melissa called and confirmed lunch, and Chuck called within a few minutes.

"Well, Big Boy, you sure made a favorable impression on Bivins," Chuck started.

"I'm glad to hear that," Luke said, trying to sound sincere.

"He was very impressed with you. He's a good person to have on your side."

"It was nice to see Mr. Frost."

"Save your charm. He's history. Bivins is the one that counts." The conversation concluded with no real business being discussed.

Near noon the bond market activity was even calm. "There's no one in the pits," John Elliott told him from Chicago.

Luke drove along Lewis Avenue and slipped down a broad residential boulevard. The course was gentry as only two or three large estates with grand trees consumed the oversized blocks. Luke veered south and slowed as he entered a quaint shopping district of one- and two-story rock-and-brick buildings, accented with Mercedes, Jaguars, and BMWs. He stepped out to a background of greenery, retail shops, and restaurants nestled within the city. The Avignon Café, a bistro, sat on a corner. Luke maneuvered around a group of ladies carrying bags. The glare of the sun forced him to squint as he entered.

Melissa was waiting to be seated, and Luke greeted her as he searched almost blindly in the reduced light. She was wearing high heels and yet barely reached his shoulders. Luke thanked the hostess and felt the pressed linen serviette in his hand. He raised his eyes, now clearing, and realized again how lovely Melissa was. The sunlight through the windows glistened on her blond hair. Her blue eyes radiated from her flawless white skin and neckline above the brilliantly colored summer dress. She appeared both seductive and virginal above the pure white tablecloth and bordered by reflections from the sparkling stemware. "Hi," Luke said as she came into full view.

"You already said that," she said and smiled back.

"Well…" Luke pursed his lips before continuing, "How are things in the Executive Banking Center?"

"Boring. I'm setting up children's trust accounts and making boat loans for doctors. Tell me about you."

"How's Chuck?" Luke deflected her request.

"Chasing some older lady for her money."

"I thought you were dating him."

"Heavens no."

"Well, he brought you to the lake."

"He asked me to go to the lake to meet you. He promised it was worth the trip and I could catch some sun." She paused. "I'm glad I went."

Luke waited a bit. "Well, I'm certainly glad you made the trip," he finally said. He immediately changed directions. "So, Chuck is really dating Cindy Cleugh? I'm a bit surprised. I could never have visualized him with her."

"Oh, it figures," she said. "She has everything he wants."

"Really?"

"And won't get," Melissa finished. "His act is geared more to the young, giddy secretarial types. She's happy to have a younger man with a body builder physique squiring her about. She likes displaying her new toy to her friends, but she doesn't take him seriously. Besides, the lady is a bitch. She's a bitter divorced woman—past her prime and pinching every penny she has and waiting for her father to die."

"Ouch." Luke faked pain. "You like her."

"Not really. And she's ruining my lunch. Tell me about you."

"I thought you were supposed to sell me some financial services."

"I have already completed my call report. I met my quota. Tell me about you."

"You first," he said. As she spoke Luke listened intently, almost enthralled. He found her confident but not brash, smart—not only in dress—and strong beneath a hint of fragility. Her honesty was refreshing, and she was not the spoiled, selfish, rich daughter he had expected. She had depth, a broad vocabulary, and clear crisp perception.

She had never been married but had been engaged once three years before to a medical student. "Doctors are boring," she said. "I was engaged for all the wrong reasons. I was tired of being single and looking for security. A broken engagement is easier than a divorce." Her eyes danced, and she continued, "Divorce for someone like you may be painful and extended, but happiness is the reward. Someone special will understand, and you can be together in the meantime."

"It will be years."

"You can still have fun. Or you could just give your wife what she wants. You could sell everything, give her some money, and have plenty left to begin a wonderful life."

"I have two children to consider," he said.

"Believe me, children are resilient and observant. They know what parents don't tell them. I'm sure your children are darling. Tell me about them," she prodded.

By the time the waiter had taken the orders, served lunch, and cleared their plates, more than an hour had passed. Luke no longer saw Melissa as a one-dimensional beauty and found himself strongly drawn to her when he suddenly realized it was almost two o'clock, and the futures market would soon close. He excused himself, grabbed a pay phone in the back hallway, and handed his credit card to the passing waiter as he dialed the toll-free number. The markets were quiet, and he signed the lunch tab as he ran through the memorized list of bonds he watched. He was relaxed when he arrived back at the table. The restaurant was almost empty now, and the only other guests were just standing to leave.

"I guess we should go," he said.

"I'll get the check," she said.

"Oh no, this one is on me. I already got it."

"I have the bank's account."

"This one is on me. Besides, I apologize for keeping you so long," he said as they stood.

"Oh, I'm done for the day." She turned toward the bistro entrance. "I'm not going back to the bank," she said over her shoulder as his eyes followed her.

He reached to open the door, and both emerged into the sunlight. A thousand phrases crossed his mind, but none found his lips.

"Thanks for lunch," she said and paused. "I may just look into a few shops before I go home."

"The pleasure was mine," he replied, looking straight into her eyes. He wanted to kiss her. He wanted to know when she could go to dinner. He wanted to touch the golden halo of her hair. He wanted to lose himself in her eyes. She lingered, knowing he was looking for the next line. "Thanks again," he said, helplessly falling to the sudden fear of two entangled relationships—one refusing to end, the other unable to bloom, and two children and his heart caught in between.

She took his response as shyness. "We can do it again."

"Of course. I'll give you a call."

"Please do." When he said nothing else, she smiled. "Well, I'd better go. Have a good afternoon," she said and turned away.

He stood, watching each movement of her step, and suddenly called her name, "Melissa," as he took two steps toward her. She stopped and turned to see him wavering and nodding and finally saying, "Thanks again. I enjoyed it."

"Call me," she said. She smiled and turned, still under his watchful gaze, and disappeared into the crowd.

Luke pivoted, embarrassed, and headed straight to his car. He called the bond market as he drove to the office.

"The future's pit was a tomb at the close," John Elliott told him. "Yours are the only calls I have had in the last half hour. The cash market in New York is dead, too. If there is another trade today, it will only involve a couple of minor-league players—the markets are asleep."

Luke hung up as the Mercedes pulled from the residential boulevards and into the brisk traffic of a city thoroughfare. By memory he quickly punched the numbers.

"Hello."

"Ginny?"

"Hi, there."

"I'm calling."

"Yes, you are. Where are you?"

"I'm on my way to the office."

"I'll have to call you back."

"OK," he said.

Soon he was back in his chair. He stared at the green diode numbers reflecting bonds prices on the black Telerate screen and replayed each sway of Melissa's splendid retreat. He knew he could not call her. She was single. Time would cut today's softness with jagged edges of disappointment. He searched for every reason not to call her, knowing he had been thoroughly charmed against his will.

He finally became productive and tackled the notes on his desk and the stream of calls. The office emptied as usual, and the hollow feeling that came each Friday evening abated until he realized Ginny had not called. He had decided to grab the loan production reports and go to the lake, when he saw the white BMW pull past his window and slip into the parking space next to his car. He walked to the rear lobby. He unlocked the outside door, swung it open for her, and locked it quickly; he followed her toward his office.

She stopped at his doorway. Luke walked past her, toward his desk, and turned when he heard the sound of the sliding cords. Ginny finished pulling the drapes closed on the glass panels looking into the office. She closed his door and set the deadbolt. She stepped to the windows and closed each of the four blinds looking outside and smiled and floated toward him.

She was ravishingly beautiful with her curled, black hair, full lips, teasing green eyes, and runway legs. "What are you doing?" he said without inflection.

"Quick. I told them I had to go to the store," she said, kissing him between words. He felt her hands on his suit pants, and he heard the zipper move. She knelt and he felt her hands on his hips. He stroked her hair and felt the softness of her mouth. In a few moments, she stood and slid out of the skirt.

"Do you like these?" she asked.

"Yes."

The white satin panties were cut high over the hips. Slowly she spun around exposing her hips, highlighted by a new tan line. She peeled away her blouse, and he reached to kiss her breasts. She slid her panties to the floor and reached out her hand, pushing papers to one side of the desk. "I've been thinking about this all afternoon," she said, pulling him toward her.

He felt her warmth and arms around him. He was with her. There was no office. There was nothing beyond the sudden den she had created. He hurled himself beyond everything he knew, no longer trapped by a role or detachment, and he was and with another.

Afterward they laughed and became paranoid about the noises outside. "What's that?" she asked and then peaked out the drawn blinds to see only their two cars. No one else was there. They kissed and began sorting the wildly discarded and intermingled clothes on the floor.

"Do you like them?" she said, modeling the panties again.

"Yes. Yes, I like them." And he did.

"Do you like me?" she asked.

"Yes," he said, and he did. They avoided the other word.

"I'm going to get killed. I told them I had to go to the store."

"Who is 'they'?" he asked.

"Oh, my sister and her husband are over. She knows where I went."

"You told her?"

"Not that I was coming here. I told her a few days ago you had moved out, but I didn't say anything when I left. Just that I had to run to the store. But I could tell she knew. She probably thought I was going to call you."

"Oh."

They kissed again, and she draped the tie around his neck.

"Are you going to the lake?" she asked.

"Maybe tomorrow."

"Don't go until noon," she ordered. "Let me guess: there's no phone and no sheets."

"No, I have a telephone," he said.

She turned a pleased eye toward him, eyebrows slightly raised, and grinned as he wrote the number for her.

"Don't forget," she started, "I don't want some excuse like you forgot and went to play tennis or drove to the lake."

"No, I'll be there. You can call that number or the car, either one."

"Just be there, OK?" she said without waiting for an answer. "Tomorrow," she said and kissed him and started toward the door.

He followed, unlocked the doors, and watched as she drove away. He trailed back to his office, sat for a moment, recalled the rush of energy, searched for the last traces of her light, and then left. He stopped at the bookstore on his way home, without the empty feeling, and looked forward to tomorrow.

Ginny arrived early the next morning with bran muffins, coffee, the *New York Times*, two pillows, and new, freshly laundered linens.

For the next three hours, they rolled and played and talked. He felt alive and unthreatened. She told him all the things he needed for his place but that they both knew he would not get. She paused at the door, and he kissed her passionately. "I have to go," she said. "That's what you like about me most. You like that I have to go."

"No, I don't," he said.

"Yes, you do. Maybe someday you won't. But now I have to go."

He kissed her again; his hands drifting on her hips, and he hugged her closely.

"Don't go fall in love with someone," she commanded. "You belong to me."

"Don't worry," he breathed.

She winked, squeezed his hand, turned seductively, and drifted out the door.

CHAPTER THIRTEEN

Luke glanced again at the yellow legal pad and surveyed the list of things to do with the telephone cradled to his ear. Andrea leaned inside the door and softly stated, "Doug Turney is on line four." Luke covered the speaker and asked Andrea to have him hold. Doug Turney was Luke's brother-in-law, married to one of Beth's sisters, and also a director of Winney's bank. Luke presumed Turney knew the divorce had been filed and wanted the latest gossip.

"Tell me about her," Doug Turney started.

"About who?"

"Whoever it is that got you to file for divorce again."

"There's no one."

"Right, there's probably two or three," Turney snickered.

"Sorry to disappoint you."

"Oh, I'm not. I'm sure word will eventually get out. Say, let's have lunch. Can you do it? Vern and I have a deal to run by you."

Years before, Luke had done a couple of real estate deals with Turney and his partner Vern Brindley. Those had been sold. "We can do lunch, but I'm not much in the market now, with the divorce."

"This is a good deal. Besides, you won't be getting divorced for a while. Let's eat those greasy burgers at Dimby's."

"Sure," Luke replied.

Dimby's Hamburgers had sat at the same intersection for thirty years with a free, faded red, dented, metal banner littered with soda trademarks. The sizzling of burgers grilled in butter and grease was enough to raise one's cholesterol on entering. Customers turned past the cashier and chose between one side with booths or the other with a series of stools below a long, vinyl countertop, brushed clean for a new arrival and decorated with ketchup bottles, napkin holders, and glass salt and pepper shakers. Luke slid into a booth, gingerly so as not to squeak on the high-gloss red, plastic seat covers. Within minutes he saw Turney and his partner Vern Brindley walking up the sidewalk. The two together made Luke smile.

Vern Brindley was a slight man, razor thin and short. He was in his late forties and dressed neatly but in obviously cheap clothes. Vern had money because he had never spent any. He had parlayed a high school education into a pawnshop in the poorest section of Sand Springs. The pawnshop bought a used-furniture store, which grew with stocks of closeouts and factory returns, mostly sold at above-retail prices with in-house financing to poor credit risks. Vern kept his profits in savings accounts and lived in a small, frame house that needed painting and had an old wire antenna on the roof for television. Three television stations were plenty, he would say. He ignored PBS. His wife worked as a secretary at a plumbing company, and they lived on her earnings. She purchased the groceries and clothing. The mortgage on the two-bedroom home had long since been paid. The furniture store was where he had met Doug Turney, then a regional furniture salesman.

Turney had proposed a rent-to-own furniture and appliance store. Vern had backed Turney in the venture, acquiring a 50 percent interest for his capital, and watched Turney drive the opening of new stores. Locations were now spread across Oklahoma, Arkansas, and Missouri. Only prodding by Turney had forced Vern to exchange his no-frills, bottom-of-the-line Chevrolet for a midrange Oldsmobile with air conditioning.

Doug Turney stood almost six feet tall and hovered over his partner. He was always dressed in a suit, but none ever fit. His legs were short, and his trunk long and thick. He had a cheeky, oval face and an evangelist's smile. His ties were usually slightly off center, dangling to one side of his short-sleeved shirt, and never reached his belt, resting instead on his huge stomach. Vern often heckled him about his belly and joked Turney was carrying the child low. Sometimes the belt buckle would tilt forward and face the ground, failing to restrain the girth, and the white inside liner of his slacks would be visible as the waist gave way.

Unlike Vern, debt was Turney's friend; he spent everything he made and a little extra. Vern would not let the company borrow money, so Vern calculated monthly Turney's half of the inventory. Vern owed nothing, and Turney owed more than $2 million for his half, split with Winney's bank and others.

Turney and Vern spotted Luke and slid into the other side of the booth; a middle-aged waitress approached with a ready pen, a small, green-lined, white pad, and a distant glare. They all ordered burgers and fries. Only Luke asked for "no onions." Turney's eyes were fixed on Luke, and he began as soon as they had ordered.

"Who is she?" Turney asked as Vern watched intently.

"There's no one." Luke's forehead wrinkled.

"Sure, sure." Turney winked. "Just give me the castoffs."

"I thought you had your hands full?" Luke replied. Despite being married to Beth's sister, Turney was in the midst of a long-term affair with his secretary. He had even purchased a large new house, with a large mortgage, for her and her two children. Everyone knew Turney was paying for her house and the tuition, so her children could attend the same private school as his.

Turney's eyes never blinked. "They're never full. Busy sometimes, but never full," he laughed, and Vern giggled, his shoulders moving up and down like a cartoon character with only the "tee-hee" caption missing. "You're the one with single hands." Turney and Vern laughed again.

"I'm not single," Luke sighed.

"And you won't be for a while," Doug Turney added.

"Just be like Doug," Vern said, looking at his partner. "He thinks he's a Mormon." He and Turney laughed in unison.

"Oh, he would need too many houses," Turney chimed.

"OK, OK," Luke intervened.

"Besides, after we talk you won't want a divorce." Turney grew serious, and the words shot from his mouth. "Why don't you become a banker?" He glanced at Vern and then back to Luke. "Listen, we're buying a block of the bank."

Vern edged forward but said nothing.

"Really?" Luke knew both had purchased a few shares but thought their combined interest was around 5 percent.

"We're going to straighten the bank out. Winney is in trouble and catching it from some stockholders. He bought a bunch of government bonds years ago to get a high yield, but the value fell as interest rates climbed—he's underwater. He can't sell them without taking a loss, and the rates are less than what the bank has to pay for certificates of deposit. He's got some bad loans, too. So the bank is hurting for income, may have to write off some loans, and can't liquidate the bonds without taking more losses. We're buying stock from some of the complaining stockholders and looking for others who want to sell. We've hired this new guy, Paul. He's a former bank examiner, so he can run operations, but he's not the type to run the whole thing. We need a president to run the bank. We're going to kick Winney up to chairman but without decision-making responsibility. Then we stop the dividends to build the net worth; that'll probably drive more shares our way if we want them. Ultimately we'll sell our shares."

"To whom?" Luke asked.

"Either another bank or another investor."

"Slow down." Luke raised his hand. "Wait. How much are you putting in?"

"Four million. Two million each. I'm borrowing mine, and Vern's putting up cash. But we'll split it three ways with you," Turney said as he popped a folded sheet from his suit pocket and slid it across the table. "Here—this is a list of the shareholders and their shares. I've checked the ones wanting to sell. We already have a deal with the circled names. We have enough commitments to get control."

"I don't want to be a banker," Luke said. "But hold on. I want to get a handle on this. Does Winney know what you're doing?"

"Of course," Turney responded. "Winney's helping me get a loan from Stone Bank. They want the bank's correspondent account from Malson. Winney wants to move to Stone also. Malson is squeezing him because he can't pay his interest, but I don't think Stone Bank will loan him as much as he owes. Winney likes the idea of Vern and me coming in, but he only knows the part about us buying stock. The board of directors is complaining because he's losing money.

He needs to write off loans and liquidate the bonds, but if he takes the loss, he has to shrink the bank and can't renew his stock loans. The directors aren't happy, so Winney keeps paying dividends to buy time. He sees our coming in as solving his problem with the shareholders."

"But once we're in, we'll stop the dividends," Vern said flatly.

"But Winney doesn't know," Turney continued. "He needs the dividends. Vern doesn't need the dividends, and my share of the stores makes enough to pay my interest."

"Wait," Luke interrupted as the burgers arrived in green, plastic, latticed baskets with wax paper liners. "OK, Winney doesn't know you're cutting out the dividends. Who's Paul?" Luke placed napkins around the hamburger bun to soak up the grease.

"We had Winney hire him. He's an operations guy, an ex-bank examiner. Winney liked the idea of having someone take paperwork off his desk. But he's not a long-term president. He can babysit it, but that's all."

Vern jumped in. "Guide us through the change of control with the regulators. Regulator stuff."

"You just said you're going to make him president?" Luke challenged.

"Unless we can get you in the deal. For him, it's just a title. He's not a go-getter. No sales ability. We're going to run it unless we can get you," Vern answered.

"I don't want to be a banker," Luke said slowly and firmly. "And I'm divorcing Winney's daughter."

"Sure you are," Turney said and smirked, and Vern chuckled. "Be realistic. She's not going to give it to you. It's going to be years. It's going to take a while, if you ever get it, and we can do this deal in the meantime."

"You want me to do a deal on Winney's bank while I'm divorcing his daughter?"

"It's business. Besides, if you're in the bank, he's going to need your help to cover his bank debt," Turney said matter-of-factly. "Look, you're going to pay her attorney bills either way. Winney's not really going to influence the divorce except to tell her to ask for more money, which will drag it out. She's going to do that anyway."

"If you're in the bank, Winney will need you more than you need him. He's got problems and huge debts," Vern quickly added.

"Think what you could do with a bank," Turney started again. "Maybe you would want to buy us out eventually. You're a business guy. You know how to make money. Paul is not a moneymaker, but he can take orders."

"My focus is getting a divorce," Luke started.

But Turney interrupted, "Look, with your financials you can borrow the money from Malson or Stone Bank." Turney slid the list closer to Luke.

Luke picked up the list and spoke without looking at it. "I don't want to buy into the bank." Luke shrugged.

"The big banks are paying a premium now; once we have controlling interest, we can double our money. We help Winney in the short term and help ourselves in the long term. In and out in a year or two," Turney stated.

"Less time than your divorce will take." Vern widened his eyes.

"Yeah," Turney added.

"I don't think so." Luke shook his head. "No thanks. My hands are full with FRM."

"Winney thinks it's a good idea." Turney flashed his preacher's grin.

"He knows you're talking to me?"

"Sure, he thinks it's a good idea for you to buy some stock."

"You've got to be kidding me," Luke said to the ceiling. "One more asset to fight about in court."

"But he doesn't know we want you to run it. He thinks he has a few years left." Vern offered. "He just wants some new shareholders."

"That's because he doesn't know the whole deal," Luke answered.

"Keep the list, and think about it," Turney said.

Luke folded the list into his coat pocket. "I don't want a bank," Luke said. "I want a divorce. I don't think it's a good idea for me to get mixed up with the bank."

"Think about it." Turney smiled. "You can get the bank easier than the divorce. And being married doesn't slow you down." Turney winked.

"Never has." Vern's head was steady.

The conversation wound to a close as Luke continued to sidestep personal issues. Luke shook hands with both Turney and Vern on the sidewalk, and then Turney hauled himself as Vern skated along toward their car. Luke called the bond markets as he steered back to the office.

CHAPTER FOURTEEN

Federal regulators closed two rural banks in western Oklahoma on a Thursday a few months later. The news was buried in a one-paragraph article. Almost two years earlier, a large energy bank in Oklahoma City had been closed in front of television crews and with detailed national coverage. The energy bank had grown quickly, packaging drilling loans for New York, Pacific, and Midwestern banks. The high interest rates, high inflation, and high energy prices of the late 1970s had fueled euphoria as lenders poured millions of dollars into fracking oil wells. The energy bubble burst in the early 1980s, leaving the perforated wells in the Southwest and their higher operating costs uncompetitive. The big banks took large losses, and a silence fell. A slow ripple drifted through the regional economy carrying unpaid consumer and business loans. Unemployment rose and defaults increased. The newspapers downplayed the closing of two rural banks as an unrelated aberration.

The two shuttered banks were in remote locations and far from Tulsa. Luke read the news with a cautious eye. The bank closings represented more uncertainty, and he had plenty of risk with the pending divorce. Business had been strong all summer; however, his divorce would cost cash. Selling some servicing would set a market price he could use in the divorce proceedings and give him added flexibility.

The next day Luke selected a list of $50 million of loan servicing to sell. FRM monthly income would drop from lost servicing fees, but Luke felt confident new loan production would soon build the portfolio. The schedules for the servicing were delivered to a broker, and an auction was set for two weeks later. Within three months the sale closed at 2.54 percent, and FRM added over $1.2 million in cash after expenses.

Chuck called in the afternoon. "Hey, Big Boy. How's everything?"

"Good, Chuck. Good."

"Hey, the renewal for the loan is coming up at the end of September. I'll have Cindy send a list of what we need. Just routine."

"Not a problem. You can have her call Harold. He can handle it."

"Sure, if you don't want to talk to Cindy…But I know who you need to talk to."

"Melissa."

"Yeah, her too. But you need to give Bill Bivins a call."

"Oh, I already finished the United Way thing over a month ago."

"Not the United Way. You need to talk to Bivins. Listen, Big Boy. He likes you, and he thinks the bank should expand into some new areas. You're the guy."

Luke paused, unsure how to respond. "Chuck, I'm flattered, but I have my hands full here."

"Look, think about it. What are you worth now anyway? Eight or nine million?" Chuck asked, shooting a low number. "What are you—thirty-three? Do you realize you could sell your company and get a five-year deal at a nice salary? Who knows where you could go."

"Chuck, you're dreaming. I don't want to sell. I'm truly committed to the people here."

"You know what—think about it. I haven't even talked to Bivins about it. But I think it's the kind of deal that could be done, and you would be a very wealthy man. Besides, you could get your divorce."

"Well, it wouldn't solve the real estate part of the equation," Luke said, trying to change the subject. "Beth is going to fight over those values, too."

"How's that going?" Chuck asked.

"I get to see the kids regularly, so that's good. I offered her half of everything, huge separate maintenance money for seven years—regardless of whether she remarries—huge child support, and of course I would pay tuition and other stuff. In fact, I'm going to call Melissa and get some information on setting up a trust to pay tuition. But, here's the deal breaker. She wants me to pay her fifty percent of the value of the company and all the real estate and still pay her fifty percent of the profits from the company for ten years with each year's payout guaranteed to at least equal the previous year, adjusted for inflation. Then she wants to have the company valued again in ten years and get fifty percent of that value. And she wants me to guarantee the value of the company doesn't diminish."

"What? That doesn't make sense."

"Of course not. She's stalling."

"No judge would do that."

"I know. So, we are getting the appraisals together. I should be divorced after about five or six more United Way drives," Luke sighed.

"No, Big Boy. You sell out and that solves that problem."

"I'm not interested in selling, and no one is interested in buying."

"Think about it. I'm not saying it could happen, but think about it. Bivins likes you. I think I could put it together."

"I will," Luke lied.

"Yeah. And talk to Fluffy about something besides tuition," Chuck suggested.

"I don't know."

"She thinks you're bashful. Are you slipping?"

"Let's see…I need to come on to Melissa. I need to call Bivins. Do I need to clean my room, Mom?"

"Joke if you want. Think about Bivins."

"I will," Luke lied again.

Luke had dismissed the thought before he hung up the telephone. His life had become relatively tranquil. The first years of coping with the hectic growth of a new company, dangerously volatile mortgage rates, and domestic strife had been temporarily replaced by a moderate expansion of the business and calm in the financial markets.

While his settlement offers to Beth were always rejected, Luke remained optimistic. Luke routinely wrote two checks to his attorney each month, one for the legal fees and expenses and one for the transfer to Beth's attorney for her spending money. The court had only awarded a small percentage of the allowance she requested. All of the monthly housing, utility, tuition, clothing, medical, and other bills were still sent to Luke. Luke hoped Beth would meet someone and become more realistic in her demands.

Luke's weekly schedule had settled into a comfortable routine. He still worked late hours, but he saw his children at least one evening each week and one day on the weekend. He even served as an assistant coach on his son's baseball team.

Melissa called a few days later. They met for lunch at the Summit Club in a busy see-and-be-seen setting of Tulsa commerce. Again,

Luke was taken by Melissa's beauty. She was nattily attired in a conservative business suit that still showed her feminine lines. Luke steered the conversation through trust and tax questions, seeking the best vehicles for his children's tuition. Melissa was moderately informed and promised to research Luke's questions. Her eyes still danced, but Luke was on guard and reserved. Twice she suggested selling the company would allow him to pursue a new life. Twice he told her he felt a huge commitment to his employees. Twice she asked if he was seeing anyone. She arched her eyebrows when he said no. He never mentioned Ginny to anyone. Luke and Melissa separated at the ground floor with her promise to call with some answers.

A few times each week, Ginny and Luke stole moments together. She was never cautious about her car being seen at his condo, and a rendezvous after the futures market closed was punctuated by Luke's call to check the cash market. Occasionally, they sneaked a drive to the lake condo and spent the late afternoon and early evening there. Sometimes they simply met in a park, sat under a tree, and talked. Only occasionally did Ginny speak of her husband, complaining of his late-night drinking with friends surrounded by scantily clad, spotlighted dancers twirling for dollar bills and his weekend ritual of playing golf and watching televised sports. She fretted about his bills and a pending IRS lien for back taxes. Luke listened and lamented his own disappointments with Beth. Suggestions of a relationship were cautious, playful, and carefully probing. Ginny asked about his divorce but never pressed.

Luke did not know if he loved her, but he knew he loved their time together. He lost himself with her and felt free. He knew it was a fantasy without the stress of mundane matters. He questioned whether his attention was enough, or whether she needed the adulation of others? And why did she stay with her husband? He thought wistfully of Ginny and then withdrew, fearful of exposing himself until the divorce was settled.

Chuck called with updates on the credit-line renewal, but the conversations always carried suggestions about Bivins's receptivity and that Luke should give him a call. Luke dismissed Chuck with politeness. Chuck promised to have the documents ready two days before the deadline, and Luke arrived at the appointed time.

Luke signed the thick stack of papers but sensed tension. Each of the past few Thursday's had been accompanied by the closing of one or more small banks. "Are you all right?" Luke finally asked.

"Of course," Chuck answered.

"You seem on edge. How are the bank closings affecting everything?"

"They're great for us. We can buy banks cheaper now. The bankers had been asking twice book value, and the purchase regulations were stringent; but now the price is softening, and the regulators are loosening the rules to find someone to buy their problems. At first we had to go to bankers for deals, look for the one having trouble paying their bank stock loans, or find controlling interest groups that wanted to sell. Now they are coming to us."

"Oh, I thought maybe the bank failures were causing problems. It seems to be spreading. I mean, I would think all of the banks face losses on loans from the oil shakeout."

"No, Big Boy, bank closings are good for us. We're growing."

The balance of the conversation was pleasant, but without Chuck's usual jostling. Everything had gone routinely, and Luke was unconcerned as he exited the building.

As instructed, Chuck called Bivins's secretary as soon as Luke left his office. In a few moments, Bivins came on the line and instructed

Chuck to hold the loan documents until Wednesday and to let him know when Luke called.

Harold Rhoden came to Luke's office on the following Tuesday morning with a confused expression but without panic. Harold had sent the daily funding requests, but no money had been advanced, and Cindy had not returned his calls. Harold had called Malson's Loan Operations Department and was told the credit line had expired, and they were waiting on the new agreement. FRM had enough cash in its accounts to close loans for a few days as long as the markets stayed quiet and no margin calls arose. Luke gave Chuck a couple of calls, but none were returned. Luke became concerned on Wednesday morning and finally left an urgent message saying he would be there after lunch. Chuck called within a few minutes.

"Luke, I sure have a lot of pink message notes from you. What's up?"

"Harold said Cindy's not funding our advances, and the Loan Operations Department said they don't have the renewal. I thought this was taken care of last week."

"Why are you calling Loan Operations?" Chuck sounded defensive.

"To find out what's going on."

"Don't call them. I'll check on it, but you're not the only customer we have."

"Are you guys that busy?" Luke asked.

"Yes. Listen, Big Boy, I'll get it taken care of. It may take a day or two, but I can get it taken care of."

"Chuck, we don't have a day or two. We have loans to close."

"Hey, a day or two shouldn't make a big difference. Look, the bank has been good to you, and you've made a lot of money."

"We signed this deal last week."

"You've been spoiled. You're running your business as if you have money any time you want it, and we need to put our money where we make the most money."

Luke leaned back in his chair. He hated the "our money" statement. The bank had its own money, its capital, but more than 90 percent of its money came from people's deposits. In Luke's mind, that didn't qualify as "our money." Individuals and businesses loaned money to the bank by making deposits. The bank had this opportunity only because the government had given the owners a charter, a license, and guaranteed the depositors the money was safe. It wasn't the bank's money in Luke's eyes. They were custodians with a role to play. Luke filtered his thoughts and focused on the delay. He had just signed a new one-year agreement, and yet Chuck had signaled more was to be done. "What's going on here? Did we close last week or not?"

"Oh, we closed. We'll get everything set up. It should be ready in a day or so."

"Chuck, I don't have a day or two. We have to be able to fund loans as they are set for closing. If we don't close, our creditability is damaged, and our business suffers. I have to meet margin calls as the market moves. It's in my best interest to not have problems, but it's also in yours."

"Hey, we have to run our business, too. It's real estate, Big Boy. Secure the collateral and collect the payments."

"It's not real estate, Chuck," Luke sighed. "Our collateral changes every day, and the value changes constantly. When can we advance?"

"I'll check on where everything stands, and I will call you after lunch."

Chuck called Bivins to gain favor and promised to stretch Luke for one more day. After lunch, Chuck told Luke he had personally ensured the line of credit would be activated on Thursday. The conversation was cordial, and by Thursday Luke thought all was back to normal. That evening he heard reports of another small, rural bank having failed. Luke still did not recognize the new era.

CHAPTER FIFTEEN

The dark gray, heavy skies of December had fallen, and Chuck Rail was frustrated. Luke Boyd had never called Bill Bivins, despite Chuck's increased pressure. Banks were struggling to find good loans, and bad loans continued to grow. The strategy of the day was to develop new streams of fee income from services, such as insurance, brokerage, and mortgage banking. Bivins was intent on starting a mortgage operation but had no interest in Osage Mortgage or Tremble Mortgage. Those operations were decaying, and FRM and Luke Boyd were on the rise. Chuck peered out his window over the north Tulsa landscape of bare brown limbs, dingy roofs, and small bare yards dusted with dead leaves. He thought of Sid Fullmer in his office with a view of the Arkansas River and a desk covered with bank acquisition deals. As Bivins had instructed, Chuck reached for his phone and called Luke Boyd.

"Luke," Chuck started, "I want to give you a heads-up on an announcement before the fact."

"You're getting married," Luke interjected.

"Well, you know the bank has a policy on that sort of thing, so one of us has to leave if we get married. We have talked about it, but it may be a while."

Luke immediately thought, "Marry her and get her out of the bank." Cindy now rarely called Luke, but Harold Rhoden constantly complained about her. Instead, he politely replied, "That serious?"

"Oh, yeah. This is the one for me."

"Well, I hope everything keeps going well. You sound happy."

"I am, but that's not the reason for my call. Listen, the bank is entering the mortgage business. The holding company that owns the bank will own the mortgage company. I've talked to Bivins. They've chosen a guy from consumer banking to get the approvals and that sort of thing. He only knows how to make car loans, so it's just an interim step. We won't be operational for a while."

Luke sat up straight. He had no fear of competing with the bank in a contest to attract mortgage loans. He competed with big companies every day. Still the change rang alarms. "I see," Luke said.

"Look, Bivins wants to talk to you, and quite frankly he's offended that you haven't called him."

"It's not my call," Luke answered. "Not that I have any interest, but why would I call to tell him I am not interested in a deal that he hasn't offered."

"You've got to understand Bivins and how these deals work." Chuck paused. "Look, talk to me. Tell me what you want, and I'll go to Bivins with it."

"I want to do what I'm doing. Chuck, please understand, I started this to prove it could be done. There are some people here who went out on a limb for me. They left their jobs to join a guy staring at his thirtieth birthday and starting something from zero. I owe them." He paused. He knew he would never wear a logo pin, but he didn't want to offend Chuck. "I wouldn't fit in there. I don't have the skills and patience needed to educate a board of directors in a new business."

"You don't have to," Chuck countered. "Look—you sell, you get your eight or nine million in bank stock, you get a six-figure salary for five years, and you move on."

"I don't want bank stock," Luke answered before realizing it sounded like a negotiation. He stopped from saying Chuck's value was at least $2 million below the value of the servicing alone and included nothing for the operations.

"Well, you can get cash, probably not as much, but you can get cash."

"Chuck, I shouldn't have said that. I don't want cash or bank stock. I don't want to cool my jets for five years waiting to go do something different. Most importantly, I can't sell out the people here. I owe them."

"No, you don't. Listen, you sell the company, you take the stock or cash, you sell the real estate, pay off your wife, and look where you are. You're young. You'll net four million or more on your share from us, another three or four million from your share of the real estate. You can earn three hundred thousand a year on the interest. You'll have a great position, nice salary, lots of perks, and a great life with someone like Melissa. You can train someone, oversee them for a while, and then fade out and start something new. But, I know you. I know you'll love it; you'll love the challenge, and you'll get involved. You could be president of this place."

"Chuck, it's just not me. Why doesn't Bivins look at another company?"

"Look, we have two guys begging us to buy them. No way. We don't want them. All they have is an old portfolio and a trickle of business. You have what Bivins wants."

"I'm flattered," Luke said but suddenly felt threatened. "Chuck, I want a divorce, but I can't sell the company to get it. I can't do that to these people."

"Listen, Big Boy. You're too good to them. You're overpaying those people. You've given them company cars. How many of them? Ten? That branch manager of yours is extremely overpaid."

Luke stood. "Phyllis?"

"Yeah, with the solid cheerleader figure. She's cute, but, Big Boy, you're paying way too much. Rhoden, too. Hell, you pay them more than our department heads."

Luke breathed deeply as the line lay silent. The FRM financials submitted to the bank did not include individuals' salaries. Chuck had to have researched the payroll checks to know the employees' compensation. "Chuck," he said and paused again before continuing, "I expect a level of productivity and commitment from these people that other organizations don't get. That has led to our success. I don't throw money at people, but I will reward people who produce. I want to be the best. I want to work with the best. I want my people to make money; I don't want to make money off my people."

"Whoa," Chuck jumped in, "I hit a nerve. Listen, I know you feel this huge commitment to them, but you pay them more than they would make anywhere else. You know that."

"Yes. And it is by design."

"OK. OK." Again there was a pause. "Listen, think it over. Remember, it's going to take several months to even get the approvals, desks, and space—that sort of thing—for the mortgage department, so this doesn't shut the door on doing something with you. But think about it, because you need to do this. I know you're sleeping on a sofa in one of your rental condos, six hundred square feet of empty carpet with a bed and a sofa. Probably don't even have a television."

"Chuck, I don't need a television."

"You'll get money or stock or both; you pay off your wife, get your divorce, and start frolicking with the Fluffys of the world. You're still in the mortgage business."

"Chuck, I'm not interested. But just for the sake of argument, is Malson going to take all of these people and pay them what I'm paying them?"

"Listen, we can take some of them. We can't pay the salaries you pay. You know that. You're paying some of those women too much. All of that would have to go through the personnel department. And they will have to get their own cars."

"There you have it, Chuck. I can't turn these people over to a personnel department and put them back where they were before they came here. I gave Phyllis, Amy, and some others a chance and a challenge, and they did it. They earned it. I can't do that to them."

"They'll get used to it," Chuck interrupted. "Look, what else are they going to do? You're the only one who will pay those salaries. So they take a short-term cut. Soon they forget; inflation happens; within a few years, they can't figure out whether they were making more with you or more with us. There's nothing to compare to. Memories are short, and these people won't have many alternatives. They'll adjust."

"Chuck, honestly I can't do it. It's not right for me. It's not right for the people here." He paused. "And I can't call Bivins. I'm not interested."

"Think about it, Big Boy. You need to do this."

"I won't, Chuck. I'm sorry."

"I'll call after Christmas. By the way, Cindy had tamales flown in from San Antonio. Yours should be delivered today."

"Thanks, Chuck."

"And thanks for the Tecate."

"You're welcome."

"The cases of pretty green bottles showed up at the office yesterday, and Cindy loved the Puligny-Montrachet."

With that Chuck and Luke exchanged their season's greetings. The tamales arrived in the afternoon, and Luke set them in the large kitchen area in the back. The staff took turns popping them in the microwave amid the harvest of turkey, ham, dressing, potatoes, green beans, salads, and desserts the caterer had spread across clothed tables. The staff crowded into the center section and exchanged glee and chatter and gifts and let the red, green, and gold paper drift to the floor. Eventually, all gathered their gifts, grabbed some leftovers, and stepped into the cold winter air. Luke was the last one there and sat alone in his chair, staring at the shadows of an early winter sunset beyond the dark December clouds rolling in ever-deeper shades. Luke stood, walked to the kitchen, grabbed some leftovers from the refrigerator, and headed for the exit. He knew he had to find a new bank.

CHAPTER SIXTEEN

Luke spent the Christmas holiday visiting with the children, sneaking a couple of hours with Ginny, and sitting alone in his lake condo. His was the only car parked in the resort, and the wind off the lake was arctic. For the first time in decades, the lake had frozen, and Luke stared through the bare limbs of trees, heard the creaking of ice, and thought of the daunting task of finding a new bank.

The smattering of bank failures continued throughout the winter. Increasingly, the failures inched toward the state's two urban centers. Each news story promised accounts were protected by FDIC insurance and assured the bank's operations would continue under the control of regulators. Promises of a stronger, consolidated industry better able to serve the communities capped each news release.

The four larger Oklahoma banks gobbled up the best locations from failed institutions, grabbed the deposits, and left the loans for regulators to collect. Usually, regulators would call the notes due and force borrowers to scurry to find another bank. The surviving small banks struggled with loan losses, which raised their capital requirements and left them unable to make new loans and faced with government orders to downsize. Within several months Malson Bank acquired five small banks in Oklahoma City, seven locations in Tulsa, and almost twenty locations around the state.

The remaining smaller banks were under siege from the bigger banks. The four large banks flooded into their markets with radio and television campaigns and hawked their growth. Bright banners were strung across old bank signs touting the change. The message was clear: bigger was safer and smaller was riskier. The value of the smaller banks' stock shrank as closed banks glutted the market. Regulators became more aggressive, requiring more loan write-offs, further diminishing bank values. The banks' owners were ordered to raise new money to meet increased capital requirements. They searched for new money, only to find the big banks hesitant to renew their existing loans. The avalanche rumbled faster, accumulating more banks.

After the holidays, Luke's first daily priority was to find a new bank and to keep his search a secret. He knew two of the three other large Oklahoma banks had their own mortgage companies. He called all three anyway, but all said they were not adding new accounts. That left the out-of-state banks, and many had ruled out lending in the region after the oil bust. The Malson line of credit expired in September, and Luke feared he would need all of that time to find a new lender. In the growing shadow of failing banks, time was a foe.

Luke contacted the larger Dallas and Houston banks. Most openly acknowledged their troubles and need to shrink. Others simply stated they were not making new loans. Even though they agreed to accept loan application packages, they advised his efforts would be best spent elsewhere. He heard, "You're wasting the postage," and "I can't make any new loans," and "We'll probably merge with someone within the next year." Luke had bright, glossy brochures printed and sent them with introductory letters, loan requests, and FRM's financial statements. The rejections complimented FRM but cited the bank's inability to make new loans.

Luke contacted the New York banks known for financing large mortgage bankers in other regions. Luke was warned the credit committees had blacklisted Oklahoma and the other COLT states. Undeterred, Luke flew to New York, armed with FRM's audited financial statements and his company brochures; he added his own financial statements. Luke hailed taxis, grabbed available pay phones for quick market checks and calls to the office, and made his best pitch to the only two New York banks that would see him. In each meeting, he was told Oklahoma was off-limits for now, but he would be called when his requests could be considered.

Both New York banks had relationships with Malson and pressed him about Malson's growth and how Malson had avoided losses. Luke was as puzzled as they were and left those meetings thinking the bankers had only met to ask about Malson. He wondered if it signaled an interest to buy Malson or concern for their loans to Malson.

In between meetings, he ran in the cold of Central Park, breathing the energy of the New York rumble, and heard the high-pitched cries of a single street person, dressed in layers of cast-off clothing, alone on the amphitheater stage, wailing his own unwritten play. Luke felt like the homeless man and knew both were struggling to find an audience.

He called Frank Ryan and met him at a small Italian restaurant on Fifty-Seventh Street. Frank confided he had accepted a position with Keegan Securities and would have a new mortgage bond department developed in a few months. He assured Luke that Keegan Securities would aggressively compete with Stiller Stevens. Frank thought liquidity in the cash mortgage market was improving, and he said he planned to offer FRM a cash trading line, eliminating the need for selling futures to cover loan applications. This would simplify Luke's marketing and eliminate margin calls. When Luke expressed his need for another credit line, Frank suggested a few banks. Luke added those to his list, and after a return to Tulsa, he soon boarded flights to Boston and then Chicago.

Two Boston banks scheduled appointments but questioned Luke about Malson and told him Oklahoma was on the blacklist. Luke planted seeds for the future and headed to the Whitehall Hotel in Chicago, found more barren fields, and ran the cold, windy streets of the Gold Coast, past the grand old houses of the previous century's industrial age set among the huge bare tree limbs lining Astor and State Streets.

By the end of February, Luke had logged additional miles to Kansas City and Denver. In each location, he searched for pay phones for hurried calls to the bond markets and the office. The airline's premier lounges became an instant office. He flew to Houston and Dallas and personally visited the banks that had sent rejections. He flew to Atlanta, Minneapolis, and St. Louis, but Oklahoma was off limits.

In hotels and airline lounges, Luke waited for faxed reports of the loan production portfolio, matched prices, and punched the keys of his HP12-C calculator. Interest rates had begun to creep lower, and the news was a two-edged sword. Lower interest rates meant an increase in loan applications and new business, but the lower rates brought higher bond prices and futures market margin calls.

The traveling limited Luke's office time. Phyllis often entered and joked about his having an out-of-town girlfriend, plopped onto the sofa with her loan files, and shot questions before he could answer.

Chuck Rail's calls increased, and he pressed Luke to call Bill Bivins, but Luke refused to discuss the issue. The travel schedule strapped Luke to his desk on nights and weekends as the wet, cold, windy Oklahoma winter howled outside.

Luke scripted more loan request packages to lenders in Arizona and California. It was a cold, overcast February morning when Andrea handed Luke a message with Pete Winston's name on it. Luke recognized the scrawled "FCBA" as a large Los Angeles bank.

"Pete Winston," the voice said after the first ring.

"Hi, Pete. This is Luke Boyd, with FRM in Tulsa. I just received your note."

"Great. Thanks for calling me back so soon. Luke, our California people sent your loan package to me. I'm in Houston. We opened a loan production office here, since we can't have a bank in the state. We can make loans, but we can't take deposits. It's just a couple of clerks and me. I handle loan requests for the southwest region, so they sent me your package. Do you have a few moments?"

"Sure," Luke said, tempering his eagerness.

"Looks like you have had some phenomenal growth, good profits, and a nice servicing portfolio of low delinquencies. What are you looking for?"

"We have a good relationship and a thirty-five-million-dollar line with Malson; that's their legal limit. We sell most of our bonds to Stiller Stevens. They use repurchase agreements to fund on delivery instead of waiting for the settlement date, so we get paid early. That gives us some added liquidity. Our preference would be to get a larger line of credit to replace Malson or, as a second choice, a smaller line to supplement Malson."

"Frankly, we would prefer to take out the other line. We make two calculations to determine the credit line size. We require a cash ratio of five percent of the mortgage line of credit, so with your cash position, we could go up to a forty-million-dollar line. A forty-million-dollar line is about as low as we want to do.

"We also do a second calculation, using a value of two percent for your loan servicing plus your net worth. We know you can sell it for two and a half percent, but we use eighty percent of that for loan value. With your net worth and servicing, we could go up to one hundred million dollars, but we use the lower of the two calculations; so we're looking at forty million dollars."

Luke scratched the numbers on a pad. He wanted to smile but did not allow himself. Knowing how to structure future growth was encouraging. "That sounds reasonable. The ability to grow would be extremely valuable."

"Good. Tell me a little about FRM. How do you originate so many loans?"

"People," Luke paused for emphasis. "We are a company of relatively young loan originators. I have been very lucky in assembling a group that understands the business, has great energy and desire, and works very hard. We've gradually added people who want to excel and be the best. This is a high-energy place, and everyone understands we are in the business of making and selling loans. Every loan has to be documented without flaw to mortgage-backed bond standards and processed as quickly as possible. So far, we have never originated a loan that could not be sold." Luke tapped the wood trim of his desk three times.

"Well, you've certainly done very well." Pete paused for a moment. "Are you going to the Mortgage Bankers Conference in Los Angeles next month?"

"Yes, as a matter of fact."

"Great. Why don't we set up a meeting with a couple of our West Coast people—maybe breakfast or lunch? I know everyone will have a packed schedule. Let me check ours and then set something up. I may need some more information in the meantime."

"Sure," Luke said. "Let me know what you want."

"I'll fax a list. I have your number here."

"Not to be presumptive," Luke said, "but how long is the process if you decide to go forward?"

"Probably forty-five to sixty days to go through the committee approvals and document preparation. I can tell you this is the type of deal we're looking for. We don't do energy loans or commercial real estate lending in the southwest region. I already have your last three audited financial statements and your interim statements. I'd like to make a trip to Tulsa and then have you meet some of our California people. So, we could have loan committee approval within thirty days and then another two to four weeks or so to draw the documents and close."

"Would you pay off the Malson line of credit when we start funding with you?"

"Yes. That's easier for us. Is that OK?"

"Sure. That seems easier to handle."

"It takes some coordination up front, but it's a simple process. We would get Malson to sign a collateral transfer agreement, and then we pay them off."

"That sounds good," Luke said.

"Great. Let me get that list out to you, and I may have some questions as we go."

There were two calls on hold, and Luke asked Andrea to watch for Pete Winston's fax before he took the calls. Within minutes Andrea had laid Pete's list on Luke's desk. By the afternoon, the information had been compiled and sent. Luke called Pete to confirm his receipt and scheduled a breakfast meeting in Los Angeles on the first day of the conference.

At least once each year, Luke took or sent Phyllis, Harold, and Amy to a conference. He viewed their trips as a reward and an opportunity to learn more about the industry. They had already chosen the Los Angeles conference, and their reservations had been made before Luke spoke with Pete Winston.

Luke decided against letting anyone know of his breakfast meeting. If Pete visited the Tulsa office, he would say FCBA was interested in buying loan servicing. He did not want to raise eyebrows or questions; he wanted to keep the deal a secret until it was done.

CHAPTER SEVENTEEN

Pete Winston called early the next week. "Luke, this deal looks really good. I hate to say 'slam dunk,' but I just did."

Luke flipped the hair over his collar. "Sounds good."

"Luke, I want to keep this moving. I'm going to be in Dallas next Wednesday and can get into Tulsa Thursday morning, but I need to be in Houston that night. How's your schedule?"

"Not a problem. Just let me know when you'll arrive, and I'll pick you up at the airport."

"Oh, don't worry. I'll grab a rental car, and we can meet in your office."

"Are you sure? We have a couple of branch offices close by. I could give you a tour and take you to lunch."

"Lunch sounds good. I probably won't have much time. Just want a quick stare at the bricks to complete my due diligence. Let's say around ten thirty on Thursday morning?"

"Sounds excellent." Luke felt tinges of relief. He cautioned himself: FCBA was an opportunity but still not a deal.

Pete Winston arrived twenty minutes late. Luke had told Andrea he was expecting someone, so he glanced through the interior office glass each time she reached for her telephone. He was watching as Andrea nodded, and he quickly slipped out the door.

The lobby was filled but not cramped. Buyers and sellers sat comfortably but nervously next to their realtors on the stuffed, curved sofas and chairs. A few seats were available, but Pete Wilson stood to one side, a leather folder in hand. He carried a linebacker's physique. His cheeks were full, making him appear younger than his forty-plus years. He was confident but not overbearing. Luke liked him immediately.

"How about a tour first?" Luke asked.

"Sure."

Luke watched the staff's eyes as they made their way through the loan origination area. A few heads looked up but none stared, as the hum of typewriters and telephones set the background. Luke escorted Pete back into the central office, and they walked down a row of low-walled, silver-capped workstations with more loan processors and the Shipping Department.

The conference room lay ahead, and the door opened, a sign the most recent closing was exiting the other door into the reception area. Luke steered Pete into the room. Huge smiles adorned everyone's faces. Luke waved to the realtors but did not speak; they were consumed with their clients. "This is the conference room for closings," Luke said. "Tulsa is one of the last markets where lenders still close their own loans. One company is trying to start a closing service, but it hasn't caught on yet. Title companies handle our closings in the Oklahoma City market."

Luke steered Pete back along more glass-walled offices of the accounting section. Nancy Washburn, the accounting manager, had her head down preparing closing schedules for Malson. The same hum of typewriters and twill of telephones prevailed. The two turned past the dot-matrix printer, its staccato and whirl working on the green-and-white paper, and Luke opened a large, solid walnut door. "Our computer room," he announced. The IBM 36 sat in the center of the tiled room. "We were using an outside service to process our loan servicing, but we brought that in-house in the past year. We batch entries and print reports at the end of the day. We still use an outside service for accounting. That's also a batch system; we get the updates each morning. We've purchased a new software package capable of handling processing, closings, servicing, and accounting. The installation is set for the first of May, and then we will be on one system with live information."

"Excellent," Pete responded.

"We moved our fiscal year from March to June, so we could do the annual audit after the software is installed. We didn't want to install software and do an audit at the same time."

"That's smart. How much setup is involved?"

"A bunch. We'll send the data from the end of March to start. Then they'll be onsite at the end of April. They told us to plan for two weeks of training in May, but I'm planning on it taking the entire month. That gives us the full month of June to become competent with the system, and then we'll have time for the annual audit."

"You have your work cut out for you, but it should be worth it. Most companies haven't made the transition yet."

"We're excited."

Pete nodded, and Luke closed the door and led him through another row of low-walled workstations to the Loan Servicing Department. More glass-walled offices lined the exterior. Then they curled to find another row of low-walled workspaces for servicing and closing assistants. Luke pointed to the glass-walled offices for the loan closers on his side of the building. The intense pounding of typewriters was audible through the open doors. No heads rose. "We have quite a few closings today," Luke said.

"I've noticed." Pete nodded.

Luke finished by introducing Pete to Andrea and showed him into his office. Luke offered coffee or soda as they were seated, but Pete declined. Pete collected himself on the sofa as Luke took his customary seat with a view of the office. Pete spoke first. "I like what I see, but I have one problem."

Luke tried not to stiffen. "OK."

"Your competition doesn't like you."

"That hurts my feelings." Luke smiled, but he was tense.

"I talked with a few of your competitors. They say you are the competition in Tulsa and Oklahoma City, and you have a strong organization. That's a good sign. They actually said very nice things about you."

"I'm glad." Luke relaxed. "We get our fair share of the market and try to hold it."

"Looks like it's working for you." Pete turned and looked through the glass panes. "Looks like a newspaper room in a movie—only more nicely finished."

"Thanks; it's very functional." Luke paused. "The communication isn't always…formal, but it is effective." Both smiled. "Say, if you like, we can drive by one of the branches on our way to lunch."

"Actually, I booked an early flight, so I drove by both this morning. I noticed you keep the same color theme at your locations."

Luke knew it would have taken almost two hours to have made the circuit. "Yes. We want things to be convenient and consistent. We like them to be crisp and well kept."

"Oh, they were. I walked in both and asked for directions. They were helpful, even though they were busy."

"I know they have some closings today."

"Yes, I noticed. How quickly could you submit loan documents to us?"

"We deliver to Malson the day after closing. Each day we call with the day's closings and advance amounts. They lend us nine-ty-nine percent of the commitment price, and they deposit into our general account the same day. We transfer the money to the branches' funding accounts to issue checks. How would this work with FCBA?"

"Same way. We allow three days for receipt, so you would have more time."

"Do we write checks on your bank or bank locally for our Tulsa-area closings?"

"Whichever you prefer. We can wire to a local account, so you can do your internal transfers and issue local checks."

Luke saw the FCBA system would be easier and took Pete's talking about mechanics as a good sign. "Are you hungry?" Luke asked.

"Starved. I ate a quick breakfast early this morning."

Luke asked Pete for preferences and settled on a continental restaurant. Fountains plumed in stone lined lagoons outside the windows. The conversation was light, each asking about the other's background and hobbies. Pete was a Dodgers fan, relatively new to Houston, and making the transition without much culture shock. The food was good, and time sped by.

Luke asked for the check as the waiter cleared the table. "The bill is mine," Pete insisted and waited as the waiter nodded and moved away. "Luke, I have to get California approval, but this deal is done. My trip was a formality—a kick-the-tires visit. I always get a prelim approval before I make a visit. I'll submit a final report to California tomorrow, and I'm confident the committee will approve this. Your interest rate will be based off our prime rate, which is the same as the major New York banks. That's one percent less than Malson's rate."

Luke smiled politely. "Malson gives us credit for our cash balances, which makes our effective interest rate much less."

"Oh, we'll do the same."

"Sounds good." Luke nodded. The lower rate would add almost $400,000 a year to FRM's profits.

"Glad to hear it. As I said, I need the final approval, but I don't see a problem. I want you to meet the California people at the Mortgage Bankers Conference, another formality. I think we can move this thing along and be ready the first week of April." Pete extended his hand, and they exchanged firm grips.

CHAPTER EIGHTEEN

Luke was eager for the March conference with FCBA Bank, but he dreaded LA traffic. He managed the distance from La Guardia to Manhattan in a half hour, but the drive from LAX would take much longer. The Tulsa flight departure was scheduled a few minutes after noon on Wednesday. That morning Luke made the usual calls to the bond market. Interest rates continued to decline slowly, so there was a small margin call. Luke transferred the call to Nancy Washburn, the accounting manager, to arrange the wire with Cindy Cleugh, as usual. Luke continued tying up the loose ends on pending deals. He called Chuck Rail to tell him about the Los Angeles trip. The conversation was brief, and Chuck did not mention Bill Bivins.

Luke met Phyllis, Harold, and Amy at the Tulsa International Airport, and they all laughed at the name. Most flights traveled to Dallas or some other regional hub. After scanning the schedule, the group decided Little Rock, Arkansas, was the only international destination. The mood was cheerful, and Luke's attitude was light. He viewed the FCBA meeting as a formality; Pete Winston had said things were proceeding well. The flight to Dallas was short, and the group made the quick connection for the Los Angeles flight.

After a few circles of LAX, the group climbed the Jetway at close to five o'clock local time. Phyllis was excited and reminded Luke he had promised to find her a spot with umbrellas in the drinks and movie stars. Luke smiled and pledged to do his best.

The rental car counter featured a trainee in his early twenties with dangling gold chains and the top two buttons unfastened on a bright, broad-collar shirt. A man in his forties with twice as many gold chains, three buttons unhooked, a nest of dark chest hair, and a slight paunch gave instructions. The group decided the trainee would pop open the third button upon graduation. After fifteen minutes Luke finally got the car and slowly inched along I-405, exited on Santa Monica, and drifted toward one of the convention's hotels.

Luke convinced the group to stay close for the evening. He wanted to call the bond market early and before the FCBA breakfast. After checking in, they dined at Ma Maison, a French restaurant, and Amy and Phyllis presented a list of places they wanted to see before their return. After dinner, they stopped in the hotel bar for a nightcap, and Amy and Phyllis had their first star sighting.

Luke arose at five thirty, because of the time differential, to check the bond market with John Elliott. The market had been steady, and the same was predicted for the day. Luke completed the call and jumped into the shower. Over the course of the next few hours, he stared out the window, checked the bond market, called the office, and sat waiting. Ten minutes before the meeting, he caught the elevator downstairs.

The FCBA group was early and waiting for Luke. Pete Winston introduced Luke to three men, all in dark suits, white shirts, and red ties. Pete and Luke were dressed similarly, and they all laughed about being in uniform. The breakfast was light and leisurely. The questions were general and mostly came from Austin Farrell, who Luke determined was the senior member of the group. Luke was accustomed to the questions of how he had entered the business and his relative youth; he calmly answered each and made most of his eye contact with Farrell. The congenial conversation continued until each glanced at his watch and mentioned the next appointment or scheduled session. Pete Winston called for the check and signed as Austin Farrell started his summation.

"Luke, Pete has done a good job packaging your application, and I'm quite confident we will be able to offer a line after our next committee meeting. That will be next week, I think," he said and sought a nod from one of his associates. "Yes, next week. Of course, I can't officially commit to anything until the committee approves it, but this deal is going to happen and on the terms Pete has in the package. We're going to go ahead and start drawing the documents to save some time. Pete will go ahead and get you a listing of the transition documents, so everyone's prepped. I think we can have this ready to close in two or three weeks, if that's OK with you."

Luke succeeded in not seeming overly eager. "Sounds very good. I have enjoyed working with Pete and really look forward to working with him in the future."

"Well, good. Excellent. You know, we really like to develop long-term relationships with our customers, and we think you and your company will be an excellent customer for years to come. So, we are excited to have this opportunity."

"Long-term relationships are the only types I want to have," Luke said. "That's very important to me, also."

"Well," Pete jumped in, "sounds like we have a deal."

"I think so," Austin said, elevating his voice for emphasis. "When do you go back?"

"Saturday morning," Luke answered.

"Well, enjoy your stay. Pete can do the closing in Tulsa. In the meantime, if you have any questions, here's my card. You can always call me if you can't reach Pete."

The group exchanged cards and strolled toward the registration area. They shook hands again and then dissolved into the sea of dark suits and white shirts.

Luke started for the lobby to meet Phyllis, Amy, and Harold. Luke was a few minutes late and found the three searching for him. They agreed to go to separate meetings and meet for lunch. Each shuffled through the registration lines, found his or her nametag, searched the list of sessions, and swam through the crowd in the hotel hallways to find the meeting room. Before noon each had returned to the lobby. The hotel pay phones were packed as convention participants called their offices. Luke spotted an open one, grabbed the black receiver, and called John Elliott.

"Not much going on," John told him. "I guess all the buyers and sellers are in LA. I can't make any money."

"I'm sure most are here," Luke said.

"Hey, by the way, we didn't get your margin call yesterday."

"You're kidding me."

"No. The back office called a few minutes ago. We have to get that today."

"Not a problem. I know we gave the info to the bank yesterday. I'll call the office, but it should be there. It was around sixty thousand dollars, right?"

"Yes. I'll check with the back office again to see if they have it," John said.

"It's what…just after one o'clock there, right?"

"Yes."

"OK, give me a few minutes, and I will call back."

Luke next called the office and asked for Nancy Washburn. "Hey, John says they didn't get the margin call money. Did that go out?"

"Should have. I talked to Cindy yesterday."

"Please make sure they sent it."

"Not a problem. I gave her the amount yesterday. I'll call her now."

"Sorry, I don't mean to yell, but it is loud in here. Everyone is trying to call their offices, so we're shouting over each other."

"I understand. I'll take care of it."

"Thanks. Can you give me Andrea?" Luke asked and was soon connected. Nothing of great importance loomed; he handed the phone to Phyllis, so she could check if anyone needed her. Luke searched for another opening along the bank of phones in the long corridor. Soon, he found one and hurriedly dialed Chuck Rail's direct line. Chuck answered on the first ring.

"Hi, Chuck; it's Luke."

"How's Los Angeles?"

"It's not New York."

"More sunshine?"

"More sunshine and a lot of gold chains and chest hair," Luke said.

"Explain that."

"It's a long story; I think I rented from Disco Car Rental. They seem stuck on bad fashion from the 1970s. Anyway, on a serious note, we need to wire sixty thousand dollars to Stiller Stevens immediately. I mentioned it to you yesterday, and Nancy says she called Cindy about it, but the broker says the money hasn't arrived."

"I'll check it out."

"Please do. It's really important. I don't want them to close out our position. Nancy is calling Cindy now, but I need you to make sure it gets there today."

"I'll take care of it. Stay away from guys in gold chains out there."

"I'll do that."

Luke hung up and called John Elliott. "I just talked to my banker. He'll make sure it's there."

"All right," John concluded before they closed.

Luke hung up the phone and began looking for his group. Harold and Amy were finishing their calls. Phyllis stood with her head cocked to one side. "I don't want to go to meetings this afternoon."

Luke smiled. "OK. Let's have fun. Where's lunch?"

"Rodeo Drive," Phyllis said without hesitation.

They dropped their things in their rooms, met in the lobby, and grabbed the rental car. Within minutes Rodeo Drive surrounded them and offered its finery. Phyllis picked a café with a light menu, and they basked in the sun. Afterward, they meandered; Phyllis and Amy checked out the boutiques, Luke looked at art, and Harold watched the shoppers. The mortgage business and Oklahoma faded in the California sun.

Back at the hotel, the concierge recommended a restaurant and promised movie star sightings. The tab was heavy, but Luke enjoyed watching Phyllis's and Amy's heads pivot as if on a swivel. "You're not supposed to stare," he mentioned several times to no avail. After a nightcap at the hotel bar, Luke was in the room minutes after midnight. He opened the blinds, turned off the lights, and let the city's neon filter into the room. The FCBA meeting could not have gone better, and he could taste the new credit line. Now he would focus on the divorce. His thoughts drifted to designing a new offer for his attorney to submit. Luke slid the drapes closed. He was tired; his day was ending its nineteenth hour. Tomorrow was Friday, and the conference would have a brief meeting in the morning and then close. He had promised Phyllis, Amy, and Harold more sightseeing. He decided to sleep in for once, left no wakeup call, and slept deeply.

CHAPTER NINETEEN

uke awakened refreshed and delighted as a thread of the morning's rays slivered between the curtains. The prospect of the deal with FCBA made him more confident, and he had dreamed he was flying. He glanced at the clock and noted it was almost nine o'clock California time. He rolled over, spun his legs onto the carpet, and walked to the windows. He took in the morning vista, turned to the nightstand, grabbed the telephone, and called to check the bond market. John Elliott's voiced boomed in his ear.

"Where in the hell have you been?"

"Asleep," Luke said with a yawn. "And it was great."

"Well, wake up. Your position has been closed, and the market is in a free fall."

"What?"

"We never got your margin. I called your banker trying to get a wire, but he never called me back. Our credit guy closed your account yesterday afternoon on the close. About thirty minutes before the market opened, Alfred Horowitz changed his view on the economy and said it was heating up, inflationary pressures were building again, and the Federal Reserve would have to tighten money supply. Bond futures are down limit."

The two point swing meant huge losses for FRM. Luke's only hope was that his position had not been closed before the market decline. "OK, let me get this. You closed my position this morning at what price?"

"It was closed yesterday before the sell-off. Grissom, our credit manager, closed the account. We never got your margin wire, and he closed your position before the market closed. Then Horowitz makes his announcement this morning before the US markets opened. The London markets did an immediate free fall. So, we opened down limit. There was no chance to get you covered today."

"So, I couldn't have covered this morning anyway, since the market had already sold off," Luke said for confirmation. "I got exposed and screwed because you didn't get the margin call, and my position was closed yesterday."

"Right. That left you uncovered, and—wham!—Horowitz hit the wire with his forecast, and the markets cratered," John's voice was full of adrenaline.

"I've got to sell some futures to cover my position." Luke's voice echoed panic. He had to cover his loans before the market dropped lower.

"I can't take an order, pal. They closed your account. You've got to talk to Grissom and get the account turned on." John's voice was frantic.

"Then give me Grissom."

"Hold on."

In the next ten minutes, Luke waded through secretaries and assistants before finally getting Jim Grissom, the credit manager for all futures accounts. Grissom matter-of-factly explained, "Mr. Boyd, I had to close the account. Your margin was due on Wednesday, and we didn't receive the wire. We waited an additional day, and I even called your bank to check on the wire. I left messages with your bank officer yesterday, but no one returned my call. I left a message at your office to call me. I had no choice under the rules."

"I'm in California. I didn't get a message. How do I get the account reactivated?" Luke asked.

"I still need the margin sent."

"But if you closed out my position, there's more than five hundred thousand dollars in our account."

"Yes, there is. But under the rules, you have to make the margin call that was due before I can renew the account, and that margin must be made with newly received funds."

"So, I have to get a wire from my bank to you and get the account renewed; then I can cover my position again."

"Yes."

"OK. To confirm: the wire needs to be for sixty thousand dollars."

"Actually, it is $56,145."

"OK. Let's call it sixty thousand dollars. I need your direct number," Luke said and insisted until he overcame Grissom's hesitancy. "You'll hear from me soon," he closed.

Luke touched the numbers, asked for Chuck Rail, and was told he was out of the office until Monday. He asked for Cindy Cleugh and was told she was out of the office until Monday. He asked the secretary to arrange the wire but was told only Chuck or Cindy had authorization on the account. Urgency swelled in Luke's chest. "Can you transfer me to Sid Fullmer?" he asked.

Luke sat on hold for several minutes before Sid answered the line. "I've got some problems, Sid. I needed a wire sent to Chicago on

Wednesday. Cindy didn't get it done, and I talked to Chuck yesterday. The wire still hasn't been sent, and Stiller Stevens closed out my position. The market has had a huge sell-off today. I can't get coverage for my loans until the original margin call is made. Both Chuck and Cindy are out of the bank until Monday."

"How much is the wire?" Sid asked.

"Sixty thousand," Luke said.

"Let's see…" Sid paused, laid the phone on his desk, and returned in a couple of minutes. "Well, your general account has more than enough, so I don't know what the problem is. Can it wait until Chuck gets back?"

"Sid, it has to be today. I need your help."

"OK," Sid replied, "I might still have authority over the account, but Cindy and Chuck can initiate the transfer first thing Monday morning."

"That's too late. I have to get the wire today. They've closed my account, and I've lost my market coverage on most of the portfolio."

"OK. Give me five minutes."

"Thanks, Sid." Luke heard the knock at the door.

"Get off the phone, and when are we going?" Phyllis howled as Luke cracked the door and peered through the gap.

"I'll be down in a bit. Get some coffee."

"We've had coffee. We want Venice Beach and sightseeing." Phyllis heaved.

"Give me twenty minutes," Luke answered.

Phyllis retreated, and Luke quickly shaved. He called Sid Fullmer.

"I can't get the wire out. I am not authorized on the account anymore, but Chuck will be here first thing Monday morning. Sorry I couldn't do any better."

"What?"

"I can't send the wire." There was frustration in Sid's voice.

"I have a ton of money in your bank, and I can't get it out!"

"Looks like your wires now require their approval. I'm not in the department anymore, so I guess some things have changed." There was a silence, and then Sid added sheepishly, "You can cash checks or get certified funds."

Luke's eyes glared; he paused, breathed deeply, and restrained his voice. "I can't come to the bank counter, get a certified check, and overnight mail that to Chicago. This is a futures account. You know that, Sid."

"Yeah, I do." Again there was pause. "I'm sorry, Luke. Chuck and Cindy are the only ones who can sign off on a wire. I can't override that."

"Is Bivins in the bank? Surely he can send the wire."

"Oh," Sid answered calmly, "probably. I'm not sure if he's here."

"Sid, you know what it means when the market goes down and I don't have coverage."

"Sure. How much is it off?"

"Down limit. Two points. Does Bivins know what that means?"

"Two points!" Again Sid paused. "I'm sure Bivins understands the markets." Sid paused again. "Sorry, Luke, but I can't do anything."

"OK, Sid." Luke sighed. "Can you give me Bivins's number?"

"I'll transfer you to his secretary," Sid replied. "Let me give you the number in case you're cut off."

Luke reached Bivins's secretary to learn Bivins was out of the office. Urgency and appeal were wasted on the imperturbable secretary who said she doubted if "Mr. Bivins" would return. Luke left a detailed message asking Bivins to either initiate the wire or authorize Sid to send the wire. Luke left the telephone number for the hotel and his room number.

He frantically showered and went straight from the shower to the telephone with towel in hand. He dripped on the telephone as he called Jim Grissom. "I can't find anyone in the bank with the authority to send the wire. But they can confirm the balance and how much money we have. Will that get the account turned on?"

"No," Grissom bristled. "Listen, if you don't have the money, you won't be the first to have a liquidity problem. I have a few of those today. Don't try to feed me some story about why you can't make margin."

"Liquidity problem?" Luke yelled. "I've got five hundred thousand dollars in an account with you and more than that in an account in Tulsa." Luke's face was red and his pulse fast. He took a deep breath and tried to slow his voice. "Listen, the people with authority to send the wire will return Monday. If I get the wire there Monday, will you activate the account, so I can buy coverage the same day?"

"Yes," Grissom replied crisply. "But don't call me again unless we've received your wire. I won't expose the firm."

"You'll get a wire—either today or Monday—and you'll hear from me."

As he dressed, Luke made more calls to Bivins's office only to be told "Mr. Bivins" was not in.

Luke called John again. "Down limit," John replied. "It won't recover. We're calling the market to open at least a point lower on Monday. It may be down limit again."

A lower market open on Monday would stack more huge losses on FRM before Luke would have a chance to buy coverage. "I can't sell anything," he muttered out loud. "OK, John, I'll call when I know something."

"Call me later in case the earth moves again," John said.

Luke stood for a second, ashen in disbelief. He did not see the bright sunshine filtering into the room. The colors had bled, and the room was a fuzzy outline of gray objects and vacant spaces. FRM had taken severe losses, and Luke knew without calculating that today's loss would be more than $2 million and would take all of FRM's cash. Another market drop on Monday would leave the company insolvent. His only hope was for the market to stabilize on Monday so he could sell coverage again.

He grabbed the loan inventory reports and hammered on the calculator to confirm his fears. He knew when rates spiked up, more applicants closed to take advantage of the now below-market rate they had been guaranteed. That would drive his losses higher. He factored the number for John's prediction for Monday, and the potential loss grew beyond $4 million. He said the number out loud and exhaled.

Luke glanced at the clock and finished dressing. His fingers were suddenly thick, and he struggled with the buttons on his shirt. "Be calm," he whispered. Phyllis called the room, and he dismissed her, saying he would be in the lobby at noon. He alternated between calling Bivins's office and John Elliott in Chicago every few minutes. Nothing changed. The market stayed down limit, and Bivins never returned. Finally at noon, two o'clock in Chicago, all hope expired as the futures market closed. There was nothing Luke could do until Monday. He put on his best face to entertain the others, but the tension churned his stomach and gripped his chest. His mind reeled. The elevator carried him down to Phyllis and the others, staring at their watches.

Luke fogged through Friday and the Saturday-morning trip to the airport. Phyllis and the others gawked at Venice Beach and the hunks and skaters whose thickest garment was a headband. Luke found the group dinner at a place with continental cuisine and two movie star sightings. Luke barely sipped the wine. He saw little, tasted less, and would never recall the day's conversations. In the hotel bookstore, he grabbed a historical account of Custer's final battle and the Indians' struggle to save their culture. Luke consumed pages during the return flights, headphones in place, and did not talk to anyone. Within minutes of landing, he was in the office, reviewing his market position. He sifted through his mail and phone messages and found the pink note labeled "Please Call" with the name of Jim Grissom and a 312 area code. The slip was marked Thursday at 1:55 p.m., and the message portion of the note was blank. Grissom's name would have meant nothing to Luke or anyone else without more information.

Luke drove to the office Sunday night to watch the Asian markets open dramatically lower. The dollar was in a free fall: interest rates were higher, and bonds were still falling off the cliff. He twice called Chuck Rail at home, but there was no answer. Cindy Cleugh's number was unlisted and he did not know where she lived. He watched the screen until after midnight, read the stacked mail, and cleaned out the tray that held assorted junk, such as Doug Turney's stockholder's listing for Sand Springs Fidelity Bank. His desk was clear. The market never improved. The London markets would open in another hour, but Luke knew it would be more bad news. He turned the office lights off and made the short drive to his condo.

CHAPTER TWENTY

uke was back in the office an hour before the Chicago market's opening. The staff noted his early arrival. The London markets had continued the sell-off. Luke knew his first priority was to stop the losses and then he had to meet with Chuck. He called John before the open. "Looks like down limit there. Right?"

"Yep. We're calling for down limit. But we may get a bounce off the bottom."

"How much?"

"Half a point, maybe three-quarters—hard to say."

"OK. I'm in the office, and I'll be watching. Keep me in mind—I need coverage. And I will get you a wire, but the bank can't send before nine o'clock."

"I'll call you right after the open," John said as he clicked to another line.

Luke called Chuck Rail. The switchboard answered, and Luke left a message. Luke watched as the market opened down limit, increasing the loss.

Luke finally reached Chuck an hour later. "Where have you been?" He held the scream from his voice, but the anger oozed through.

"New York. Cindy and I made a quick trip and got back last night. Had a great time."

"Chuck, Cindy never sent my margin call to Chicago. My position was closed, and the markets have cratered. I need a wire sent this morning. Right now."

"Hold on, Big Boy. We'll get your wire sent. New York is great. Expensive, but great. No wonder you love it."

"Chuck, I've lost a lot of money. That wire has to be sent."

"I heard interest rates really moved. Bivins mentioned it in the morning meeting. He told me you called. Don't worry, Big Boy. We will get the wire done. What's the amount? Oh wait, I see the note here. I'll give it to Cindy, and it'll go this morning."

"Sixty thousand, right? It has to be there in fifteen minutes."

"OK. We will do it now."

"Chuck, we have to meet. Today."

"Can't do that. Maybe dinner or drinks tomorrow night."

"As soon as you can. I can be there any time."

"Let's say tomorrow, but I will call to confirm."

"Get the wire sent. I'll call Chicago. Got to go." Luke hung up without awaiting a response.

Within an hour John Elliott's office had the wire, Jim Grissom reinstated the account, and FRM was free to trade again. Luke watched the Telerate machine, but the market never bounced; there was no opportunity to sell coverage. The futures market closed down limit again, and the cash markets continued to sag, indicating the futures market would be worse the next day and the losses would grow.

Luke answered the constant flow of calls and stared at the Telerate machine. The tasks weaved a comfortable fabric of normalcy into his day; however, as the calls slowed and the office emptied, the loss rumbled in his stomach. Chuck Rail had not called to confirm a meeting. Luke was certain Chuck and Bivins both knew he had taken large losses. The markets' moves were front-page news in the *Wall Street Journal.* Luke seethed and questioned whether Malson would acknowledge its culpability. The thought that Chuck had intentionally not sent the wire began to swirl in Luke. He believed Cindy to be clueless; and since Chuck had taken over the account, there seemed to him to be a pattern of delays, snafus, and complications interrupting the funding of loans—and now a delay in sending wires. The hovering questions magnified Luke's anxiety as he sat alone with his the only lit office and the rest of the building dark.

Luke knew FRM would soon be illiquid. Losses would be incurred with each loan closed and realized as loans were sold and settled in the cash market. The losses would exceed FRM's cash reserves. Luke mentally tried to estimate the cash drain, measure the outflow, and chart a course, but he still did not know how much would be lost.

Luke stepped through the darkness of the condo living room, vacant except for the sofa. He undressed in the darkness of the bedroom with only the blanketed mist of the outside lights. He flipped on the light and tried to read, but he could not concentrate. He lay in the darkness and glanced at the red numbers on the clock. He tossed, stood, and peered through the window at the night's calm. He was tired but his mind raced. He grabbed a blanket, lay on the sofa, and slept in fits. When he finally rose, he was exhausted.

By Tuesday morning the market crash and interest rate hikes had jumped to daily newspapers and morning television news. More analysts echoed the call for higher interest rates and slower growth. The news coverage frenzied realtors and buyers; they scurried to telephones to confirm applications were locked at the old rates and surveyed lenders to find the lowest rates for new applications. The calls outnumbered FRM's telephone lines, and the busy signals added to the fray and stretched the staff for the next few days.

Luke arrived early again on Tuesday. He called John before the open and hoped for a bounce off the bottom. The London markets were eroding and forecasted another down limit opening, increasing FRM's losses.

Luke placed an order to sell contracts a quarter-point off the down limit price. Even if the order was filled, FRM would take another loss of around $2 million. Luke sat watching the green numbers flash on the Telerate screen, oblivious to everything else. A bounce off the down limit open began, and Luke snatched the phone to call.

"We're close?" Luke said.

"Yep. Yep. Looks good."

The green diode numbers continued flashing higher, and suddenly the screen blinked, showing a trade at Luke's offer price.

"Did they hit?" Luke immediately asked. The screen blinked again slightly higher. "They had to hit," Luke breathed.

"Must have. Hold on." John balanced a telephone on his shoulder, held another in one hand, and stared at the speaker box, his pen ready to note a trade. Luke could hear the trade numbers in the background and exhaled when John's voice boomed, "You're done."

"Thanks, I'll call," Luke said. He knew the losses were far more than $6 million. He looked around his office, but he saw nothing. There were no colors or dimensions, only the gray outline, empty spaces, and the tatter of his thoughts.

Luke reached for the phone, and Chuck Rail took his call. Chuck insisted he was booked all day, but said he was available for dinner. Chuck selected a posh seafood restaurant known for flying in fresh fish daily.

Luke stared at the Telerate machine as if his money were inside. Suddenly, he thought about the arbitrage variance. Bonds moved independently and traded at different prices in the cash and futures markets. Usually, the variance was small as arbitragers bought and sold the difference, booked a small profit, and brought the markets closer together. Horowitz's statement had moved the markets erratically. A wider spread could increase or decrease the losses. Luke grabbed his pen and watched the Telerate. The cash price was falling as the futures price held. His hedge had been placed too soon relative to the cash price, but it was his only option. He knew he could not have waited to see if the market would hold. He had to have the coverage in case the market collapsed further. Luke leaned back; he knew the variance would ultimately narrow, and his losses would be around $7 million.

Luke's face was pale, but Nancy Washburn was buried in her thoughts as she stormed into his office and began unraveling, "I don't know how much money we have. I haven't known for a while. Cindy hasn't been telling us when we receive wires from selling loans and bonds. I don't know how much she is depositing to fund the new loan closings. I don't know the balance because I don't know all of the transactions," she heaved and gasped. "It has been this way for the past few weeks. I don't know what's been coming into our general account. I transfer money to the branches to cover the loan closings, but I don't know how much is in the main account. I give her the closings each day, but I'm not getting the deposit confirmations. I tell her which settlements we are supposed to get, but I don't get a confirmation we received the wire. I thought she would send the info, and then you were out of town and now…" She was finally out of breath and did not finish.

"How much money do you think we have?"

"I'm not sure. I don't know what they've done. I don't know how much she has deposited for advances. I just know she doesn't do it every day. The same thing for loan sales. I don't know what has come in, so I don't know what to pay off. They must be putting some money in the account because they haven't said we're overdrawn." Her shoulders drew up in a question.

Luke knew the company's general account should be fine now but would begin burning cash as the new loans were sold at a loss. "So, how many transactions are you missing?"

"I don't know. I don't know what I'm missing." She twisted her strawberry hair around a pencil.

Malson had always provided a daily summary of wires received from loan sales. Nancy would reconcile the wires to ensure the right amount had been received and then identify which Malson advances were to be repaid. Cindy had stopped sending the daily summary. Since Nancy did not get the wire notices, no reconciliations had been done, and advances had not been paid off. Cindy had not noticed.

Previously, the bank verbally confirmed each day the amount advanced to FRM for new loan closings. Nancy would then transfer money to the branch accounts to fund the closings. Since Cindy no longer advanced daily and no longer called to give the amount of the deposit, Nancy had no way of knowing how much money had been put into the general account. Random deposits were going into the general account without notification and without being verified or reconciled.

Luke knew they had to ballpark a number and get the information quickly. He asked Nancy to have Cindy fax a record of transactions. Luke acted calm, and Nancy was flustered but appeared to settle with Luke's instructions. The missed margin call seemed to escape her. He spared her the magnitude of the marketing losses that were coming.

Luke started, "Well, we sent a wire to Stiller Stevens for the sixty thousand dollars. We already had over five hundred thousand with them for previous margins. Call John Elliott, and have three hundred fifty thousand sent back to us. That should bring in some cash." Nancy smiled at the thought of being able to write a deposit into her ledger. Then Luke became concerned the market might whipsaw, suddenly run back up in response to the steep decline, and require a significant margin call. He didn't really know his cash position, and he no longer trusted Malson to transfer money on request. "On second thought, let's transfer back a hundred thousand and leave the rest up there." The difference didn't seem to matter to Nancy. She seemed pleased with the thought of cash coming in and left with a smile.

Luke glanced outside without seeing the morning sky. He dropped his eyes, stared at face level, and calculated. Luke didn't see the stream of FRM employees walking by his windows and watching him stare. His eyes were fixed and the numbers were etched in his head. FRM had lost around $7 million and was going to be short $5 million in cash when all of the pending applications closed. The loan applications would close within the next sixty days, but Luke knew the company would be out of cash within a few weeks. He had to get Malson to pay for the losses.

CHAPTER TWENTY ONE

The day had been brutal, but Luke's engine pounded as he walked into Jimmy's Seafood to meet Chuck Rail. He had a vague negative memory of his only previous visit. The restaurant, located in an aging shopping center, was one of Chuck's favorites. Jimmy's had an old-money clientele, deep red walls, lowly lit sconces, and heavy baroque drapery. The faint light forced Luke to squint as he entered even though the sun was setting outside. He glanced and saw Chuck sitting at the dark bar with intermittent light from overhead spots and the slight glimmering of the brass railing. Chuck finished a sip of his martini and placed it lightly on the bar. The ice shards shimmered opaquely as the olive, cloaking pimento, danced in the glass.

"Hi there, Big Boy," Chuck started with a broad smile.

"Hello, Chuck," Luke responded flatly and noted Chuck's confidence.

"Have a martini." Chuck's teeth flashed at the end of the word.

"Don't drink them." Luke looked behind the bar. "Now isn't the time for a Perfect Rob Roy," he thought. "Maybe some wine with dinner," he said.

Chuck was jubilant about his trip with Cindy, giving Luke all the details of the sights, the dinners, the sex, and how much money Cindy had. Somewhere during the stories, Luke finally ordered a glass of wine; he rarely spoke as Chuck relished in the recounting. Chuck nodded for a second martini, and Luke mentioned getting a table. Within moments they were led through the drapery and into the dining room, framed with paintings of light oval faces in black borders lit with a single bulb better suited for night reading. Luke motioned to a table farther from the others. Chuck leaned comfortably into his chair and fingered the huge, leather-bound menu.

"Why wasn't the wire sent last week?" Luke started.

Chuck's eyes peered over the menu and then dropped to resume his perusal of the fare before replying, "You know, you expect a lot of people. We have lots of customers. We can't always be focused on one person. Cindy was busy, and the wire didn't get sent. We took care of it yesterday though."

"Chuck, why didn't anyone send the wire? Nancy called Cindy on Wednesday and Thursday. I called you Wednesday and Thursday, and it didn't happen. I called Sid Friday, and he couldn't send a wire. Bivins never called me back."

"Look, we were busy trying to get out of town. We had to low-key the whole trip. No one could know we were together. Employees in the bank—that sort of thing. Sid's not in the department anymore. And Bivins? He's president of the bank. He can't get involved every time you need something. You never call the guy; then you expect him to drop everything for a special request. Don't call him like that."

"I wasn't trying to go over your head. I needed the wire sent."

"Don't worry about going over my head. Bivins loves me. He knows everything." There was a long pause as Chuck caught Luke's stare. Chuck's eyes darted to the side, dropped for a second, and came up on the other side. He began talking without looking at Luke. "Bivins is going to grow the bank, and he knows I'm going to help him."

Luke opted to change directions. "How does Malson continue to buy banks and dodge all the losses? Everyone else is in trouble."

"We know what we're doing. Bivins is buying smart. The bank will grow and become a regional player. As nationwide banking opens, we will sell out to a New York bank. We will all make plenty on the stock. You might be president someday. Our stock is at twenty-one dollars plus, and it could double in the next year."

"I don't want to be president, and I don't want to sell." Luke shook his head emphatically. "I have a lot of people to think about. I can't bail on them."

"Sure you can. We'll hire some of them. You and I both know you have some good people. You just pay them too much. They'll adapt."

"I can't do that." Luke paused. "Chuck, we lost seven million dollars or more when the margin call didn't get made. We're still counting. Cindy apparently quit telling Nancy about the daily transfers weeks ago, so we're not sure when and if they are being made. We've called Cindy to have her fax summaries since the last bank statement, but we don't have them. We're not sure where we are." He paused as the waiter arrived.

Chuck ordered only after probing for the freshest items. Luke ordered quickly and was set to resume, but Chuck spoke first. "We know you got hit. Heck, we got hit on the bonds the bank owns. So you lost a few dollars. You're still a rich man."

"I don't think you are hearing me. We lost around seven million dollars, maybe more."

"Ouch. I didn't know it was that much." He paused as if the number was sinking in, but he rapidly recovered. "So, you're worth three million or so," Chuck said, shooting a low value. "That's still a pretty good price. And Bivins is still ready to buy."

"Bivins knows we took a loss?"

"Sure. How could he not know? Don't be an amateur. The markets got hit."

Luke took a deep breath. "I don't have that kind of cash."

"Sure you do. You can sell some servicing; raise your cash. What's it worth?"

"It's selling for around two-point-five percent and will go higher since the market moved."

"Wow. That's more than I thought." Chuck paused for a second. "Let's say a flat two percent for round numbers." Chuck paused again. "Now, you can sell some servicing to raise cash and go on, but why do that? Let's talk about taking a deal to Bivins. You can still get around three million dollars, and that's a lot of money. Face it. You've relied on us to be there every day to take care of your wires and transferring your money. Then we all go upstairs and have to explain how this kid is making millions, borrowing money from us, and doing something we should be able to do. That doesn't look good."

"You're a bank. That's what you're supposed to do. I provide deposits, a lot of free deposits, and I pay good interest. That's what's supposed to happen. People put money in your bank, and you make loans."

Chuck smiled wryly. "Really," he said and smirked. "That's how it works? Well, you have counted on having easy access to capital every day. That's not going to be possible forever. It's our capital. We're giving you the money to finance your business. You have the chance to make a lot of money, and you seem to be caught up in platitudes and visions of how things should be. Come on, Big Boy. You're still a rich man. Look, we are not liable for your losses. Don't even think about that. You know you will never get anywhere in this town with that approach. We have the connections. You don't have the politics. Where are you going to get a credit line, and how are you going to run your business? You'll lose everything and get nothing. We need to talk to Bivins about a deal, or you need to cover your losses and cut back your operation."

"Your capital? It's not your money. It's your depositors' money. Chuck, I lost seven million dollars, maybe more. Doesn't that bother you as a lender?"

"No," Chuck said nonchalantly. "You lost, not us." He sliced a piece of fish and took a bite as Luke stared in disbelief, watching him chew. Chuck continued, "Bivins doesn't have to loan you money. We don't have to loan anyone money. It's our money." Chuck took a sip and lowered the glass only halfway. "It's business. You pledged collateral, and I secured it. I can't go wrong."

Luke sat in silence and watched Chuck eat. He was shocked when Chuck had said it was their money. He knew Chuck was wrong about securing the collateral. Malson had only the closed mortgage inventory as collateral and the value changed constantly. None of FRM's stock or the servicing was pledged to secure the loan, but Luke had personally guaranteed $5 million of the FRM line of credit. Luke sifted through the maze. The losses would make FRM insolvent and Malson could call the loan. Luke could sue, but FRM would be out of business.

Luke watched as Chuck bragged about some of the bank's recent moves and downgraded a few of its customers. A few words registered, but Luke mostly watched. "Idiots," Chuck said, referring to Tremble Mortgage. Luke drifted during Chuck's monologue and tried to focus on options. He watched Chuck savoring the catch of the day, unconcerned. Luke had the information he needed for now.

Chuck waxed again about the trip and Cindy's old-money connections. Luke nodded without listening, pushed his knife and fork into the center of his barely touched entrée, sipped only a taste of the wine, and waited for the next pause. He begged off Chuck's suggestion for after-dinner drinks without displaying his shock. Chuck quickly grabbed the dinner tab, saying, "This one's on the bank."

They walked together toward the exit, and Chuck stopped at the bar entrance. "Think about it. Get some quotes for the loan servicing. Bring us the quote, and let that be the starting point in getting a value for the company. Don't worry about your people. You know we want to hire the good ones. At first the money may seem different, but over time they won't know the difference. People adjust."

"Short memories, eh," Luke replied distantly as Chuck nodded.

Chuck reached for the white bar phone as Luke reached for the door. Luke did not ask whom Chuck was calling; his thoughts scattered as he was engulfed in night air. Chuck's cockiness and lack of concern had caught him totally off guard.

Chuck's words rang in his ears: "Access to capital." He had heard the words from Bivins before and thought them strange. Capital had meant bonds to Luke, the ability to sell mortgages on the secondary market. Suddenly, Luke knew Bivins and Chuck Rail were using the term to describe working capital, lines of credit, and the financing to run the business. Luke recalled the one- and two-day delays in depositing advances from the line of credit, glitches in sending wires, and delays in renewing the line of credit. Did Bivins and Chuck know about FCBA? Had Pete Winston called Malson for a reference? He struggled to remember Bivins's words, "How will you continue your business without access to capital?"

"Was that how he said it?" Luke wondered out loud over the drone of the radio he did not hear. His mind raced under the streetlights, as the car slowly traced the right lane and cars whizzed by. He knew he could not go to battle with Malson now. A legal battle would be costly, and any judgment would come years later after FRM had been driven out of business. He knew he needed a plan. He knew he had to sell servicing and have Nancy verify the transactions in the general account.

He polished off the remainder of the drive and finished the book of the Sioux and Lakota Indians' futile fight to save their civilization. His mind painted visions of the captured Indians confined to small cabins under the US Cavalry's supervision, reliant on sacks of government allotted food, and staring at beckoning horizons they had once roamed and dreams they had once lived. Between short spells of sleep, he stared at the devilish red numbers on the clock.

CHAPTER TWENTY TWO

Sunshine and blue sky always brightened Luke's mood. He did not see either the next morning. He sensed only a glare and felt the fatigue of the restless nights. He settled into his chair and reached for the report of the servicing portfolio. Luke knew the value of his servicing had probably jumped above 2.5 percent with the market's move, even though Chuck always quoted 2 percent. That was the loan value FCBA had used, and he now knew Malson hoped to buy FRM cheap, paying a discounted price for the servicing and paying nothing for the value of the operations. Luke knew the company was worth much more, but Luke did not intend to sell the company and surely not to Malson.

Luke's pen circled pools of servicing to be sold. Surely rates would decline in the coming months, he concluded. He believed the interest rate movement was a whipsaw, ratcheting interest rates up and then down, producing the volatility traders loved and lived by, and rates would decline with the weak economy. He had selected more than half of FRM's portfolio before he had enough to cover the losses.

Luke called Harold Rhoden into this office and waited until he was seated. "Here's the deal. Malson didn't send the margin money last week. Our futures position was closed, and we lost our coverage. We are going to take a hit of around seven million dollars as we market these loans."

Harold's face fell flat; he wiped at an imaginary Fu Manchu and stuttered before he spoke. "What are you going to do? Are we honoring the quotes on the deals waiting to close?"

"We quoted it; we'll live with it."

Harold seemed relieved. "Well, that will keep business coming."

Luke smirked. "Things are going to be tough for the next few weeks. Maybe you can come spend your time here. No trips to Oklahoma City."

"Sure. I've been seeing someone, so that's not a problem."

"How about putting Mike in charge of everything over there?" Mike Eckridge had effectively been running the Oklahoma City production offices for months.

"He can do it." Harold seemed relieved.

"Let's do that then. That'll let you focus on shipping and my next problem: Nancy's lost track of the banking transactions. It's been happening for a while. She needs your help." Luke was thinking as he spoke. "Let's get Nancy in here, so we can go over a few things." Luke buzzed her on the intercom and sat quietly before he spoke again. "Your friend you're seeing—anyone I know?" he asked Harold.

Harold smiled. "I hope not." It was Luke's one smile of the day.

Nancy breezed into the room at full stride with a legal pad and pen. Luke handed the circled servicing portfolio report to Harold and waited as Nancy settled on the sofa. "We're going to sell some servicing. I've marked the pools to be sold. I'll need this fast, so we can get it to some brokers and attract bids. I need both of you to work on this."

Both Harold and Nancy silently nodded. Neither spoke.

"OK. As for Malson, Nancy, we have to figure out what is happening with cash. Harold, you have to help her. Call Cindy Cleugh and get some sort of record for daily transactions, cash going into and out of the accounts. We have to verify we received money on the loan advances from the bank and the loan sales."

"Have you talked to Chuck?" Harold asked.

"Oh, yeah."

"And?" Harold twitched.

"Chuck knows where we are and how we got here." Luke paused. "The new computer system…" Luke stopped. "We need to put that off. Let's see…" He recalibrated. "OK, let's reset the installation for October. It's got to be after the audit. Harold, give them a call and reset the date."

"Do we need to pay them an additional fee?" Harold asked.

"No way. We're paying two hundred seventy-five thousand dollars, and we've already deposited half of that. The delay shouldn't cause them a problem."

"I'll check." Harold showed apprehension.

"Set it for October," Luke restated for emphasis. "So, let's see what we can get done." As Harold and Nancy sprang to their feet, Luke sighed, "And thanks."

Luke sat calculating. Malson had no intention of paying for the losses. He knew it would be ninety days before the servicing sale closed, and FRM would run out of cash before then. He recalled the dinner conversation. Chuck had flatly stated one option was to sell the servicing and cover the losses. Chuck did not appear to have any urgency or understand how the cash worked. Cindy certainly had no idea. A direct assault on Malson would end up in a lawsuit and FRM closing. Luke decided to sit quietly in the trap, sell the servicing, get a new line with FCBA, and then sue Malson.

Luke knew he had to bring Pete Winston up to date. "I want to be up front. We got creamed last week. Malson didn't send a margin wire. I didn't know since I was in LA, and our position was closed Thursday before the market moved. We have taken some huge losses; I have to sell some servicing to get us back on our feet."

"Horowitz blew up everything. People say his firm got short the day ahead of the announcement."

"Probably. We were covered, but when the margin wire wasn't sent, we were exposed."

"What do they say? Why didn't they send the money?" Pete waited.

"We made several calls, and they said they would send it. But they didn't."

"How much of a hit did you take?"

Luke took a breath. "Around seven million dollars."

"Oh." Pete exhaled. "Will they make good?" His voice hinted he already knew the answer, so he continued. "Are you suing?"

"The loan officer left town and apparently forgot to send it. That's their story. I don't know what really happened. We called them Wednesday and Thursday and they said they would do it. Frankly, I don't know what's going on with them." Luke paused. "If I can sell the servicing before the end of our fiscal year, we will still show a profit and have enough cash and net worth, if you will still approve us. Then I'll deal with them."

Within the hour, Pete called again and told Luke FCBA was still interested in talking once the servicing had been sold and new financial statements were ready.

Luke stared thinking. The servicing sale had to close before June 30. The audited financials would be dated as of June 30 but would not be ready until mid-August at the earliest. The Malson line of credit expired in September. That only left Luke with a tight window of around forty-five days to get a line approved and closed with FCBA. Luke finally saw Andrea staring at him. She raised a stack of pink message slips and he waved her into his office.

The servicing brokers were responsive and a bid date was set. Within two weeks, Socoast Savings and Loan in Mississippi submitted a bid of 2.72 percent. A mid-June closing was set, the contracts were signed, and Socoast made a deposit with the broker.

If the sale closed before June 30, Luke still had a chance of moving to FCBA. If the sale closed after June 30, the audited statements would show a loss, killing the FCBA deal, and putting FRM below the Department of Housing and Urban Development (HUD) minimum net worth requirement. Without HUD approval, FRM was out of business.

While the servicing bid process went smoothly, the Malson cash reconciliation was a growing disaster. Millions of dollars were flowing through the general account without detail. Deposits were piecemealed irregularly and not grouped by a day's activity. Deposits were being made only every few days regardless of FRM's requests. Nancy said Cindy had complained the process took too much time and there was plenty of money in the account. The bank statement showed only a dollar amount of the deposit without a memo tying the amount to any group of loans. The previously simple process had become a maze.

The once constant calls from Cindy were a memory. Nancy and Harold struggled to reach her, and she seemed unconcerned and deferred all requests to an indifferent clerk. The clerk faxed activity ledgers with dates and amounts, but no other details. The ledgers presented a puzzle of finding what combination of transactions would fit what combination of loans.

Nancy set up spreadsheets on oversized green ledgers, trying to reconstruct the past and track the new transactions. Her once organized office became littered with curled faxes of blurred numbers, clipped with heavy black binders, tagged with bright yellow and pink sticky tabs, and scarred by large red and green circles. Heaps of daily green-and-white dot-matrix paper bore marks where she tried to trace sales and wires and deposits. Her once straight hair now spun like a nest as she constantly wound the sides.

For the next few months, an eerie silence loomed. Luke had expected a follow-up call to his dinner with Chuck, but none came. Luke quit calling Chuck. He had told Chuck of FRM's losses and presumed he knew servicing was being sold. He was surprised Chuck no longer called and suggested Luke talk with Bivins. He doubted Malson would be renewing the line of credit. He thought Chuck was letting him dangle.

Nancy and Harold punched their calculators but made no progress. FRM closed loans, and Cindy continued the same irregular funding routine. Luke knew FRM should be running out of cash, but Cindy said the balances were fine. Nancy said Cindy was still weeks behind in notifying her about receipt of the loan sales. Luke assumed money from loan sales had to be sitting in the general account.

The stillness and quiet advanced.

CHAPTER TWENTY THREE

For decades, Snickel Fitter, one of the eight largest accounting firms, had been preferred by financial institutions and regulatory agencies. The accounts in the closed banks were insured up to $100,000, but those with bigger balances—bank creditors and shareholders—lost money. Agencies were left red-faced as they distributed their reserves and booked their own losses to shut down institutions they had certified as being solid. Attorneys looked for deep pockets to recover damages for their clients. Plaintiffs and agencies pointed at Snickel Fitter as a defendant with cash and insurance and filed lawsuits. By early May, most regulatory agencies had announced they would no longer accept Snickel Fitter's audited reports.

FRM had always engaged Snickel Fitter and now had to search for a replacement. Leggett Knoiser, a second-tier regional firm, was actively soliciting Snickel Fitter's clients, and after a quick meeting, Luke retained them. Leggett Knoiser noted the HUD September 15 deadline but agreed when Luke insisted on a completion date of August 15. He knew he needed time to move to FCBA before the Malson line of credit expiration date. While a new auditor had been selected, Luke was still on edge. He no longer had accurate financial statements to manage the company.

Some bright moments flickered. Frank Ryan had landed at his new company, Keegan Securities. One of his first moves was to offer better terms to targeted companies; FRM was on the list. In early June, a Keegan Securities broker called and offered a cash bond trading account. Luke could now sell his pipeline of loans into the cash market. He no longer needed to hedge in the futures market, make margin calls, and roll out of the hedges as loans were packaged into bonds.

Around the time of the Keegan Securities call, interest rates started a new decline. The retreat was slow but steady, and Luke knew he was lucky he did not have to manage margin calls. New loan origination business grew. Luke had calculated correctly on the trend of interest rates, but the decline meant the value of the package he had sold to Socoast was declining. He had to be sure the transaction closed at the sales price.

Despite no longer managing margin calls, Luke still had to stay on top of the market. He was always within range of the Telerate machine or a telephone. Luke knew the stress was eating at him. He played tennis rarely, devoted less time to his divorce, and spent even more time at the office. He went for runs close to midnight to be able to sleep. His divorce attorney's bills arrived promptly the first week of the month. More bills came for the real estate appraisals needed for property settlement proceedings. Beth had never made another offer, and Luke had stopped also. He knew once he had the new financials, his next offer would be much lower.

Luke tried to conceal his stress, straining to display the same smile and keeping the dilemma to himself. He attended the same business functions and even added new ones to ensure he was aware of any rumors. He stayed busy to harbor hope, but doubt played with him in the quiet time.

Luke saw the stress's impact on Nancy Washburn and hired two temporary clerks to help. The working mother of two returned in the evenings for a few hours, trying to reconstruct the web of transfers. The stacks of paper grew, as did her frustration. Her husband, a mechanic, questioned why she was inattentive, working late hours, and picking up fast food. He brought the children to the office in the evenings for the first few weeks but tired of watching Harold and Nancy calling out names and keying calculators until long rolls of tape snaked on the floor and were gleefully ripped and carried as streamers by the skipping children.

Nancy Washburn tried, but the challenge was over her head; her best estimates were two months old and had limited value. She complained Harold Rhoden was not a good helper. Cindy's random transfer system had exposed a weakness. Luke needed to know where the company stood but was hesitant to hire someone and expose them to the risks and uncertainties of the next ninety days. Luke needed an exceptional talent, and he hoped Wilt Sanders could help him find someone for the job.

CHAPTER TWENTY FOUR

Wilt Sanders was fortyish with slightly thinning black hair, pale skin, a narrow face, and a nervous air. When embarrassed, he would occasionally stutter. He was quiet, compassionate, shy, and brilliant. After college and securing his CPA, Wilt had moved from Missouri to Tulsa and spent ten years with Snickel Fitter, where he had first met Luke through a mutual friend. Wilt had then started a new firm with three other CPAs, long before Snickel Fitter was blacklisted from regulatory audits. Wilt prepared FRM's and Luke's personal taxes. The two had bonded designing tax and corporate structures and challenging each other with history and geography questions.

Luke grabbed the phone with a smile and a brief reprieve from the mounting tension and recalled a spring day when Wilt had brought the tax returns for review and signature. Wilt had slid through the door with his typical quick step, sweeping lightly side to side, and his sheepish smile. Wilt had given Luke the tax returns, sat on the sofa several feet away, and reviewed the returns, quoting numbers precisely, as his eyes darted around the office and glanced out the exterior windows. Each number flowed briskly and firmly in his summary as if he read from a teleprompter, even though he had no copy in front of him. Wilt knew the incomes, the deductions, and the details of each schedule and then made recommendations for structure changes with the tax impact of each. Luke was more than impressed. Wilt concluded nonchalantly as if everyone had this ability and asked politely if Luke would call him a cab.

"Why," Luke had inquired, "how did you get here?"

"I took a taxi. My car is in the shop."

"Where are you going?" Luke had asked.

"Downtown," Wilt had responded.

"I'll take you," Luke had offered. Wilt had refused several times, but Luke insisted, and Wilt had finally conceded.

Wilt blushed as he slid into the Mercedes. "My car's not in the shop. I lied."

"Where is it?"

"I don't know." Wilt had answered.

"You don't know?"

"I don't know. I don't know where I left it. I was in a hurry and parked in a different parking garage downtown than I usually do. I can't remember which one."

"Well, let's look for it," Luke had offered. "Was this last night?"

"No, uh…" Wilt hesitated. "It was about a week ago."

Both had burst into laughter, gained composure for a moment, glanced at each other, and then laughed again. Luke had again asked to help Wilt find his car, but Wilt had another appointment.

Luke smiled to himself, recalling the story, dialed Wilt's number and quickly passed through the receptionist.

"Hi, Luke," Wilt answered. "How's it going? I was going to call you."

"What's going on?" Luke asked.

"I'm leaving the firm."

"Really? When? Why?"

"Oh, I don't like managing people. I just want to do some consulting. I will still do taxes and things, but I don't want to be tied down."

"Let's talk."

"Lunch?" Wilt asked.

"I can't today. Maybe you can come by late or something?" Luke asked.

"How late?"

"I'll be here," Luke replied.

"OK. I'll be there after hours," Wilt answered.

The office staff had only slightly thinned. Luke sat reviewing marketing reports when he heard the carpet whistle at the door.

"Sorry I'm late," Wilt opened as he entered.

"Not a problem," Luke replied. "I'm here for a while."

"What's going on?" Wilt looked through the glass panes. Almost half the staff was still there, and the sound of typewriters and rustling papers sounded like the middle of the day.

Luke shook Wilt's hand and walked past him to shut the door. "Do I have a deal for you…" Luke said as Wilt eased himself onto the sofa. Luke dropped into his customary side chair.

"That bad?" Wilt smiled.

"That bad," Luke breathed. "Look, I need someone desperately. But I can't hire anyone full time. I don't know that I have a full-time job." Luke paused. "Actually, I don't know how long they would have the job. I called you today to ask if you knew someone who could help us, but if you are available, I would love to find a way to bring you into the company."

"Oh, oh…" Wilt's head shook. "I don't know."

"Don't turn me down yet." Luke smiled. "You haven't heard the worst part. It's much worse than you think." They both laughed. It was the last light moment as Luke narrated the missed wires, missed margin call, staggering losses, and the quagmire. Luke watched closely as Wilt hung onto each word; his social nervousness faded seamlessly into concern and understanding.

"You don't know where you are." Wilt shook his head. "How could you?"

"I know we're in trouble. We are in default on the loan agreement and Malson could cut us off at any time. We would obviously sue them, but we would be out of business as soon as we lost the credit line, and these people would be out of jobs. I had to sell servicing, and it has to close by June 30 to get a clean audit and keep our approval with HUD, or we're out of business. The auditors will be able to give me accurate numbers as of June 30, but I won't have their report before the middle of August. Once I have a clean audit, I know I can go forward as long as Malson doesn't pull the line of credit. Then I could safely bring someone in full time. In the interim, I need someone to help me get the numbers under control." Luke had intentionally omitted his talks with FCBA. Both paused as Luke cocked his head slightly and breathed. "What do you hear about Malson?"

"Nothing." Wilt shrugged. "They're doing great and expanding."

"I don't know how. It doesn't make sense." Luke sat silently as though sorting through a puzzle. "Anyway, can I talk you into helping me?"

"Of course. It's doesn't make much sense to have me here when the auditors are here. I wouldn't be adding anything. It would be best for me to come in after the audit is complete. That would also let me finish up some stuff at the firm. Then I can help you find someone to run the accounting department."

"How about you?" Luke added. "I mean, if we survive. How about you?"

"Oh, no," Wilt said as he squirmed. "I don't want to manage people."

"Think about it."

"Oh, no. I just like the numbers and doing the work."

"OK. I'm just being greedy."

"I take it as a compliment."

"It is." They both nodded to each other. "How about some pizza? We ordered plenty."

"Oh, no. Thanks." Wilt stood. "I need to run. Who's doing the audit?"

"Leggett Knoiser. We had to change since no one will accept Snickel Fitter."

"It's crazy. One of the largest firms in the country is going down. They had the bank audit market locked up, and now they're being sued on almost every bank that fails. They won't last much longer."

Luke looked through the glass panes. "I don't know how long we will last. I can raise the cash, but without a credit line, the game is over."

"You'll make it." Wilt smiled.

"I hope so." Luke paused. "And I'll need your help."

"Call me when the audit's done or if you need anything else."

The two shook hands, and Wilt retreated through the rear of the building. Within minutes the pizzas arrived, and the staff popped the boxes open and spread the slices on paper towels. Gradually, they returned to work, closed their last files, placed plastic covers on the adding machines and typewriters, and filed out the backdoor. The cleaning crew entered, wrestled with waste-can liners, and rolled sweeper cords. The vacuums' hums filled the air, and one by one, each brightly lit office fell black as the cleaning crew finished, turned off the lights, and moved closer to the rear door. Finally all the office lights had tunneled to blackness except for Luke's and he was alone.

CHAPTER TWENTY FIVE

The waiting wore on Luke. The daily work masked the dilemma, but he knew it was a false sense of security, and he felt the uneasy undercurrent. Even after running, he awoke in the night. FRM could fail at any moment and the angst of waiting for the servicing sale wore on him.

Luke had begun tracking Malson's stock price. The bank traded "over the counter" with a variance between the bid price, the price buyers were willing to pay, and the ask price, the price sellers wanted. A small group controlled most of the shares, so trading was thin with little daily volume. The stock stayed in a tight range of twenty-one dollars to twenty-two dollars. It was like trying to track a star moving through the night air.

Luke recalled Chuck's forecast that the stock would double. Still, Luke could not understand how Malson had dodged the losses hitting other banks and why they were so quiet knowing FRM had taken a hit in the market. He doubted Malson was waiting for him to calculate damages and make a demand. Chuck had threatened him about bringing a law suit. He thought instead Malson was waiting for the renewal date—to gobble up FRM. The company was already in the web. The thoughts careened in front of Luke as the stream of asphalt melted under the slate gray Mercedes.

Luke pulled into the shopping center parking lot, a large Walmart anchored the scene and a row of local retailers lined neatly to one side. The center stood on the outskirts of Tulsa and less than an hour from the lake condo. The white BMW stood out, parked a hiker's walk from the stores. Luke stopped the car, and Ginny glanced at her watch and then stared to denote his tardiness. She paused for another second, grabbed her purse, and slid out of her car.

"About time," she opened with a smiling huff.

"Sorry, I didn't get away as quickly as I hoped."

"That's OK. I'm glad you got away." The afternoon meetings had been erratic and rushed in the past few months. It was even more unusual when he had suggested they go to the lake.

"I actually wanted you to have a chance to do some shopping, so I took my time."

Ginny's eyes darted as she glanced around. "Not here, darling. Not here."

"Oh, OK. I guess we can go then."

The banter continued for a bit and blended into conversation. Luke stole glances as he drove. Her eyes were greener than the summer flora flashing by the car. Her beauty stirred his emotions and yet calmed him. Sunlight cloaked the two through the open sunroof as the air jetted overhead. The anxious nervousness of the servicing sale veiled his thoughts. The closing was a week away, and Luke knew he could do nothing but wait. Ginny was here, and he wanted to talk with her.

Her legs glistened below her yellow shorts. "Great tan," he said, sliding his hand along the svelte curve of her thigh as the car gripped the curves toward the condo.

"You see a tan; you don't touch it." She leaned to his touch and kissed his cheek. She placed her hand on his and stroked it to keep it attached to her thigh.

"When do you need to be back?" Luke asked.

"I can stay late."

"That's good."

Luke pulled the car in front of the condo, and the two held hands down the stairwell to the front entry. Luke unlocked the door and turned as Ginny dropped her purse on the sofa and started toward the stairs leading to the downstairs bedroom.

"Do you want something to drink?" he asked. He opened the drapes, revealing the hue of the lake framed in broad, green oak leaves beyond the upstairs deck.

"Not now," she said, turning on the step. She stood just below him. Her pale blue blouse was opened at the collar and tight at the waist; it danced when she moved.

"Come here." Luke motioned to the sofa. "Let's talk for a minute."

Ginny paused, surprise reflected in her eyes. She moved to the sofa as Luke moved her purse to a chair and slid to the far side away from her. "I need to talk to you about some things."

"Are you pregnant?" she asked.

"Yes."

"OK. I'll marry you," she said and stood.

"Sit down. I want to talk to you about something."

Ginny leaned backed and eagerness rippled across her eyelashes. "OK."

"I don't know how much longer I will be doing what I'm doing," Luke said, stumbling. "Let me start again." He paused. The words weren't coming.

Luke retreated to the stereo and put on a classic jazz album. John Coltrane's saxophone played softly as Luke took a deep breath and returned to the sofa. "Look," he started again, "I want to be sure you know who I am and what's really important to me."

Ginny widened her eyes. "What's going on?"

"Ginny, I'm not the young businessman everyone thinks I am. I think you know that. All I need are three things: my books, my music, and a place to sit."

"Like that ugly sofa you have?"

"Yes. I could even have a 1970s beanbag chair and be happy."

"Need a lava lamp?" She smiled, and suddenly the air was easier.

"No lava lamp, just a beanbag chair." He sighed lightly. "Ginny, I love being with you, and I wonder if we would ever have a chance together. Our time is fantasy time, playtime. I'm not sure you know who I really am."

Ginny almost smirked. "So you think we should get married?"

"I don't know. Look, I will eventually be divorced."

"Not soon."

"Whenever. At some point I'm not going to be Luke the mortgage guy. I was just doing the mortgage thing to pay my way through law school. Halfway through I decided I wanted to start a company. I've told you that. The business is something I wanted to prove…prove the talent in the business rested with the people doing the work and not the old money that owned the company."

"You and your social agenda…" Ginny floated her eyes away.

"Yes. That's important to me. Not the money. I can't see me doing this for much longer. Maybe a couple of years at the most. Maybe not that long. I want to do other things."

"Like what? Practice law?"

"I don't know that I want to practice law. I knew that halfway through law school, but I thought I should go ahead and finish. I don't know what I'll do, but I'll find something interesting and I'll make enough money. If I practiced law, I would be one of those people representing ideas instead of being focused on the money."

"Always wanting to be the rebel…" She looked at him motherly.

"C'mon. I don't need a lot of money. It seems to have come with the deal. You remember when I started this. I told you it wasn't about the money."

Ginny looked at him without expression.

"And I don't need to be the focus of everything. I'm not really that outgoing."

"Oh now, really. You seem rather outgoing to me…and everyone else."

"That's part of who I have to be to build the business, the sales part. I don't like social events; I don't like being in the social scene. I'm not the type to go to galas."

"I like galas."

"I don't. I have never been as lonely as when I have been surrounded by tons of people at some event. I would rather be with a few people I truly know than in a group of people where everyone acts as if they care. That's phony. I don't share myself with anyone but you."

"We don't share everything."

"I know. I can't share everything with you now, and I don't even know if we would be good at it. I guess…I'm wondering if we will ever find out."

"I like parties, social events. I like mixing with people." The room lay quiet, and the notes of the music were more distinct. "I don't want to be alone."

"I've never felt as alone as when I've been places where I think everyone is smiling only for the hope of what they can get. Maybe it's recognition that others want, recognition that someone cares or notices or approves or whatever. That's not me. I am lonely. But there are worse things. I would rather be lonely than be trapped in a bad marriage."

"I want to have friends. I want to be in the right social circles. That's what I want in life." Ginny's lips flowed. "That's what I want for my life."

"You know that's not me."

"You think it's not you, but it is. You say you're doing this for some hippie social agenda or whatever, but you like the attention. What's going on? You're just stressed with work and the divorce. This will pass."

"I don't think so. Ginny, I may not be doing this much longer. Mortgages. My life may change, and when it does, I want you to know who I am and how I feel. I don't care if I lose a lot of money."

"What's going on? Is the divorce really getting close?" Ginny's eyebrows flared.

"In a way, maybe." If Malson pulled the credit line, the company would fail and he would sell the real estate.

"I don't think so. She will never let you go. She's going to hang on forever. And she's going to use the children in every way she can. She knows that's your weakness."

"I know. Still, at some point it's going to happen and then…"

"And then, we'll talk about it." Ginny smiled, pulled her knees onto the sofa, covered the space between them, and draped herself around his neck. Her kiss was warm and deep, and he could smell her soft scent. "You belong to me," she whispered. She kissed him again. He fingered her hair and found her narrow waist. She rested her chin on his head, and Luke kissed her neck. Slowly, Ginny leaned back, opened two more buttons of her blouse, and leaned toward him. Luke kissed her breasts as she cradled his head. Ginny sighed deeply, leaned back, and took his hands. "Upstairs, downstairs, or here?"

Luke watched every step as they moved downstairs and Ginny finished unbuttoning her blouse. He loved to watch her walk, and she floated on staircases. Luke opened the bedroom drapes to expose another broad, green-leaf-framed tableau of the lake. By the time he had turned, Ginny was pulling back the bedspread, her nude beauty drawing him in. Everything vanished into her hair, her eyes, and the tender rhythm of her heart beneath her firm white breasts, beating slowly faster until her green eyes fixed into his and released her deepest, warmest breath and covered him.

CHAPTER TWENTY SIX

Luke often said there were three crises before a deal closed. Buyers and sellers twisted through these before finally getting the deed or the check they wanted. Luke had heard their anguish. He had been through the same ride in his personal transactions, but he was always detached by his mantra: it was just one deal, and there would always be another. The servicing sale did not fit Luke's philosophy. This was the only deal, and this deal had to close.

Luke had watched the declining rates—good for new business, but bad for the higher interest rate servicing he had sold. As rates moved lower, owners were more likely to refinance, paying off the mortgages early and terminating the servicing income. The value of the servicing was dropping along with interest rates. Yet, the buyer, Socoast Savings and Loan, had not raised any issues and the closing was now three days away.

Luke was pensive as he walked into the office on Monday. He was already fully abreast of the bond market as he slid into his chair and swiveled toward the screen. He bent to slide the marketing reports from his briefcase and heard Andrea's voice, "Joe Conti, for you."

Luke recognized the name of the New York broker for the servicing sale. "OK," he said to Andrea. He picked up the line and said, "This is Luke," and leaned back.

"Luke, Joe Conti. Wanted you to know we got a fax this morning from Socoast Savings saying you missed some deadlines, and they are cancelling the contract."

"What deadline?"

"They say they had been waiting for some delinquency schedules. Your people sent some but not all. They have the right to cancel if you fail to provide the information, and they have given us the required notice."

"How much do they want to cut the price?"

"They're not asking for a reduction. They're cancelling the contract. They have put me on notice and want their deposit refunded."

"Not going to happen," Luke calmly stated as he grabbed the folder and thumbed through the contract. "We supplied the documents. They know rates are down; they think values are lower, and they want either a better deal from me or from someone else. Have you faxed me a copy of their letter?"

"I wanted to call you first. I can fax it right away."

"Please do." Luke took a breath. "I will be sending you a notification of their breach and put you on notice to hold the deposit. Either they close, or we are going to claim the three-hundred-eighty-thousand-dollar deposit."

"I have to release the money," Conti replied.

"Now..." Luke was still thinking. "Do they want a reduction? Is that the deal?"

"They've told me to look for other packages. They're gone."

"No, they're not. They're going to get sued."

"They want the deposit."

"C'mon, Joe. Now that I think about it, you're probably going to get sued to ensure you don't release the money. If you give it to them, you are going to be held liable for that part, if not more."

"Don't threaten me."

"It's not a threat. You know that. You can probably pay the money into the court and let Socoast and FRM duke it out. If you don't, then I have to assume you're in bed with them."

"I'm calling as a courtesy to let you know what I have to do, and you're trying to threaten me. It's not my fault they walked. Your guy never sent them the reports."

Luke was getting mad. Conti had no way of knowing what had been sent; his posturing told Luke that Socoast Savings must have plans to buy lots of servicing, and Conti viewed FRM as a onetime deal. "We sent them the stuff. Please send me their letter. Ours will follow. Don't let that money go." Luke took a deep breath. "Are you in this with them? Is this your idea they can now get a better deal?"

Conti almost squealed, "How dare you!" The rest blended into a stream that Luke let slide as he walked to the phone beside the sofa, covered the receiver in his hand, and paged Harold Rhoden on the intercom of the other phone.

When Conti stopped for air, Luke interrupted. "How many times did you tell them they would have to forfeit the deposit to me?"

Conti was silent for a second and then shot back, "You didn't send the schedules."

"How do you know? You don't. Sounds like you love them more than me. Here's the deal. I am going to sue them for a lot more than the deposit. I don't want to sue you. If my attorney says we have to sue you to freeze the deposit, we will. I'm not mad at you now, but you're getting there. These guys are not taking a free walk."

"Understood." The line was quiet. "I don't like you accusing me of being on their side. They are just using their cancellation rights under the contract."

"Hold it!" Luke stood and saw Harold Rhoden stop at the door and flinch from the anger in Luke's voice. Luke's fingers shuffled through the contract, looking for the remedies for a breach of the agreement. "Why don't I hear you saying they are trying to walk because interest rates are down and values are softening for this package? Didn't hear you say that once. Why am I not hearing how hard you tried to keep the deal together? Why I am not hearing how you told them the deposit was going to be frozen? You sound like you are on their side. I keep hearing their side of this. I haven't heard much that sounded neutral.

"There it is," he mumbled to himself before talking to Conti again. "We have the right to put you on notice regarding the deposit. I see that in the contract. They may be bigger, but I am madder. And we will sue Socoast Savings and anyone taking their side."

"OK. OK. Calm down. The fax is on the way. You have a response time in the contract, and we won't do anything so long as we hear from you in that period."

"That's much better, Joe. And we will want acknowledgment of our notice."

"OK. I can do that when it is received."

"Thanks."

"Read the letter. Get back to me. Let me know what's going on."

"You will hear from us today."

"And Luke, if you want us to remarket this package, we would love to do it."

Luke softened his voice. "So, we're still dating?"

"This isn't our doing."

"Wasn't mine either. We'll talk later."

Luke hung up and motioned a wide-eyed Harold to come in.

"What's going on?" Harold asked.

"Conti is sending us a fax. Socoast Savings is backing out of the deal. Do you mind seeing if we have the fax?"

Harold's face dropped. "Sure."

Luke tried to collect his thoughts as Harold vanished around the corner. Within seconds Harold returned, reading as he walked. "They said they had everything they needed. They just wanted some follow-up information." Harold handed it to Luke.

"When was that?" Luke asked.

"Last week. The guy said there was no rush."

"Probably trying to set us up to claim we breached the agreement. But that's not the real reason. The value of that servicing has probably dropped with interest rates falling. They're going somewhere else, but they're not getting the deposit back."

"What do we do?"

"Sue them and get a new buyer."

"How long does that take?"

"Suing them will take years."

"I mean the new buyer."

"Another two or three months." Luke breathed deeply as neither spoke. There was not enough time to get a new buyer, get audited financials, and move to FCBA.

"Any way to get these guys to close?" Harold asked.

"I'll try, but Conti says no. Start getting the info together again."

"Are we sending it to Conti?"

"Probably. We'll send them to three brokers and see who steps up. Let's include the same loans, so we will be able to show the variance in price for the lawsuit. Wait." Luke paused and wondered if the new price would be enough. "OK, let's include the same loans."

"OK." Harold stared at Luke for a second, waiting to see if he would say anything else. Finally, he stood and turned toward the door. "OK."

"OK," Luke mumbled. "Guess I'll find us a lawyer."

FRM had seven days to claim the deposit, so there was time to find an attorney. Nonetheless, Luke handwrote a letter and had Andrea type it and then fax it to Conti. He attended his regular routine and flipped through the Yellow Pages, reviewing Tulsa law firms. The only attorneys Luke had ever hired were for his divorce and to incorporate FRM. If the servicing sale did not close, he needed someone who could sue Socoast Savings and help negotiate with Malson. He needed a firm with experience in finance and plaintiff's litigation; additionally, the firm could not represent Malson or one of the other large banks. The choices were narrow. The name Morton-Ingles was familiar. He had heard good things about Jake Ingles.

Conti sent a fax acknowledging receipt. Luke called quickly, "Find out what they want. Let me know what it takes to do this. I'm not saying we'll do it, but we'll listen."

Conti agreed but gave Luke little hope. Several hours later, he called Luke, and his voice was almost a whisper. "I'm sorry. They're moving on."

Luke thanked him for trying. "Harold will be in touch about updating the package. We'll sue them for the difference in sales price and our expenses."

"I'll waive our commission to reduce the damages," Conti said.

"Thanks," Luke chuckled. There was no commission due unless the sale closed, so Conti's waiver was a message to Socoast that Conti wanted no benefit from the suit. Luke was now sure Socoast was buying more than one package from Conti. The facts would come out in the litigation. "You know the drop in rates is the problem. They think the price has declined for this package." The line sat quietly for seconds.

Conti finally spoke. "I'm sorry."

"I am, too. I'm not in the habit of suing people," Luke said flatly.

Luke hung up. Luke had always found a way to resolve issues; his divorce was his first lawsuit. Now he was preparing for his second, and Malson loomed as a third. He called a few people who had mentioned Jake Ingles. The referrals were good. He took only good clients and good cases and went to the courthouse only as a last resort—this was the synopsis. By the end of the day, Luke had left a message for Jake Ingles.

Gradually the staff began filtering through the backdoor. Harold Rhoden drifted in and sat as always in the side chair that faced outside. "So what are we going to do?"

"Sue Socoast."

"What about our HUD approval?"

"Looks like I have to talk to Malson." Harold waited, and Luke continued, "Get a lawyer. Sue Socoast. Find a new buyer for the servicing. Get the June 30 audit done by late August. Get Wilt to track the changes from June 30 to September 1. Close the new servicing sale by the middle of September, so we have the net worth again. Get the auditors to update the financials and include the servicing sale. Get HUD to approve the exception. And get Malson to renew the credit line."

"What do you think?"

"Piece of cake," Luke laughed.

"Really?" Harold's eyes were hopeful.

"I don't think so," Luke said softly. "But, that's the plan. Any thoughts?" Luke asked as he watched the remaining staff going at full speed.

"No," Harold said as he looked outside at the pastels of the early-evening sky.

They sat quietly.

CHAPTER TWENTY SEVEN

Jake Ingles called early the next morning. Luke liked the sound of his voice, casual and professional with no hint of huffiness. Luke was straight to the point. Luke agreed to fax the contract, and Ingles said he would do a review, have an initial meeting, and make recommendations free of charge. Luke was surprised when Ingles said he could be at FRM's office in the afternoon.

Jake Ingles was dressed in gray slacks, blue blazer, and collegiate striped tie and accompanied by two associates. Ingles handled the introductions, and the three settled into the huge sofa. "Spread out," Luke offered, and they scattered on the chairs and sofa, and Luke stayed behind his desk.

Ingles gave a brief summary of the firm: thirty-five attorneys, practicing in commercial litigation, insurance defense, product liability, estates, bankruptcy, and foreclosures. Ingles appeared to be in his late forties. His frame was wide, with a hint of a paunch, and light skin wrinkled on his brow and cheeks. His hair was black and full. He smiled often, genuinely, with none of the hammering bluster plaintiff attorneys often wore to audition toughness. Luke liked Jake Ingles immediately.

"So, looks like these guys breached the agreement. Any clue why?" Ingles asked.

"The value of the servicing has dropped along with interest rates. If the loans are above the market, they pay off quicker, shortening the income stream. The servicer loses the monthly income and the interest-free deposits on the escrow accounts."

"So, the value includes some projection of the life of the loan?"

"Yes. I'm sure they've plugged those projections into their pricing models."

"OK. So how much do you want to sue them for?"

"Dave Winfield money," Luke said, referring to the major league player who had just signed a two-million-dollar contract, a new record.

"Two million," Ingles answered.

"So, you're a baseball fan."

"All sports. I have no problem suing them for two million or more. Couple of issues. We can freeze the money by putting Conti on notice. Your letter was fine. Well written. We'll send a letter from the firm putting Conti and Socoast on notice of the breach. We'll get the three-hundred-eighty-thousand-dollar deposit paid into the court. We'll sue for the full value of the contract plus punitive damages. Sound goods, but the most we can expect is the difference between the contract price and whatever you can sell it for now. So, you'll get the difference, plus interest and your costs. If we can show bad faith on their part, which looks probable, we can get the punitive damages tripling the amount."

"We have already started looking for a new buyer. My guess is three times the difference in the new price will be around two million dollars."

"Good. Now, I typically ask for a contingency fee of thirty percent. Legally you have to pay the filing fees, which would be a couple of hundred dollars. There would be no other up-front expense on your part." Ingles paused. "But, I'm willing to take the case for a twenty-percent contingency fee for a couple of reasons. First, you're in the mortgage business, and we have a foreclosure practice. Our firm would love the opportunity to do some foreclosure work for you." At this, the male associate nodded his head and looked at Luke. "Secondly, I'll file in Tulsa and get the earnest money frozen, but I think Socoast can ultimately get this transferred to Mississippi."

"I knew that was a mistake when I agreed to their jurisdiction, but we were in a hurry to get the deal done."

"Not a problem. Your contract is solid, and it's pretty obvious they made a decision to cut their loss and walk away. Instead of taking a loss on the day of closing by overpaying, they lose the earnest money and put off losing the rest until they are forced to go to trial in a couple of years."

"Everything sounds good, but I don't want to lead you astray. We don't have many foreclosures. Our only foreclosures are on HUD loans."

"Oh. I thought maybe you had some of your own loans like the banks and savings and loans do."

"No, that's a popular misconception. We sell everything. Plus, we have a much lower foreclosure rate than others. It's about one-half of the industry standard and far below the other Oklahoma lenders."

"Wow!" Ingles paused only briefly. "We would still take the case at twenty percent. In reality, we don't think we are the ones who are going to ultimately handle the suit. I think we will end up helping you find a firm in Mississippi. But we can file the suit, get the deposit money paid into the court, and argue jurisdiction."

"But you wouldn't be getting paid for that."

"That's OK. Maybe we get the Mississippi firm to split some of the fee. More importantly, we would like to build a relationship with you. You have a good name in the community. Your company's growth is impressive, as are your offices," Ingles said, turning to look into the interior office. "You're the kind of person and company our firm would like to represent for years to come."

"Thank you. I appreciate that."

"I'm being sincere." Ingles nodded. The two associates seemed less genuine in their nods, but Ingles was the one that mattered to Luke.

"One question," Luke said. "You mentioned foreclosures. Do you represent any banks?"

"Not right now. We do foreclosures for a couple of savings and loans. Honestly, they are some of the smaller ones. We don't do any for Tulsa institutions." Ingles turned to the two associates, who gave negative shrugs.

"That's good," Luke said.

"Just let us know when you want us to start." Ingles smiled.

"Start." Luke grinned and came around the desk and shook hands with Ingles and the two associates. Luke walked the group back to the lobby, exchanged handshakes again, and headed back to find Harold Rhoden and Nancy Washburn waiting in his office.

"Attorneys?" Harold asked.

"Attorneys."

"Leggett Knoiser wants to come by tomorrow," Harold said.

Nancy Washburn's face crinkled. The frustration of trying to track Malson had festered, and she knew the servicing sale had collapsed.

"Good," Luke added nonchalantly. "You guys make the arrangements."

"They want to see where they're going to set up, get a schedule—that sort of thing. They will be back next week to get started," Harold added.

"Good. We need them to get started. They should probably save most of their time for after July 10, so we have the most recent bank statements."

Nancy jumped in, "They want some preliminary numbers. What do I give them?"

"What you have," Luke answered. "They'll figure it out."

"How?" Nancy said.

"I don't know," Luke said. "That's what they do. They have until mid-August." Luke paused. The mid-August date was no longer as critical. The financials were going to show huge losses. Socoast's breach had killed any hope for getting to FCBA. Still, Luke needed lead time to save the HUD approval and negotiate with Malson.

"OK," Harold said. "Well, they'll be here tomorrow morning at ten. We'll set up some space. How long do you think they'll be here?"

"On and off for four weeks, maybe five. They agreed to a flat fee, so the quicker they move, the more they make." Luke turned toward Nancy. "We don't pay them until we get the audited financials. That's the deal. So don't let them bill you early or get a progress billing. Once the new servicing sale closes, we will need them to update the financials." He stopped and thought about the deal he had yet to find.

Nancy curled her hair, and Harold wiped his face.

"OK, we need to move the computer installation again. Looks like…" Luke rolled through the months, "Let's say early November." Harold had already reported the software company was elated to push back the delivery. Their schedule was crammed full with installations of first-generation software.

"I'm sure they'll be OK, but I'll confirm," Harold said.

"Anything for me?" Nancy said, standing.

"No. But thanks for what you're doing. I know it's tough."

"It'll get better." Her jaws clenched into a grin.

The office gradually thinned as the summer's late sun continued to fall. Harold stopped by an hour before dusk to say the new servicing packages had been sent to three brokers and Joe Conti. Within a few minutes, the last of the staff had departed, and Luke noticed he was alone. He looked at the long shadows.

He reached for his briefcase and started toward the exit. He wished he could go pick up the children and take them out for hamburgers. Beth wouldn't allow that. He wished he could call Ginny and go to dinner with her, but that wasn't an option. He thought about the fights with Beth, the affairs, and the way he lived.

He flipped to the back pages of the *Wall Street Journal* and found the bid-ask price of $21½–$21¾. Malson stock almost never moved. He scrolled through the pages of the Telerate but found he had no access to stock quotes. He looked at the cost of that service and decided against adding the expense. He was hungry, and he needed a new book. He ordered a pizza, stopped at the bookstore on the way, and selected a biography of Mary Shelley. He headed home; the car's stereo was silent, and he did not notice.

CHAPTER TWENTY EIGHT

The following morning Luke arrived at the office shortly before nine, as usual. He nodded to Andrea and said, "Good morning." He glanced at the Telerate, eyed the morning sky, and turned to the back pages of the *Wall Street Journal*. He looked at the paper again, pulled a ruler from the drawer, and aligned the Malson symbol with the price to ensure the small print had not sent him astray. The price was right: $17¼–$17½. Malson stock had dropped over four dollars in one day.

Luke leafed hurriedly through the paper looking for an article or announcement regarding Malson. He saw earnings reports for larger and regional banks across the country but none for Malson. There was still time before the meeting with Leggett Knoiser, and he headed out of his office. "I'll be back in ten minutes," he said to Andrea. His stride was long and fast, and his focus so intent he was oblivious to those looking at him. They were accustomed to seeing him leave in the afternoon, after the market closed, and enjoyed speculating whether it was really a business meeting. His departure after having just arrived seemed strange.

Luke drove to a convenience store, slid a quarter in the slot, and pulled out the morning newspaper from the red metal machine. There was nothing in the front section or the business pages. He scoured up and down the columns of each page and then across to make sure he missed nothing. There was no article regarding Malson. The business page had a box devoted to local, over-the-counter stocks. Malson's name was there with the same stock price: $17¼–$17½.

Luke drove back and tossed the newspaper on the coffee table next to the sofa. He glanced again at the Telerate machine. He had several pink messages stacked on his desk. His quick jaunt had thrown him behind schedule. A new set of variables began pulsing through Luke's thoughts. What if Malson was in trouble? What would Luke do if Malson failed?

A few minutes after ten, Harold Rhoden stood at Luke's door and asked where they should meet with the group from Leggett Knoiser.

"We can meet in here for a few minutes. Then you can show them the area you have set up for them."

Soon Harold and Nancy arrived with two brown-clad accountants. Luke recognized the difference between the Snickel Fitter crew and this one. While Snickel Fitter had leaned toward bold colors and contrast, Luke concluded Leggett Knoiser seemed to target the most shades of brown possible in one ensemble. Then again, he thought, Snickel Fitter was being sued by almost every bank regulator, and Leggett Knoiser was picking their bones.

Edgar Dinsen was the head of the Auditing Department. He was tall and chunky and in his late forties. The overflow from his waist covered his belt. He had thick brown hair, thick eyebrows, and a five o'clock shadow even though he had shaved only hours earlier. He introduced Robert White, the head of the audit team. White was also plump but a few years younger than Dinsen. His belt was also hidden. Both wore light- to medium-brown suits, white shirts, striped ties of different shades of brown, brown shoes, and black socks.

Edgar and Robert sat on the sofa. Edgar's hairy calves were exposed between his short socks and tight suit paints as he crossed his legs. Edgar was extremely formal and spoke with a bit of a gurgle. He covered the scope of the audit and the price and expressed confidence in satisfying the August 15 deadline. Edgar said he had a list of items needed to begin the process. Robert White opened a satchel and palmed a stack of papers.

"Let Harold and Nancy go through those with you," Luke interrupted. "They will be the ones putting that together. Besides, they'll want to show you the workspace."

"Of course," Edgar responded, and Mr. White slid the papers back into the case.

"One thing—no, really, a few things I want to point out," Luke continued. "First, our records are a bit of a mess. Malson has not been timely in reporting transfers. The information comes more slowly and with less detail than before; therefore, it takes longer to produce financials. Nancy has done a good job of trying to keep up; she and others have worked long hours, but our records aren't current. You'll need to document the June 30 numbers, and we won't have their raw data until around July 10 or so."

"We can work with that timeframe." Edgar nodded firmly as he spoke.

"Good. Second, we expect we'll have some significant losses for the year. At the same time, we are in the process of selling servicing to make up for the losses. The first buyer is going to breach the contract."

"How do you know that?" Edgar questioned.

"They told us," Luke answered, although he almost laughed at the question. "We will find a new buyer, but the closing will be after June 30. Is there a way to do a footnote or an update?"

"We can't include the value of any servicing you own unless you paid a third party for it. That's a FASB rule—Financial Accounting Standards Board. On the other hand, if you have realized the income from the sale before the release of the audit, we can note the transaction. If it's after the audit, we can do an update."

"Good. Now, how do we update the audit?"

"We would prepare a new report with a new date. We would need to review and verify any other financial results during the period."

"How much of a fee do you need?"

"Not much. Say two thousand. We would only have to review a few months or less."

"OK." Luke nodded to the group. "Let's see how the new sale plays out, but let's plan on doing the update and the additional fee." They all exchanged nods. "A quick question: are you guys going to be the new auditors for Malson?"

"Oh no. They're too big for us. I would guess Craig and Foster, one of the big eight firms will get their work. We've picked up some of Snickel Fitter's smaller accounts."

"Do you know much about Malson?" Luke asked.

"They're big. They look like the strongest bank in the state."

"Wow. That's good." Luke smiled but didn't believe it. "Well, one last thing: schedule your resources for July 10, that's when most of the data will be available. Let Harold and Nancy get you and Mr. White whatever you need."

"Sounds good," Edgar Dinsen said, and Robert White nodded.

The group adjourned. Luke walked them to his door, grabbed the phone messages Andrea held out to him, and headed to his desk. He muttered to himself, "How do you know they're going to breach? I have a fortune-teller!"

Phyllis walked through the door as he slid into his chair. "A meeting here, a meeting there. Oh, aren't we Mr. Important?" She smiled.

"Do I need to talk to you before I return any of these calls?"

"Let me see…" She flipped through the pink slips and displayed a cocky grin. "I think so."

Luke sneaked glances at the Telerate as Phyllis reviewed files. She noticed everything. "I see you got a morning newspaper. Anything up?"

"Wanted to check the baseball scores."

"Yeah. Baseball is boring." With that Phyllis grabbed her files, curled around the door, and swished past his windows. Luke's smile evaporated as he grabbed the telephone and resumed the day. Before he dialed the first number, the direness dug into him. FRM had huge losses. Socoast Savings had walked on the agreement. He still did not have a new buyer, and the HUD approval might be lost. Somehow he needed Malson to renew the line of credit, but now they might be in trouble. Their stock had dropped almost 20 percent in one day. FRM might be out of business within the next ninety days, if not sooner.

It was Wednesday, and Luke called Beth hoping to see the children. The line was busy all day. Late in the afternoon, he drove again to the convenience store and bought the evening newspaper. He again raked over the pages but found no articles on Malson. The stock prices were from the previous day. He drove back to the office but left the newspaper in the car. He worked for a bit, but Beth's line remained busy.

There were still almost two hours of sunlight. He drove to the country club. The parking lot was emptying as most had finished their rounds, and only the stragglers were on the course. He changed into a golf shirt and shorts and took a cart to the range. He was the only one there. His swing was quick—too quick—and his focus blurred. He tried to take the club back slowly, maintain balance, keep his head still, and accelerate through the ball. It wasn't happening. His body jerked as if drawn by an invisible puppeteer. He flailed at a few as hard as he could and tried to get the adrenaline out of system, but it didn't work. He took a few deep breaths, admired the azure summer skies, the pure white clouds scattered thinly, and the sun becoming a bigger orange in descent. Still, his shots were errant and scattered. "Thank God I'm not on the course," Luke thought. Again, he set up. He tried to relax and swing through the ball, but it squealed hard right off the tee—the dreaded shank. He looked around to see if anyone had seen it. He was still alone. Two, three, four, five times in a row, Luke shanked the ball dead right. He walked a few yards up the tee area, walked in circles, and returned. He had not shanked a ball since he was a kid first learning the game. He shanked the next five balls, each leaving the club in the same pattern, rising normally and then taking a hard right turn: the pitchout, the lateral. No one was safe when someone had the shanks. Luke shook his head and thought, "What else could go wrong?" He loaded his bag on the cart and headed down the path to the huge, white brick clubhouse. He made passing small talk without breaking stride to the few drifting out of the men's locker room and toward the black leather chairs of the lounge to settle their bets. He grabbed his suit without changing and headed to the car. His thoughts sprayed like the golf balls. "Tennis and running—that's all for the next few months," he thought. He started the car and pictured the dark condo, a cold slice of pizza, a night of reading the biography of Mary Shelley, and the wait for the morning newspaper. The car phone rang before he reached the black-and-gold gate to the club.

"Where are you?" Ginny asked.

"Leaving the country club."

"Get home," Ginny commanded.

"Where are you?"

"Calling you from pay phones. How long before you get home?"

"I'll see in you fifteen minutes."

"Hurry up."

"Will you be saying that in fifteen minutes?"

"No," Ginny giggled.

"Good." Luke smiled.

CHAPTER TWENTY NINE

uke slid into the parking slot, shut down the engine, bought the morning newspaper from the machine, and retreated to the car. He flipped to the business page and found a full column devoted to Malson bank. The headline celebrated Malson's growth, and paragraph after paragraph reviewed the number of banks added to the fold, the growth of assets, and the promising future. Buried near the bottom lay the announcement Malson had taken a quarterly loss of $89 million. The loss was attributed to a onetime expense for bank acquisition costs and an additional reserve for loan losses as a precaution. The next sentence recapped the operating income Malson had generated, excluding the adjustments. The final two paragraphs restated Malson's positive outlook and strength. Luke thought the article must be a verbatim reprint of a press release. The small box for local stock quotes listed Malson at $17.25–$17.50, no change from the previous day.

Luke headed to the office and snatched the *New York Times*. He found a one-paragraph article on Malson. The article reported the $89 million loss. The article bore none of the glowing praise of

Malson's stability and strength. Luke knew the *New York Times* had culled the Malson press release for the salient facts.

Luke looked again at the local paper. The third paragraph listed Malson's net worth after the loss at $356 million. Luke grabbed his calculator and briskly tapped the buttons. Malson had lost approximately 20 percent of its net worth, equal to the drop in the stock price. The stock price had dropped a day ahead of the announcement. Obviously, some had known to unload the shares before the press release.

Luke folded the newspapers to their first pages, laid them on the coffee table, and looked into the interior office area. He realized he had not said good morning to anyone as he had entered.

The Socoast Savings closing date passed quietly. The date Luke had watched like a child awaiting a birthday now had little meaning except for legal filings. Jake Ingles filed suit, and Conti agreed to pay the deposit into the court. Luke expected the money to sit for years until the suit was resolved. Jake Ingles called regularly giving Luke updates; the more they spoke, the more Luke liked him.

By early July, FRM had received new bids on the servicing package. Interest rates had continued to decline, and Conti again had the highest bidder. Corn Savings of Iowa bid 2.49 percent, but September 24 was the quickest closing date Luke could negotiate. It was still quicker than normal, and none of the other bidders would close sooner. The new price was about $650,000 lower than the Socoast Savings price, and Luke knew it would not cover all of the loss from the missed margin call.

The September 24 closing date was a problem. The HUD approval had to be obtained by September 15. Leggett Knoiser would need time to update the financials. Luke now needed an extension from HUD to allow time to close the sale and get updated audited statements. The extension of time from HUD was problematic. FRM had already received one extension to move its fiscal year date from March 31 to June 30 to install the new computer system. If HUD declined the request, FRM would be out of business during the interim. Losing HUD approval would cause FRM to forfeit all of its servicing rights, and both the $6 million servicing sale and the remaining servicing, worth more than $4 million, would be wiped out.

Calamities and roadblocks raced through Luke's mind. Visions of Malson waiting to snatch the company weaved around him. Luke wanted the servicing-sale money in hand prior to confronting Malson. He wanted to be in a stronger position, but September 24 was too late. Luke knew he had to meet with Malson when he had the audited financials and knew where he stood. Luke's divorce was tethered to FRM's financial problems. No progress could be made until a value was established, and he did not want to publish FRM's predicament. Everything was moored together.

On the evening Luke executed the contract with Corn Savings, he sat alone after everyone had left. He scribbled notes on the canary-yellow pad. The servicing sale would decrease FRM's annual income by $1.2 million. There was no way to keep all of the personnel without suddenly making the company unprofitable.

He stared through the glass panes and mentally walked through the rows and saw the faces of employees: Connie, the loan processor he had hired out of high school when he worked at PCT; Pat Duron, the shipping clerk and single parent; Jenny Jensen, who had two children and had worked with him before FRM and had helped him start the company; and Phyllis, who had once told him, "You can't start a new mortgage company." He thought of the four single mothers who lived in his apartments and paid only half the standard rent.

Luke glanced at his watch. There was a real estate dinner scheduled for the evening. If FRM failed, he would be able to get a divorce. A wry smiled crossed his face. FRM would be gone, and he would merely sell the real estate—but how could he face the employees? His lips dropped. He stood without packing his briefcase, corralled a deep breath, and headed to the meeting.

CHAPTER THIRTY

The call to HUD offices in Washington did not go well. Luke reached Ray Fontenot, the regional manager of compliance. Luke's verbal request for an extension to October 8 was quickly denied. "You've already had an extension," Fontenot answered, without asking why FRM needed more time. "We gave you an extension for your computer system installation. The deadline is September 15."

"That's still a problem," Luke answered. "We've had to delay the installation."

"Doesn't matter," Fontenot responded robotically.

"Can we make a written request for an extension?"

"Sure, but it'll come to me. I'll turn it down. You had an extension."

Luke was nervous. "What happens if we miss the deadline?"

"You will be suspended until we have received audited financials with acceptable net worth."

Luke cringed, expecting the worst. "We are in the process of selling some servicing. We will need the sale included in our net worth. Can the auditors certify as to our net worth after June 30 and after the sale is complete?"

"Yes. But you have to have enough net worth and have the statements here by September 15." Fontenot's voice was detached.

"OK, but what if we are under the net worth level on June 30, but we have a supplemental audit showing we are over the net worth as of September 24?"

The line was silent. "Well." Fontenot was thinking. "That would be nine days too late. There is usually a ten-day grace period before the suspension is done, but I won't guarantee it. You would have to have it here by September 25, but I won't guarantee the grace period. The suspension may be done before then."

"If we are suspended, how long does it take to get reinstated?"

"We have up to sixty days to make a decision."

Luke saw the hemorrhaging of being shut down for months. The servicing would be gone and the company would have to close. "I need a few more days. I think the accountants will need a couple of weeks to update the financials. Can I get a week or so past September 24 to give the accountants some time?"

"No."

"OK. Can I still send a written extension request?"

"If you wish, but I will turn it down."

"I don't want to make you mad."

"It won't." Fontenot's voice remained curt. "You should probably do that to cover your bases with your shareholders."

"I'm the only one," Luke thought. He said OK instead.

The ten-day grace period was still too tight and too tenuous. Luke doubted he could get updated audited statements to HUD one day after the closing, and Fontenot would not guarantee the grace period. Luke could not risk FRM being suspended. He had to confront Malson before the HUD deadline of September 15.

He first needed the numbers from Leggett Knoiser, and then he had to make Malson step up and pay for the losses.

Luke grew more impatient. The bank statements arrived by July 10, but a week later Leggett Knoiser had still failed to move in the full audit team. One accountant came sporadically and stayed only a few hours. Edgar Dinsen blamed the influx of new clients for the delay but assured Luke the deadline would be met.

Luke grabbed the telephone. "Wilt," he began. "Hey, this is driving me nuts. We didn't get the servicing sold prior to June 30, so our net worth is going to be under the minimum. And Leggett Knoiser is still not here full time."

"What do they say?" Wilt asked.

"Scheduling problems, but they promise they will meet the August 15 deadline."

"They can do it. There's plenty of time."

"So, why don't we get started early? We can pay you as a consultant. We have the June bank statements, so we can let Leggett Knoiser track the stuff up to June 30, and you can start tracking July," Luke offered.

"Does that help?"

"Yes. Can you set something up to track Malson and determine where we are?"

"I can start with a zero balance for everything and track since July 1. Once I have the audited numbers, I can plug them in." Wilt made it sound easy.

"Let's do it. I've already talked to them about updating the financials once the servicing sells."

"When's your computer system getting installed?"

Luke paused. "That's put off for a while, maybe forever."

"Do you want to get a couple of the new IBM personal computers? We could set up spreadsheets on the computer and simplify the process."

"How much are they?"

"Around eight thousand. IBM just released a new model. The firm ordered a couple. They're much better than the older models, and there's new software. We can build some spreadsheets to track loan closings and funds advanced by Malson. You could track loan sales, too. You'll catch on in no time. It won't integrate with the software you're buying, but in the meantime, it can help."

"You're going to have to train some people."

"Oh." Wilt paused. "OK. You'll catch on quickly. It'll probably take a week to get one."

"If it will help, let's do it."

A week later three heavy boxes were delivered. Wilt arrived after hours, and Luke led him to an empty office, where the boxes waited next to scattered stacks of accounting records. Luke left Wilt to tear open the boxes, and within a couple of hours, Wilt had set up the system, loaded the spreadsheet software, and dragged Luke back to test the system. "We can save the data on this," Wilt said, holding a palm-sized black disk. "It's called a 'floppy.'" Wilt waved the thing, so it curved but never folded. "The programs will be saved on the hard drive, but your data will be stored on these." Wilt began showing Luke how to do a spreadsheet.

"Did you get one of these?" Luke asked.

"No, I can't afford it." Wilt looked disappointed. "These things cost as much as a new car."

"You're going to have to do this. I don't have time right now."

"OK. I can teach Nancy, but you'll want to play with it. This would be great for your real estate stuff. Plus, you'll get hooked."

"We looked at a word processor last year, but it was over ten thousand, and all you could do was type documents. It was a fancy typewriter."

"Sure. This is a lot quicker, and now there's some software."

"Yeah," Luke said absently. The new computer occupied half the desk. Luke stood, walked back in front of the desk, and leaned against the wall. "What do you hear about Malson?"

"They took a hit last quarter." Wilt seemed unconcerned.

"Their stock dropped about twenty percent before they announced the loss," Luke added, but Wilt said nothing. "It held steady for the first ten days or so and then dropped suddenly. It's lost another three. It's down to fourteen."

"I haven't paid attention," Wilt said, staring at the computer screen.

"The bigger banks are getting hit. Lowe National is down to nineteen; it used to be around thirty. ANC Bank has dropped from forty to under twenty, and CPT Bank was thirty-five, and now it's seventeen."

Wilt turned. "I didn't know you followed them."

"I don't. Rather, I didn't. I called a broker to see where they were at the start of the year, and I have been watching them lately. Malson has to have some losses."

"They still have a ton of capital."

"I know," Luke said with a shrug.

The room fell silent as Wilt fingered the keyboard. Luke stood and scooted his chair beside the desk. Wilt began, "Let me show you this. You can copy a range and paste it somewhere else."

Fifteen minutes before midnight, Luke and Wilt suddenly noticed the time. Luke tossed the notes he had taken onto his desk, grabbed his suit coat, and saw Wilt waiting for him at the backdoor. "Thanks, man."

"This was fun." Wilt had a big smile.

"Say, can you get us another one of these?"

"I knew you'd want one."

"Nancy needs one. You'll need one when you're here. I may get one later."

"I knew it," Wilt laughed. "You can put your real estate on the system."

"Sure, but I can track the loans in process and the closed loans, too. It will be easier to calculate our marketing position."

"Right." Wilt's eyes could not get wider.

"Can you order another one tomorrow?"

"You bet." Wilt beamed.

CHAPTER THIRTY ONE

The second computer arrived the next week. Leggett Knoiser's staff finally landed and unpacked near the end of July. Soon Nancy, Harold, and the accounting clerks were working triple-duty. In addition to the daily routine, they packaged the servicing reports for Corn Savings and pulled the records requested by the accountants. Wilt came by several nights a week.

"I'm not sure I'm doing you any good," Wilt opened. "This Malson system is…ah…not good."

"You're helping. I trust your numbers. Nancy's under a lot of stress, and I think the job may be bigger than she can handle."

"Maybe…" Wilt was never one to criticize. "She doesn't have much background."

"I know. I thought she could grow into the position," Luke conceded. "Once the auditors are gone, can you show her how to track this on the computer? Teach her a little bit. It's teaching, not managing."

"Sure. I'll do it," Wilt agreed.

Edgar Dinsen came to check on the audit team. Luke was anxious to catch him and invited him into his office. Edgar started the conversation, "I was hoping to talk to you."

Luke took the lead. "And I wanted to talk to you. I don't expect our net worth to be enough for HUD. The first buyer breached the contract, but we have another buyer, Corn Savings of Iowa. It's set to close by September 24. We're going to need you to supplement the audit after the Corn Savings deal closes."

"Oh, we can do that. We verify it closed, see the money transferred, and issue a supplement audit."

"What about the income statement between July 1 and September 24? How do you review that?"

"How much are you selling the servicing for?" Edgar asked.

"Should be over six million after expenses."

"Well, you can't lose that much in two months." Edgar looked unconcerned.

Luke tried to show no facial expression and concluded Leggett Knoiser had not dived deep enough to understand the scope of FRM's losses. "Well, in this business you can." Luke pressed his lips together. "So, what do we do? Wilt Sanders had his own firm for a while. He's helping us computerize some things. Can he help?"

"Sure, he'll know what we need—trial balance, that sort of thing."

"OK. And we talked about this earlier. The fee is two thousand?"

"Yes." Dinsen said eagerly.

Luke thought Dinsen reacted like a door-to-door salesman who had sold extra sweeper attachments. "Put this in your plans. It's important."

"Now," Edgar jumped in, "I have a question for you." He tried to stretch taller on the sofa. "I know I said we could do this by August 15, but we really need some time."

Luke was anxious to know where FRM stood, but the August 15 deadline had been drawn to move to FCBA. That deal was dead. "What do you need?"

"Two more weeks. The first of September should be good."

Luke paused for a minute. The delay would keep him waiting longer and give him less time to confront Malson. It would not have an impact on the HUD approval. Luke paused longer. Why was Malson not calling? He couldn't remember the last time he had talked to Chuck. Malson stock had declined again and now stood slightly above ten dollars per share—a 50 percent drop in two months. He realized he had never answered Edgar. "Sure, that's OK."

"Thanks," Edgar exhaled.

Luke saw Edgar's relief. "Labor Day is coming," Luke cautioned, looking for the calendar.

"That week. That week. We'll have them that week."

"Not that Friday."

"Tuesday or Wednesday." Edgar's head bobbled.

"OK." Luke watched as Edgar's ensemble of brown wrinkles stood and headed back to his team. Luke dropped his eyes and looked at the form letter rejection he had received from HUD. A faded blue signature stamp bore Ray Fontenot's name.

The bulk of Leggett Knoiser's team was gone by mid-August. Thereafter, Robert White or another staff accountant came occasionally, asked Nancy for a few documents, and left. Before the end of August, the visits stopped, and Luke presumed the final review was in process.

Wilt Sanders had the second computer running. Once Leggett Knoiser packed up, Wilt started coming in the afternoon. He coached Nancy on the spreadsheets and taught her the keystrokes. Only a few others still lingered when Wilt walked into Luke's office late one evening. "How's it going?" he started.

"You tell me." Luke's face relaxed.

"You know, this isn't going to solve your problem."

"Wilt, I have more than one problem." They enjoyed a brief laugh.

"Sorry. OK, I don't want to criticize." Wilt fought off a stutter. "I really don't want to criticize, but I think Nancy is in over her head."

"That's my fault. I put her there."

"Well, she means well, but she is not catching on to the computer. And I think"—Wilt paused to select his words carefully—"she has trouble understanding the basic concepts of accounting. She doesn't understand how things fit together. She's chasing numbers."

"I'm not an accountant, so I can relate."

"She feels bad she let it get out of hand. Now, in reality, there was no way for her to keep track of things. You have to have a clean cutoff, and Cindy destroyed that. But she knows she can't handle it." Wilt took a deep breath. "She doesn't want to let you down."

"Is she a good number-two person to back up someone else?"

"I don't think so. She's so frustrated she's ready to quit, but she feels bad about where everything stands."

"Did she quit?"

"No. No. She won't quit until you bring someone else in. She'd be relieved. She's not going anywhere, but she knows the job is more than she can do."

Luke rested silently. "So when do you start?"

"Not me."

"Come on," Luke pretended to plea.

"Not me." Both broke eye contact before Wilt spoke again. "You know, Marie, one of the new clerks, she shows promise. She has the background, and she could be the top assistant, but you need to find a degreed accountant with controller experience."

"What do I tell them? 'You may have a job tomorrow or next week, or you may not?' I can't do that." The room fell silent. "OK, I'll know something within four weeks. Until then, can you keep chasing the numbers? And if we survive, I'll have to find a replacement."

"I don't mind."

"How much to hire you?"

"No." Wilt started to talk but nothing came out. "No. I don't think so." The white BMW drove past the window. Luke caught the car out of the corner of his eye.

"Could you manage with Marie in the second slot instead of Nancy?"

"Don't take this wrong. I don't want the job. I think you need a new person, and I think Marie should be the number two person. Nancy will help with the transition."

"OK. I understand," Luke allowed. "So, how are the daily transfers? Are you able to track Malson?"

"Yeah. It looks like they are advancing within a week, but there's no pattern. It takes a couple of weeks or more for Cindy to send notifications on loan sales. It takes hours to figure it out, and there are always loose ends. I don't think Cindy's very smart." Wilt looked uncomfortable with his comment.

"We used to balance daily before Cindy. We call her Cindy No-Clue." Luke stated as Wilt tried to fight off a laugh. "You know she's Chuck's girlfriend. Do you ever see him?"

"She doesn't sound like his type." Wilt shook his head. "I haven't seen him in a long time. Couple of years. I used to run into him when I was with Snickel Fitter, but I've been gone for—what?—five years or so." A comfortable pause settled. "So, how's your pipeline schedule coming?" Wilt asked.

"It's cool. Really cool. I've played with it a few times, but I still need a cheat sheet to remember the key strokes. Maybe if we get through September, we get another computer, and you can teach someone to track this data."

"That's a deal. I can do that." He glanced through the inside office panes. Everyone was gone. "I guess I need to get going."

"Thanks." Luke stood. "Thanks for everything."

Wilt almost blushed.

Luke headed to his back office, grabbed the rent schedules, hustled to Wilt's area, and flipped on the computer. He began arranging rows and columns and inserting data. He answered each ringing line until she called.

"So you're still there," Ginny started.

"I saw you drive by. Where are you?"

"My sister's. Sorry, I didn't see the other car there; it was blocked by yours."

"Don't worry about it. How long are you out?"

"I have to go home in a little bit."

"What are you doing for Labor Day?" Luke asked.

"We're going to his parents' house in Oklahoma City. Football season is starting, so I'm sure they'll watch every game. His parents have a pool, so I will get one last tan for the season. We'll probably cook out Monday and then drive back. Are you going to the lake?"

"I don't think so. There'll be too many people. I'll stay around here."

"What if I run errands Saturday morning?" Ginny asked.

"I'll be home."

"How about tomorrow? Can you get away?"

"Probably after the market closes—around three o'clock."

"Good. I'll be at your place."

"Ginny…" Luke paused. "Can you get away in two weeks—I mean, get away for the weekend?"

"Oh, I don't know."

"Let's go somewhere."

"Where?" Her voice rose.

"I don't care. We could leave on Friday and be back Sunday."

The line was silent. "I've wanted to visit a friend in Kansas City. I could say I'm going there."

"Good."

"Where are we going?"

"I don't know. I want to spend some time with you." Luke paused and thought about destinations. "Let's go to New York."

"Are you serious?" Ginny almost giggled.

"Can you do it?"

"Yes." Her voice sounded like his question was stupid.

"I'm serious."

"So am I."

"OK. See you tomorrow," Luke said softly.

CHAPTER THIRTY TWO

Luke spent a lost holiday weekend. Beth and the children were with her family. Luke's family lived hundreds of miles away and knew little of his circumstances. He struggled balancing the details of his life without trying to explain them to someone else, so he acted as if everything were normal. The lake and country club would be packed with celebrations of the last weekend of summer. After Ginny's Saturday morning visit, Luke took three long jogs, played in his Sunday-night tennis league, read, and worked at the office.

Tuesday came, and Luke did not expect a call from Edgar Dinsen. Luke's experience had taught him accountants spent time as though it were infinite. Snickel Fitter had always seemed to rush at the last minute. Wilt usually showed up a day or two before the deadline with the tax returns. Dinsen had already missed one deadline. Still, Luke expected Dinsen to deliver the financials on Wednesday.

Malson had usually contacted Luke forty-five days before the renewal date; the expiration was less than thirty days away, and Chuck had never called or asked for financials. Getting the audited statements from Dinsen by Wednesday would give Luke a couple of days to review and to confirm his numbers and cash flow. He planned to set appointments with Jake Ingles and Chuck Rail for Friday or Monday. Then he would take his financials and the Corn Savings contract and hammer out a deal with Malson. Luke expected it would take a couple of weeks to finalize a Malson deal, and he did not want to stew over the weekend. FRM would keep him occupied during the week, and the weekend with Ginny would help him relax.

Ginny called early and asked if Luke could meet in the afternoon. She complained of her weekend but had arranged to get away, and her friend in Kansas City had agreed to cover for her. Luke booked their flights, arranging to meet Ginny in Dallas. Luke usually stayed in the center of the block at the Park Lane Hotel. Instead, he splurged and booked a room at The Plaza.

Dinsen had not called by late Wednesday, so Luke called him but was forced to leave a message. He left another later and three on Thursday until Dinsen finally called in the afternoon. The audited statements were still not ready. Dinsen said he needed to talk to Robert White.

The fuse was burning. Luke continued his routine, but his eyes were constantly drawn to the clock sitting on one of the end tables. He glanced through the long panes and watched the staff. Everything looked so normal, and yet Luke knew differently.

Dinsen called and said Robert White would not be finished until early next week. Luke had already resigned himself to another delay. The pause was long, and Dinsen repeated himself before Luke spoke. Luke kept his calm. He pedantically explained why he needed the financials immediately.

The next morning Dinsen called and apologized for being behind. He blamed the volume of work. He said he had talked to a clerk at HUD, and she had said sometimes it took ten days to process the audited statements, so they might wait until September 25. Luke heard line peeling off the reel and finally Dinsen started his request for more time. Luke shot out of his chair and cut him off, "That's not guaranteed. We are not waiting until September 25." He faced the outside windows, and he shouted the words slowly, "When… will…I…have…them?"

"Next Tuesday." Dinsen's voice barely trickled out.

Luke spent a horrible weekend waiting. He called Dinsen twice on Monday to confirm the Tuesday delivery. Neither call was returned, so he drove to Dinsen's office. Neither Dinsen nor White was there, and Luke left his card and bluffed, saying he would be back in thirty minutes. Dinsen had already called when Luke reached his office. Robert White had finished the drafts. The review committee would complete its work on Tuesday, and Dinsen would deliver the statements Wednesday afternoon.

Dinsen called Tuesday morning and promised Wednesday's appointment was still solid. "Luke, the review committee has finished, and the finals are being prepared," Dinsen started and paused. "You know…these don't look very good."

Luke almost laughed. "What was your first clue?" he wanted to say. He took a breath. "I didn't expect them to look very good, but I need to know what the statements show, so I can deal with it."

"Well…" Dinsen paused again. "OK."

"Two o'clock tomorrow," Luke said before they hung up.

Dinsen showed up promptly. He handed Luke a copy, set a stack on the coffee table, and seated himself on the sofa. Luke stayed behind the desk and flipped through the pages. Dinsen started the review. "You took some large marketing losses." Dinsen started reading income and expense numbers from the income statement.

Luke ignored Dinsen's voice and bored straight to the bottom-line. FRM had lost $6.9 million dollars. He stared at the number. He had hoped operating income would have lowered the loss more. Luke had not seen an accurate financial statement since February, so he assumed costs had to have increased more than he thought. The operating profit was over $400,000, except for Malson not having sent the wire.

Dinsen's voice continued in the background, and Luke's fingers flipped to the balance sheet. His eyes fixed on the equity column. FRM's net worth was a negative $4.9 million dollars. Luke saw the previous year's net worth as $2 million, so that made sense to him.

He searched through the balance sheet accounts for variances. His eyes landed on fixed assets. The number was only a few thousand. The deposit on the new software system was not included. Luke flipped back to the income statement and read again through the numbers. The office expense category looked high. "Did you expense the deposit on the new computer software?" Luke asked.

Dinsen seemed taken aback, his head moving slowly to one side, and then flipped to the back. After about a minute, he finally responded, "Yes. That's footnote eight."

"Shouldn't that be capitalized and amortized?"

"Well, I don't know that you will complete the purchase." Dinsen tried to sound professorial and started again reciting numbers.

Luke again tuned out Dinsen. The software deposit was over $100,000, but it was not going to make or break the deal, so he dropped it. Luke's eyes scanned the income statement and balance sheet again. Quickly, he ran through the footnotes. He would study the details later.

Luke stared at Dinsen without listening. His eyes drifted outside and then lit on the yellow legal pad. The servicing sale would give the company more than $6 million, enough net worth to satisfy HUD, but almost $1 million less than the company had before the missed margin call. He needed operating cash to fund the credit line equity, the early settlements, and operating expenses. The company needed a cash infusion.

Dinsen was still talking. Luke needed a chief financial officer. Luke penned $120,000 in a separate column to cover salary, payroll taxes, insurance, and benefits. FRM still owed one-half of the software purchase and would have conversion expenses. Luke estimated $180,000. FRM was going to have less income in the next year once the servicing was sold. Luke estimated the lost income at $1.2 million and wrote the number on the pad. Luke sneaked a peak through the panes looking into the offices. FRM was burning, but there was no parade outside his office. The normal hum and sway of the office continued. Andrea wasn't even watching him. He turned to the pad. The reduced servicing portfolio meant FRM would have fewer escrow balances, and the net interest rate charged on the line of credit would be higher. Luke grabbed the HP-12C again and punched the numbers. The difference would be another $350,000. He wrote the numbers on the pad and mentally added them and wrote $1.85 million. Luke needed a cash infusion of $1 million to operate, and net income needed to improve by a $1.85 million in the next year! Luke was going to have to sell more servicing or shrink the company or grow the company or some combination.

Luke estimated FRM would have $170 million in servicing after the Corn Savings sale. He calculated the value and wrote $4.25 million on the pad. After closing with Corn Savings, FRM would have about $1 million in cash, plus the servicing value. He thought about the next offer to Beth.

Luke raised his eyes, looked over the still-talking Dinsen, and saw the afternoon shadows crawling beyond the bushes. The outline of Beth's face flashed in his memory and beyond Dinsen's soliloquy. How much money did he need personally to pay the attorneys for the divorce? He wrote $150,000 a year in a new column. How much would the court give her? He wrote a question mark on the pad, slid the pen on his desk, and leaned back.

Dinsen finished the numbers and looked up. "I saw you grab your calculator. The numbers add up."

Luke smiled. "I'm sure they do."

Dinsen cleared his throat, turned to look around, and then faced Luke. "How much would you take for the car?"

"Pardon," Luke replied.

"The Mercedes. I'm sure the company will be selling it, in view of your losses."

"You want to buy the car?" Luke spoke slowly.

"Well, it would depend on the price." Dinsen almost looked cocky.

"It's not for sale. It's a 500 SEL; you can get a new one for a little over forty thousand."

"Well, with the losses I have reviewed, the company will have to sell assets."

"The company doesn't own the car," Luke spoke slowly. "Look at the financials you prepared. The company doesn't own the desks, the typewriters, the furniture, the copiers, the signs, the building or the autos we provide. All of that is owned by separate companies I own. Those items are leased to FRM. You reviewed that." Luke shook his head.

"Well, you have these losses. Surely, you're going to shut down and sell off the assets."

"Edgar…" Luke took a deep breath. "We've sold servicing to Corn Savings and should net around six million dollars. That's why I need you to do a supplemental audited statement after the sale closes."

"Oh, yes. Let's see…" Dinsen flipped through the financials and took a credit-card-sized calculator from his shirt pocket. "That would give a net worth of over one million dollars. That's more than enough to satisfy HUD and the other agencies."

"We have to close the sale and have you certify the new net worth."

"Oh yes, that's the additional two-thousand-dollar fee, and we have agreed to do that."

"Yes. We've discussed that." Luke thought they were now on the same page.

"I merely thought you might be interested in selling the car," Dinsen repeated.

"There's a dealership in town."

"But, I thought you might be willing to offer a," Dinsen swallowed deeply, "a discounted price in view of your position."

Luke did not know if he should laugh or get mad, so he stared at Edgar for a moment and decided to be kind. "I don't think so." Dinsen looked away. "Besides, that's not really the color you want. I think you'd prefer something in obtuse instead of gray."

"I don't know if I've seen that one."

"Probably not. Now, I need to get these to Malson. I have Wilt Sanders working on our financials since June 30. Can you accept his work papers?"

"I'm sure we can find a way to do that."

"Good. I'll ask Wilt to call you. Take his call—this is important, and I can't afford to have any more delays."

"It's been a busy time for us." Dinsen lowered his eyes, and Luke thought his ears almost drooped.

"Wilt can coordinate the update of the financials and whatever you need to confirm the sale."

"We will need copies of the sales agreement, confirmation from the buyer acknowledging the purchase, and a copy of the closing statements. We also need to verify receipt of the money into your account."

"You should have copies of the sales agreement, but let's get you another one before you leave." Luke stood and led Dinsen to get another copy and then led Dinsen to the front door. Luke hustled back to his office and slipped into his chair. The numbers on his notepad glared at him. He combed the numbers again, glanced at the clock, and reached back for the telephone. Chuck Rail was not in his office. Luke left a message and went back to work.

Wilt came by in the evening, but he was in a hurry. He handed Luke a copy of the preliminary income statement for July, and Luke gave him a copy of the audited financials. Wilt sank into the sofa. Luke watched Wilt's shoulders sag, and then his body retook its shape. "How much servicing will you have after the sale?"

"Around a hundred and seventy million."

"Well, you still have more than four million in servicing value, plus another million in net worth after the sale. And you made money in July."

"Some salve for our wounds." The company had netted around $90,000.

"So what's your next step?" Wilt asked.

"I'm trying to get an appointment with Chuck."

"I'm close to having August finished. The missing information should come next week, so I can finish by Friday. I can finish the July balance sheet now that the audit is done."

"Good. I need for you to give Dinsen a call." Luke found the number and scrawled it on one of his own business cards. "Here. Please call him and make arrangements for the supplemental audit."

"Sure. I'm busy the rest of the week, but I'll call him. I really have to run."

"Thanks," Luke said genuinely. "I am gone this weekend. I'll call you after I meet with Chuck."

Wilt wished him luck, told him he wouldn't need it, and lingered a second before he left.

Chuck Rail had not called the next morning, so Luke called again. Chuck's voice was stale as he took the call.

"We have our financials. I thought I might bring them and visit with you when you have time. We have a servicing sale set for the end of the month."

Chuck seemed unconcerned. "Tomorrow's not good, but getting together is a good idea. We need to go over a couple of things. There may be some minor changes administratively. Let's do Monday. What time?"

"How about nine? Anything big?"

"Housekeeping and compliance stuff. We need to modify a few of the calculations on the line of credit. We can go through that. Let's say ten."

"OK. See you then."

The numbers still vibrated on the pad. Luke had not told Chuck of the negative net worth amount. Chuck had not asked about the servicing sale, and Luke wondered if he had presumed FRM had already sold servicing. Luke was almost flabbergasted that Chuck was talking about renewing the line of credit, but Chuck's casual mention of modifying some terms set off alarms.

Luke pivoted to his credenza, thumbed his card files, and found Jake Ingles's number. Jake's calendar was full for Friday, so an appointment was set for eight o'clock Monday. Luke planned to give Jake a narrative of the Malson relationship before meeting with Chuck.

After the market closed, Luke headed to the laundry. He was leaving with Ginny tomorrow and needed to take care of his errands now. He returned to the office and finished the day's business. Once everyone had left, he grabbed his pen, pad, calculator, servicing schedules, marketing schedules, and financial statements and headed to the office Wilt used. He started estimating cash flows and income using the spreadsheet he had started. It made him feel better.

CHAPTER THIRTY THREE

uke was early to the office on Friday. His suitcase was tucked in the trunk, and the staff seemed not to notice his early arrival. He closely watched for any signs of panic. The cadence and sounds were the same. Even Harold Rhoden and Nancy seemed content and secure.

Luke flipped through the *Wall Street Journal* and found Malson's stock hovering slightly above eight dollars, significantly down from the twenty-one dollars per share of three months earlier. The huge drop at the end of June, after the loss announcement, had been followed with further dips. Luke expected Malson to announce another loss at the end of September.

Ginny called before noon. Luke felt the excitement in her voice and arranged to meet her at the departure gate in Dallas. The day was lively. Luke stayed as late as he could, and no one seemed concerned when he announced he was leaving early. Luke made a mad dash to the airport; he was almost the last one on the plane. After a brief flight, he found Ginny with a bright smile, a plum outfit, and a tan suitcase. She looked beautiful, and he noticed others at the gate glancing at her. Within minutes they were seated in first class.

Luke relaxed and let the whirlwind float away. Ginny was looking out the window as he took her hand. She turned, smiled, and said nothing. Luke looked at her and then the people barreling down the aisle toward their seats. "Is this how it would feel?" he wondered. He was excited for the weekend. He saw the excitement in the eyes of the staff when they left on Fridays. He knew the excitement he felt when he drove to see his children. Briefly, Beth's image flashed, playing the role of protector of the children; Luke batted it away. He wished the children were with him, and he was excited to be with Ginny. "Are all these people excited by who they're with or where they're going?" he wondered. He squeezed Ginny's hand lightly.

The connection to LaGuardia left on schedule. Luke and Ginny snacked lightly on the shrimp cocktail and passed on the entrée. They arrived on time. Luke led Ginny to the cabstand, and soon they watched the lights of Manhattan as they crossed the Triborough Bridge, snaked along the FDR, and made the jagged climb to The Plaza. The room was on an upper floor and faced Central Park as Luke had requested. The bellman dropped their bags. Luke opened the windows, and the sounds of the city gushed in. "I'm hungry," Ginny said with a solitary nod.

Luke found the Italian restaurant on Fifty-Seventh he remembered from his dinner with Frank Ryan. The dinner crowd had thinned, but the service was leisurely; the pasta, veal, and scallops were excellent, and the vela of the candlelight danced in Ginny's eyes. After midnight they strolled back to the hotel, their arms around each other. The cars, horns, and sirens of the city came blaring through the open window; Luke closed it and turned to find Ginny watching him. This time there was no hurdling beyond his solace to be with her. He was already with her, and the moments blended into a tender mélange. Later he lay in the room's darkness, gathered the silhouette she cast from the muted city lights, and knew he had never seen a more beautiful moment.

The morning's sun breached the room's stillness slowly. Luke closed the drapes, threw on his running togs, kissed Ginny good-bye, and started for the door. "See you in a bit," he said as she smiled sweetly into the pillow. Once downstairs Luke found the sundry shop, grabbed the *New York Times*, and flipped to the back of the business section. Malson stock still stood above eight dollars. He slid the newspaper back into the rack and headed for Central Park.

The earbuds played the spinning cassette's tunes, but Luke's early strides were stiff and fitful. His burden was inching forward: the stock price, FRM's loss, the $1 million operating capital he needed, the $1.85 million improvement needed to break even, the pending sale to Corn Savings, the divorce, and the Monday meeting with Malson that could end FRM. Soon his gait relaxed, the business faded, and the notes of Neil Young's "Southern Man" became more distinct. Central Park was already alive but not yet at full bustle. The amphitheater sat quietly without a homeless person performing a play. He ran a familiar circuit and stopped only when he had circled back to the light at Fifty-Ninth and Sixth. He walked along Central Park South, crossed to The Plaza, and climbed aboard the elevator, the earbuds still in his ears.

Ginny was up when he returned. She sat in a white robe, loosely tied, her black hair draped on her shoulders. "I ordered breakfast," she said. "Take a shower."

Luke emerged to find Ginny primping in her robe and the white-clothed room service table with melon, strawberries, blueberries, muffins, juice, and coffee. He walked behind her, saw her eyes in the mirror, and kissed the back of her neck. The reflections of their eyes met, and his hand slipped inside her robe. Ginny said nothing and dropped her eyes. They nibbled on fruit and had coffee later. Ginny slipped on her flats, saying, "I know you will want to walk."

They emerged from the hotel and headed into the park. Softball games and joggers joined with dogs and Frisbees and strollers in a holiday revue beneath perfectly smooth, blue skies, and lightly placed, pure white clouds. The pair wandered through the paths nestled in the shade and drifted beyond bridges and trestles as the huge trees dampened the city's sounds and rained colors on them. The lake came into view; Luke rented a boat, and they climbed aboard. The green-hued water lapped quietly and seeped over the oars as Luke pushed them out, bending at the turns and leaking away from the other boats. At the farthest point, they drifted, watching the leaves dance in the wind, the turtles diving around them, and the towers outlining the park. Comfortably, Luke rowed to the dock, and they lunched on the deck still adrift in the day.

They came out on the park's east side and waltzed south on Fifth Avenue. Soon the condominiums and co-ops gave way to Tiffany & Co., Bergdorf Goodman, and the sparkling midway of the retailer displays. They strolled through a few stores and aisles but never selected anything. The windows and offerings were merely a part of the tour, and most of the time was spent on the sidewalk. Near Forty-Second Street, Luke pulled Ginny toward the curb. "I want to go to Tower Records. Do you mind?"

"You can buy an album anywhere," Ginny said.

"Not this one; I can't find it. Tower Records is huge. If anyone has it, they will."

"Sure," she said with a puzzled air.

Luke stepped off the curb, hailed a cab, and they slid inside. "I've looked for this tune for years, but I never find it. I'm sure it's out of print. It's an old Sam Cooke song."

"Sam Cooke?"

"He was a pop singer in the late 1950s and early 1960s. He had a velvety voice and a lot of dance tunes that were popular. He was really before my time, and I didn't much care for his songs, but I remember when I was twelve or so, he had a song, 'A Change Is Gonna Come,' that I really liked. Most of his songs cracked the top ten and stayed for a while, but this one came and went quickly. It had an orchestral start and then a gospel sound, with an outsider's lyrics. Looking back it was a civil rights song, but when it played on my old AM radio, I guess it struck me as an outsider's lament," he said, still thinking.

"I hope they have it." Ginny's eyes were sympathetic as she watched the traffic coming at all angles and the buildings slowly parading by. "I've never heard of him."

"I think he died soon after the song came out. I can't remember. He was shot. I think in a motel room."

"Really?"

"Yes, I'm not sure. I didn't know at the time, but years later, in college, some of us were talking, and someone said he was married but with a different woman at a motel when he was shot by a third woman."

"You're making this up."

"No."

"Sounds like your kind of guy." She tapped his arm.

Luke laughed but quickly replied, "I'm not really that way."

Ginny dipped her chin but held her eyes level, so she was peering up at him. "There were times I thought I could see you as a fifty-five-year-old man frisking about with women half your age."

"That's not me."

"I don't think it so much anymore."

Luke launched himself from the cab with Ginny in tow and hurried into the half-block and three stories of Tower Records. The clerk feathered the thin publishing sheets and said the tune was out of print. It had not been released on cassette. Compact discs were new, and only the current releases were available. The clerk suggested the basement, where the older, vinyl recordings were stored. They took the stairs and dropped to a level with some natural light sifting from the clouded sidewalk windows and incandescent bulbs hanging from the shorter ceilings and found another clerk who pointed them to the most likely area. Luke draped his hands atop the album covers and skipped over the tops, his hands alternating and the labels reeling by in rapid succession. Ginny appeared interested and looked randomly. Everything was old, and the basement was darker; it had a few customers and a full layer of dust. Luke found a box of Sam Cooke's albums under a table, knelt on the floor, lifted each album, flipped to the back cover, and searched the listing of songs. Within a few minutes, he smiled. He tilted the album to the light and scanned the bottom and read the publish date—1968. It was a collection of hits after Sam Cooke's death. He wondered how long it had sat in the crate.

Ginny smiled benignly as Luke paid the four dollars for the album, and they regained the street. It was the only purchase of the day. Luke asked if there was anything she wanted, but she said, "That's not why I came. When you buy me something, it's going to cost more than that." They both laughed.

They made their way back uptown and then grabbed a cab as the shadows grew longer and the sun began yielding to the high-rises. It was still hours before sunset, so they found a glass of wine close to the hotel. The prized album rested in a yellow plastic wrapper with bold red print in a chair beside Luke.

"So, tell me about this song," Ginny said.

"It's an outsider's song. Sam Cooke was black."

"I saw the cover," Ginny said.

"OK. The singer says he was born by a river and, like the river, has been running ever since. The lyrics talk about going to the movie and going downtown but being told not to stay." He saw Ginny's eyes watching him. "When I was young, I knew I was poor, and I knew there were places I wasn't welcomed. Small towns are that way. Some of the city fathers think they are better than you because their families own something or run something. It's their town, and they think they are entitled to control things and not be challenged. They decide who is given opportunity and who is not. Being successful becomes subjective—subject to their determining who they want." Luke drifted with his thoughts. "Sometimes I thought I was running, looking for a place where I could be comfortable." Ginny watched him and let him think and talk. "I think you have to be comfortable with yourself. Others can't give you that." He paused, still searching for the words. "The singer's sad, but he knows better days are ahead. He knows a change is coming. It's an upbeat message. It didn't play on the radio for very long, but I really liked the song."

She smiled at him. "So where are you running?"

"I think the singer's running to acceptance, but that's not what I'm trying to find."

"You want social acceptance."

"I don't think so. I don't need a lot of attention."

"You want acceptance."

"I don't think so. I love coming here because I can walk around and be me instead of being Luke the Mortgage Guy."

"You like being noticed."

"Not so much…" he said, and his voice faded. "I prefer to be anonymous. Now, you enjoy being noticed."

Ginny smiled. "You noticed me."

"Yes, I did." He leaned and kissed her cheek. "You are beautiful and smart."

"You didn't notice me because I'm smart."

"Maybe not, but I wouldn't want to be with you if I didn't think you were."

Her eyes were reflective. "I think I understand the song I've never heard. I remember the feeling of being an outsider. I think we all feel left out at one time or another. When I was young, I was never invited to the right parties; I wasn't part of the right crowd." She paused. "I wanted that very much."

"You need that?"

"I want that. I really want that." Ginny paused, and slowly the petals of her eyes opened. "Once I grew older, people said I could sing, and I performed. And then the competitions—I really loved that. I loved the events."

"You loved the recognition."

"Yes."

"You didn't win just for singing." He smiled at her. "You're beautiful."

"Thanks," she said without embarrassment. "Yes, once I was noticed for my looks and voice, there were more parties and events and functions. You know."

"You miss that?"

"Yes," she answered wistfully. "I want to be more social. I don't so much want to sing, although I enjoy it, but I want to be more social."

"Like see your picture on the society page, standing and hugging and mugging for the camera?"

"Don't be so callous," she almost snapped at Luke's words. Her lips softened. "Yes, I want that."

"That's not for me." Luke's lips were straight. "I'd rather know and be close to a few people than to have lots of people around me." They sat for a second, gazing in different directions.

They retreated to the hotel, opened the windows, sat on the windowsill, and watched the colors burn and darken richly through the sun's last rays. They made love again. Ginny's eyes locked into Luke's as he lay beneath her. His entire world lay in the green of her eyes, the beat of her breast, and the rhythmic waving of her hair as he gazed up at her, his hands riding her hips. Her rhythm flowed until her eyes closed slowly and her chest heaved. Then she looked down at him with her body still pulsing and her green eyes stealing his. Luke felt a part of his soul being pulled away steadily into her eyes, yielding to the magic she made. They lay together, the city's sounds gradually returning to their world, warm with love. Luke sipped the scent of her neck, kissed her lips, and pulled back to let their eyes meet.

"I love you," she said softly. "And I think you love me." Her lips waved with a tremble as she spoke, and she kissed him again before he could answer.

They changed for dinner and headed for the highly reviewed restaurant Ginny had suggested. They found the tiered entry, approved of the lively pastel walls, appreciated the artistically presented courses, and surveyed the tiny servings. "Why are the tables so close together?" Ginny complained in half voice.

"Real estate is at a premium, and rents are high."

"The review of this restaurant was glorious, and I don't want to complain—"

Luke interrupted, "But you're disappointed."

"Yes."

"I'm sorry. You were so excited. I'm sure it's one of the places to be seen." In the corner of his eye, Luke caught a glance of the lady at the nearest table. She was obviously eavesdropping and appeared offended as though their critique had diminished her evening.

They lingered only briefly. Luke grabbed a cab, and they headed to a steakhouse he knew on East Forty-Sixth, on the other side of Park Avenue and close to Third. The bar had a festive rumble; the piano played the classics, and conversation was comfortable. Ginny liked it better, and they both ordered wine.

Luke took a deep breath and put his hand on Ginny's. "My life may be changing soon." Ginny's face fell serious. He leaned back, pulling his hand away. "I may have to make some hard choices, or they may be made for me. The company may struggle."

"You're not broke," she said dismissively.

"No. If I sold everything, I would still have some money," he started and then chewed on the pause as numbers rolled in his head. "There's a chance that I may be selling everything, including the real estate." He scanned her face for any sign of emotion. "Some of the commercial property may take longer, but once it's sold, the divorce could be done." One eyebrow of Ginny's darted up slightly. "I could be divorced in a year." He paused and watched her, waiting.

Ginny's hair lilted to one side. "Do you really want a divorce?"

"Of course. I miss my children, and I hope they understand when they are older."

"Are you sure that's what you want?"

"Why do you ask that?" He didn't wait for a response. "I wouldn't be here with you if I intended to stay married. I'd be divorced now, but I haven't found a way to balance the business, the money, and those issues."

She touched his hand. "Don't get me wrong. I love you. We're lovers. I'm not sure you really want a divorce. I'm not sure you don't need someone on the side for fun."

A part of Luke was offended; another part, compliant. "I understand how you get that impression, but it's not who I am." His voice strengthened. "I'm not married because I want to be." The moment lingered. "I know why I'm still married. I can't get her to agree to the divorce, and I can't kill the company."

"The business is more important than your divorce."

"Why do you stay married?"

Ginny's eyes stayed fixed. "I don't know. I hate him sometimes, but I know he will never leave me. It's not like with you." She stopped. Neither spoke for a moment.

"Why do you stay?"

"I don't know." The two were silent, and Luke felt he had crossed a line. He decided to change the subject, but she spoke first. "I know why he goes out. He has goals. He wants to be 'someone.' That's very important for him. He wants to have friends and opportunities. He spends more than we have, but he wants to be with the right people and get ahead. I know there's this IRS thing, and it scares me. I see the envelopes, and I know he owes some back taxes. It makes me wonder if we'll lose the house. He struggles, but he tries. I don't trust him with other women, but I trust him to come home. I know he can't do better than me. Does that make sense?" She didn't wait for a response. "He wants to go to the right places and know the right people. I want that, too."

"You don't trust me."

"I don't know that I could trust you to stay with me. Sometimes you have this wild, radical thread that drives you."

"You mean you really want to see your picture on the society page." Luke smiled humorously, trying to lighten the moment.

"Yes," Ginny shot back. "What's wrong with that?"

"Nothing," Luke said apologetically. "It's not me." Their eyes swept around the room before he pulled her back, saying, "I'm trustworthy. I'm not happily married, and I don't want to live a lie."

"I hope you mean that."

"But I am who I am."

"That's part of what I love, but there's a part of you that I think will destroy you. I thought I could see you with someone half your age when you were in your fifties. Sometimes now I think I can see you alone and lonely. I don't want to be alone."

"I don't think you will be."

She kissed him as the words left his lips. "I'm getting tired."

He watched her fall asleep in the crook of his arm and gently pulled his arm away, turned on his side, and faced the closed windows. She spooned closely, draping her arm around him. The day's bliss replayed before him, and the tape of the night's conversation rewound. Luke was sure he loved Ginny. He thought he only needed to find the path to bring them together. Sometimes we feel love when we do not see what is so obvious to others. He slept deeply without thinking of FRM or Malson.

CHAPTER THIRTY FOUR

The tenderness of the weekend was stripped away. The financial losses and uncertainty replaced the slow soft recess of Ginny's hand as they parted at the Dallas airport. Luke's eyes whispered the sadness his lips could not say. Ginny caught the earlier flight, and Luke sat alone in the airline lounge, staring at nothing and feeling the swelling void as the separation gnawed away the wholeness he had felt with Ginny. He wondered what she was feeling. He forced himself to focus on FRM and Malson. If Malson pulled the credit line, FRM could fail in the next twenty-four hours. Luke stopped by the office Sunday night, checked the bond markets, and ensured he had adequate coverage. He left Andrea a note saying he would be in around noon or later.

Luke had called the bond markets by the time he pulled into the downtown Tulsa parking garage. The tension pulsed through Luke slowing each moment until he felt his breath and looked without clarity. He found Jake Ingles waiting with a nondescript slice of Tulsa's skyline in the background. Jake was dressed in slacks and an open-collared dress shirt. His tie and sport coat hung behind his door and came into view as Luke seated himself and Jake closed the door.

"I have a ten o'clock appointment with Chuck Rail at Malson," Luke started. He handed Jake a copy of the audited financials, the July income statement, and a copy of the contract with Corn Savings. He explained the missed margin call, the sudden movement in the markets when Horowitz made his projections, the huge market losses taken by FRM, the dinner with Chuck, and the eerie silence that had followed. Jake Ingles showed no emotion, and Luke wondered if he was displaying coolness under pressure, indifference, or detached objectivity since the results would not affect his own life. Luke recounted Chuck's obsessive references to Malson's buying FRM. Luke recalled the slowness in renewing the line of credit and the change in processing loan advances and notices of loan sales since Sid had left the department. He described the accounting chaos that had followed.

"If you lost all this money, how are you still making loans?" Jake asked nonchalantly.

"I don't know," Luke paused. "Cindy Cleugh has to be putting loan sale proceeds into our account and not paying off the advances on those loans. We probably owe them for advances on loans that have already been sold."

"Out of trust," Jake said.

"Out of trust?" Luke asked.

"It means collateral has been sold without repaying the debt," Jake answered. "But, sounds like they did it to themselves." Jake did not wait for a response. "What do you want?"

"I want them to pay for the losses. And I've got to have the credit line to save the business." Luke's response was calm and clear. "They pay me and fund loans until I get another lender." Luke then recapped the dance with FCBA and his hopes to move.

Jake offered his first display of emotion and took a deep breath. Jake asked more questions and made notes on his pad. After an hour, Jake picked up the phone, called Malson's attorneys, and said Luke would be late for the meeting with Chuck. After another hour, Jake looked at his watch, said he needed to be in court, and asked if Luke was comfortable going by himself or wanted to wait until he could go with him. Luke said he was fine going alone, and Jake asked Luke to call him after the meeting. "I'm going to call Malson's firm and let them know you're on the way."

Luke walked the three blocks to Malson, swung into the building, and headed to Chuck's office. One of the clerks led Luke to a windowless conference room in the interior of the building wedged between elevator shafts and a fire exit. Luke had never been to this room. Four scarred walls were painted in cheap, light orange, and the sheetrock showed in the divots. Stacks of supplies and brown boxes sat in two of the corners. A battered, stained, oval-shaped conference table sat askew, and a few nonmatching fabric chairs were scattered about the room. Luke paid no attention to the surroundings, set down his leather binder, and fixed his eyes on the door.

Chuck swung open the conference door and entered with two of the bank's attorneys. Chuck made introductions and left. Luke shook hands with the attorneys, and one introduced himself as Phil Sandifer, a partner in the firm. They said they had been in contact with Jake, and the bank wanted some of its officers to research the relationship. They excused themselves.

Luke thought of the bond market, looked, and found a telephone sitting on top of one of the unopened brown boxes in the corner.

Luke called the market, finally surveyed the room, and understood he was being stored until Malson could formulate its plan.

An affable man a few years older than Luke entered with a pad. He introduced himself as vice president of operations. "Well, tell me why you're here?" he started.

"I think Malson wanted to buy me, tried to squeeze me, failed to transfer money when it should have, caused huge marketing losses, and now has a large outstanding loan without enough collateral. It cost me more than seven million dollars. FRM's net worth is below the HUD minimum, and we'll lose our approval by September 15. We've sold about six million dollars in servicing, but that won't close until September 24, and that's too late to save our HUD approval."

The man set his jaws into a fixed smile. "How did this all happen?"

Luke began with Malson's suggestions to buy FRM and the changes in the relationship. He detailed the missed margin call in March. He referred to the changed relationship since Sid had left the department.

The meeting continued past noon, and sandwiches were bro-ught in. Finally, after another hour, the man took his notes, asked Luke to wait in the room, and left. Luke was alone and again grabbed the telephone to check the bond markets. The markets were steady and would remain so for the week. He called Andrea and said he was be-hind schedule; he told her he would return to the office but might not arrive until everyone had left.

Within minutes Sid Fullmer walked in. Luke trusted him, and they shook hands warmly. Luke started on Sid immediately, "You re-member me calling in March, don't you?"

"Yes," Sid said.

Luke pressed to know why Malson was intent on taking over FRM and why Malson had disrupted cash flow and record keeping.

Sid was stoic. Luke saw the distance one creates to protect his own as Sid said he knew nothing about Malson wanting to buy FRM; Luke believed him. "I know you called. I know the losses are from the market swing. There are a lot of people talking about this in the bank. They talked to me, and I wanted you to know what I said." Luke could tell Sid wanted out of the room. "I don't think Chuck understands the collateral," Sid finished. He shrugged his broad shoulders and edged out of the door.

Luke glanced at his watch and realized he had been in the room for more than four hours. He exited, stood by the door, and saw the vice president of operations approaching.

They sat again in the room, and the man started, "What do you want?"

"I want the seven plus million dollars for my marketing losses, and I want my line of credit renewed."

"We can't do that." The man flashed a chagrined smile.

"Not yet," Luke said.

"We need to verify why you lost money and how you lost so much. We are verifying now how much collateral we have and how much we're owed. We want to determine how we lost our collateral. This will take some time." He continued by going through the audited financials and Wilt's income statement for July and asking questions regarding the servicing sale. He knew of Wilt Sanders and seemed pleased he had reviewed FRM. He stayed more than an hour, and then he was gone.

Luke had barely stood to stretch his legs when three other bank employees entered. They introduced themselves as members of the Auditing Department. Their dress fit their descriptions, and they nervously asked if Luke could identify the FRM employees who could help them collect information. Luke detailed Harold and Nancy's responsibilities and told them of Wilt Sanders's role. They made notes of processes and procedures, and Luke told them how things had changed with Chuck and Cindy. After more than an hour, they took their notes and left the room. It was after five o'clock.

Luke followed the audit team out of the conference room and saw Chuck and Phil Sandifer, the attorney, waiting for him. "Let's go upstairs." Chuck smiled around his teeth with eyes boring straight at Luke.

The three rode silently in the elevator, entered the plush law firm offices, and started toward a vacant office with the light off, an unused desk, chairs, an empty bookshelf, and windows opening onto the Arkansas River. Luke suddenly realized it was the first time he had seen natural light in almost seven hours and walked to the window. Chuck turned to Phil Sandifer and scoffed, "Give me a minute." Sandifer retreated with a grin and shut the door. Chuck's cockiness filled the room. "You picked a good attorney, Big Boy," Chuck started. "Good for you. You chose one who is reasonable instead of some hotshot all fired up to sue somebody."

Luke now knew Jake had probably had conversations with Malson's attorneys during the day. "Who was the operations guy—the one that I met this morning and ordered sandwiches?"

"You won't see him again. He's going to be the operating president over all the banks soon. He's managing coordination of the banks now. He was there to get information for the board." Chuck parted his lips slightly, showing his teeth. "You can stop that takeover bullshit. No one ever tried to pressure you, do you understand?" Chuck paused, and his lips rose at the corners. "You know, the board wants to send you over to Judge Filcher now. Get this in federal court and get rid of you."

Luke stared at Chuck, held the leather folder in one hand, and fingered the leather chair with the other. "I'm not afraid to sue you guys."

"You should be. You're not going to like Judge Filcher," Chuck sneered. Chuck stepped closer to the desk and leaned on it. "You need to shut down the company, sell off the assets, and pay off the loan."

"You don't have the collateral."

"Yes, I do."

"No, Chuck." Luke stepped around the chair, closer to the desk, and looked down at him. "You're short on collateral. You shorted yourself. You don't have enough mortgages to cover the advances you've made, and you don't have a security interest in the servicing. I guaranteed only a portion of the loan."

"It doesn't matter. You'll go down once we get to federal court."

Luke saw Chuck's confidence, but he returned no expression. His words were slow and even. "I'm not going down. I'm not going down."

Chuck cocked his head again. "Just shut it down. Let the numbers fall where they fall and walk away."

"I'm not going down."

Chuck stared at Luke, his outline framed by the light from the window, and Luke fixed on Chuck's eyes and a background of dark paneling in the unlit room. Finally, Chuck turned back and grabbed for the door. Luke rounded the desk and followed him. Chuck twisted the door lever, stopped, and turned toward Luke, "Fuck you."

Luke took another step until his chest rested a few inches from Chuck's face, looked down on his forehead, and breathed, "Fuck you, Chuck. Open the door."

They emerged into the hallway and started toward the law firm's lobby. Chuck's face softened in a false display of civility. "We'll be in touch with Jake Ingles," he said, as if planning lunch.

Luke made his way to the elevators. It was after hours, and most of the offices had cleared. The tower's lobby was vacant, and the first of the cleaning crew had arrived. Luke walked alone down the suddenly empty street being swept by the wind, and toward the parking garage. His pace was brisk, and he wondered if Jake Ingles was still in his office. He started the car and lifted the telephone, but it rang before he could dial.

"Hello."

"Luke, Jake. We've got a meeting with the bank tomorrow at ten. Can you be here an hour earlier?"

"Sure." Luke took a breath. "Am I still in business?"

"You did well. We have some work to do tomorrow."

CHAPTER THIRTY FIVE

Luke found FRM's offices empty when he returned. He had hoped some staff would still be there, so he could get a whiff of the office mood. He wondered what they knew, or thought they knew. He hadn't talked to Ginny and answered the phone each time it rang as he sifted through the mounds of paper stacked on his desk.

Ginny called after a couple of hours. "Have you forgotten me already?"

"No. Just the opposite. I was afraid I wouldn't get to talk to you. I had a rough day."

"I never caught you. I thought you might want a break from me."

"No, I don't. I wasn't here. I won't be in much this week." He explained he was tied up with the renewal of the line of credit but offered no more. He told her to call or come by anytime. He left a couple of hours later.

The next morning Luke was in the office early. Cindy Cleugh had so irregularly advanced on new loan closings that neither Harold nor Nancy had noticed Malson had failed to advance funds on Monday. Luke saw no apprehension in anyone's eyes until he said he might not be out for the day but would call before noon. Malson's stock was listed at slightly more than six dollars, a drop of another two dollars.

Jake Ingram started talking as Luke entered. Luke noted he was wearing his tie and jacket. "Let me start here. These guys know they have done wrong. That's clear. That being said, they have no intention of rolling over. If you want money out of them, we're going to have to sue, and it's going to take years."

"That puts me out of business," Luke answered.

"You can start another company. Start smaller and grow again."

"I need a credit line. Without the credit line, I'm out of business."

"Can't you get another?"

"Maybe a small one or two. I don't know. If I'm in a lawsuit, maybe no one will want to touch me. Even if they do, I need a big credit line. With a few small lines, I would have to lay off a lot of people. I can't do that."

"They're not going to roll over. They're probably going to threaten you and who knows…" Jake did not finish.

"They already have. Who's Filcher?"

"Judge Filcher?"

"Yeah."

"The meanest federal judge around. He loves beating up on attorneys."

"It seems they to want me to meet him."

"That's what I heard. The rumor is he's in their pocket, but you didn't hear it from me."

Luke's eyes betrayed him. "What's the deal?"

"Not sure. He's also known as Judge Socks. He traded some favors for the appointment, but I don't think it was what he thought it would be, and it didn't give him the lifestyle he wanted. The money didn't go as far as he thought it would. He's tight and ornery, and some think he's mean because he knows the lawyers make more than he does. So, he likes to beat up on them."

"Judge Socks?"

Jake thought for a moment and decided to tell the story. He grinned throughout. "He's tight, and he would take his girlfriend to his house when his wife was gone. The wife wanted to catch Filcher and hired a private investigator and gave him a key. So, many have seen the pictures of Filcher nude except for his socks. His wife got some money, and that left him with even less. He didn't think his full salary was enough, and half the salary has been much worse."

"Wow" was all Luke could muster.

"Not a pretty picture. He's pretty fat, and the black socks were drooping around his ankles. But you didn't hear it from me. She wasn't too cute, either."

Luke merely shook his head.

"OK." Jake grabbed his pen. "Tell me who you saw yesterday and what they wanted."

Luke recapped the parade of questioners. "I didn't see Cindy Cleugh."

"Probably won't. I think she's either being reassigned or maybe resigned. Not sure."

"And Chuck?" Luke asked.

"Fighting for his life. I understand you guys are friends."

"We were."

"He doesn't think much of you now."

"I reached the same decision about him a long time ago."

Jake asked Luke to call around noon, and Luke walked through downtown. Luke arrived at Malson's law firm office as directed and was led to a large, packed conference room with a board lining one wall. Numbers were scribbled all over.

"Looks like you're about eleven million short," Chuck Rail started.

"No way," Luke answered.

"Tell him." Chuck nodded to one of the members of the bank's audit team.

Within seconds, Luke knew the guy did not understand how the relationship worked. Luke debated challenging the misstatements as they occurred but decided to wait until the auditor had finished.

"The money for the sellers, loan payoffs, and expenses is in the branch disbursement trust accounts. We've verified those are OK. The problem is Cindy didn't tell us when she advanced money, and she didn't tell us when we received wires on loan sales. We only need to ensure you fund all the loans and account for all of the loan sales. Once you do that, our numbers will hold. We'll be short around five million."

"Not seeing it," Chuck shot back.

"No surprise there." Luke shook his head for emphasis.

Phil Sandifer stepped in, "We need to work with your people to verify the numbers."

"You want me to call them?"

"Yes. Who are our leads?" Sandifer turned to the bank's auditors.

Luke used one of the telephones and gave Harold and Nancy the names of the audit members from the bank and told them to supply whatever the auditors requested. The auditors left, making it apparent to Luke that this was a command post and not the room where Malson was doing its work.

Phil Sandifer started again, "Mr. Boyd, the bank is obviously investigating ways it can be paid in full. As you walked over, we had a call with Jake Ingles; you probably want to give him a call. The reception-ist can find an office or conference area for you."

Luke soon found himself in the same vacated office from the pre-vious day. Jake told him the bank wanted to get repaid and termi-nate the relationship. The bank was asking for an assignment of the proceeds from the sale of servicing. Luke quickly said, "No way," and Jake indicated he had anticipated the response.

Within minutes Luke was asked back into the conference room with Chuck and the bank's attorneys. Sandifer started again, "Mr. Boyd, we want authorization to speak with the accounting firm that prepared the audited financials."

Luke raised his palms. "It's 'Luke.'"

Sandifer smiled. "Luke."

"Now, who are all of these people?" Luke asked. Sandifer made introductions, and something told Luke he liked Sandifer, even if he was the opposition. The bank had four attorneys present, but Phil Sandifer was obviously in charge.

Luke called Edgar Dinsen and gave him authorization to talk di-rectly with the bank's representatives. He turned to Sandifer. "Do you want me to call Wilt Sanders, so you can talk with him?"

"Wilt's working on this?"

The statement let Luke know that Sandifer knew Wilt Sanders. "Yes. He prepared our July income statement. He should have August com-pleted this week, and he's using the audited financials to bring our balance sheet up to date. He's helping us to track Cindy's transfers."

Sandifer looked pleased and turned to Chuck. "That's good."

Chuck dodged the comment. "We're looking at ways to still pro-vide a credit line, but the other banks will have to come into the deal. We going to meet here at two, and they will probably have some questions. How much are they owed?"

"I'm not sure. I'll have to check." Luke knew he had asked Nancy and Harold to stop using the smaller banks, but he had not verified it.

"Well, the other banks will have to come into the deal. That's a deal breaker," Chuck huffed at Luke.

"They can do as they please. This is between us," Luke answered.

Sandifer again cut in, "Can you meet with us at two o'clock?"

Luke took this as a request to leave. "See you then. I'll call Wilt."

Jake Ingles called as Luke raced to his office. "A lawsuit is going to be a prolonged endeavor. Can you live off the remaining servicing?"

"No. If we lose our HUD approval, the servicing would be pulled. That would be the end. If I can close the Corn Savings deal, we'll have plenty of net worth, but the HUD deadline is September 15," Luke answered. "There might be an additional ten days, but it's not guaranteed."

Luke walked into the office and saw the uncertainty. The usual traffic in and out of his office was only a dribble and most tried not to look at him. Occasionally, he caught someone glancing at him furtively with a hopeful air, straining a smile, and moving on. He checked with Nancy and Harold and grimaced when told they had advanced a bond with one of the small banks. Luke knew he had to avoid Malson trapping the money. He told Harold to change the wire instructions for that bond, raced back to the Malson meeting, and wondered why Chuck was still in the picture. Cindy was gone, but Malson seemed to be relying on the man who had mangled the relationship.

The room was packed. Representatives from the other banks joined Malson's attorneys and Chuck. Luke shook hands with the bankers and saw apprehension. He turned to see George Winney step into the room, his feet spread farther apart than his shoulders to bear his weight. Doug Turney and Vern Brindley followed him. Winney seemed pleased and comfortable, and Turney and Brindley wore the mischievous smiles of elementary students going to the principal's office.

Chuck started the meeting. "Mr. Boyd advised us yesterday he was out of trust on his line of credit and unable to determine the amount. Malson has dedicated significant staff and resources to getting a handle on the relationship."

Luke almost rose out of his shoes but then decided to listen. Chuck's explanation sounded like a prosecutor's opening argument. Luke bit his tongue and watched the impact it had on the bankers. George Winney's smile widened. Doug and Vern glanced at Luke as if they were proud of him.

Chuck's soliloquy continued. Malson was willing to continue funding and would manage a $20 million line of credit, but Malson would only put up $15 million; the other banks had to put up the other $5 million. In addition, Malson would loan FRM $6 million with the Corn Savings sale proceeds repaying the loan. If the banks refused to put up $5 million, Malson would refuse to fund FRM, causing the company to fold. If FRM failed, Malson would sue the other banks for any principal payments they had received in the last ninety days.

There was a pause as the bankers looked at each other, and Luke jumped in. "Malson caused the problem by not properly managing the account," he said hurriedly, grabbing the floor and then slowing his speech to collect his thoughts. "No one has any exposure to losses. No one has funds advanced except you." He turned to the one of the bankers. "Your loans should be funded in the next week. Malson has not been advising us when it advances money and when it collects on loan sales. They also caused us to miss a margin call, which caused the losses. And they know it."

The first banker stood, explaining he wasn't owed money and had no interest in Malson's deal. Besides, he added, Malson had agreed to manage the documents, and it would owe his bank for any loss caused by its mismanagement. His comments let Luke know the bankers had been prepped by Malson prior to the meeting. The banker shook his head at Luke and walked out. Luke could tell the banker did not care what had really happened. The prospect of a loss, regardless of who had caused it, had quenched his appetite for business from FRM.

The second banker stood and stared at Luke. "The bank expects to be repaid when the loans are sold," he said. He turned to face Chuck fully. "Malson holds the documents in trust for us. If you don't pay us, we will sue." He threw Luke a disgusted look and walked out.

George Winney, Doug Turney, and Vern Brindley were now the only bank representatives in the room. George Winney spoke first. "We aren't owed anything, so this seems like it's a matter between Malson and FRM." He glanced at Doug Turney.

"That's what it looks like to me," Turney added.

Winney, Doug, and Vern stay seated as though they wanted to know more. Chuck restated his argument and gave a quick lecture on the bankruptcy code. FRM would fail if Malson withdrew funding, and Malson would sue the banks in bankruptcy court to recover any money they had been paid in the last three months as a preference item.

Turney's smile grew. "We don't have any preferential transfers. FRM hasn't used the line, and besides you have been holding documents in trust for us, just like that other guy said." He glanced at

George Winney and Vern. "I guess we should let these guys work this out."

Luke could see the trio had enjoyed their outing and felt used until Turney walked by, placed a hand on his shoulder, and winked as if he would be willing to help.

Luke could see Chuck deflating. "What's the twenty million? Where did you—"

Chuck cut him off, "Our legal lending limit has been reduced by the regulators from thirty-five million to fifteen million. That's all we can do."

Suddenly Luke saw the first impact of Malson's losses: as their capital decreased, their legal lending limit dropped. The bankers' exit left Luke more collected. "I told you yesterday, but I'll remind you: if we lose HUD approval, they can take the servicing away from us."

Chuck's faced softened, and Sandifer spoke. "Will the Corn Savings deal close?"

"I think so. Interest rates have held. I don't think they will walk away like Socoast." He saw some relief in Sandifer's eyes. "But, this six-million-dollar deal won't work. We need more working capital for the one percent equity in the line of credit and operating expenses."

"Then shrink," Chuck jumped in.

Luke turned to Chuck. "No."

"You're going to have to shrink; the equity on any line of credit is going up to five percent if we do a renewal."

"What?"

Sandifer and Chuck looked at each other. Sandifer spoke. "If the board agrees to extend a line of credit, the equity requirement will be five percent of the amount advanced."

"Why is the board doing that?"

"The board is responding to requirements from federal regulators." Sandifer's face was earnest.

Luke knew now the bank was in deep trouble, but so was he. "I can't live with five percent." He began calculating the additional cash required in his head. Further, the small credit line would restrict loan production, and Luke had already estimated he needed to grow to break even and keep the staff. "And we can't live with a fifteen-million-dollar credit line."

Chuck's spewed disgust. "You're lucky if we fund you at all."

Sandifer did not allow a moment to lapse. "The bank is looking for alternatives within its capacity." He forced a brief smile. "Give us some time, and we will be in contact with Jake."

"We have new loans to close. You have to start advancing money tomorrow."

"Don't tell me what to do," Chuck snarled.

"Give us some time." Sandifer strained. "We will be in touch."

"We have to have HUD approval to keep operating. We lose that on September 15. Without that, we can't make new loans, and we lose the servicing."

Sandifer and Chuck looked at each other before Sandifer spoke again. "We will be in touch with Jake before the end of the day."

Wilt Sanders called in the late afternoon and said the August income statement and balance sheet would be ready Wednesday. Finally, Jake called and said Malson would fund new loans while an agreement was negotiated.

Ginny called hours after everyone had left. "Tomorrow afternoon?" she asked.

Luke told her he was tied up, and she said she would try to come by the next evening. The two days had thrown Luke far behind, and he worked until midnight.

CHAPTER THIRTY SIX

Jake called early the next morning. "We're going to meet at Sandifer's office, but here's the deal." Jake explained Malson had proposed to renew a $20 million credit line with the 5 percent equity required. Malson would loan FRM another $6 million on a separate note to be repaid from the sale of servicing. Luke said he would reject the deal, but Jake finished, saying, "Let's talk and see what happens. I don't think they have the authority to write you a check."

Jake and Luke walked into Phil Sandifer's office, and Jake and Sandifer made small talk as the group waited for Chuck. Luke interrupted the conversation, "Where's Cindy Cleugh? I haven't seen her."

Sandifer stretched his neck. "Cindy is leaving the bank."

"Oh. Another question: can we get Bill Bivins in these conversations?"

Sandifer stretched again. "Actually, Mr. Bivins is taking a position with another bank. I trust you will keep that to yourselves. It won't be official until the end of the month. He's wrapping up a few things now."

"Who's taking his place, the vice president of operations I met?"

"Oh no. He's coordinating the integration of the branches. He works more directly with the board. Actually, Todd Weldon will become president and Nelson will be chairman. That's not official, either."

Luke processed the information. Cleugh had been fired, and Bivins was out and had most likely been looking for a new position for months. Obviously, the bank's leaders had known for months it was losing money. That explained the lack of communication recently from Chuck and his pleas to contact Bivins. The small talk returned until Chuck Rail entered the room.

Once Chuck was seated, Sandifer directed the conversation. "The bank is not able to pay any money to FRM for a number of reasons. First, we would have to document the amount of the alleged loss and verify the origin. Our internal review hasn't shown any evidence that the bank created a loss, but we can see how a missed margin call would have led to some substantial losses. We would have to document what loans were being held, how much the loss was on the loans, look at the market movements and trades, and verify the bank caused this and not FRM. We can't just accept your word you lost over seven million dollars because of us."

Luke jumped in, "Chuck knows he didn't send the margin call, and he knows I told him about the losses."

Chuck showed bluster but did not speak. Instead it was Sandifer who started anew, "Well, I said the bank couldn't pay for a number of reasons. The second is that the regulators will not permit it." Chuck's vigor evaporated. "I can't go into the specifics, but the bank has to consult the FDIC and must get approval for any agreements. The bank's maximum loan to one borrower is now fifteen million. We are working on approval to do another five million from some of our new banks that haven't been consolidated yet. We have special-exception approval to do a six-million-dollar loan to be repaid from the servicing. That's the best we can do."

Jake looked at Luke. "It doesn't solve the problem," Luke said, thinking out loud. "A loan doesn't increase FRM's net worth. We only have until September 15, and that's next Monday."

"What if the bank makes the loan to you and you put capital into FRM?" Sandifer asked.

"That solves the net worth issue, but it's not enough money. FRM will have only around one million dollars in cash, but we have commitments on software, and we are going to struggle after the servicing is sold. With your new five-percent equity requirement, we won't be able to use all of the credit line and would have to shrink substantially."

"How much do you need?" Sandifer asked.

"Give me the seven million you cost me, and I'll work it out."

Sandifer smiled at Jake and then glanced at Luke. "It's not a possibility. I'm being very candid." He waited a moment before beginning again, "How much of a loan would enable you to continue to operate?"

Luke looked at Jake and could tell he wanted him to give them a number. He calculated the software purchase, the equity in the credit line, and rounded up for the drain on cash flow after the servicing was sold. "We need about eight and a half million."

"So, if we could arrange a loan of eight and a half million dollars, then you could repay six million when the servicing sells and still operate."

Luke did not like the way the conversation was going. He looked at Jake and saw him nod his head slightly as if saying, "Take it." Luke changed the subject, "You're reducing the credit line by almost half. Fortunately, we have a bond broker doing cash trades and funding on delivery. But that much of a cut is going to cause us to struggle."

"Maybe the bank's Bond Department could help." Sandifer turned to Chuck, but Luke spoke first.

"The bank's Bond Department doesn't offer as good a price as the New York houses. We are both selling to the same brokers." Luke stopped and looked at Chuck. "We have equal access to that capital."

Jake spoke next. "Let's all talk among ourselves and get together this afternoon."

Jake and Luke caught the elevators and headed through the lobby. Melissa Marin was slicing her way through the crowd and heading for the exit. She saw Luke, but Luke spoke first, "Hi."

She gave him a quick "Hi," a forced smile, and continued on.

"Who's that?" Jake asked.

"Melissa Marin."

"She's pretty," Jake said, raising his eyes.

"She used to think I was cute," Luke said sarcastically.

"You dated her?"

"No. She works for the bank." Luke waited until they were farther from the crowd and added, "I think she knows something's going on."

"Oh, I'm sure rumors are moving around the bank." Jake nodded.

"That's why I'm not so cute anymore. She's noted my declining net worth."

No business was discussed, and Luke was left with his thoughts; both nodded to acquaintances without stopping as they passed down the street.

Luke leaned against a wingback chair, and Jake started talking as he seated himself behind his desk. "The bank is in trouble, and the regulators are calling the shots. If you don't want to start another business, it's best to take their deal. I think the bank may become judgment proof because of their losses. The suit will take years and lender liability is new theory. There aren't any Oklahoma cases. Even if we win, I doubt we will be able to collect the judgment because they'll be broke."

"I have to solve the HUD problem by Monday."

"Then we have to make a decision."

"What about Chuck? Why is he still in the discussions? Why wouldn't they have someone else around? Why not Sid?"

"Not sure. I would guess they think he knows the most about the facts. I would think once this gets solved, they will have someone else manage the relationship."

"If we can do this quick enough to not lose the HUD approval, I'll do it," Luke answered.

On the drive to the office, he wrestled with his own words. Taking the Malson deal was saying good-bye to $7 million, but in fact it had been gone for months, and Luke had never counted on that money for any reason other than to maintain the business. Luke now knew Malson was wobbling. Even if he won the suit, he might never recover any money, and FRM would close in the meantime.

Luke found the office relaxed. Harold and Nancy were almost giddy since Malson had advanced funds and had matched the detail as in the days before Cindy Cleugh. A stack of notifications on wires from loan sales had come in as well. Wilt was coming by with the August financials. Luke had told them nothing about the negotiations with Malson, yet he sensed they all knew something big had happened. They did not know the crisis still loomed.

Jake Ingles called in the afternoon. Malson hoped to have approval by Friday to do the credit line and side loan to Luke. Jake thought the documents could be ready by the middle of next week.

"That's too late," Luke said. "HUD has to have the statements by Monday."

"Go see them," Jake suggested. "I'm tied up in court on another case. Are you comfortable going alone or maybe I can have an associate go with you?"

Luke thought over the options. He knew it would take valuable time to educate another attorney on the facts. "I can handle it," he answered.

Within the next two hours, the plan hatched. Phil Sandifer, Chuck Rail, and Edgar Dinsen would go to HUD to meet with Ray Fontenot. Sandifer and Chuck would promise HUD the financing was being arranged, and Dinsen would present a letter saying the new financials were being prepared and would show sufficient net worth. Luke called Fontenot, who was evasive but finally agreed to a Monday meeting.

Ginny reached Luke in the early evening. "Can you meet at the condo?" she asked.

Luke left immediately and saw her car in the lot. They climbed the stairs together, and Ginny breathed, "He's still out but probably only for another hour. Tomorrow is girls' night out." She winked.

Luke opened the door, and she headed toward the bedroom before he caught her arm. "Sit with me on the sofa," he said.

She raised her eyebrows. "OK."

The living room was empty except for the sofa. There was an unblocked view of the vacant dining room and a portion of the bare kitchen counters. Nothing hung on the walls. There was no lamp or overhead light, and the room was growing darker. Luke bore straight ahead. "I want to be with you, but I want to be clear about where I'm going."

"OK."

"I don't know how much longer I'm going to do the mortgage thing."

"Are you in trouble?" she asked.

"No," he lied. "I think I'll be doing the mortgage thing for another year or so, but I don't want to do it for long. I only wanted to prove the best people could join together and beat the companies owned by the old money. I always said I would be out of it by forty. I will end up doing something else."

"Like what?" Ginny looked concerned.

"I don't know. I would like to teach someday. Maybe I will practice civil liberties law. I don't know."

"Really?"

"And I won't live here."

"Why?"

"It's a big world. I just happened to have gotten the idea of starting a mortgage company while I was going to law school. I liked the challenge. But I don't want to live in Tulsa."

"But this is where we live."

"For now. There are so many other great places. I don't want to stay here."

"But, you have a business here. You like the lake. What's going on?"

"The lake is nice for here, but the water is dirty. It leaves a film, a greenish brown stain on your swimsuit. There are many more beautiful places. It's a big world and there are places with beautiful blue water and nice beaches and more things to do." He paused. "And I'm not going to spend my life in the mortgage business. I want to be more than one thing. It seems people spend their life learning one thing and concentrating more on what they know than what they don't know. I want to keep learning and keep growing. The moment we quit learning, we start dying."

"Here you go," she said and frowned, "off on some crusade."

"Maybe. Maybe not. I'll still be doing this for a while, but not forever. We are two different people, but I love you. I want to be with you. I'm not divorced, but someday I will be. In the meantime, we can be together and see where it goes."

"What?"

"Can you see us being together once I can get out of this thing?"

"Why can't you keep the mortgage company? Why can't you stay here?"

"Because I want to do more things and this isn't where I want to live."

"I want to live here. I want to have friends here. I want to join organizations here."

"Ginny, that's not me."

"And I'm not a crusader," she exhaled. "I want to live here. There are things I want here." She paused as if thinking it over but then asked, "Teacher?"

"Maybe. There are lots of things to do, and I don't need a lot. Look around."

"This is short-term, isn't it?" She shook her head. "You know what's important to me."

"I won't always live like this. I've always worked and I have always made enough money. I always will. I may not make as much, but I'll make enough." He looked around. "This is a little bizarre, isn't it." There was no question in his voice. "I won't live like this. I'll make enough money, but I can't promise you society pages and galas."

"I know. That's why I stay married."

"What?"

"That's why I stay married. He and I want the same thing."

Luke's chest emptied, but his body was still. Time stopped, except for the flutter of her hair and the breathing of her chest. Suddenly Ginny's eyes were cold and flat. Her lips seemed to wave, drawing him in, but the hardened eyes kept him back. Her words hammered in his head. His eyes darted around the room as though searching for help. She tilted her head and brushed her hair to the side with bored indifference. He leaned back; the adrenaline drained from his body, and he felt stupid.

"That's what I want," she repeated, a timbre vibrating with each word. She watched him reeling in one place. "You knew that." The silence was too loud for him to speak. "Maybe you're tired. You said it's been a rough week." Again the silence hung. "And you won't feel so rushed tomorrow."

A long time passed before he spoke. "Yeah. I've had a lot going on."

"I'll call you tomorrow." The corners of her lips drifted lightly.

Luke wanted her. He wanted her now. He wanted her lips to quiver, her eyes to dance, and her touch to take him. He felt the excitement building in him, and he wanted to touch her neck and let his fingers drift down her arms. He sighed, "Yeah, let's try tomorrow. It's been a rough day."

He walked her to the car and saw the fullness of her breasts as she slid behind the wheel. He walked upstairs, sat on the sofa, and breathed the last of her scent. The hollowness bore through him; he filled with foolishness from having overlooked the obvious and then emptied again in the darkness.

He grabbed his shoes and ran three miles. The music played in his ears, but he heard nothing as his mind burned with the conversation on the sofa. He knew Ginny was the same as Melissa. When drawn to Melissa, he had called Ginny, playing it safe. He should have known what she would say but still couldn't accept the words. The sound of "I like you married" flirted in his memory. "You belong to me" teased his desires. "It's not like with you," had given him hope. "That's why I stay married" had crushed his chest. He barely slept.

CHAPTER THIRTY SEVEN

Ginny went to Luke's condo Thursday night. She seemed not to notice the distance between them, or maybe it had always been there, and the illusion had been ripped from Luke's heart. He watched her and never felt the rush of breaking from his loneliness as they had sex. The stark bedroom, the empty rooms, and the lone sofa flashed when he closed his eyes and reflected the cold and rejection he felt. The rush of escaping into her allure evaded him. He regretted opening the window into himself, and now it was closed. He had poured his energy into being an outsider and building a mortgage company whose ripples had lapped the pool's edge and attracted a predator. He had to face Malson and try to save the company before he could allow himself to think of living another life.

Malson had reported progress on Thursday, and Chuck and Phil Sandifer called Luke on Friday. Luke heard the scratchy background as they shared a speakerphone. Edgar Dinsen had met with the bank's auditing department, and the bank had approval for the line of credit and the side loan. The group agreed to stay at the Madison Hotel in Washington, DC.

"This Dinsen…" Chuck coughed. "Edgar Dinsen. Where did you find him?"

"We needed an auditing replacement for Snickel Fitter."

"He looks like Deputy Dawg and sounds like him, too," Chuck laughed.

"Yeah, a bit." Luke could hear Sandifer chuckling in the background.

"Is he going to get the updates done in time? He makes me nervous," Chuck said.

"Me, too," Sandifer echoed.

"Yes. I have to ride him. He always wants more time, and he hates to commit."

"Deputy Dawg better commit on Monday." Chuck mimicked a cartoon laugh.

"OK."

"Do you have to fly with him?" Chuck asked.

"No, I booked a different flight for me."

"We've greased some wheels before the meeting." Sandifer's voice was sure. "Congressman Wheeler is a good friend of the bank. Our meeting should go well."

"OK," Luke said, leaning into his desk with eyes popped wide open. Congressman Dee Wheeler was the House majority leader and one step from being Speaker of the House of Representatives. Luke could only muster another one-word response. "OK."

"That'll smooth the conversation," Sandifer said confidently. "Let's get together at the hotel before the meeting."

"OK." Luke was still thinking about Congressman Wheeler.

Luke churned through the weekend. He drove to the lake Friday night; Labor Day had passed, and the lake was less crowded. Luke waffled between confidence and uncertainty about Monday's meeting.

He drove to see his children on Saturday but returned to the lake Saturday night. He saw them again on Sunday, caught the last flight to Washington, read the *New York Times*, noted Malson's stock stood at four dollars, and checked in the Madison Hotel.

Luke was up early, although the meeting was scheduled for the afternoon. He had not left a wakeup call and was surprised when the phone rang before eight. He casually answered, "Hello."

"Luke, this is Congressman Dee Wheeler."

Luke stared at the white light of the hotel phone. "Yes, sir. Good morning."

"Good morning, Luke. I want you to know I have spoken with HUD, and your meeting should go well today. I'm sure they will extend the time needed, so the bank can get its documents arranged. I wanted you to know I have spoken with them, and they will be amenable."

"Thank you."

"I didn't want you being concerned. I understand there are some issues, but I think those have been worked out."

Luke remained silent.

"My office will be verifying the meeting goes smoothly."

"Thank you."

"Now, enjoy your day in the city," the congressman added before he said good-bye.

Luke slowly cradled the phone and turned and sank into a stuffed chair. A new power hovered in his life and sapped his energy. He ordered breakfast and a newspaper. The phone rang again. It was Phil Sandifer asking if Luke had talked with Congressman Wheeler. Luke agreed to meet Sandifer and Chuck before noon. He called Edgar Dinsen and arranged for him to meet the group. Luke showered, ate, and walked around the city. The call from the House majority leader spun in his head.

The four gathered in the lobby and reviewed the key points. The audited financials showed a negative net worth of $4.9 million dollars. Malson was loaning Luke Boyd $8.5 million dollars, which would be invested as new capital into FRM, raising its net worth to $3.6 million dollars, far above the $100,000 level required by HUD. Malson would close the transaction by September 17, and Dinsen would provide the updated audited financial statements by September 25. The servicing sale of $6 million was not a condition of the deal.

The others asked about lunch, and Luke recalled a Greek restaurant within a couple of blocks. They scaled down three steps into a packed room of suits and good cuisine. Sandifer, Chuck, and Luke looked anxiously at each other, slicing the servings thinly. Dinsen dived into the offering. Chuck tossed disgusted glances as Dinsen ate. The other three left their plates half full.

They grabbed separate cabs, Luke hauling a gaping Dinsen as the accountant's head swiveled. "I've never been to Washington, DC," he repeated every few minutes as they wound through the city with the Capitol dome looming overhead. They uncoiled in front of the Eisenhower-era HUD building, its 1950s architecture encasing cold, pale green, tiled floors and vacant concrete corridors. The building reminded Luke of an oversized elementary school, with gigantic hallways and gargantuan classrooms. An attendant led them at a pace so slow Luke paused between steps as he passed empty rooms with more than twenty desks, each with a typewriter, most shrouded in plastic and only a handful uncovered and as yet silent as four or five staff chatted away.

The group sat in wooden chairs and waited until Ray Fontenot casually entered from the hall, greeted them, shook hands, and led them to a cavernous conference room with gray-and-white tiled floor and off-white walls, vacant except for a small, pale, wooden square-legged table and a few thick-legged wooden chairs. No one sat. Sandifer looked relaxed, Chuck puffed his chest, Dinsen's mouth was open, and Luke sensed trouble. Fontenot stiffened. "Do you have the financials?"

Dinsen handed him a copy of the audited report and a letter stating the pending transactions would increase the net worth to $3.6 million within a few days. Dinsen's letter said new financials would be ready by September 25.

"Mr. Boyd, you missed the deadline." Fontenot's words echoed in the den of hard flooring and bare walls.

Luke quickly recapped the transaction, current negative net worth, his borrowing of money, and the sale of servicing.

"I don't care where you get the money or how much you borrow. FRM has to have enough net worth." Fontenot glared at Luke. "You told me you needed to change your fiscal year to install software. That looks like a lie."

Luke was conciliatory. "That was the reason for the delay. Some other problems arose. We had to delay the software installation."

Chuck explained the bank was committed to loaning the money, but obtaining approvals and drawing documents required time; he said the transaction would be complete in two more days. Sandifer nodded and voiced his agreement.

"So you found out about this in the last week. That's why you have to rush to help Mr. Boyd."

"Yes," Chuck answered.

Luke cocked his head. "Wait a minute." Luke started to air the differences but then stopped. "The bank has been aware of our situation for a while."

"Whatever differences we may have, the bank is ready to provide the financing," Sandifer interceded.

Fontenot set his sights on Edgar Dinsen. "Does he have the net worth now or not?"

Dinsen wavered. "No."

"Are you going to certify he has the net worth?"

Dinsen looked around the room and stammered, "I will certify what the net worth is." He then paused, pulled at his collar, and muddled on, "After the loan." He looked at everyone. "But I can't certify it now."

"Will it be enough?" Fontenot demanded.

"I don't know." Dinsen's words sloshed in his mouth. "You see, there…are so many…accounting rules, under the FASB…provisions, the Financial Accounting…Standards Board, and me…we must…must…follow each of these verifications of—"

Fontenot cut him off, "So you don't know what the net worth will be. Sounds like Mr. Boyd's out of luck."

Luke jumped in, "Wait a minute. I haven't lied to you, and I've been straightforward. Dinsen's letter shows what the net worth will be. It's way over the minimum. You'll have the statement by the twenty-fifth." He turned to Edgar Dinsen. "Right?"

"Yes, I can do statements by the twenty-fifth; I just don't know what the amount will be." Dinsen was starting to perspire.

"That doesn't do me any good," Fontenot said. "Are you going to do what your letter says?" Fontenot demanded of Dinsen.

"Well, you see, we have so much we need to review and…"

"What is this?" Fontenot jumped in. "Either he has the net worth, or he doesn't."

"Luke, can we have a moment?" Sandifer asked. He saw the shock on Luke's face but continued, "Please, you and Edgar go outside for a second."

Luke paused. Dinsen was mumbling and crumbling before his eyes. Luke sensed Fontenot did not appreciate being forced into this meeting and obviously blamed Luke. Further, Luke now knew Malson had prepped the congressman and Fontenot with their version of the ordeal. "For a second," Luke said. He looked at Chuck and Sandifer. "You know where I stand," he said and lingered. Chuck glared back, and Sandifer smiled with a nod. "Come on Edgar," Luke said to Dinsen.

Luke led Dinsen out of the room and closed the hollow-core door behind them as Dinsen began muttering about everyone needing to understand the Financial Accounting Standards Board and procedures and limitations. Luke put Dinsen in a chair facing in the opposite direction and said, "Be quiet." Luke walked back and leaned his ear against the door. He could hear Chuck's voice echoing in the room.

"Congressman Wheeler has told you the bank will make this good. You'll have the financial statements by the twenty-fifth, or the bank will take over FRM's assets. We already have HUD approval, and the servicing will go to us," Chuck said.

"I'll give him until the twenty-fifth. That's a ten-day extension. I understand you have a letter regarding Malson stepping in to ensure HUD's interests are protected." Fontenot's voice sounded cordial.

"We have the letter," Sandifer said matter-of-factly.

"OK. We'll wait until the twenty-fifth." Fontenot's voice trailed away.

Luke heard steps and moved away from the door, heard the knob turn, and said to Dinsen, "This is a huge building."

"I know," Dinsen said, as Chuck, Sandifer, and Fontenot exited the conference room. Luke turned to face them.

Fontenot started, "We're going to give you a ten-day extension. That's until the twenty-fifth, but that's all." He stared at Dinsen, still seated. "The letter will go out today. But I must receive the updated financials by the twenty-fifth."

Dinsen stood and started to gaggle about the process. Luke interrupted. "By the twenty-fifth."

The four headed downstairs unaccompanied, struggled to find the right elevator, and found themselves on a different side of the lobby and cut off from where they had entered. They separated into two groups. Luke led Dinsen toward a busy street where they could catch a cab. "I still have several hours before my flight," Dinsen said, looking up at the Washington Monument towering above the Potomac River. "I've never been here before," he said again. "I wish I could see some monuments and things."

Luke searched for a cab. "They're impressive."

"Gosh, I really wish I could see some of them."

Luke hailed a taxi, opened the door for Dinsen, and watched him slide across the seat. Luke leaned inside the cab and caught the driver's eye. "How much to do a monument tour?"

"Forty."

Luke reached into his pocket, pulled out three twenty-dollar bills and handed them to the driver. "Show him some monuments."

"Aren't you coming?" Dinsen asked and acted as if he were lost.

"Enjoy. I'm going to catch an earlier flight." Luke shut the door and waved the taxi away.

CHAPTER THIRTY EIGHT

uke's mind raced faster than the jet that carried him back to Tulsa. The Grateful Dead and "Fire on the Mountain" shot through the headphones. The majority leader of the House of Representatives had called his hotel room. Chuck and Sandifer had given a letter to Fontenot stating Malson would take over FRM and its assets on September 25 if the net worth issue had not been resolved. Luke wondered how much of the conversation he had missed and what else he did not know. He knew he was deep in a trap and Malson's political connections were now part of the seal. He could fight Malson now and lose FRM, or he could sign the deal and try to escape later.

The next morning Malson stock dropped to below two dollars, a drop of more than nineteen dollars from the price a few months earlier. Luke had called Jake Ingles to tell him about the HUD meeting. Jake did not seem surprised. By noon Jake Ingles had called to say the closing was set for Wednesday afternoon.

Wilt Sanders arrived as scheduled and brought the July and August financial statements. Luke asked how to transfer money from FRM to himself to pay on the Malson loan without incurring a large tax liability. Wilt had officially left his firm but knew one of the partners could handle the issue. He called from Luke's office and arranged for the formation of a holding company.

Luke watched from behind his desk as Wilt sat on the sofa, finished the call, and replaced the handset. Luke smiled. "OK, do I have a deal for you!" He watched Wilt closely. "You're officially out of work, and it looks like we are going to make it. How about becoming our chief financial officer?"

"Oh, I don't know," Wilt started. "I don't want to manage people."

The answer was better than Luke had anticipated. "You won't have to manage people. We will get you people who can do the work. You oversee it. Help us with the computer conversion. You'll love that. Computerize everything. We need that."

"That would be fun. But, how do I not manage people?"

"We'll figure that out." Luke paused. "Look, we give you a hundred thousand dollars a year and a car, and you tell me what you want." Luke was raising his overhead, but a poor accounting department had left him vulnerable. He needed Wilt's expertise to deal Malson and turn the company over to the key people.

"Wow." Wilt liked the money. "You know I want to consult, but I haven't lined up any clients. It might give me time to transition. I wouldn't want to do it for more than a year."

"A year's fine. If you want to stay, you can stay; if you want to go, you can go. Anytime." Luke spread his arms. "How easy can I make it?"

"Can I think about it?"

"Sure. But if you decide to not do this, tell me why and let me try again."

"OK." Wilt was thinking.

When Wilt accepted the job on Wednesday morning, Luke broke into his biggest smile since he thought he had landed a line of credit with FCBA. Within two hours Wilt was onsite. Harold was elated, and Luke saw the relief in Nancy's eyes. Luke left for the meeting with Malson, confident he was better equipped for battle.

The war resumed as soon as Malson presented its documents in one of the law firm's conference rooms. The agreement required Luke's full guarantee, instead of a partial guarantee. Luke's personal liability was increasing from $5 million to $28.5 million. The documents provided FRM had to hire a new chief financial officer acceptable to Malson within the next thirty days. Neither of the terms had been previously discussed. Luke looked at Jake Ingles, who said two words, "Sign it." He left out the words "you really have no other choice."

Luke probed Chuck on the chief financial officer provision. "This isn't much notice. We have to recruit someone, and then they will want to give at least two weeks' notice, if not more. Who's going to be acceptable?"

"That Nancy is out," Chuck started harshly and switched to a smile, "but, we can help you." He glanced at Sandifer. "If you can't find anyone right away, we have a great person in mind. Betsy Simpson, a bank officer with another bank, recently earned her accounting degree, and she would be a great choice."

Luke was shocked at Chuck's transparency. Betsy Simpson was married to a Malson employee who did not know his wife had an on-and-off affair with Chuck. Malson wanted to plant a spy in FRM. Luke had not seen this coming but was thankful for the timing. "You think she's a good choice?" Luke asked.

"Oh, yes." Chuck smiled as if he thought Luke would agree.

"Well, you certainly know her."

"Yes," he said, the two sharing the inside joke.

"Would Wilt Sanders be acceptable?" Luke said, picking up a pen.

"Sure," Sandifer spoke first.

"Of course," Chuck said, shrugging, "if you could get him."

"He started today," Luke said nonchalantly. For a few seconds, Luke thought the silence in the room was worth the $28.5 million guarantee and the $7 million loss. He quickly got over the feeling. On the way back to the office, Luke processed what the bank regulators must have been told and was sure the blame had fallen on Nancy and him.

By the next morning, Thursday, Edgar Dinsen had verified the capital infusion. Wilt guided Dinsen through the July, August, and September transactions, and by Friday morning, the updated audited financials were ready. Luke called Ray Fontenot at HUD to tell him the updated financials would arrive on Monday, days before the deadline. Luke couldn't tell if Fontenot was disappointed or unconcerned as he said, "Be on time next year." On Monday Fontenot acknowledged receipt. The HUD extension letter Fontenot had promised in their meeting arrived two weeks later.

Ginny called and went to Luke's condo on Thursday night. It had been a week since they had seen each other. "Are you avoiding me?" she asked, unbuttoning her blouse as she entered.

"I guess we want different things. That's what you told me." He hoped she would take back her words.

Instead, she crushed him again. "So, we want different things. Don't be so serious. We still have fun." She smiled flirtatiously as her skirt dropped to the floor.

Luke went through the motions but the magic was gone. Afterward he watched her getting dressed and she knew something was different. She saw the fatigue in his eyes and noticed he had lost weight.

"Are you trying to get rid of me?" She peered at him. "You'll call me. I know you will." Her eyes showed a trace of doubt.

Friday morning Nancy walked into Luke's office and resigned. Luke had already been warned by Wilt. Luke offered her another position, but she declined, and he felt guilty for her leaving. Luke thanked her as regrets filled the room.

On the same day, the local newspaper carried Malson's announcement that Bill Bivins was leaving and had joined another bank in Georgia.

Doug Turney had left several messages and finally reached Luke. "I see you're still around," he started. "Pulled it off, huh? I knew you would."

"Beth should have taken one of my offers. She's lost some money," Luke said.

"Oh, you'll get it back. I mean, I'm sure she'll get it back. You'll have made it all back and earned more by the time you get divorced," Turney concluded.

On Friday afternoon Luke felt himself decompressing from the turmoil. The summer's greens had yet to turn, but the air was cooler; the evenings had the hint of a chill. He planned a quiet weekend at the lake. He would run and read and relax. Luke was surprised when Andrea signaled Chuck Rail was holding.

Chuck's voice sounded as if he was trying to sell life insurance. "I want you to know Malson is solid; the bank will be here, and the board already has a strong plan."

"OK," Luke said.

"Now, we are going to announce a loss today. But as I said, we want you to know the bank is solid, and Malson will still be here." Chuck's voice halted. "There will be some changes, but these are only going to make us stronger."

"Who will be managing our account?" Luke waited as if a child were being born.

"Tom Cook, from correspondent banking, is moving into my department. He will be your loan officer."

Luke heard only "my department" and "your loan officer." Chuck had survived and was still managing the relationship. "Who?"

"Tom Cook. He was in correspondent banking."

"OK." Luke recalled the name from the luncheon with Bivins.

"I want you to know the bank is strong, and we will be here to fund your loans under the agreement."

"OK."

"Great. Now have a great weekend," Chuck concluded as though his voice were being recorded.

Luke sat in disbelief. The conversation had seemed comical. He grabbed an evening newspaper but found nothing regarding Malson. He decided to wait and pick up the *New York Times* on Saturday morning and then drive to the lake. He ordered a toasted bagel and coffee and leisurely fingered through the business section. A full column was devoted to Malson's announcement that it had lost $353 million in the last three months. Malson now had a net worth of only $3 million dollars—less than FRM's! The article included quotes from federal regulators assuring the bank would remain open, and operations would continue despite the losses as a restructuring plan was developed. Malson had announced losses of $442 million in the last six months. The stock price was $0.25.

CHAPTER THIRTY NINE

The staff knew something huge had passed, even if they did not know all the facts. There was plenty of talk in Tulsa as well. Inaccuracy and lack of knowledge have never kept people from talking. Competitors tried to find an advantage, but FRM was still there and appeared solid. With others Luke polished the veneer and avoided the facts, which were far less interesting than the rumors.

The servicing sale to Corn Savings closed on schedule. FRM netted $6.2 million and the proceeds reduced the side note down to $2.3 million. Joe Conti thanked Luke, asked no questions regarding the Socoast suit, and asked when FRM might want to sell more servicing.

Wilt Sanders was a master. Luke suddenly had better financial reports and worked fewer hours as Wilt artfully guided the software installation. Personal computers were installed to track loan applications, loan closings, marketing reports, and loan sales. Luke even had time to computerize his real estate business.

Harold Rhoden seemed to fit the slot heading the Loan Shipping Department. The pressure of loan originators, branch managers, and realtors had been too much for him. The new role required less decision making. He worked well with Wilt, and Phyllis liked the change. Luke let Phyllis, Amy, and the other Tulsa-area branch manager report directly to him. Mike Eckridge had done a good job managing the Oklahoma City region for the past six months. Luke believed he had a team to take over the company. First, he needed a more solid credit line.

Tom Cook, the new loan officer, was overwhelmed by the responsibility. Correspondent banking had traditionally been a good-ole-boy job—shaking bankers' hands, telling stories, and making routine loans on bank stock, where collateral value was rarely questioned and principal payments were even more unusual. Correspondent Loans was a dying department as big banks gobbled up smaller ones. Real estate lending was a challenge for Tom Cook, and mortgage banking was quantum physics to him. A few weeks into the relationship, Cook became testy and made a comment about "creditability" and "FRM having misappropriated money" while talking with Luke on the telephone. Luke exploded from his chair and would remember little of what he said other than, "Malson and Chuck Rail caused this," and "Don't ever question my creditability." Luke knew he had unleashed an onslaught of profanities from the festering hatred he harbored for Malson. The line was quiet for a long time as Luke recomposed himself, looked through the glass panels to find Andrea staring at him, and then sat back in his chair. Thereafter, Cook watched his words, rarely called Luke, and dealt primarily with Wilt and Harold, who both viewed Cook as a lightweight.

The search for a new bank had begun immediately. Luke called Pete Winston first. FRM's cash position was back above $2 million, but the marketing loss in the past year was a concern. "The bank is going to want to see one solid year without those huge marketing losses, so they know it was an aberration," Pete said. He recommended Luke start the process after the next audited reports.

In the first weeks of Luke's new search, banking news deteriorated. By the end of October, all of the large banks in Dallas and Houston had failed. Suddenly banks from North Carolina, New York, California, and Ohio had taken over landmark buildings in Texas, and the temporary banners that had waved across rural Oklahoma now dotted major cities. The conquering banks took the deposits and made no local loans. The first twenty-four-hour cable news network focused on the demise of Texas and the brave new era of interstate banking. Oklahoma and the rest of the region drew ancillary notice. Luke knew his hunt was more of a long shot this time.

Business was steady, and the lower credit line with Malson was always a problem. FRM had to regularly sell loans individually, giving up the servicing, to stay within the limits. The sales ate into FRM's income, since the servicing was discounted at least 1 percent or more when sold individually. The shipping was more cumbersome, and additional clerks had to be hired. The salary expense and overnight shipping fees gnawed into profits, and Luke grimaced as he saw income draining out the door with the FedEx couriers.

It had been almost two months when Luke saw Ginny again. She had quit calling two weeks before and he hesitated before finally touching the numbers. They met in the afternoon. She was beautiful, but he did not lose himself. He felt smudged and distant. Afterward, he watched her glide down the stairs and float across the parking lot, her steps pulling him toward her as she faded away. Somewhere before she reached the car, the veil tore and the vision vanished. He did not call her again.

A false semblance of civility returned when Chuck called Luke in early December. It was their first conversation since Chuck's September call to warn Luke of Malson's loss announcement. Chuck called with a mundane question Luke detected as camouflage to learn more about the mortgage business. Malson Mortgage was adrift and not a factor in the market. Luke figured Chuck needed the information to curry favor upstairs and gave him half-accurate answers. He took a moment to probe, "How are you doing?"

"Big Boy, I'm fine. The bank is going to be fine. Some changes. A little less money, but Chuck can change."

"So, you're solid?"

"Sure." He dropped his voice. "You know, I'm not seeing Cindy, but I can still find a friend here and there."

"How's Sid?" Luke asked.

"Oh, Sid left the bank. He left in early October. He joined a small banker who's trying to assemble a group of rural banks. It'll never work."

"Oh," Luke said, thinking Sid must have been planning his move when Bivins was jumping ship and as FRM and Malson had been scuffling in mid-September. Chuck must have been Malson's only mortgage banking option.

The December holiday season approached, and the short days and cold, wet, bare-tree Oklahoma winter descended. Bank closings were now a weekly Thursday event. Two of the small banks Luke had used and who had been summoned by Malson to one of the meetings had been shut down by regulators. Winney's bank, Sand Springs Fidelity, seemed to be surviving, and FRM had to use it regularly because of the lower credit line. Luke hoarded earnings, made no principal payments to Malson, and paid only the interest. Luke wanted the cushion; he was unsure of Malson's future. Beth knew of the losses; she stalled and insisted there would be no divorce. Her spending was still out of control, and the cadre of sitters grew. His divorce was going nowhere slowly.

Malson's stock remained at a mere $0.25, and Luke wondered if an out-of-state bank deal was in the works. There had been no AM radio voice call from Chuck, so he assumed the bank had stabilized. Three days before the year ended, he found full-column articles in the *Wall Street Journal* and the *New York Times*. The articles announced Malson had posted a loss in the most recent quarter of $373 million—larger than the last three-month loss! The bank now had a negative net worth of $370 million. Both articles said the bank would remain open under an operating agreement with the FDIC.

CHAPTER FORTY

In early January, Luke increasingly knew he was stuck with Malson. The reception from out-of-state banks was even colder than the previous year. The regional bank failures and FRM's losses barred doors. Keegan Securities' early settlements helped, but FRM was at Keegan's limit, and Luke hoped to find others to offer cash trades and early settlements. Early settlements would make up for part of the reduced line of credit with Malson and would be simpler and more profitable than selling individual loans. Luke decided to start his search with Stiller Stevens.

Almost all of Luke's business now went to Keegan Securities. John Elliott had jumped to another firm a few months earlier and moved to Los Angeles to market junk bonds for mergers and acquisitions. Fred Lawson had taken Elliott's place and called frequently, trying to regain more of the account. Luke decided to pitch the idea of Stiller Stevens matching Keegan's deal. An appointment was booked, and in late January, Luke caught an early plane to O'Hare, dropped his luggage at the Whitehall Hotel, and grabbed a taxi south to the financial district and the Stiller Stevens office.

Fred Lawson was in his early thirties, medium height, and slightly built. Fred was eager to build his business and knew Luke produced good volumes. They visited the Chicago Board of Trade, and Luke watched the animated traders and the clutter of paper in the pits and explained his deal with Keegan.

Fred promised to talk to Stiller Stevens executives about offering a similar deal. Alex Stewart had retired. Luke offered to meet directly with the decision makers if that would help. Luke noted the young broker's age; it was rare for Luke to deal with someone his age or younger. Fred was obviously still learning and wanted to talk more about the industry. They agreed to meet for dinner at Cricket's, a popular restaurant in the Tremont Hotel.

Cricket's décor of toys and overhead trains, all reminiscent of the 21 Club in New York, drew an attractive crowd. The food was good. Luke thought Fred was earnest, and the conversation was lively. Midway through the entrée, Fred's eyes darted to the left, and he waved sheepishly toward the reception area. Luke instinctively turned.

A tall blonde, dressed in a tapered green dress and high heels, waved back to Fred. Luke's eyes locked on her. The blonde leaned to her friend, a somewhat shorter blonde, and whispered. The two walked toward the table, and Fred and Luke stood in unison.

Luke watched as Fred enjoyed a courteous hug with the tall blonde and then another with the shorter one. Fred made the introductions. "Denise, this is Luke Boyd. Luke, this is Denise Patrick." Luke smiled and disappeared for an instant in the brilliance of her round eyes. He never heard the shorter blonde's name although he knew he said, "Nice to meet you." His eyes floated back to Denise Patrick. She was five feet nine, and the heels made her taller. Luke did not know her dress was a size four, but he liked the dress.

Denise and her friend had stopped by for a cocktail. They had both worked with Fred as broker's assistants at another firm before Fred moved to Stiller Stevens. Denise was now a broker, and her friend was still serving as an assistant. Luke nodded and turned his head at the appropriate times, but he always found Denise's eyes and smiled. Only later would he wonder how stupid he might have looked.

"Please join us," Luke offered, but Denise and her friend said they were going to the bar. "Join us after dinner," Denise said. Luke's appetite was gone.

Luke and Fred finished their meal, and Denise was the topic. She was thirty and single. Luke had a clear view of Denise and her friend as they sat at the bar. Occasionally, Denise would look over her shoulder and smile. Fred said she was smart and knew the commodities markets. Fred grabbed the dinner tab, and Luke flipped his hair over his collar and offered to buy drinks in the club. Denise glanced twice as Fred paid and moved on her stool as Fred and Luke approached.

Luke ordered a Perfect Rob Roy, stirred, strained, and up with a twist. "What's that?" Denise asked.

"Scotch with equal parts sweet and dry vermouth. I like these more than they like me. Two's my limit."

"Why?" she asked with a smile.

"I like them," he said and smiled back.

Fred was gone in a half hour. Denise's friend stayed a little longer, and then they were alone. She was from Long Island; she had moved to Chicago five years earlier. She had started as an assistant to an older broker, who had built a clientele of grain elevator operators, farmers, and buyers whose livelihoods were tied to wheat, corn, soybeans, and pork bellies; they traded futures to hedge their crops, purchases, and contracts. Her broker had retired at the end of the previous year, and she now had the accounts. Excitement danced on her lips as she talked, but she was well grounded.

She asked Luke about mortgage banking. She did not know the operations side but knew all about GNMA bonds, FNMA bonds, Treasuries, and T-bills and the cash and futures markets. Luke talked about the industry, and Denise raised the question of the bank failures; she knew of the problems spreading in his region. She was well versed, but Luke never mentioned Malson. The business talk merely traipsed on the surface.

"Are you married?" she asked.

"Yes," he said and waited.

"Children?"

"Two. A boy and a girl. I love them to death."

They talked for a few minutes about his children, which led into a discussion of her family. Her father had worked in Manhattan and had commuted for years. Her mother stayed at home. Her parents had since retired to Naples, Florida, and Denise flew there several times a year. She had one sister still in New York.

"You haven't mentioned your wife," she said.

Luke took a deep breath. "Well, that's a long story and…"

"And?"

"I don't think you want the whole story."

"Try me."

"You're going to say I'm making this up, but here goes." She furrowed her brow as he talked about Oklahoma requiring a property settlement prior to granting a divorce. Her eyes widened when he described his condo. She seemed sympathetic when he told her he had been separated for almost two years this time. He mentioned the prior separation. He talked about Beth's spending, the unkempt house, the endless stream of nannies and cleaners, but he never mentioned her affair.

"So, girlfriends?" she asked.

"No," he lied.

"C'mon."

"I've had a few affairs," he admitted. He took a deep breath. "Mostly with married women." He winced, expecting her disgust.

Instead she followed with a question. "Because?"

He took a sip. "They're safer. I have one huge problem already. I'm married, and I don't need the complications and guilt single women put on me." His eyes stayed on his glass.

"I don't understand," she pressed.

"Married women have a home, a life, a future. They're bored. They want to have fun." He thought of Ginny. "There aren't any strings. My life's going to be tied up for a while."

"Don't you feel guilty?"

"About their husbands? Yes. I don't feel good about it."

"What's wrong with single women?"

"They want to make plans. I can't make plans. It may be years before this thing is settled. I guess that's why I never fix up the condo or get a better place."

"What do you mean you can't make plans?"

"They want families and children and houses and stuff, and I'm not going to be able to make those types of plans right now. I'm trying to get out of one deal, and I'm not anxious to get messed up in another. Dating them becomes a second hassle."

"So, you've dated single women," she said and gave him a knowing smile.

"Yes. That hasn't worked well. It can get bad." He regretted opening the topic.

"How bad?"

He looked away from her and then swiveled back to his drink. "Well, let's just say they get angry; sometimes they get depressed. I've heard I'm destroying their life. Maybe it's the stigma of seeing a married man. They call Beth, thinking I'm there. One would even call me in the middle of the night and say she was going to kill herself."

"Sounds like you've been hanging around too many Southern belles." She cocked her head, and the blond hair bounced and floated like in a shampoo commercial.

"Southern belles? That's the Deep South, not Oklahoma."

"Sounds the same to me."

"How?"

"Sounds like you prefer women who are dependent on you—who need you. Women that rely on men for support, money, status. I don't hear much about career women in your discussion."

"Well, some of them worked," he said defensively.

"They don't sound like independent women. If they were secure in their life, maybe you wouldn't have these issues. Maybe you need women to be dependent on you. Maybe you need that for your self-esteem."

"I don't know about that."

"Doesn't sound like you can handle independent women. Must be too threatening."

"I don't think that's the problem." He gave her a big smile. "So, you majored in psychology?"

"No," she lied.

"Well, I'm not real complex, but I'm a little more complex than your analysis."

"Yes, I did major in psychology."

"Are you having fun?"

"I'm just goofing with you," she said and laughed. "You didn't tell me about growing up in Oklahoma."

Luke mentioned growing up in a small town, selling magazines door-to-door, mowing yards, and summer jobs working with blue-collar workers for minimum wage. He mentioned the heavy influence of Protestant and Pentecostal religions and the times he had visited a friend's church as a child where the congregation spoke in tongues. He admitted he no longer attended but he still believed we were judged by how we used our talents. He mentioned the "Love it or Leave" mentality where questioning things was unpatriotic. "Oklahoma has not fully accepted the Renaissance," he joked.

She laughed. The bar was thinning, and she mentioned she had an early day. "How long are you in town?" she asked.

"I leave tomorrow."

"Too bad," she said. "There's a great little place close to the Board of Trade. I know you would like it."

"I'm not leaving until tomorrow evening," he lied. He had a morning flight.

"If you have time, we could meet for a late lunch."

"I could arrange that," he smiled.

They walked toward Rush Street to hail a taxi. He heard her tell the driver to go to State Street and then turn onto another street he didn't recognize. He closed the door and watched the cab blend into the sea of lights and reflections. He glided down Rush Street and turned the corner to the Whitehall Hotel.

The next morning he called the office and said he would return that night. He began calling Chicago banks trying to arrange an appointment, but he struck out. There was no interest. He met Denise Patrick, and the daylight showed the fineness of her complexion. A hint of freckles danced below her eyes when she spoke. Her thick blond hair swooped from one side to the other in the 1980s fashion, and her lips were full but not thick. She was striking, and heads turned as they moved through the restaurant. She played tennis and loved snow skiing and music. She had one customer in Tulsa who she knew did business with other brokers. She was planning a trip in February to capture more of the account. Luke gave her his card and told her they could play tennis at his indoor club.

CHAPTER FORTY ONE

By February all of the major banks in Oklahoma were in trouble. Lowe Bank had a negative net worth and announced it was operating under an agreement with the FDIC. The other two large banks had stock prices hovering around two dollars and also had operating agreements.

Pete Winston's voice was subdued as he said FCBA was pulling in its horns. While his office was staying open, the bank had placed a moratorium on new commercial loans from the Southwest. Pete mentioned the ratcheting uncertainty, the collapse of the regional banks, and the general slowing of the economy. Pete tried to buoy Luke's spirits and promised to stay in touch.

Luke knew the savings and loans loved the interest-free escrow accounts that came with mortgage loans. He hoped the promise of interest-free balances could land a credit line. He found they were only interested in buying servicing. Some had wicked proposals. One Texas institution wanted to pay Luke $200,000 dollars to buy $10 million in loans on March 26 with a promise to buy them back on April 4. The institution would even loan Luke the money to do the deal. The transaction was a sham to fool the regulators of the troubled institution.

Luke told them no and then refused their calls as the offer increased to $250,000. The industry was running scared.

Luke's visit with Fred Lawson brought some relief. Stiller Stevens agreed to match Keegan's deal but set a $5 million limit. Luke increasingly knew he had to be able to renew with Malson again in September. He needed Malson to survive but to be too weak to muster another attack. The unsettling prospect shadowed every day.

The Reagan administration lobbied publicly for lower interest rates to stimulate the economy. Critics warned the Japanese would quit buying US bonds; still, the Fed eased, and long-term interest rates started a historic decline. Single-digit rates returned. Residential sales were stagnant, but Luke saw an opportunity.

The mortgages on the books were suddenly far above the current market. FRM had never advertised, always relying on realtors and builders to funnel their business. Now Luke bought half-page ads in newspapers heralding the drop in interest rates and the huge savings available for homeowners. FRM was months ahead of others in pursuing the strategy, and FRM's telephones exploded with calls.

Processing refinances was expensive. Borrowers needed more handholding to guide them through the process. More staff was needed, the profit margin was thinner, and Luke needed more credit capacity to meet the demand. Still, Luke knew seeking refinances was the best way to maintain and build his servicing portfolio.

Andrea's note brightened a February day. Luke moved Denise Patrick's message to the top of the stack. She was arriving next Tuesday; she had a midday appointment and was available for tennis later. She was flying back to Chicago on Wednesday.

She looked like a model, spinning from the Hyatt's revolving doors. She clasped her sheathed racquet next to her burgundy warm-ups. Within minutes they arrived at the tennis club. She was crisp in her short tennis skirt as they emerged onto the brightly lit indoor court, and the white outfit highlighted her large breasts. Her femininity quickly vanished into a whirlwind of energy. Her forehead was heavy and hard. Her serve was fast and spun and kicked. Two hands joined firmly as she ripped topspin backhands crosscourt and down the line. Denise Patrick was an outstanding tennis player, and Luke had to play his best.

An hour and half later, they sipped juice, and Luke asked her to dinner. In another couple of hours, her long legs again swirled through the Hyatt's doors, this time below a short raspberry ensemble. The couple headed to Luke's favorite restaurant, a French bistro on Fifteenth Street. The sconce-lit, dark green walls highlighted her eyes and hair. She ordered carefully, avoiding heavy sauces and butter. She was gleeful about the vegetables and ate lightly from the broiled fish. They shared a bottle of Puligny-Montrachet, and the candlelight flickered in the glasses. Time melted warmly.

The night was dark, and a wisp of light misted from the street lamps. She turned as they reached the car, and the faint glow framed her face. Luke stopped, reached with his left hand, and lightly swept her hair. She smiled, and he leaned and kissed her. He felt the softness of her lips, and she was firm in his arms. She smelled like spring. Slowly he opened the car door; she took a half step and then turned. Her eyes softened, and he kissed her again. He leaned back, and her round eyes opened; he saw her fragility as she slid into the car. Luke started for the hotel, and for the first time all night, the couple was quiet.

"Would you like to come over?" Luke asked, surprised at his calm cadence.

"And see this beautiful vacant condo you've described?" She focused straight ahead. He waited, and she let him off the hook before he responded. "No, thanks. I have a nice room," she said, glancing out the passenger window. She turned to him and touched his hand. "Why don't you come share it with me?"

He never answered the question. He always remembered the cascade of chandelier light on her hair in the lobby and the slow ascent of the elevator as they stared at each other. She reached into her coat pocket, removed the key, and unlocked the door. Once through, she turned, and his lips found hers; his hands cradled her hair. They swayed together, stripping each other and finding each other at the same time. His fingers drifted on her narrow, tapered hips and the fullness of her breasts. Their caresses stroked and drove their thirst. He melted into her; their eyes locked and searched. Her rhythm was like the sea, wave after wave, taking him, drawing him, until both were spent. Her warm, soft lips kissed him as he came and then she draped herself around him.

They slept embraced as one as the twinkle of the city's lights played on the bare windows. The first late light of the winter morning spilled across the room, and she fidgeted, opened her eyes, and fingered his hair. He awoke to her touch and took a deep breath as her fingers trailed his abdomen and her lips followed. His eyes rose to the ceiling and then into themselves as he vanished into the softness of her mouth. He stroked her back and shoulders until she raised herself above him, and they made love again. Their eyes were wide open in the morning light and he wanted all of her. He lost himself in her and she held him and squeezed him. He sucked and stroked her breasts, while one hand pulled her hips toward him. Her hips rolled faster and deeper and faster until she shuddered and her warmth spread over him. They fell silent as one.

They had hardly spoken since they had first entered the room. Luke whispered softly, but the words echoed in the moment. "What time is your flight?"

"Why don't you come to Chicago for a weekend?" she answered.

CHAPTER FORTY TWO

A comfortable pattern unfolded and furled around Luke. At five o'clock on Fridays, he rushed to the airport, hustled onto the plane, and landed at O'Hare shortly after seven. Within the hour, he taxied to Denise's high-rise apartment and dropped his bags, and they headed to dinner. He unwound before her eyes; the layers of FRM and the mortgage business peeled away. Malson, Tulsa, Beth, and the divorce receded with the undertow below the waves of Lake Michigan and drowned in the noise of the city. He met her friends and was even anxious for their reviews. They shared her favorite restaurants, searched out new ones, and found foreign movies on blustery afternoons with her red beret set against the wind. They made love to the hiss of the radiator, shielded from the cold. Monday mornings he rose early, bounced in the cab to O'Hare, and hustled to be in the office before nine.

In the beginning he alternated weekends. On the Fridays he stayed in Tulsa, he spent time working, seeing his children, and waiting for the next weekend. He was hesitant to introduce Denise to his children, concerned to increase the confusion in their lives.

In March, he realized he had not skied in two years. Denise met him in Denver, and they flew to Aspen. She was a strong skier and attacked the mountain. The crust flew off her edges as she skipped over the moguls. They caught the early lifts to the top, chased each other to the soundtracks from their earphones, and lunched surrounded by huge, brilliant blue sky with the quaint village far below. The afternoon brought more vistas as their ski tips pointed at the horizon below them and then broke hard to cut between the white, snow-burdened limbs, still edged in green, and slip onto another run. They caught the last lift of the day to the top and waited for it to close. They breathed the majesty as the others headed down. The mountain was now theirs alone, and the last run of the day was long and fast and cold as the peaks pierced the sun and the shadows flattened the groomed snow.

Soon Denise would come on the Fridays when Luke did not fly. She shook her head at the first glance of his condo and trudged through the night. Thereafter, they celebrated her Friday arrival with dinner and then made the hour-long drive to the lake. On those Saturdays the boat glided in the summer sun and found a secluded cove. They drifted below the lake's high cliffs. They read and sunned and made love to the sways of the waves. She flew on Sundays to make the Board of Trade's Monday opening. He filled the Sunday evening void of her leaving by seeing his children.

Amy and Phyllis had chosen a conference in San Francisco, and Luke asked Denise to join the group. Phyllis gave Denise the once-over, and forced her eyes wide as if to say to Luke, "Oh my, what have we here?" Amy merely smiled. Harold sneaked glances at her long sculpted legs, tight waist, and abundant breasts. Suddenly, the three knew the reason for Luke's changed routine. None seemed to disapprove.

Tulsa was a small city, and soon Ginny called. She had heard reports of sightings of Luke with a tall blonde. "Have you found her?" she asked timidly before asking, "Are you in love?"

"I'm still married," he answered simply. He declined her offer for a reunion at his place. "I really can't," he said. He had learned the end scrapes away the magic and chars the memories. Scars conceal the wound, and yesterday's glimmer melts and fades and glows in bittersweet moments. The reunion seeks the élan long lost, but new light exposes the sad truth: *was* can never *be*.

He shared his music with Denise. She knew him and understood his affinity. She listened and laughed and loved and humored some of his tastes. They listened to jazz and pop and new and old, and the music followed them. Increasingly, he flew almost every weekend. Chicago was where they both wanted to be.

The towers were casting long, fading shadows, and they were sitting on her sofa watching the evening come when he opened up about the last two years with Malson. He told her about Bivins asking him about "access to capital" and the sequence that followed. The telling stoked his energy and his resolve. She smiled sadly at him. "Get out," she said matter-of-factly. He told of his commitment to the people who had taken a chance and his faith that if he tried hard enough FRM would succeed, and she gave him the same sad smile and said, "Get out." He told her he hoped to have a new credit line in a year and then leave when things were stable. She shook her head. "You became a big fish in a small pond. They will bury you. Come to Chicago. If you want to make money, you can. If you don't want to, do something else. But get out of Tulsa." The need to finish the job drove him. She admired that in him but saw it as a weakness. She did not tell him that faith is merely hope for those who did not know the truth.

Through the summer her confidence and her accounts continued to grow. They loved walking Chicago's Gold Coast near her apartment; Astor Street was her favorite, with narrow sidewalks and abundant trees. The mansions of another era lined the street while nannies wheeled children in prams.

They turned a corner to find the three-story brownstone on State Street. The top floor was for lease. The large living room was airy and bright with huge windows onto the street and a marble fireplace centered against the far living-room wall. The second bedroom offered an opportunity for workspace, and the french doors opened onto the deck, soon trailed with spices and herbs and vegetables in wooden planters. They tanned on the deck, and he saw the pride she felt at her accomplishment. It was her place, and she refused his offers to share the cost.

Denise and Luke brought pink to each other's cheeks. He shared each new episode of the Malson story with her and valued her counsel. She was smart, but there were some things he could not do, despite her warnings. He saw his life after FRM, and he was eager and ready and wanted to speed the process. He was younger than he had ever been.

CHAPTER FORTY THREE

Malson announced a $16 million loss in March. What once would have been failure seemed like shining success compared to the $815 million lost in the previous nine months. Malson's press release touted the stabilized condition of the bank. Tom Cook called shortly thereafter looking for principal payments on the $2.3 million loan to Luke.

Luke didn't like debt. Paying principal would decrease the interest expense, but he wanted Malson to have a reason to keep FRM alive. Luke feared Malson would pull the line of credit once his side note was paid. He told Cook he could most likely pay some principal early next year.

Chuck Rail then called and was direct; regulators were demanding the bank shrink. Malson's net worth was negative by hundreds of millions of dollars, and its legal lending limit to one borrower was now an arbitrary amount set by regulators. They had established $10 million as the cap. The combination of FRM and Luke's notes was over the limit and noted on monthly reports to regulators. Chuck complained about having to explain the FRM relationship every thirty days.

Luke countered FRM could not generate the profits needed to make principal payments without a larger line of credit. Malson's problems had forced Luke to sell loans individually, squandering profits. The standoff continued.

In early June, Chuck called again. Luke's radar deployed when Chuck said the bank had an offer: Malson's bond department would provide early settlements if FRM would sell its bonds through them. Malson and FRM dealt with the same New York dealers, and Malson wanted to mark up the price by $1,250 per million. Luke balked. Malson cut the markup in half. Luke calculated the increase in servicing value would more than offset the additional costs. "We'll still need to renew the line of credit and the note. We probably can't start paying principal until after the first of next year," Luke allowed.

A meeting was set. Luke had not been in Malson's building since September of the previous year. The starkness struck him. The once plush lobby was Spartan. Once busy elevators sat vacantly on the ground floor with the doors open. He rode alone and found the real estate section, once vibrant and loud, quiet with empty office cubes and stacks of brown cardboard boxes. The employees had distant, vacant looks, except Tom Cook, who appeared unaware. Chuck's office had none of its former panache. The plants were gone, and the carpet was soiled and tattered.

Chuck looked hopeful but battered. "We're going to make it. The bank is reorganizing," he professed. "It's about fee income now," he said, enthusiastic about the fees to be earned in the Brokerage and Insurance Departments.

"What kinds?" Luke asked.

"All kinds," Chuck accelerated. "For now, we're just brokers. But in the big picture, we can provide hedges and commercial reinsurance and trade stocks for our own account. The banks will be unleashed."

Luke muzzled himself, so as not to say, "Sounds like the 1920s and the decade before the Great Depression." Instead, he nodded. "When will this be?"

"Oh, a few years away. But it's coming. For now we can only serve as brokers."

Luke relaxed. "OK."

In a few minutes, they stepped onto the fourteenth floor. A couple of desks occupied a small corner. In New York alone, Stiller Stevens had thirty traders buying and selling mortgage-backed bonds and nothing else. Malson had one. Luke met Tim Hastings for the first time. "Call me 'Butch,'" he said. Hastings had been lured from a local stockbroker, and he didn't specialize in anything. He placed and sold orders for everything—mortgage bonds, corporate bonds, municipals, stocks, mutual funds, and you name it. His job was simple: find a buyer or seller and get the trade. He spent his day dialing for dollars and stock-trading accounts. He was decades older and carried a tall, large frame, topped with thin strands of hair pulled into a comb-over. Luke noted his Southern accent, inquired, and heard, "Birmingham, Alabama," with half the syllables missing.

Malson offered the same interest rate on early settlements as Keegan Securities and agreed to take all the bonds FRM could deliver, since regulators did not classify early settlements as loans. Of course, Luke still preferred Keegan Securities and Stiller Stevens, but the Malson bond deal offered added capacity. Tim "Butch" Hastings could not hide the glee from the opportunity he had been handed.

Wilt and Harold liked the deal. The FedEx driver was no longer chatting with the receptionist as the last boxes were filled and tabs stripped to affix the adhesive. The staff now notched their duties into the regular office hours, and overtime dropped. The office hummed again with the resonance Luke recalled before the missed margin call and chaos had ruled. Luke's future beyond FRM teased him.

In late June, Edgar Dinsen was in the office again. The annual audit process began, and Luke laughed, thinking of the "Deputy Dawg" moniker. Even Wilt admitted the resemblance. The Leggett Knoiser staff marched as slowly as the year before, but Luke's urgency was gone. Luke wanted to downplay income, and Wilt agreed to book as many expenses as possible to reduce profits. Luke was not so much concerned with taxes as with keeping how well the company was doing from Malson.

As usual, Dinsen missed deadlines, despite Wilt's help. The audited statements were ready in late August, ten days later than Dinsen's promise but with plenty of cushion for HUD approval. Ray Fontenot gave Luke a sterile, "Yes, we have them," when Luke called HUD three weeks before the deadline. Luke could almost see the smile as Fontenot added, "You don't have to call me every year."

Malson routinely approved the renewal of the line of credit. The relationship sometimes seemed almost as it had in the beginning. The audited returns showed the servicing sale income and another $500,000 in operating income; Malson wanted all of the operating income applied to the side note. Wilt prepared statements showing $150,000 of the profit going to the software purchase and tax liabilities of $200,000. Malson agreed the value of the collateral had increased, accepted a $100,000 principal payment, and the side note balance dropped to $2.2 million. Luke now had a shot to find another bank.

Luke and Wilt picked $40 million for a servicing sale offer in September to build cash for a move to FCBA and then pay the side note to Malson. That was the first time Luke saw it in Wilt's eyes: The computer software was in place, and the processes and systems had been standardized. Wilt's days revolved around answering questions and settling disputes; Wilt was annoyed and bored.

Increasingly, Wilt mentioned Marie La Dell, his top assistant, saying she was capable but recommended Luke find someone with a stronger background. Susan Nichols worked at Osage Mortgage, had an accounting degree, was studying for the CPA exams, and had called looking for a job earlier in the year.

Wilt again started talking of consulting. "You know, it's been about a year," he would say. Luke knew butterflies fly when they reach their peak and he could not hold on to Wilt. By November, Wilt had yielded the reigns to Susan Nichols and was gone, saying, "I will stay in touch. I'm available when you need me, and I'll still do taxes."

Luke called Chuck to let him know Wilt was leaving but would still be consulting. The latest renewal had not required Malson's approval of FRM's chief financial officer, but Luke presumed Malson would want to know. Chuck was unconcerned. "I don't know her, but that's fine." Luke thought the call was a good sign.

CHAPTER FORTY FOUR

The last three months of the year were a breeze. Luke enjoyed an October weekend with Denise in New York. He mentioned Tower Records, and she knew the address. They walked out with sacks filled with Lou Reed, Pat Metheny, The Cure, and more. Most Friday's he flew to Chicago and made early-morning Monday returns. Denise made a few weekend trips, and they watched the reds, oranges, auburns, and yellows shimmer on the trees around the lake. They had the balconies and the restaurants to themselves. He spent Thanksgiving in Chicago, and they cooked vegetables and turkey, played tennis, and ran along the lake. The season drove snow down Michigan Avenue. They shopped and bundled against the wind; gloves, topcoat, and scarf were de rigueur. The couple's cheeks burned bright red but then thawed a rosy pink by the brownstone's fireplace.

The end of the year was spent in Snowmass. A three-bedroom condo was arranged. Luke wanted Denise to spend time with Harold Rhoden and Mike Eckridge, the Oklahoma City regional manager. Harold had married that year, and his wife and Mike's wife came along. Luke wanted Denise's opinion of Mike and Harold.

She found both pleasant enough but endorsed neither. "They're not you," she said.

Luke took it as a compliment. "They don't have to start it," he answered. "They only have to run it."

Denise's eyebrows told him she had her doubts. "I like Phyllis's spunk. Amy seems OK. Mike is your better pick, but he's weak. I don't like or trust Harold."

For the third year in a row, Luke began the year hunting for a credit line. He had spoken with Pete Winston before the holidays, and Pete thought FCBA might soon lift the moratorium. They agreed to talk in the middle of January. Pete called a few days ahead of schedule, and Luke's heart raced with anticipation. He took an extra moment and a deep breath before answering.

After a casual greeting, Pete said, "The bank is going to start looking at some commercial loans like yours in the Southwest. Can you get your financials together?"

"I can do that."

"It will take us forty-five to sixty days or so—so around the first to the middle of March."

"Sounds great," Luke said and leaned back. "Look, we're selling some servicing. We're profitable. Last year was good, and this year has started better. The servicing sale will generate some additional cash."

"How much?"

"We should net around a million dollars, but we are profitable without that. We will pay some on the stock loan with Malson."

Pete sounded his approval, and Luke sent the updated financials the same day.

The celebration was short-lived. Tom Cook called within hours. He wanted principal payments on the $2.2 million side note to satisfy the regulators. Luke reminded Cook the note was not due for another eight months, and the bank had already agreed the collateral value had increased. He said a $400,000 payment was budgeted within the next month or so, but did not mention the servicing sale.

Luke knew Malson would learn of the sale when FRM made arrangements to transfer the files. Luke grabbed the phone and called Chuck Rail. "What's the deal with Tom Cook demanding early payment? That's not due until September. Right?"

Chuck started talking about liquidity and regulators and cleaning up the bank. "We're trying to position for a new buyer."

Luke wanted Malson interested in FRM's survival and planned to leave a portion of the side note unpaid until he moved to another bank. Then, when FRM was safe, he would sell more servicing and pay off the note.

Chuck's mention of a new buyer sent a chill down Luke's neck. "Listen, I have a deal to sell some servicing, and we have a principal payment of $400,000 in the budget. We need the rest for liquidity, so we can grow servicing. Then we can sell more servicing later in the year and pay you off around September. That's the plan."

"That's our collateral," Chuck started.

"No, it's not. We didn't pledge the servicing. We can't. And besides, we'll still have enough servicing. We're inside the covenants."

"Maybe I need to look at it again," he said, wavering.

"Read it, Chuck."

"Yeah. I'll take a look." Chuck's voice was calm. He called later and sounded excited to be getting the $400,000 principal payment.

Luke again lived with the urgency of moving to FCBA. He had asked Chuck who was buying Malson, but Chuck said he only knew someone was working on a deal.

Pete Winston called within two days. The financials looked good, and he was confident the loan would be approved. He would plan a trip to Tulsa as soon as he had cleared the first set of reviews.

Luke wanted confirmation. "I still owe two-point-two million on a note with Malson from the restructuring. They have our stock as collateral. We had planned on taking some of the servicing sale proceeds to reduce the note. Does that matter to you?"

"No. That won't impact our deal, and we're not concerned about the stock loan."

"So, I don't need to pay off the Malson side note to do a deal with you."

"No. That's between you and Malson. We're doing a line of credit for mortgages."

"Great. And spending the servicing sale proceeds won't affect the loan."

"Not at all. With your financials we can still do the forty-million-dollar credit line," Pete answered.

The servicing sale was on schedule, and Harold called Malson a few days before the closing to arrange the transfer of loan files. Tom Cook called within a few hours. "I heard you're selling servicing. That money needs to be paid against the side note."

"We've already talked with Chuck. We will pay four hundred thousand dollars on the side note after the sale. You need to talk to Chuck." Luke finished.

Soon, Chuck called, virtually begging for more money. Luke reminded him that FRM was not obligated to pay anything. "We'll pay you four hundred thousand after we close," Luke offered. "Give me a few days after the closing to get everything settled."

Chuck quickly gave in. "It's a deal." Chuck sounded elated, and Luke sensed Chuck would gain favor with those structuring the Malson sale.

The servicing sale closed on a Thursday in late January. FRM netted slightly more than $1 million after expenses, and Luke told Susan Nichols to hold the money over the weekend and to make the principal payment on Monday.

The next day Pete Winston called, reported he had the initial approvals, and scheduled a visit for the next Tuesday. "I should have final approval by the middle of February, and we'll close this deal in early March. I'll bring a list of the things we'll need with me." His voice was confident.

Luke let out a shout when he hung up the phone, caught Andrea staring at him, and smiled back without speaking. He grabbed the late Friday afternoon flight to Chicago. Denise's eyes and the smattering of light freckles on her cheeks played before him as the white billows of clouds grayed, charcoaled, and faded into black night air. Luke could see his escape and charted the future, as Peter Gabriel's "Shock the Monkey" spun in the headphones. He thought he had assembled a good team. He would start the transition in the first six months after moving to FCBA. He would move to Chicago and wait out the divorce.

CHAPTER FORTY FIVE

Susan Nichols ran into Luke's office on Monday afternoon with startled eyes. "They took it all," she started.

"What?" Luke needed to hear the words again.

"They took all of the money from the servicing sale. All of it."

"Where did it go?"

"I don't know."

Susan had called to verify the balance before making the transfer. The balance was lower than expected, and she requested a transaction summary from the clerk. The report showed money leaving the account on Friday.

An hour later Susan confirmed Tom Cook had debited the account for the full amount. The side note balance had dropped to $1.2 million. Luke was calm when he reached Chuck. "Cook took all the money. You can keep four hundred thousand—we'd planned to pay that today—but put the rest back into the account."

Chuck voiced surprise. "Let me find out what happened."

Luke asked Susan to check the other accounts. The general account held FRM's money, and the remainder carried the word "Trust" in them, designating the account held money for others, such as borrowers' escrow accounts, loan disbursement accounts, and the payroll account for employees' salaries and payroll taxes. Susan found no debits from other accounts.

Chuck did not call back on Monday, and Luke spent an anxious night. Malson's taking the money would not affect the deal with FCBA, but Luke knew something was happening with Malson. Pete Winston was flying in on Tuesday, and Luke planned to spend the day with him.

Luke called Chuck twice Tuesday morning but never reached him. Luke did not want to talk to Chuck with Pete in the car. He called one last time from the Mercedes, turned off the telephone, and then picked up Pete at the airport. Luke tried to appear relaxed and calm, but Chuck's not returning his calls gnawed at him. He drove Pete to the office but did not walk him around as he had almost two years earlier. Luke casually flipped through pink notes on his desk, looking for a message from Chuck Rail, and then sat in his customary side chair and visited with Pete. Luke had asked Andrea to give him a signal and to take a message if Chuck called. Luke stole glances at her, but the signals were negative.

Pete handed Luke an overview and a list of documents needed prior to the closing. "We should be ready around the first of March," Pete assured. FCBA wanted Malson to sign a collateral transfer agreement, pledging to forward the mortgage loan documents to FCBA when the Malson credit line was paid. On the day of closing, FCBA would pay off the Malson line of the credit and Malson would begin transferring the documents. Pete recommended having arrangements made by the middle of February. "We'll handle the collateral transfer agreement. As soon as I have final approval, I'll call Malson, let them know we are stepping in, and arrange everything.

"Great," Luke said. Shortly before noon, they headed to lunch at the restaurant with the fountains dancing from the rock lagoon.

Luke hid his anxiety, and the meeting went well. The conversation was mostly about baseball and the dawn of spring. The two had done this duet before. They lingered after lunch; Pete seemingly wanted to kill time until his afternoon flight. Luke offered to drive him by the other offices, but Pete said there was no need. They were among the last to drift out the door.

"It's good to see you again," Pete said. "You're a survivor."

"Thanks," Luke responded. "Maybe you can stay longer next time. I know a couple of great places for dinner."

"I'll do that, and we will celebrate the closing. Should be in about four weeks. We'll get this done for you," Pete finished.

Luke parked in front of the terminal, and they visited for a few minutes. Once Pete entered the terminal, Luke eased the Mercedes from the curb, hit the power button, and waited for the phone signal. Luke rounded the curve and punched in Chuck Rail's numbers. When he heard, "He's on another line," Luke responded, "Tell him I'm on my way to the bank, and I will hold until I get there."

In a few moments, Chuck Rail answered. He started on the defensive, "Cook got all excited about being able to report a big collection. He jumped the gun."

"OK. Put the money back."

"Well, there's a problem." The line was quiet.

"What's the problem?" Luke subconsciously hit the accelerator. "I'm on the Crosstown Expressway. I want the money in the account, or I'll be there in ten minutes."

"Look." Chuck paused. "This is me and you talking, OK."

"OK."

"Cook reported the collection as a loan pay down. We can't make a new loan to you without some approvals."

"Well, get Weldon to approve it. He's president now, right?"

"Well, actually he resigned last week. He's leaving the bank. But even he couldn't approve it. It's an extension of credit, and we have to get FDIC approval to give you the money back since you are over the legal lending limit."

"What?"

"It's not a line of credit. We can't advance on it. It's a note, and we processed and reported a principal payment, and if we give you the money back, it's like getting approval to make a new loan. We're trying to get an exception."

"Are you serious?"

"Yes."

"You made a mistake. Fix it." The line was quiet. "Just tell them you made a mistake, and put the money back."

"I can't do that."

Luke questioned if he should fight over money he intended to eventually repay. He needed one more month to make the break. "I need that money."

"Give me a couple of days. Let me run some traps. Let me see what I can get done. They're reading it now."

"Who?" Luke asked. "Your law firm?"

"Yes."

"I need to call Jake. Talk to you later."

Luke exited the expressway, called Jake, covered the details, and headed to the office. Jake Ingles called in a few minutes. "Malson's in a jam. They can't give the money back without FDIC approval, because it would be like making a new loan. They have someone looking to buy the bank, too. They're trying to find justification for taking the money. They might have a position that will hold up: the right of offset."

Luke racked his brain for the term. "I'm not in default," he said.

"No, you're not. But the bank has the right to offset an account and take money from your account at any time and apply it to your indebtedness. They always have that."

Luke suddenly realized Jake was right. Unless waived, banks could draft money even if no payment was due. Banks only did that when they were in trouble or wanted to end a relationship. Malson qualified on both counts. "Are you kidding me?" Luke said.

"Now, I've talked with Malson's attorney, Phil Sandifer, and he says they will try to replace the money; if they can't, they'll agree to let you sell more servicing and keep all of the money."

"Who's looking to buy Malson?" Luke asked.

"I don't know, and I haven't heard anything."

Luke had never told Jake about FCBA. "Look, I have another bank lined up. It's not official; it's not done; but I may be able to change banks in another four weeks or so."

"Do you need the cash to move?"

"No. I just don't trust Malson."

"We'll tell them to give us the money; if they don't, we'll get a letter that says you can sell servicing and keep the proceeds."

Luke and the Mercedes were now sitting outside FRM's office. "OK. But I want them to refund the money."

"I think they're in a jam. They're scrambling to justify what they've done."

"OK." Luke ended. "I don't want them screwing up my new deal."

"Why would they? They can't do that."

"I don't trust them. They don't want me in the mortgage business. They wanted to buy me, and I wouldn't sell. I don't trust them." Luke's voice was intense.

"I think they're on their heels, and most of those people are gone. Sounds like someone else is buying them. You're the least of their worries." Jake tried to calm him.

"I hope so."

Luke went straight to Susan Nichols's office. "I want to open an account with another bank." He thought for a moment. "National Bank over on Seventy-First. How much can we transfer?"

"A couple hundred thousand," she said, looking confused.

"What's the best way?"

"Write a check." She shrugged. "Malson probably won't notice. Is that what you're asking?"

"Yes. Let's do it. Go over, get the account forms, and let's do it."

"They aren't giving the money back, are they?"

"I don't think so." He looked around. "Go ahead and get the forms. Let's sit down later—you and Harold and me. We need to talk."

Luke called Jake Ingles, who confirmed the loan agreement did not preclude FRM from setting up accounts with other banks.

Susan's concern had turned into cockiness when she returned with the bank account forms and sat on the sofa. Harold joined them. They called Mike and put him on the speakerphone. Luke started by bringing Harold and Mike up-to-date on Malson's taking of the money. "I want to put some money aside because I don't trust them," Luke explained. "Jake says we can do it. We need some cushion and I don't know what's going with them." Harold and Susan nodded their heads. Mike voiced his support.

Luke paused, "Now here's the real news. I've been working with FCBA, and they are probably going to give us a forty-million-dollar line." His face was solemn. "Don't celebrate yet. Let's keep this to ourselves."

CHAPTER FORTY SIX

The new bank account was set up with National Bank. Malson said it could not return the money, but Phil Sandifer was working on a letter authorizing FRM to sell more servicing and keep the proceeds. Luke and Jake spoke daily, and Jake said Sandifer needed a week or so. Luke pressed, even though he had no intention of selling the servicing now. He wanted Malson on the defensive, while he moved to FCBA. He was nervous about Malson's sale and called Chuck to confirm Sandifer was working on the letter; he probed for more information. Chuck appeared relaxed and ready to talk.

"So," Luke started, "who's buying you?"

"Dolph Malthers is taking over," Chuck answered.

Luke was shocked. "Dolph Malthers? Dolph Malthers the half owner of Malthers-Nelson?"

"Yes. He has to approve everything now. Just like the regulators."

"But he's the vice-chairman."

"Sure. He's always been on the board."

"Doesn't he already own half the bank?"

"Not quite that much. He owns forty-two percent or so, a little over. Nelson has about forty-eight percent, and the rest is split."

Luke was in shock. "How does he sit on the board and manage and own a bank that gets in trouble and then buy it?"

"He's put a deal together the regulators will approve, and he will own one hundred percent of the bank."

"Wow," Luke said in disbelief. "How much money must he have? I mean, you guys lost almost nine hundred million, so he has to come up with that much to cover the losses and have the new capital to keep the bank open."

"The government is financing the deal." Chuck's voice grinned. "The government is taking over the bank and then selling it to him. They will loan him five hundred million to restart the bank."

"What happens to the nine-hundred-million-dollar loss?"

Chuck's voice rose. "It goes away. The old corporation goes away, the government takes the loss, and Malthers restarts the bank with a loan from the government." Chuck paused before the finish. "And we keep the same name."

"You've got to be kidding. That's what that new tower cost—nine hundred million! The government is taking a loss and forgiving it?"

"Sweet, huh?"

"Is Nelson in the deal?" Luke asked.

"They may have a side deal, but only Malthers will have stock. It's a different corporation. The government owns the name now, and he gets it back in the purchase. We'll still be Malson," Chuck finished with big flair. Luke was in disbelief and said nothing. "We have to go to the regulators and Malthers with everything. They're trying to close the deal in the next ninety days. That's why we can't put the money into your account," Chuck concluded as if it made total sense.

Luke was still stunned as he hung up the phone. Malthers was a large shareholder in Malson; he had been on the board that brought in Bill Bivins and wanted to move into the mortgage business. Now Malthers had swung a deal where the government was giving him money to restart the bank. Luke thought again about the phone call from the House majority leader in his hotel room in Washington, DC.

Luke stewed for two more days about Dolph Malthers before Pete Winston called. The FCBA line of credit had been approved by the home office, and the closing was set for early March. Pete asked for a contact at Malson to coordinate the payoff of the line of credit and to transfer the collateral packages. "Call Chuck Rail," Luke said and gave him the number. "He may refer you to Tom Cook, but that guy isn't reliable. Let me know if I need to call Chuck."

Luke hung up the phone with a huge smile but did not want to jinx the deal. He decided against a celebration until the closing, but he was looking forward to sharing the news with Denise over the weekend.

Pete Winston called back in two hours. "Malson seems to be a problem. I spoke with Chuck Rail and told him we were doing a line of credit with you. I told him we needed a collateral transfer agreement giving us the documents after we paid off the line of credit. He seemed OK, and then Tom Cook calls about an hour later and says you have to pay off the side note before you can move."

"What?" Luke could not believe it.

"They said you can't move the line unless you pay off the side note. That's another two-point-two million. Is that right?"

"It's down to one-point-two million, but there's nothing in the agreement about that," Luke answered. "I'm sure of it."

"Well, Tom Cook says that's their position. Do you have a copy of the agreement?"

"I'll get you a copy." Luke started scrambling in his credenza. "I'll fax you a copy. There's nothing like that in there. Let me call Chuck and try to clear this up."

"All right. I don't want them squirreling the deal, but now we'll have to have our Legal Department review your loan agreement with Malson, unless they back off their demand on the side note. I will still need them to sign the collateral transfer agreement."

"OK," Luke said before ending the call.

Luke punched Chuck's number, and he answered on the first ring. "We need to get paid," Chuck started. "We need to get loans off the books, and Malthers wants your loan off the books."

Luke knew another fight was coming. "There's nothing in the agreement allowing you to stop my moving to another bank."

"I'm a soldier here," Chuck offered. "I have to do what's in the best interest of the bank."

"You're a whore," Luke shot back.

"Where's that going to get you," Chuck came back.

"I've been straight with you. Where's that gotten me?"

Within minutes Luke had called Jake Ingles, and Jake had promised to call Sandifer. Soon the battle began. Malson wanted the side note paid in full as a condition of allowing FRM to move to FCBA. Jake countered Malson's loan agreement did not prevent FRM from moving the line of credit. Malson raised the ante and said they wanted the side note paid in full and also wanted to charge a fee to transfer the files. They said they would determine the fee in a few days.

"Can you pay off the personal note?" Jake asked.

"Sure, if I sell some servicing, but I can't sell it soon enough. It takes three months to do a deal, and Malthers is taking over the bank. No telling what happens then."

"There's some new case law in the area of lender's liability. There's a major case in Texas where the federal court held a lender interfered with a business, made decisions that took control and were outside the loan agreements, and caused losses. It was a manufacturing company, but the same concepts apply, and Malson is doing the same thing. The courts held the bank liable and awarded treble damages. It's a different circuit, but it might work for you. We can bring suit, but that will take years, and there's a question about the value of the judgment. If the government technically closes Malson and sells the name to someone else, then our Malson no longer exists, and the judgment will be uncollectable."

"I don't know how, but I have to get rid of them." Luke stopped. He told Jake about the deal Malthers had cut with the government.

"Wow. Sweet deal," Jake said simply.

Luke made an offer. "Tell them I'll agree to sell servicing to pay off the side note, but they have to let me move the line of credit to FCBA now."

"Give me time. Sometimes these things take time. I'll send a demand letter. They'll either sign the collateral transfer agreement or make a response."

After a week, Malson had still had not responded. Due to the delay, Pete Winston said the closing would have to be moved to mid-March. "We're still ready to do the deal," Pete started. "Our legal review doesn't show any restriction on your doing the line of credit with us. But, honestly, it makes the California office a little nervous. They don't want to be caught funding money and not getting collateral."

Pete's words replayed as Luke sat on the Friday flight to Chicago. Jake had made no progress, still insisting Luke be patient. Luke was anxious to tell Denise of the battle, knowing she would tell him to make a deal and "Get out." Still, he was excited to see her.

They caught a cab and found a restaurant near Lincoln Park they both enjoyed. Luke unwound over a glass of wine, and Denise let him give the blow-by-blow details of the stalemate. He did not hear the words he expected. "I think they'll blink," she concluded.

"You think?"

"Yes, for now. But I don't think you've heard the last of them. They'll try to jerk you around and scare off FCBA. Eventually, they will give in, but I don't like it in the long run. You got too big. You're on their radar. In a city this size, no one would care. But millions there are more noticeable than millions here."

Luke then told her about the Malthers deal, with the government forgiving the $900 million loss and loaning him another $500 million to start a new bank under the same name. Her eyes got big. "You're messing with the wrong people. Make a deal and get away from them." The both chewed on her comment before she changed the subject. "How's your coverage?"

"Bonds? Commitments? We're covered."

"Don't be long," she said. "Don't get caught holding loans without coverage."

Rates had continued to drop for the past year, driving more refinances, but real estate sales had only slightly improved. "The economy's weak. I don't see it turning and interest rates going up."

"Don't be long," she repeated. "Some big players in the pits are going short. They're legging into big positions, selling on every little rally."

"But the economy's weak," Luke said and paused to think. "I know Reagan is talking hard about trade sanctions on the Japanese; he's trying to show he's tough since the trade deficit keeps getting worse. Still, I can't see him doing sanctions. The Japanese would retaliate by selling our bonds." He thought some more. "That would not only drive rates up, but that would really hurt the economy and raise the deficit. I can't see the government playing politics to look tough and wounding the economy now."

"I don't know about that. I do know some big players are getting short." Denise was serious. "Be sure you're covered."

"I am." He looked into her eyes, and the weekend began.

CHAPTER FORTY SEVEN

L uke watched as bond prices improved slightly Monday morning, and the markets appeared stable. Denise's warning lingered. His applications and closed loans were covered with bond sales to Keegan Securities and Malson's bond department. Luke knew more applications would close if Denise's prediction was right, so he sold a few more bonds to raise his percentage of coverage.

By midmorning Luke had heard no news regarding Malson, so he called Jake Ingles. Jake had not received a response to his letter. "Be patient," he advised Luke.

Luke called Pete to give him the update. "We just need to know they will transfer the collateral and not create havoc," Pete said. "We can wait for a bit."

Malson had still not responded by Friday. Beth's family had weekend plans, so Luke was not going to see his children. He made his late-afternoon race to the airport, caught the last flight, watched the bright orange sun drop and burn a scarlet arc on the clouds, and grabbed a taxi at O'Hare. He carried his bags into the brownstone. Denise looked beautiful. Her cheeks had a bit of glow from the soft light, and her hair reflected like gold. She greeted him with soft lips and the warmness of her caress. Luke felt like he was home. She kissed him again and then pulled back. "Did you hear the news?"

"No."

"Reagan's doing trade sanctions on Japan. They announced a few hours after the market closed."

"That's going to be huge."

"Really!"

"The bond market's going to get hit Monday." Luke thought of the Horowitz announcement and the market volatility of two years earlier. "Bond futures will be down limit. Thank God I'm not in the futures market."

"I'm short," she smiled.

"You are?"

"Yes. I knew some guys were getting short, so I took some of my money and traded for my own account. I'm short some contracts. I should be good," she giggled.

"Great."

"Are you covered?"

"Yes. I was fully covered, but after you warned me I bumped my coverage to be sure."

"Good." She was beaming.

"Dinner?"

"In a little bit." She kissed him again.

CHAPTER FORTY EIGHT

Reagan's sanctions brought a tsunami. Luke was concerned about the impact on new business but happy with Denise's gain. The couple was exhilarated by an afternoon of indoor tennis and Denise's trade. They went to her office Sunday night to watch the Asian markets open. Bond prices crashed and the interest rate on mortgages increased almost 1 percent. The futures market would not trade for at least two days or more unless prices improved. Denise had booked a nice profit, and Luke was glad he no longer had to cover loans in the futures market and make margin calls. They grabbed a taxi back to the brownstone, cooked pasta, cut fresh vegetables, and opened a dry white wine. They sat on the floor watching the fire, the drift of snowflakes, and each other. Luke caught the Monday-morning flight to Tulsa.

Luke called Chuck in the morning. "When can we close with FCBA?"

Chuck said the law firm was working on a response.

Pete Winston called in a half hour. "I don't know what's going on, but Tom Cook just spent fifteen minutes telling me how untrustworthy you are. He tells a significantly different version of what happened two years ago."

Luke tried to stay cool. "I'm sure. He wasn't even involved. He has to say whatever someone told him to protect Malson."

"I understand. It wasn't a pleasant call."

"You want to give me the particulars?" Luke was suddenly nervous.

"Not really. His version is that your losses are from paying too much to your staff; he said you didn't have coverage, hid the losses from them for months, and then blindsided them."

"That's not true." Luke tried to keep his voice level.

"It's OK." Pete stopped him. "I don't believe them. You were straightforward with us. We were ready to do a deal, and you called and told me you had a problem and had taken losses. I think you've been pretty candid. Further, if your losses had to do with paying too much in salaries, how did you make money last year? Their story doesn't hold up. Their call is not going to blow up the deal."

Luke relaxed. "Good. Thanks."

"Not a problem. But we need to move on this. I need the production and, California wants to know what's going on."

"May I tell them the latest ploy didn't work and they need to give us the collateral transfer agreement so we can close?" Luke asked.

"Be my guest."

Luke called Chuck Rail. "Cook's call to Winston didn't scare them off."

"I didn't know about Cook's call." Chuck's tone was tame.

"Who had him call?"

"I didn't tell him to call. Look, the firm's working a response."

Luke immediately called Jake Ingles. "They're screwing with me. I don't know who's really in charge. Cook called FCBA trying to blow up the deal, and Chuck claims he didn't know about it. I don't know if they're playing good cop, bad cop, or if they have a bunch of cowboys shooting their guns in every direction trying to impress Dolph Malthers and save their jobs."

Jake promised to call Phil Sandifer. "Try to be calm," he reassured.

The phones were crazy. Realtors who had written contracts over the weekend begged for a special deal, and others wanted appointments to plead in person. Some of the savings and loans, already reeling with losses, announced they would not close loans at the lower rates they had quoted. The panic increased. The staff was inundated with callers verifying their applications were still locked at the old rates. Luke had to wait for a line to make an outside call, and the stack of pink slips grew on his desk.

The chaotic market and deluge of phone calls continued on Tuesday. The futures market was down limit again, and Luke knew Denise had made more on her trade. He was anxious for their customary evening call. He was watching the Telerate machine and thinking of Denise when Andrea cornered his door and broke the moment. "Jake Ingles is on the line."

"I talked with Sandifer," Jake started. "He says Chuck Rail will be calling with a verbal offer. Sandifer said it's not final yet, so he doesn't know what it is. They said they should have a written response by Friday."

"Yeah, right."

"No, I believe him." Jake sounded sure. "Apparently, Sandifer has given them the firm's opinion. Chuck is supposed to call this afternoon."

Luke began stealing glances at the burgundy-and-gold, square clock on the side table and repeatedly snatched a glimpse of his watch. He alerted Andrea and the receptionist to find him as soon as Chuck called. The heavy phone traffic continued from the previous day, and he kept wondering if Chuck was getting a busy signal. Finally, in the late afternoon, Andrea said, "Luke," through the glass and gave him a nod.

"Luke Boyd," he started.

"Luke, Chuck. Here's the deal. We're glad you have another bank. We want you to pay off the side note, and we want a transfer fee of fifty dollars per file." Luke was on his feet, but Chuck continued before he could interrupt. "The transfer fee will apply to all files we hold for both the line of credit and for the servicing."

Luke sat down, punched the calculator, and wished he could see Chuck's face. "Chuck, I don't know how many files there are, but I'm guessing you want around two hundred thousand dollars."

"I can't really say how many there are."

Malson had again upped the ante. "The loan agreement says you hold the collateral documents for no charge and you signed HUD's agreement on the servicing files saying you get no fee."

"Well, we think we should be able to charge something on termination."

"You have no right under the agreement, and HUD won't permit it on the servicing." The line was quiet. "You're holding us hostage."

Chuck was nonchalant. "Make a proposal." There was a pause and then a spike, "You're the Big Boy."

"Put it in writing."

"They're working on it. Probably by Friday." Chuck was calm.

Luke reviewed the call with Jake. "They can't do that," Jake concluded. "Let's wait for the letter. You may have to make a compromise. It may cost you in the short run, but you can make it up. Right?"

Luke's mind circled. The first issue was paying the side note. Taking the money out of FRM would drop the cash position below

$2 million and kill the FCBA deal. A servicing sale would take almost ninety days, and that was too long.

The only alternative was to borrow a million dollars. The industry was in turmoil, and Luke's only other bank relationship was with Beth's father. He knew Sand Springs Fidelity Bank's maximum loan had been cut to $500,000. That wasn't enough. FCBA was only interested in the credit line. Luke was out of options.

The second issue was the transfer fees; it was ransom money. Even if he agreed, he still had the problem of paying the side note in full.

Luke looked at the clock; he was tired of waiting. He was relieved when Chuck answered. "If you'll sign the collateral transfer agreement now so I can close and move to FCBA, I will pay two hundred thousand on the side note now and agree to pay the balance by June 30. That gives me time to sell some servicing. Or, since you guys want into the mortgage business, I'll sell you one-point-two million worth of servicing to pay off the side note. Your choice. As for the transfer fee on the files, you can't legally charge it, but I'll pay fifty thousand."

"I don't think they want to buy servicing."

"I think they want to crater the FCBA deal."

"I'll run it by them."

"By whom? The president?" Luke asked.

"He'll be involved, but it's not his decision."

"Who is the president now?"

"Arthur Pierce."

"Who's Arthur Pierce? Is he new?"

"No, he headed the Auditing Department. They moved him in when Weldon left."

"Who's the chairman?

"Nelson took that over. Malthers is still vice-chairman; he'll be chairman after the deal closes with FDIC."

"So it's not Malson, it's Sonmal?" Luke said, reversing the names.

"What?"

"You guys are just switching chairs, and the government is forgiving a nine-hundred-million-dollar loss and loaning you five hundred million. The government is paying for your losses and then loaning you money so you can force people out of business and take their place!"

"Sonmal?" Chuck repeated.

"That's a slick deal." Luke started again, "And Pierce was in the Auditing Department? Not many presidents come from the Auditing Department."

"That's true," Chuck allowed.

"So you have your own Deputy Dawg?"

Chuck said distinctly, "It's most likely a transitional position."

"Arthur Pierce...," Luke made a note on his pad. "When will you call?"

"I'll be in touch tomorrow," Chuck promised.

CHAPTER FORTY NINE

The next morning, the cash markets inched slightly lower. The futures market was still down limit. Mortgage interest rates had continued to increase since the trade sanctions had been announced, as the Japanese continued selling US bonds they held. FRM's phone lines were still inundated.

Luke checked with Jake Ingles, but there was no news. Chuck finally called after lunch. "We can't exchange servicing for the note. We think the regulators would have problems with it."

Luke heard the word "think" and knew Malson had not approached the regulators. "FDIC isn't requiring me to pay off the side note to move to FCBA. Why would they care? It's got to be someone there."

"We haven't talked to them on this." Chuck's voice stopped abruptly.

"You haven't talked to them about anything. You probably didn't even talk to them about putting the money back you stole from the servicing sale. You haven't even talked to them, have you?"

Chuck backpedaled. "I haven't been in all of the conversations." There was a pause, and he tried again, "There are others involved in this. I know we are not a buyer of servicing. I think we can cap the fee at fifty thousand dollars to transfer all of the files."

"I'll pay the fee, but I can't pay the side note now. I'll sign an agreement saying I'll sell servicing and pay the note by June 30. Tell them. I will pay it then."

"They want to be paid now. That's a condition of letting you move."

"You have Jake's demand letter to sign the collateral transfer agreement, so we can move. Either sign the agreement or put your objections in writing."

"We'll have something by Friday. It may be late in the day."

"I'm sure whatever you do will be late."

Luke slammed the phone repeatedly against his desk before he hung up. He saw only gray images and vacant spaces. He stormed through the office and into the back parking lot and stared at the sky until the colors returned. He went back in, oblivious to those staring at him, and called Jake Ingles, who promised to call Phil Sandifer. Another day passed.

The bond markets were still drifting lower, and interest rates still inching up, but the pace was slower. The futures market was trading again. Denise had pocketed over $150,000 and told Luke she had closed her position and the next dinner was on her.

Chuck Rail called shortly before lunch. "We need a couple of people to sign off on some things. We'll have our written response on your moving to FCBA next Wednesday, unless you want to make another offer."

"No more offers. You need to take my deal."

"This is over my head. But then again, you once had different options."

"No lapel pins for me." Luke slammed the phone down and then called Jake.

Luke's frustration came through. "They're still stalling. It's like they want to run out the clock or something."

"I think you're right. They can kill thirty days. They can probably get by with that. Anything longer puts them at risk. But then again, a judgment against that corporation is worthless," Jake reasoned.

Luke called Pete Winston to bring him up to date.

Late in the afternoon Susan Nichols walked in shaking her head. "Malson made a mistake on an early bond settlement, and now they want to draft our account."

"What happened?"

"We delivered the certificate for a two-million-dollar bond to Malson, so Butch could fund the bond and pay the line of credit. The clerk said the amount Butch paid was two hundred thousand less than the credit line advance, and she needed to debit our account. I got a copy of the bond department's funding sheet, and it looks like they used the market price. I've called Butch, but I can't get him on the line."

Luke grabbed the phone and called Butch Hastings. "Butch, we sent a bond for early settlement yesterday, and Susan says you paid the market price instead of the commitment price."

"Well, yes, we have a little movement here. It's just temporary, but you're covered. This thing should come back. I've been watching and—"

"You are supposed to advance on the commitment price," Luke said, "not the market price."

"Well, I've got you covered. You're covered; don't worry. We'll get this worked out. As this thing moves, we can increase that advance and—"

Again Luke interrupted, "It doesn't matter how the market moves. We have a commitment. You advance based on the commitment price, not the market price."

"Yes," Butch started, and then he stammered again about "gotcha covered" and "you're covered" and "when this thing moves." He sputtered and talked, and Luke waited until he heard, "And when we get this bond sold and moved—"

Luke shot in, "This bond is sold. I sold this to you over a month ago. We have a commitment."

Butch's voice started to break. "Let me get on this. I'll call you back."

Luke was nervous. "Get the trade confirmation from Harold," he said to Susan. Luke thought again and spoke as she headed for the door. "And get a copy of all of our trade confirmations with Malson."

Within the hour, Luke became more concerned. Harold had all of the trade confirmations from Keegan Securities, but he was missing $12 million of confirmations from Butch. Susan and Harold were standing in his office when Luke called Butch. "That two million dollars goes against the trade on January 7. Susan gave you that confirmation number for the advance. I'm faxing you the commitment."

"Let me check that. I'll get back to you."

"And I'm missing some confirmations." Luke read off the numbers. "I need those."

"Don't worry; you're covered." Butch's voice sounded better.

Luke felt better, but the snafu made him nervous. "How short was the early settlement?" he asked Susan.

"About two hundred fifteen thousand."

"And they debited that amount from the account?"

She nodded with a grim face.

Luke thought. If Butch's department advanced the market price until the issue was resolved, and Chuck's department drafted the difference, FRM could face a cash crunch. Payroll was due in a few days. "Can you transfer the payroll money today? We already know the amount, right?"

"Sure."

"Do it and let me know how much is left." Susan stood and started toward the door, but Luke raised his palm. "How many more commitments do we have with Malson?" He pulled the marketing list, added in his head, and answered, "Almost forty-three million." He looked at Harold. "When do we have early settlements at Malson again?"

Harold looked at his list. "We have two million today and maybe another four million for Monday or Tuesday. We have probably about ten million next week."

Luke feared Malson would drain FRM's cash by failing to advance at the commitment price. Even worse, Malson's failure to honor even a few bond trades could cause losses large enough to kill the FCBA deal. If Malson failed to honor all of the trades, FRM would lose more than $5 million and would be bankrupt. "We have to get the other commitments out of Butch. Harold, you have to stay on him. I'll call, too." Luke looked at Susan. "Let's transfer the payroll money now. Let's transfer another two hundred thousand to National Bank. Let me know how cash looks after that."

Susan Nichols returned soon. The payroll transfer had been made, and she had deposited money into National Bank. Most of FRM's cash was tied up in the equity on the line of credit and the early settlements, and only $100,000 was left in the general account.

The next day Butch continued promising Luke, Susan, and Harold that FRM was covered, but the early settlements with Malson's Bond Department for Friday were short by $209,000, and Malson drafted the difference from the general account. Late in the afternoon

Harold, Susan, and Luke went over numbers. Chuck's department was advancing new loan closings at the commitment prices, but the Bond Department was doing early settlements at market prices. Luke looked at Susan. "If we only had a hundred thousand in the account, how did they take over two hundred thousand?"

"I don't know. I don't think there's that much float."

"Call someone. Tell him you're leaving for the weekend and just want to make sure everything is OK."

"All right." She grabbed the phone from the side table. After a brief exchange, she reported, "Cook said everything's fine, and we have about half a million in the account." The three sat in disbelief.

Luke called Butch Hastings, but he was gone for the day. "We have to get the confirmations from Butch on Monday." Luke wondered what game Malson was playing this time. He looked at Harold. "Do you have the names of some of those companies that advance money for closings?"

"You mean brokering the loans immediately?" Harold asked.

"Yes, we assign the loan and the servicing to them, and they advance the money."

"You mean like being a mortgage broker? We've never done that."

"I know."

"It's table funding. They take the servicing, and they charge a fee."

"I know." Luke looked through the windows into the offices. "We're holding a lot of loan applications."

"OK," Harold answered. "I can call some."

Luke had already arranged to see his children over the weekend, and Denise had planned to stay in Chicago. He called Denise as soon as Susan and Harold walked out. "Can you come to Tulsa?"

"Sure," she answered.

CHAPTER FIFTY

Luke saw his children Saturday morning. He made plans to take them to a movie Sunday evening. They never noticed his distraction.

Denise's flight landed shortly after noon and she waited only a few minutes at the airport before Luke arrived. As they made the drive to the lake, Luke told her about Malson shorting the bond purchases, the missing confirmations, and Butch Hastings's evasiveness. "You know what he's done—or not done," she said. "He made the trades with you, but he didn't sell the other side. He was trying to make some extra spread for himself."

"How?"

"He gets a commission on the trade and probably part of the overage. The market was moving in his direction, so he was probably making an extra eighth of a percent here and there, picking up several hundred dollars on every bond for his cut; he got caught long, and now he's down more than ten percent on the whole load!"

"I thought Malson was stuck, and he was covering for them because they didn't want to honor the trades. Maybe they needed the money or something."

"No. I doubt that. Maybe they were long, but they would have been trading for their own account. Not sure what they were doing. They probably want him selling the other side of his trades when they buy bonds from you. I think he was trading on his own, and he's caught."

"I'm caught" Luke said as the air went out of his lungs.

"You're all caught," she said matter-of-factly. "They'll have to honor it if they want to stay around. I don't know..." Luke watched her think as the scenery slid by. "If they're dumping the old corporation, they'll try to weasel out." She reached her answer. "They won't pay. These guys don't like you, and they're huge."

Luke was fine until he put Denise on a Sunday afternoon flight to Chicago. He and the children arrived moments before the movie and sat a few rows from the front. The children seemed not to care about the seats; they watched the movie, ate half the popcorn, and sipped on their sodas. Luke's mind was on Monday.

Malson's blocking Luke's move to FCBA by refusing to sign the collateral transfer agreement was an obstacle; if Malson and Butch Hastings failed to honor the bond commitments, both the FCBA deal and FRM were dead. Luke could tell Butch Hastings wanted to come clean on Monday but could not say the words. He kept telling Luke he was covered and the market move was temporary and he would get it right.

FRM delivered $4 million in early settlements on Monday and the usual day's deliveries for the new loan closings. There was no problem with Chuck's department, and they advanced using the commitment prices. Susan Nichols came into Luke's office with shock plastered across her face. "This makes no sense," she said. "The advances for new loan closings are fine again, but the Bond Department shorted us by four hundred twenty-four thousand on the bond settlements.

Chuck's department drafted the shortage from our general account. There's not that much in the account! Still the transfer went through, and when I checked, they said we had two hundred fifty thousand in the account. That can't be right! That account has to be overdrawn five hundred thousand dollars—half a million!"

"And the daily advances from Chuck's department are fine?" Luke asked.

"Yes. Yes. They advance at the commitment price, but Butch shorts us on the bond settlements. And somehow enough money appears in our account to pay off the old advances for those loans!"

"Is Butch transferring some other money to our account to cover this? How many settlements tomorrow?" Luke asked.

"I don't show any money coming into the account! We have another three million for tomorrow," Susan answered.

Luke thought for a moment. He called Butch Hastings. "Where are the confirmations you owe me? We sent you the trade numbers."

"You're covered," Butch started.

Luke only half listened. "Have it fixed by tomorrow."

Luke could not sleep that night. The settlement numbers would not be available until around three in the afternoon. Butch pleaded with Luke the next morning. "I can't advance any more today, but this will get worked out. You have your coverage."

Susan Nichols had become accustomed to the routine. Her report was in monotone. "Funding of new loan closings through Chuck's department is fine, but we were shorted three hundred eleven thousand on Butch's bond settlements. Chuck's department drafts the account for the difference, and somehow we still have money in the account. That puts the overdraft over eight hundred thousand. I checked with Tom Cook, and they show the account balances are

OK." She held her notes in one hand and opened her other palm. "What are they doing?"

Luke knew the account had to be overdrawn. He grabbed the phone and called Chuck Rail to see if he would give the same answer as Tom Cook. "Chuck, how much is in our account? Can you check?"

Luke could hear Chuck walk away to find a terminal. "You've got about four hundred thousand in the account," Chuck said. "Working on a way to pay off the side note?"

"No. I'm still waiting for you to sign the collateral transfer agreement or give me your objections in writing. Are you going to have that tomorrow?"

"Actually I was about to call you. We have a few people out of town. It may be Friday before we have the response."

Luke knew the collateral transfer agreement was no longer his most pressing problem. "Am I supposed to be surprised," Luke said and ended the call.

"What are we going to do?" Susan asked.

"Let's get Harold." Luke asked about brokering loans, as Harold walked through the door. Harold said he had found a couple of sources, but they would only take four or five loans a day, so FRM would have to delay closings.

"We have to close and deliver as many loans to Malson as fast as we can," Luke said. "If they walk away from our commitments and we have to broker the loans to someone else, we are going to lose more than ten to fifteen percent of the loan amount on each closing. That's millions we don't have. Butch is not paying commitment price for our bonds, and by some miracle we aren't overdrawn. We need to call people and push up the closing date when we can. We need to start calling now."

The room was quiet. Finally Harold spoke. "What are you going to do?"

"I'm going to see Arthur Pierce."

"Who?" Harold asked.

"He's Malson's latest president." Luke flipped the hair over his collar.

"When?" Harold pursued.

"Tomorrow morning."

"Do you have an appointment?" Harold wiped his face.

"No. I've never met him. I'll go tomorrow morning. This has to come to a head. I'm going to be Bobby Knight."

"Who's that?" Susan asked.

"He's a basketball coach that throws temper tantrums and chairs," Harold answered.

"They say there's money in the account. Let's transfer the next payroll today. Use the amount of the last payroll," Luke said to Susan. He glanced at both of them. "Let's call Mike in Oklahoma City and bring him up to speed."

Later Luke called Jake Ingles and brought him up-to-date. He told him he was going to see Arthur Pierce the next morning.

CHAPTER FIFTY ONE

L uke called Arthur Pierce at eight o'clock. He had left two switchboard messages before he reached a secretary on the third call and was told "Mr. Pierce" would be in shortly. He called again and the secretary acknowledged he had arrived. "What is this in regard to?" she asked.

"He needs to talk to me. I will be there at nine o'clock, and he needs to see me."

Luke held until she came back on the line. "He said he can meet with you, but just for a couple of minutes."

Luke made a point of riding the elevator to the eighteenth floor. He climbed the grand staircase to the nineteenth floor and was shown to Arthur Pierce's office. Luke looked around and knew the man did not fit the room. Arthur Pierce was about five feet eight and weighed at least 275 pounds. Luke guessed he had trouble matching sizes because about four inches of his belt dangled at his waist, wagging as he stood. The belt was cracked and worn; his suit was crumpled, and the dingy color of his white shirt showed its age. His tie was unevenly matched, and he looked nervous. "What do you want?" he started as though Luke were going to rob him.

Luke held out his hand until Pierce extended his, and then Luke gave it a firm shake and sat down. "I only have a few minutes," Pierce said, still waiting for Luke to speak.

Luke was surprised at his own calmness. FRM's fate hung in the balance, but he was steady and sure. Finally he spoke. "Does this bank want a relationship with me or not? If I pay off the side note, will you still advance on the line of credit?"

Pierce seemed to gain confidence. "Once we get paid on that note, we will terminate the relationship." He tried to sit taller, but he was looking up at Luke.

Luke stared and watched Pierce's eyes drift away. "Well, you have some problems. You stole money from our account when we sold some servicing, but that's not why I'm here. First, Butch Hastings and your Bond Department are reneging on around forty-three million in trades. That's more than five million you owe based on the current market. Second, your people have somehow overdrawn our account by eight hundred thousand dollars but think we still have money. Third, you're blocking my moving to FCBA because you are refusing to sign the collateral transfer agreement and you are demanding payment on the side note. Fourth, you're trying to charge me a fee to move the files to FCBA."

Pierce was hit. "What are you trying to pull? I've heard about you."

Luke put venom in every word. "I'm not pulling anything. You've been holding me hostage for weeks because you won't let me close with FCBA. You've been playing games. And now you're reneging on bond sales. It's a loss of over five million as of now. It may be growing. They're shorting us on the settlements, and somehow your people have overdrawn the account. We figure we must be overdrawn by eight hundred thousand, but they don't seem to think so."

Pierce looked scared. He turned to the phone, dropped it the first time, and then grasped it firmly. He looked at Luke and then laid the phone down and walked to the office entrance. "What's Tom Cook's extension?" he asked his secretary. He returned, tried to puff himself up, and called Cook.

Luke stood and walked around the office. Luke did not care for the décor; there was too much leather and too many hard edges. He liked a masculine room, but Pierce's office reminded him of naked Greco-Roman wrestlers, as though someone were trying to compensate. "Bivins picked out this stuff?"

"Yes. I think Mr. Bivins redid the office," Pierce said nervously. Luke admired the view from the windows. After a few moments, Tom Cook entered, noticeably shocked to see Luke standing in Pierce's office. Pierce said nothing to Cook, looked at Luke instead, and said, "What are you trying to pull?"

Pierce was encouraged by the arrival of new troops, but Luke was on a mission. He pointed his finger at Tom Cook. "This guy's prints are all over this deal. First he stole the money from the servicing sale, and now he has overdrawn the account. He's probably helping short us on the bond trades."

Cook looked at Pierce. "They're not overdrawn. Can't be." He looked at Luke. "I don't know anything about the bond trades."

"Wrong. You or someone has overdrawn the account. Maybe you didn't pay yourself off on some of the loans. I have no idea what you're doing. But I know you're short eight hundred thousand."

Pierce seemed to be able to handle Cook. He sent him off to get more information and stood. "I don't know what you're trying to pull, but I have another meeting."

"Where do you want me to wait?" Luke asked.

"We'll call you." Pierce looked toward the door.

"I'll wait in the reception area." Luke followed Pierce.

"You can wait downstairs."

"I like it here." Luke stepped to a table and made a point to finger the magazines. He selected a news periodical and settled into one of the sofas. Pierce reentered the president's office and soon emerged and headed to the elevators. Luke looked around and saw six secretaries behind oversized desks, spaced far apart from each other. Luke stood and walked the executive floor. There were only eight offices. Two vacant offices were labeled "Chairman" and "Vice-Chairman." The next office was vacant and unmarked. The secretaries barely looked up as Luke surveyed the area. He continued and found four more offices, but none had nameplates on the door, and two were vacant. Two accounting types occupied the others. There were six more secretarial stations, but only two were occupied. A couple of people glanced without taking notice. Luke walked back to Pierce's waiting area, grabbed a phone on one of the tables, dialed the office, and asked for Susan. "I'm at Pierce's office. Call me here if you need me." He gave her the extension number on the phone.

In fifteen minutes Arthur Pierce stepped off the elevator and seemed startled to see Luke. Pierce stopped for a second and then walked up to Luke. "I don't know what you're trying to pull, but you need to talk with Mr. Rail." Pierce headed toward his office.

Luke cut him off. "So, what did you find?"

"You're not overdrawn."

"Oh yes, we are. And you're shorting us on the trades."

"The Bond Department is checking on that now."

"So, are you going to honor the trades and put the money back into the account?"

Pierce stared at Luke for a moment and looked away. "The law firm will be looking at this. I don't think we'll be funding any more of your loans." He headed back to the elevators.

Luke followed him. "Oh yes, you will. You'll fund today." Pierce hurried into the elevator, punched the button, and anxiously waited for the door to close. Luke returned to the reception area, called Jake Ingles, and left a message. He walked to Pierce's secretary with a big smile. "Tell Pierce not to worry. I'll be back."

Luke headed to his car, called Jake as he drove, and brought him up-to-date. Jake promised to call back after he talked to Phil Sandifer. When Luke arrived at the office, Harold Rhoden was waiting. "Tom Cook says that won't fund us anymore. Apparently they are cutting off the other mortgage companies in ninety days. Both of them called me this morning and said Malson told them yesterday. They wanted to know if we had heard anything." Harold's voice was shaking.

Luke called the owners of Osage Mortgage and Tremble Mortgage. Malson had called them and said they were pulling out of the business and would quit providing credit lines within the next ninety days as part of the transfer to new ownership. Harold watched as Luke talked to both of them. The timing of the calls told Luke the terminations were unrelated to Luke's visit with Pierce. Malson was going to eliminate all of its local competition. "They were only funding us until I paid off the side note," Luke said to Harold after he hung up. "Pierce told me. After that they were cutting us off. They want us out of business."

Jake called and said Malson was auditing the accounts. "They say the accounts are fine. Are you sure you're overdrawn?' he asked.

"Have to be. Susan says so, and I can't figure how we wouldn't be. There's not that much float in that account. The other accounts have a ton of float."

Jake called back in an hour. "They want to meet at their law firm's office. That's all I know."

Jake and Luke walked in shortly after noon. Chuck started, "Not sure what happened. But you're right: looks like the account is over-drawn. You have to make up the difference." There was no conviction in his voice, and Sandifer's eyes slanted down as he scribbled on a pad.

Jake read the body language. "I don't think so. Sounds like you are reneging on the bond sales. That's the issue. Fund at the com-mitment price and the overdraft goes away."

It was Sandifer's turn. "The bank is looking into that situation."

"Give us our money, and live by the agreement. And we need you to sign the collateral transfer agreement to FCBA," Jake finished. In less than two minutes, the meeting was over.

Luke stopped at the door and looked back at Chuck. "You better fund today." He turned and headed toward the elevator with Jake.

When Luke got back to the office, Susan Nichols was waiting for him. "They swept the payroll account. They took another swipe at the general account, too. They must think there's money there. The payroll money went to the side note, so it's down to a million. I don't know where the other money went. Anyway, they took over four hun-dred thousand from the general account, so now it has to be one-point-two million overdrawn, and they took two hundred thousand from the payroll account. The payroll money is gone. We have noth-ing left."

Luke called Jake to give him the latest. "They're grabbing mon-ey everywhere they can. They're grabbing money that's not there. They took our payroll money and applied it to the side note. They grabbed money from the overdrawn account. They're grabbing mon-ey and going to figure it out later. We don't think they've drafted the loan-in-process accounts. Those will be all right for a few days, but I have to close loans."

Moments later Jake called back. "Send your funding packages. They will fund today, but they're not using the commitment price you show. They will only fund at market." He paused. "They want to meet late this afternoon." He paused again. "They bounced the checks presented today on the general account. Pierce ordered no more money out of the account, but that's been changed."

"What?"

"They're going to pay them. Tell the people to run them again."

"That's going to kill us—having checks returned. How many?"

"No one knows. Sandifer says they're going to pay the checks. You need to have your people run them again. Chuck's department will talk to anyone who has a question."

"He'd better play it straight."

"They'll have a clerk do it. It won't be a problem."

Harold sent the funding packages with the commitment prices. Malson funded short, using the market price instead. The proper amount had to be sent to the loan-in-process accounts to cover the closing checks. Susan called one of the Malson clerks, and they transferred money from the overdrawn general account. She was gleeful when she gave the news to Luke. "They shorted the advance for new loan closings, but when I called to transfer the money to the closing accounts, it went through! I can't believe they gave us more money. Just like that!"

Luke shook his head and the staff continued handling calls regarding returned checks and moving up closing dates.

Luke met Jake in the lobby, and they rode the elevator to the law firm. Phil Sandifer and Chuck Rail were waiting. "We cannot document your trades. The bank is eager to end the relationship," Sandifer announced.

"How many can you not document?" Luke interjected.

"We don't show you have any bond sales pending."

Luke was up in his chair. "Chuck knows we do. He was funding against them." He stared at Chuck. "Chuck, you have copies! You were funding at the commitment price!"

"Those advances were in error and will need to be corrected. They're not on our books," Sandifer responded.

"You're still drafting our accounts. You drafted the payroll account," Luke shot again. "Does Malthers know what you're doing?"

"Mr. Malthers is aware of our discussions. He does not want the bank to continue to have lines of credit with mortgage companies. That's part of his criteria in acquiring the bank. He wants to terminate this relationship." Sandifer sounded like he was testifying before a Senate subcommittee.

"I want to talk to him." Luke's voice rose. "How do you go broke, get the government to pay for your losses, get more money from the government, so you can start over, run your competition out of business, and take their business? I want to talk to him."

"I don't think so," Sandifer answered.

"Where is he?" Luke demanded.

Jake intervened. "What's your proposal?" he said to Sandifer.

"Let's end the relationship. The line of credit is immediately terminated, and FRM assigns all of its servicing. We will apply that toward the personal note and the deficiency in the accounts, and Mr. Boyd will sign a personal note if we determine a balance is still owing." Sandifer paused and waited.

Luke gave a faint laugh. "How generous!" He saw Jake staring at him. "What about the loans we have to close?"

"That's FRM's problem. If you can't close them you could close the business, and the customers will go elsewhere." Sandifer paused. "That's for you and your counsel to decide."

The offer was worse than Luke expected. "Let's get Butch in here."

"Mr. Hastings will be leaving the bank's employ." Sandifer smiled smartly.

"Did you review his copies of our trades?" Luke asked.

Chuck and Sandifer exchanged glances; Sandifer answered. "We don't have any more trades on our books."

"Do you want some copies?" Luke wished he had them all. "Chuck and Cook have been funding against them."

Chuck and Sandifer both moved in their seats. "We would like to see those," Sandifer finally answered.

Luke drew from the hip. "Oh, I'm sure there are copies all around this building. Butch has his copies, and Chuck's department was funding against them. I'll give you enough servicing to pay off the side note. And you fund all of the commitments. You sign the collateral transfer agreement, and we go to FCBA—and that's that."

Sandifer shook his head. "That's not an option."

Jake asked for a moment, and he and Luke walked to the hallway. "Do you have copies of the commitments?"

"We're short twelve million. Butch must have gotten nervous and stopped sending them. We have the rest, and we have my dated notes on all of the trades. Chuck has to have copies because his department was funding against them," Luke answered.

Jake nodded, and Luke saw Chuck exit the conference room and turn the corner. Jake spoke first when he entered the room. "Phil, I think we need to talk. I'll call you in a few minutes." He turned to Luke and said, "Let's go." The two were silent until they exited the elevator. "Fax me copies of what you have," Jake finally said. "I'm not going to give them copies, but I want to see what we have."

"They need to fund. I have to keep closing loans."

"I don't know if I can get that."

"They'll fund. If I don't close loans, I'm out of business. They fund or we sue."

"I'll try," Jake answered.

Within the hour Luke called, confirmed Jake had received the faxed confirmations, and posed a question. "I don't understand. They say there are no records of trades, but Chuck advanced against some of them. Then they say Butch is leaving Malson. If they agree with Butch, why is he leaving?"

"I told Phil you have copies of bond sales to Butch. He didn't seem surprised. I think Chuck Rail's department has them also. Apparently you're not the only one that Butch has ripped off. Some individual stock customers are claiming money is missing from their accounts. It's not as big as you. But you're not alone."

"That's good. They have to believe us." Luke was hopeful.

"This is not about believing you. The problem is they owe you too much money. It's five million instead of a hundred thousand. Five million is a big number. And they don't like you."

"So? They need to fund. I have to close loans."

"I don't think that's happening."

"I have to close loans. Everyone's nervous because of the move in interest rates. If we don't close loans, I'm out of business."

"I think you will have to wait," Jake said softly.

Luke knew if he stopped loan closings, rumors would fly; realtors, buyers, and sellers would continue to tie up the lines. Malson's having returned checks had made everyone more nervous. He ran through his options. Malson had put nothing in writing. He called

Susan on the intercom. "How many closings tomorrow? And Friday, too." Within a few minutes, he knew he had over $4 million to close. FRM had no cash at Malson; it had all been swept. He had only $400,000 in the National Bank account, and payroll was due soon. He called Chuck Rail. "We're closing loans tomorrow and delivering packages," he said and hung up before Chuck could respond.

CHAPTER FIFTY TWO

Malson had not responded by Thursday morning. Luke called Chuck, told him loan packages would be delivered by noon, said FRM would close loans on Friday, and immediately hung up. Luke was bluffing. If Malson did not transfer money, the loan-in-process accounts would eventually be overdrawn, and checks for loan closings would bounce.

Jake called in the afternoon. "They want two days. They agreed to fund loans through Friday. Are you in town this weekend?"

"Sure," Luke said, though he knew he was scheduled to go to Chicago. "What's going on?"

"They said we may need to meet on Saturday. I think they expect to have some decisions late Friday or over the weekend."

Luke knew Malthers was calling the shots. "Regulators don't work on the weekend, do they?" Luke was now certain that Malthers owned the regulators.

"I don't know," Jake said. "But make yourself available over the weekend."

Luke breathed easier knowing Malson would fund through Friday. The loan officers pushed closings forward on the schedule, so they could deliver to Malson before the weekend. Buyers and sellers were surprised but went along. The office was in overdrive and most stayed until near midnight. Employees threw Luke furtive glances and then refocused on their work. Phyllis came in the office periodically with her stack of files, but on one occasion she came empty-handed and sat on the sofa and stared at Luke. "Are we going to be all right?" she asked.

"I think so."

She heard the hesitation in his voice. "OK," she said and then bounced up.

Susan Nichols rushed in. "They bounced the check to the IRS for payroll taxes. It's about fifty thousand."

"When?" Luke surged forward.

"Probably when they swept the payroll account. The IRS check had not cleared, so Malson got the money. The IRS will be sending a letter, and they'll want a one-hundred-percent penalty."

Luke called Jake. "Add a hundred thousand to the list." He told him about Malson having swept the account and the IRS wanting the penalty.

"That can be negotiated with IRS," Jake answered.

"By whom and when? I'm underwater here," Luke answered.

Malson funded the new loan closings at the market price instead of Butch Hastings's commitment price on both Thursday and Friday. The early settlements through the Bond Department were settled short also. Despite the short funding, Chuck's department continued to transfer money to the loan-in-process accounts and further overdraw the general account. Susan estimated the overdraft at $1.9 million.

Jake called Friday afternoon. Malson wanted to meet early Saturday morning at Phil Sandifer's office. "Don't plan on closing loans on Monday. I think they're done."

Luke called Denise and told her it was going to be a rough weekend. He told her to go have fun, and she said, "Make a deal."

Saturday morning was warm, and spring flirted in the air. Luke sensed none of it. The group assembled around the table in jeans and knit shirts. Phil Sandifer started, "You are outside the covenants of the loan agreement, and we estimate you are overdrawn by one-point-nine million dollars. You personally owe us a million on the side note. We will fund no further loans, but we will purchase all of your servicing in exchange for the debt and overdraft."

Luke thought a moment; Malson wanted to avoid honoring Butch Hastings's trades. "You grabbed the payroll money out of the payroll account. You have to put that back and pay the IRS taxes."

"You're overdrawn, and the drafts were authorized by the right of offset," Sandifer stated.

"That was trust money, including payroll taxes. The account is labeled 'In Trust.'"

"I don't think so." Sandifer calmly looked at Chuck. "We'll check. In any event, Malson will need some of your servicing employees during the transition. We're willing to pay their salaries until the servicing transfer is finalized. We may even offer some of them jobs later."

Luke nodded, knowing the purpose of the meeting was to take over FRM's assets, and then Malson would make offers to the FRM employees.

"No deal."

"If you refuse, we will go into federal court on Monday morning to have FRM put into bankruptcy and have a receiver appointed, and we will sue you personally on the side note as well as the overdraft and the line of credit."

"Are you going to honor the bond sales we did with Butch Hastings?"

"That's our final offer."

Jake looked at Luke and Luke started again, "What if—"

Sandifer interrupted, "That's our final offer."

Luke started again but stopped when he saw Sandifer shaking his head negatively and heard Jake intercede, "I think they're done." Jake turned to Sandifer. "We'll call in an hour."

Once outside Luke gazed at the abandoned downtown streets. He knew Malson would never accept a deal that would allow FRM to survive. Malson wanted to destroy Luke financially. Their offer would leave FRM with debts, a large inventory of loans to be closed at a loss, and payroll and taxes owing. If Luke could not close the pending loans, the business and his reputation were finished. "I'll beat them to the courthouse and file bankruptcy first. I didn't pledge the servicing. If FRM goes into bankruptcy, the servicing will go back to the agencies."

"Are you sure?" Jake asked.

"Yes. They're not taking the company!"

"What can you do?" Jake asked. "They're ready to file."

"I'll call you in an hour."

Luke headed to the car and started toward the office. He picked up the phone, called Sandifer's office, and asked for Chuck. "You need to talk to me one more time."

"Why?"

"If you have any hope of keeping your job, you need to talk to me one more time."

"Why?"

"Meet me somewhere. Alone."

"OK." There was a long pause. "Philbrook in twenty minutes."

Luke grabbed a coffee and sat in the parking lot of the Philbrook Museum. The luscious setting, used for galas and weddings, was tranquil but failed to calm Luke. A car pulled into the lot and swung around. Chuck was in the passenger side, his face barely visible above the door, and Sandifer was at the wheel. Luke was surprised to see Sandifer but now knew Chuck was afraid to meet him. "If we file bankruptcy, the servicing goes back to HUD and the agencies. You get nothing." The color went out of Sandifer's face. "If you don't fund loans Monday, I will file bankruptcy."

Chuck tried to look calm, but his eyebrows flinched. He exchanged glances with Sandifer. Chuck said "OK" through clenched teeth, and they drove away.

Luke called Jake Ingles and told him of the conversation, as he drove to the office. Luke arrived to find shipping personnel and closers finishing files and preparing for Monday. Jake called. "They don't want you to file bankruptcy," he started. "They've changed their mind."

"Funny, huh? They won't take servicing to pay off the side note and let me go to FCBA, but they want the servicing if I'll go out of business."

"Can you still move to another lender?"

"Not unless they honor the commitments—all of them. And they have to let me move to FCBA."

"What's FCBA think now?"

"Pete's waiting on Malson to sign the collateral transfer agreement. I need to level with him soon."

"What if you had the money to pay off the side note?" Jake asked.

"I can't get the money, but that's not the issue. They have to honor all of the trades or I will take huge losses and FCBA won't do the deal."

"What about your father-in-law?"

"He's broke. He's being propped up by his wife's trust money and my brother-in-law and his partner."

"Can they raise some money?"

Luke made a decision he did not want to make. "I'll call them."

Luke knew Doug Turney and Vern Brindley worked every Saturday. He called, arranged a meeting, arrived within thirty minutes, and spelled out the recent history. They already knew there was bad blood between Luke and Malson. Luke watched their eyes. Vern Brindley wanted no part of it. Doug Turney seemed intrigued, as if looking for an opportunity. "I need about a million to have enough to pay them off. But, they have to honor the trades. If they don't, I will take huge losses and that will kill the FCBA deal."

Doug and Vern said the bank could only provide $500,000, its new legal lending limit. "Plus, Malson has to honor all of the trades, right. Otherwise, it won't work." Doug repeated. After another half hour, the meeting broke up. Doug Turney winked at Luke. "Let me know how it comes out." He paused, "Maybe if Malson is not in the picture, we can help you."

Luke counted the hours until Monday. Jake called early and said Malson would fund loans again. The negotiations continued throughout the day.

Luke wanted Pete Winston to hear the facts from him. He called and gave him a quick version, letting him know FRM had done the trades and Butch Hastings had been fired. "I don't know how this will turn out. I have to get them to honor the trades, or you can't do a deal with us."

Pete let Luke down gently. "If they sign the collateral transfer agreement and honor the trades, we can still do the deal, but everything's out-of-date because of Malson's delays. I will need new financials and probably another fifteen days for a new approval; then I can start the closing process again."

Luke promised to keep him posted.

The negotiations continued Tuesday, and Jake called in the afternoon. "Malson will fund loans today, but that's it. They know you keep cramming loans at them, and the overdraft keeps getting larger. They said they aren't seeing any settlements from Keegan Securities."

"I stopped those," Luke said. "They'll close on the regular date. I thought Malson would draft the money. We have about two percent equity in the Keegan settlements. I don't want Malson grabbing it. It's worth about seven hundred thousand dollars to us."

"Sandifer says they want all of the servicing in exchange for the balance on the side note and the overdraft. Otherwise, they are going to bankruptcy court."

"They lose the servicing," Luke countered.

"They don't seem concerned. I'm not sure what they're thinking." Jake paused. "They say they are ready to go to court tomorrow."

Luke thought about the trip to HUD, the morning call in his hotel room from Congressman Wheeler, and the closed-door conversation with Ray Fontenot. "They made a deal to get the servicing out of the bankruptcy court. They want me to go down. It's not about the money or the trades. I'll bet the government is going to take the loss on Butch's trades before Malthers gets the bank. They'll grab what they can, but they want me to go down. I'd even bet they even have something on the trades I'm missing. Butch had to have had some notes."

"Maybe. Probably. But they're not going to give them to us. Not until we're in court, and by then their corporation will be dissolved."

"And they're not afraid of court now. They've made a deal with HUD or someone. How hard is it to pull off a servicing deal after you've gotten almost a billion dollars from the government to keep your bank?"

"What do you want to do?" Jake asked.

Luke took a deep breath. The FCBA deal was dead if Malson did not honor the trades. "They honor all of the trades I did with Butch at the commitment price. I'll give them forty million in servicing to pay off the side note. They give me back the money they took from the payroll account and pay the IRS penalty. And we go our separate ways."

"They said they will pay the servicing salaries."

"Right, they pay the amount we are paying now," Luke added.

"They've already turned down this deal, but I'll take it to Sandifer."

"If they say a word about the sales to Keegan, the deal is dead. I think they've forgotten I have equity in those."

Luke was tired. Jake soon called back. "They know you have some confirmations from Hastings. I think they know you don't have them all. They will only honor the trades where you have confirmations."

"I have my notes on the other trades."

"That won't do. Apparently, they know something from somewhere. They've probably talked with Butch Hastings. But they know you don't have them all."

"So? What will they honor?" Luke asked.

"If you have a confirmation, they will honor it. That's it. That's thirty-one million out of forty-three million, right?" Jake sounded tired also.

"That's going to cost me one and a half million or more."

"For one and a half million dollars, they would rather go to bankruptcy court." Jake's voice was resigned.

"It's not about the money. They want me dead. The government is going to take the loss on Butch's trades and then give the bank to Malthers. This isn't costing them anything." Luke thought for a minute. "They don't want to buy servicing, but they want the servicing. I'll bet they've figured a way to value any servicing they get at zero." He paused. "They'll take the servicing to pay off the side note. Then they'll tell the government the servicing is worth nothing, so Malthers gets it for free when he gets the bank. Malthers gets to start his mortgage company with free servicing, and runs the competition out of business." Luke paused again. "Give me a few minutes."

Luke hung up. He was boxed. Jake's voice had told him he had no choice. He counted cash in his head. He knew the deal had to appear to kill FRM before Malson would accept it. Chuck had never appeared to understand how the cash and equity worked. Maybe that would provide an opening and Luke could find a way to survive and rebuild the company. He called Jake back. "OK."

Jake called in the early evening and said they were close to a deal. Jake told Luke to be at Chuck's office the next day and to bring a schedule of the servicing employees' salaries. Sandifer was not there. Only a few of Chuck's personal items were visible in the office. Two worn and faded, orange-fabric side chairs sat next to his desk. Chuck asked for the employees' salary schedule.

"Servicing employees only, right?"

"Right," Luke answered. "It includes the payroll tax and health insurance."

"You pay well." Chuck laid the sheet down. "Here's the deal. We pay the amount on this schedule until the servicing is transferred. We will fund the bond commitments where you have a copy. I understand you have thirty-one million dollars of those. You give us all of the servicing and we will consider the line of credit and the personal note paid in full. And we want a hold harmless agreement. No suits. You and FRM waive all claims."

"Close. You pay that schedule and honor the trades where we have commitments, and we'll do the hold harmless agreement." Luke raised his price. "But, you don't get all of the servicing, you get forty million. That's enough to pay off the side note. And you pay us for the money you stole from the payroll account and the IRS penalty."

"We're not writing you a check. That's a deal breaker. I'm just the messenger, but that's a deal breaker. We might go a little less than all of the servicing."

"I'm stuck with twelve million in underwater loans. That's a loss of one and a half million or more. And I have to find some way to close those loans, or I'm done in this business."

Chuck let out a slight smile. "That's your problem. Are you taking our deal?"

"My deal or no deal." Luke stood up and started to leave.

Jake ran after him. "That's as much as we can get. They're done. I'm telling you they're done. They're going to stop funding now. They're not funding. They're going to bankruptcy court. Sandifer's already drawn the papers. They're going to file in bankruptcy court."

"No deal. That's my last offer." Luke started toward the elevators.

Luke had reached the office parking lot when the car phone rang and he heard Jake's voice. "They'll do it."

Luke sat and looked inside the building. "OK." He sat in the car for a few moments. He walked into the office. The staff was busy, but he saw the eyes looking at him. He called Susan and Harold into the office and explained the deal.

"Can we close the other loans?" Harold asked.

"Yes." Luke counted the money again. With the equity in the trades with Malson and Keegan, the check Malson would cut, and the National Bank account, FRM could close the loans. "How many can we close a day?"

"Four or five," Harold answered.

"People will have to be patient. We can't close on demand."

"If they're not, what do we do?"

"If they wait, we will honor the quote; if they want to transfer, we will let them. It'll save us some money but cost us more in reputation."

Luke looked through the glass windows. The adrenaline was still surging but reality began taking his energy. He hung his head. "I have to tell them."

He waited for five o'clock, walked into the center of the office, stepped on top of one of the wood file cabinets, and sat on the low partition wall, his head close to the high ceilings. He called everyone together and asked the receptionist to busy the phones. More than fifty sets of eyes bore up at him. He saw the anguish in their faces, and he took a deep breath. "We're losing the credit line with Malson. We were going to lose it within ninety days anyway. They are pulling the lines from Osage Mortgage and Tremble Mortgage. As you probably know, Malson was not honoring the bond commitments we had with them." No one in the crowd appeared shocked. "I can't keep everyone," he said, and his voice started cracking. "I'm so proud of what we've done. I'm so proud of you. I'm so very proud. If this is it, I thank each of you. But I can't keep everyone. We'll have to be a smaller company. We'll have to broker loans for a while. I can't keep everyone." His voice was a whisper, and he took a deep breath. "Those of you we can keep, we'll have to pay less. If you want to go somewhere else, I understand. Malson will probably offer you jobs. They're going to buy some of our servicing." He was on the verge of losing control, and the tears welled and obscured his vision. He took deep breaths and exhaled and heard words of encouragement that only made it harder. "I'm sorry. I'm sorry," he said. His voice was barely audible, and he lowered himself from the wall.

He walked out the backdoor, across the back parking lot, and down a side street. The tears were streaming down his face, and he walked fast. Three blocks later he made a right and wandered through a residential neighborhood, winding through the streets, his pace fast and faster until he finally slowed and the tears stopped. He looked around not knowing exactly where he was. He wiped his cheeks and slowly pivoted and started finding the way back to the of-fice. He arrived thirty minutes later. Almost everyone was there and working.

CHAPTER FIFTY THREE

The documents were ready Thursday afternoon, and the group assembled in one of Sandifer's conference rooms. The bank had a few accounting personnel there to notarize documents and go over the procedures. Chuck tried to look cocky, but his voice was quiet. Harold, Luke, and Susan had selected the worst and highest-rate servicing to transfer to Malson, and Luke handed the schedules to Sandifer.

Susan had already set up a new payroll account with National Bank. New loan-in-process accounts had been opened with National Bank to handle the funding through the brokers that Harold had arranged.

Sandifer had a large of stack documents next to him. "We want a hold harmless agreement," he started. "Neither side will blame or sue the other. This settles any and all claims the parties may have against each other. And each will refrain from blaming the other for any loss in any forum. Neither party will make any negative comments to anyone regarding the other."

Jake had reviewed the documents, glanced at them, nodded his head, and passed them to Luke. Luke scanned through them. He read through the hold harmless agreement twice. The accounting personnel would track and fund loans for the $31 million in confirmations FRM had from Butch. Procedures were established to cancel the credit line and side note and tie up the details. The accounts at Malson would gradually wind down, and the residual would go to FRM. Within an hour, the agreements had been signed. Sandifer handed Luke a check for $300,000 for the payroll and IRS issues.

"A few bank personnel may want to come out and make arrangements regarding the servicing," Sandifer said.

"Anytime," Luke said.

In the car on the way back, Luke counted FRM's position and thought about the more than $8.5 million he had lost in his battle with Malson. He still had the equity in the Keegan Securities bonds, the loans being funded by Malson, the National Bank account, and Malson's $300,000 check. He had talked with Pete Winston. The marketing losses that FRM was about to take would kill any chance of a deal with FCBA for at least another year and a half. Luke estimated FRM would end up with around $600,000 cash and almost $100 million in servicing.

Luke was uneasy. He was restarting the company with less cash than when he had first started, with a lot more employees, and without a credit line. He knew it was a poor business decision. His reputation was taking a huge hit. Making a profit in the next year was unrealistic. He knew he would burn through most of the cash.

Luke gave Susan the checks and told her, "Jake says he can get the IRS to waive the fees." In fact, Jake did, and FRM pocketed the $50,000 difference.

Early the next morning, Andrea walked in and said, "There are a bunch of men up front. They asked for you."

Luke stood to go to the lobby, but the entourage had already started making its way to him. Arthur Pierce led the brigade, followed by four minions, and for a few steps, it looked like he was strutting until he looked around and saw all the people. His side-to-side wobble slowed, and his shoulders visibly lowered. Luke walked toward him, and Pierce muttered, "What are all of these people doing?"

Luke looked around before speaking, "Working."

The minions shuffled and looked at each other.

"I thought you were out of business," Pierce said softly.

Luke looked around again. "Doesn't look like it." For several seconds Luke watched Pierce try to grasp the situation. "What do you want to see? The Servicing Department?"

"Yes," Pierce mumbled.

Luke led him to the back. Stacks of files sat on the floor. "Those are yours." Pierce stood staring at the files while his followers looked around and at each other and tried to stand stiff. The victory parade had been cancelled. Luke could not help himself. "Nice suit," he said, looking at the crumpled, brown plaid cloth with lumps around the waist from Pierce's heft.

Pierce tried to save face. "When's all of this going to be ready?"

"In a couple of months. You'll probably pay us for ten to twelve weeks, and then we'll be finished."

Pierce looked around. "OK. OK."

"We need to pick up our servicing files. Do we go through Chuck or you?"

"Chuck is leaving the bank."

"What about Tom Cook?" Luke asked.

"He's no longer with the bank."

"I told you the account was overdrawn." Luke paused. "You kill a lot of soldiers."

"What?" Pierce looked confused.

"Oh, you don't know yet." Luke paused. "Sand Springs Fidelity Bank agreed to take over as custodian for the servicing we're keeping. Who do we see to get our files?"

One of the men with Pierce raised his hand and gave Luke a business card. "Me," was all he said.

Pierce and his group tired of looking at each other and the stacks and retreated. Luke walked them to the door and watched them wedge into one car. The receptionist apologized to Luke, "I tried to stop them."

"Not a problem. It was more fun this way."

Luke called Jake to tell him about the visit. Jake had news for Luke. "Butch Hastings has agreed to plead guilty in federal court before indictment for fraud and embezzlement. He lifted a couple of hundred thousand dollars from some individual stock accounts. A couple of local doctors got taken. They had apparently been referred through Malson's Executive Banking Center. He'll probably be sentenced by Judge Filcher in about three months."

"Maybe we should have held out?"

"It wouldn't have made a difference," Jake answered.

Luke agreed. He knew Malson had used its political clout to make a deal to grab the servicing. FRM would have been closed, and Luke would be tied up in court. Luke watched the local newspapers and four months later a three-line, one-paragraph article was buried deep inside. The article said a former Malson trader had been sentenced to prison for eighteen months for unauthorized trades in individual stock accounts. No other improprieties were mentioned.

Chuck called Friday afternoon and asked, "Can we meet somewhere?"

Luke was surprised, but said, "Sure."

Thirty minutes later Luke pulled into the Philbrook parking lot. Chuck was waiting alone. "If you hear of anything, let me know. I have had some resumes out for a while. I appreciate anything you hear of. Anything."

"Sure," Luke said, although he never considered helping Chuck. He never saw or talked to him again. He heard Chuck moved to Arkansas and began working in collections for a midsized bank. It was better than the collection job he had to take in a Kentucky bank a couple of years later.

Denise came for the weekend. Luke had lots of work to do and she watched him and knew he was still in shock. "How long will it take you?"

"Are you getting impatient?" he asked.

"No. I was only wondering what you thought."

"A year and a half, maybe two." He was suddenly sad. He wanted out. He didn't want to broker loans, but it was the only path to becoming a mortgage banking company again. He wanted to stop, but he couldn't leave the employees now. "Give me some time."

"It's your call," she said. "If it's going to be a while, then get yourself one of those decent condos downtown. Get a view of the river where you can watch the sunset and relax at the end of the day. Decorate it nicely—like the lake or not; it's your choice. But have a place to rest and refresh and then come home to me on the weekend."

"That's one more asset to fight over. At least I have less money now," he said, trying to be funny.

"She's going to fight over every penny, but I don't care. You can give her all of it, including the new condo. I don't care."

Denise caught the Sunday-night flight, and Luke submerged himself into FRM and the rebuilding process. Several times each day, he thought of the brownstone, the faint splash of freckles under Denise's eyes, the skip in her step, and the bounce of her hair. He was anxious for the weekend.